The Toastmaster

**Written by
Dan Peavler**

Living Springs
Publishers

Copyright 2016 by Living Springs Publishers

ISBN 978-1-953686-11-4 Second Edition
Library of Congress Control Number: 2016919990

Living Springs Publishers
www.LivingSpringsPublishers.com

Cover Images:
Copyright: <a href='http://www.123rf.com/profile_donfiore'>donfiore/123RF Stock Photo</a>
Copyright: <a href='http://www.123rf.com/profile_afhunta'>afhunta/123RF Stock Photo</a>
Copyright: <a href='http://www.123rf.com/profile_pressmaster'>pressmaster/123RF Stock Photo</a>

Dedicated to Jack Jones for bringing a different perspective to my life. He was the inspiration in developing the characters of my story.

ACKNOWLEDGEMENTS

To Candice Kearns Read for the sharing of your insight, knowledge and expertice of the written word. My novel would have been a pile of papers without your support.

To Veryle Peavler and Hank Peavler. Thanks for being fantastic partners in bringing "The Toastmaster" to fruition.

Character List

Maliki Young is Troy and Rosie's son, who along with Tanya, narrates the story. He is Sara's grandson.

Tanya Springfield is a Dallas news reporter who is writing a story about the people of Medicine Bow.

Sara Young is Tom, Troy and Rebecca's mother. She works to manage her own personal life along with the struggles of her children.

Troy Young is Tom's twin brother. He finds trouble at every avenue of his life.

Tom Young is Troy's twin brother. He finds contentment in his everyday life.

Rebecca Young is Tom and Troy's sister who faces both fame and adversity at a very young age.

Sam Blake is the head of Blake Enterprises and one of the richest men in Texas. He makes his home in Medicine Bow.

Stanley is Sam Blake's friend and right-hand man.

Jackie is Sam Blake's Personal Assistant.

Lola Dodge is a Pastor in Medicine Bow and Sara's best friend. She is the wife of Theo, mother to Delphia and Jesse.

Delphia Dodge is Lola's daughter whose positive outlook on life helps Rebecca deal with her personal hardships.

Rosie is a woman in Colorado who has a chance meeting with Troy She is the mother of Maliki.

Billy Ray Lockett is Troy's friend who travels to Colorado with him.

Larry Lover is Troy's friend who travels to Colorado with him.

Uncle Martin is Sara's deceased husband's uncle who Sara and her children live with.

Drew Fudderman is a local resident whose family owns a pig farm near Medicine Bow.

Luther Barnes, AKA: Square Shoulders, is a local man and friend / nemesis to Uncle Martin

The Ortiz family is a local family who own a ranch near Medicine Bow. Manual, Ester and their grandson Renaldo are mentioned in the book.

The Camp family is a local family living in Medicine Bow. Earl, Ethel and their sons Trey and Monty and their nephew Jimmy are mentioned in the book

Steve Dalbey owns a cabin in the mountains. He rescues Troy when he finds him unconscious in the snow.

Charley & Jennifer are a husband-and-wife Troy meets in Las Vegas.

Ed Dodd is an FBI agent who is also Sam Blake's childhood friend.

Mike King is the heartless head of a crime syndicate who Troy becomes involved with.

Vinny Barros is a career criminal who works for Mike King.

Rex Parker is a career criminal who works for Mike King.

Jimmy Marsh is a career criminal who works for Mike King.

Prologue

The sun setting over the snow-packed peaks of the Maroon Belles shot a ray of light through a fifteen-foot-high picture window at the front of Maliki Young's plush Aspen home. Tanya Springfield sat comfortably on a black leather recliner, digging her nylon covered feet into the thick carpet while sipping a glass of Pinot Noir held gently with both hands.

Maliki was holding a gold medal at the precise angle that the sunlight filtering in the window momentarily shot a beam of light across Tanya's face. He noticed the reflection and immediately moved to the middle of the large living room and set the medal down on a mahogany coffee table. He had always been in wonder of the older woman, not only because she is a highly successful celebrity, but because of her incredible beauty.

"I know my father was never normal." Maliki was searching for an angle; a meaning to the story he was about to disclose. "It's ironic that he tried so desperately to escape something that he never was."

Tanya simply listened. She had planned and prepared for this meeting for the past six months and was not about to spoil the occasion by being overly aggressive. She was very good at extracting information from men.

Maliki sat down, sinking deeply into the sofa. They had already made plenty of small talk. Although they both seemed relaxed, there was a sense of uneasiness; partly from the fact the two were going to spend the next four days alone, and partly from the uncertainty of the information Maliki held about his father and the fabled money that had disappeared. "I was born to run," he referred to a question posed to him earlier as to why he liked running.

"You certainly are a descendant of runners." She reached up with her right hand and ran her fingers through her hair, thinking that at one time everyone in the country had been chasing his father. "It sounds like you have a legitimate shot at making the Olympic team this year."

"I can only pray. It's why I'm training at altitude." He noticed that her heavy makeup couldn't cover the wrinkles meandering from the corners of her still-pretty eyes and the pitch-black hair dye couldn't conceal all the strands of gray hair.

Tanya leaned forward and placed her nearly full glass of wine on the coffee table. "Maliki. How much do you know about your father?"

"Everything."

"I find it amazing that you know everything."

"He told me the entire story."

"I have heard from several people that your father spilled his guts to you the night you were born." She couldn't help but notice that he had his father's chocolate brown eyes.

"That's right," he never blinked.

"And you remember what he told you?"

"Everything."

"You were a full month premature."

"Yep, I was only weeks away from being an embryo and little more than a heartbeat. I could fit in the palm of his hand." Maliki looked directly into Tanya's eyes. "After he confessed his life's sins, I already didn't want to be like my parents."

Tanya snickered. She had her doubts about this far-fetched story of remembering his father's confessions. There was no question he did possess much information about not only his father but about everyone in Medicine Bow, but for her to write an accurate exposé he would have to be honest with her. "You know, Maliki, every time I met your family I either said out loud, or thought, that their experiences would make a great story worth telling the world."

Maliki replied, "I've been looking forward to spending this time with you. I think you are the perfect choice to create a legacy for the Young family."

"Thank you," Tanya leaned forward in the chair. "But for us to gain an accurate picture of your family and the people of Medicine Bow, we have to be honest with each other."

"I'm sure you will be satisfied with our time together."

So confident, definitely a product of Medicine Bow, Tanya thought as she relaxed back in her chair. "Are you ashamed of your father?"

"Which one?"

"Obviously Troy."

"No, I'm not ashamed of him. I think he was very sick." Maliki picked up the gold medal and placed it around his neck.

He stood up and walked to the large picture window and looked out at the beautiful sunset. "It's so clean up here."

Tanya walked over to stand next to him. Noticing he was much taller than his father; actually, both his fathers. "Shall we start tonight, or would you rather start in the morning?"

He hesitated for a moment, "Let's get started." He turned and walked toward his bedroom. "I'll be right back."

Tanya was aware that Maliki was very successful and rich. He had made a lot of his money at a very early age in land development, with the help of Sam Blake, but beyond that she knew very little about him. Waiting patiently, she wondered why his six-bedroom, obviously very expensive, home would have such simple furnishings.

Maliki returned carrying three boxes and placed them in the center of the large dining room table. Tanya silently watched him remove the contents from the first box. He glanced toward her with a large smile. "Troy did tell me everything right after I was born." He stacked several notebooks on top of each other. "He also documented everything right before I was born. He had nothing better to do while he was in jail."

"Oh my gosh," Tanya placed her hand on the notebooks.

"Also," Maliki began pulling out several diaries from another box, "I have diaries from my mother, Aunt Rebecca, my grandmother, and even notes from Sam. I have something from almost everyone who lived in Medicine Bow."

"Why didn't you tell me you had all this information?"

"Nobody else knows. I suppose I like the myth the people of Medicine Bow have about Troy speaking to me when I was an infant."

"Where in the world will we start?" Tanya began emptying her writing materials and tape recorder from her briefcase onto the table and opened her laptop computer.

"I've been working on this for several years and have it all organized." Maliki held up the first notebook with a large number one on the outside. "With your help, we can tell a very compelling story. Let's start a couple of weeks after Troy's nineteenth birthday."

"Okay," Tanya placed the microphone in the middle of the table.

Chapter One

Dallas, Texas

Judge Murphy looked as though he had swallowed a field mouse and was afraid if he opened his mouth it would escape. The décor of his chambers was wall-to-wall oak; even the large desk he was perched behind. Troy Young was sitting calmly between his mother and lawyer. Everyone present, especially Troy, understood the futility of the judge's attempt at pretending his stern demeanor would have any long-term rehabilitative effect

"Your honor," Troy's attorney broke the ice. "Mr. Young has made considerable progress over the past three years. Completely clean until this last smidgen of misconduct."

"He broke a table, three chairs, a window, and bashed the light in on a police cruiser." Judge Murphy struggled to remain seated as he pointed toward Troy's file. "And for Christ's sake! He was naked when he did this."

"Yes, sir."

"Disturbing the peace of the law-abiding citizens of the state of Texas may be a smidgen of misconduct to you, Mr. Harvey, but I take such behavior very serious, very serious." His eyes stayed glued on Troy. "Son, you may think this is a place where only small-town justice will be administered, where you can get away with anything, but I guarantee your abysmal behavior will not be tolerated by this court."

"Yes, sir," Troy never moved a muscle.

"I understand you have some … well, medical problems. Problems that could be causing you to act in the dreadful manner you displayed last month. Am I correct?"

"Your honor, Mr. Young has been prescribed medication which, when taken properly, allows him to live a normal life. He stopped taking the medication for a couple weeks and his behavioral problems ensued," said Mr. Harvey.

"What medication is Mr. Young taking?"

"Lithium, your honor."

"Son," the judge looked sternly at Troy. "It seems you need this medication, but, if possible, this court would rather steer clear of administering any type of ruling on such a personal matter." He looked at the attorney, "I don't believe it necessary for the court to oversee Mr. Young's medication."

"I wholeheartedly agree," said Mr. Harvey, knowing full well the judge's friendly intentions.

"Mr. Young's record with the courts goes back several years."

"His problems began four years ago at the age of fifteen."

"Juvenile court at fifteen," mumbled Judge Murphy, more for his own benefit than anyone else's.

Troy glanced at his mother who was sitting with her back as straight as a washboard with her pretty blue eyes fixed attentively on the judge. He wondered if she would speak up, attesting to the fact that his troubles had started much before his fifteenth birthday. She remained quiet.

"Your honor, I would like to have this problem resolved as quickly as possible," stated Mr. Harvey, bringing the pretense that justice or rehabilitation were the recourse of the meeting in the judge's chamber. The decision had been determined by the judge after a phone call with Sam Blake yesterday, and Mr. Harvey was due at a luncheon in thirty minutes.

"Son, I give you fifty hours of civic duty to be performed at the discretion of the town folks of Medicine Bow. They are the ones who have to live with you." The judge stared directly into Troy's eyes and closed the folder on his desk. "If you come before me again, I will throw the book at you. Do you understand?"

"Yes, sir."

"What about the record?" asked Mr. Harvey.

"Bob, nothing will be on the record." The judge rose from his seat and pointed toward the door.

Troy allowed his mother and attorney to exit first and followed them through the courtroom to the adjacent hall. Sara sat down on a wooden bench.

"That's that," said Sara.

"Yes, that's that," replied Mr. Harvey, condescendingly. "I'm sure we will be in touch."

Sara allowed the attorney a malicious look as he scurried down the hallway. She turned to Troy and patted the hard wood bench. "Sit down."

Troy sat next to his mother.

Sara took in a deep breath. She was far more relaxed than she had been for his previous indiscretions. It was as though she was getting ready to give him advice for the final time and wanted to make sure to give him something meaningful. "You know how embarrassing ..." She hesitated, realizing she was about to make this time about her and not him.

Troy glared at her, "I could have handled this myself."

"I know you could have, but no matter what you think, your actions affect more than just you." God only knows that she was still lost in understanding how to talk about the alcohol, drugs, and disorder that had a strangle hold on her son.

Troy loosened his tie and pulled it over his head.

"Tom and Rebecca are worried about you."

"They can't help me, Ma."

"I can't force you to take your medication," she had noticed a glaze over his eyes. "But your actions are completely unacceptable when you are off them." Sometimes it seemed futile, but she knew that she would never stop trying to help him.

"You don't have to worry about that anymore. I'm fixin' to leave."

She turned her head and watched a group of people leave the courtroom across the hall. She didn't have to look at Troy's face, it was chiseled in her mind, and physically he was nearly flawless.

"I know I've caused you a lot of problems," he sat up straight. "I do want to apologize for that. You and Rebecca have always stood by me."

She looked at him somewhat surprised that he never mentioned Tom. He and Tom were classic twins who seemed to suffer through each other's pain. They had always been very close.

"I've taken advantage of you," he looked at his mother's tired face, "it pains me that I do."

Sara couldn't understand how his behavior could be so dreadful, as it obviously was, from accounts not only from the recent police report but from the many accounts of misdoings given to her from friends and acquaintances and then be so sensitive when in her presence.

"I'll give you one thing, Troy. You are a survivor."

"Sometimes that is not a good thing to be."

Sara jerked her head toward him. "How could you say such a thing." Suicide had been one of her greatest fears.

"I mean a person usually has to have been through some sort of disaster to be a survivor." He could sense the distress his mother was experiencing. "Don't worry; I'm not going to kill myself. I just hate being treated like some sort of charity case."

"How are you being treated like a charity case?"

"You know as well as I that Sam is the reason I was given such a light sentence."

"Aren't you happy Sam is willing to help? He was the one who found you help when you first became sick."

"I was sick way before Sam found Doctor Starr."

"What do you mean?"

"When I was hit by the school bus …" He hesitated, wondering if he should come clean with one of his deepest secrets.

"Yes, you were eight years old." Sara felt the accident was the cause of his problems, although the doctors disputed her belief.

"The bus didn't hit me. I jumped in front of it."

"What?"

"I threw myself in front of it. The driver couldn't have stopped."

"Why would you do such a thing?"

"I just had this terrible urge to jump in front of it."

"I don't understand."

"I know, Ma," he shook his head. "Nobody understands how I feel. Usually, I don't understand. Sometimes it is as though I am invincible. It's the greatest … like having so much positive energy inside and not being able to get it out quickly enough. But when the downside comes, it becomes so unbearable that it hurts. It's been that way as long as I remember."

She looked closely at her son with his high cheekbones and dark brown eyes, drawing a second look from several of the well-dressed professional women walking so rapidly to their appointments. She knew he wasn't a bad or immoral person, but at the same time she had no clue as to how she could help him.

"Let's go home."

Maliki and Tanya

"Maliki, I don't think there is any question that Sara really loved Troy." Tanya turned off the recorder that was sitting in the middle of the table.

"Unquestionably. She had sacrificed a lot for her children. Having three children and losing a husband when she was only nineteen made her a real survivor herself."

"What happened to her husband? Your grandfather."

"He was killed in an automobile accident outside Joplin, Missouri, when Tom and Troy were two and Rebecca was just a baby. He worked in the oilfields, and crashed on his way to work."

"So, Sara was only nineteen when she was widowed."

"I believe so," Tom stood up and yawned.

"Sara is five years older than I am."

Malaki couldn't help but think how good Tanya looked for a lady in her fifties. She had a sensuality about her that no other woman he knew possessed. "Would you like something to drink?"

"Sure," she looked at her still full glass of wine sitting on the coffee table. "Oh, I still have wine."

Maliki took her wine and poured it down the bar sink. "Would you rather have something besides wine?"

"Wine is fine," she had always admired a man who took control.

"It's only eight. Shall we keep going?" Maliki opened a bottle of water for himself but handed Tanya a glass of wine.

"Definitely, I'm kind of a night owl. I really am enjoying this." She took a sip of wine, "How did your grandmother end up in Medicine Bow, Texas?"

"After her husband died …"

"Your grandfather."

"Yes," Maliki sat down at the table. "After Grandfather died, his Uncle Martin insisted that Grandmother and the three kids move to Medicine Bow."

"Did she have any other family?"

"None she could count on. She was penniless and in dire straits. Uncle Martin thought Medicine Bow would be a great place to raise the three kids, so he offered her his home."

"I was in Medicine Bow about a week after they were in court." Tanya turned on the tape recorder and pulled her laptop to the edge of the table.

"It's all here."

Medicine Bow, Texas

The annual harvest festival in Medicine Bow had become a trendy place for the people of Dallas to spend a weekend away from the stress and anxiety of the city. The small-town celebration was reminiscent of the country fairs that were once a cherished part of the fabric of communities scattered throughout Texas.

The prior year, one visiting couple, on the premise of spending a leisurely afternoon at the fair, found that country life was more than a three-legged race and hayrack ride. Upon witnessing a contest where pigs were greased and then chased by the local children, they stepped in to admonish all adults within shouting range. They were quickly sent on their way. Upon returning to Dallas, they immediately reported the cruelty to a television station. The charges hit a nerve with Tanya Springfield, a local television celebrity. She, along with several members of an animal rights group, hightailed it to Medicine Bow in time for the Sunday afternoon pig chase—um, contest. After witnessing the kids chase the pigs, the activists refused to leave until they were assured the event would not be held again.

A year later, Pastor Lola Dodge and her husband Theo, the fair organizers, scheduled the contest for early in the morning. A television crew was expected to arrive around lunch time to interview the town's hero, track sensation Rebecca Young.

The early morning sun reflected off Lola's shiny black skin as she greeted everyone with a large smile. "Welcome to the fair. Don't be afraid to spend some money. Everything is a fine item, indeed." Her low, authoritative voice boomed from deep in her large belly.

Many of the people looking at the sparse selection of hand-knitted sweaters, socks, and assorted crafts situated on two long tables, sitting precariously on the church lawn, knew Lola. She was the vociferous pastor who brought them salvation every Sunday morning.

"Delphia. Go find Jesse and tell him to get over here. Now! Mr. Blake and Mr. Ortiz are getting ready to grease the pigs," Lola yelled at her daughter. "I'm going inside the church to get out of this awful heat. Y'all come in and get me before you start chasin' them pigs."

Delphia was at an awkward stage where her appearance could be described as homely. It would most definitely be a mistake for anyone outside the confines of Medicine Bow to describe her as such. Nothing was more valued in the community than the children.

"I'm goin' to catch me a pig this year and sell it to Mr. Ortiz for twenty dollars." Delphia turned to look back at her mother as she began to run away. "I bet I catch one and Jesse doesn't."

"Just find him." Lola stepped into the church foyer and fanned herself with the harvest festival itinerary. She looked down the aisle of plank flooring where she could see the sunken figure of someone sitting alone in the front pew. "Is that you, Troy Young?"

"Yes, ma'am."

"Are you in here to keep from melting in the sun, or are you prayin'? I hope if you are prayin' it isn't in order to win a bet." She pulled her blouse away from her huge bosom to let the air cool her body.

"I'm just sittin' here," he moved over to allow her room to sit.

Lola had always held a soft spot for Troy, and she always found time to converse with him. She knew he was pondering over some problem and was avoiding eye contact with her. He should have known better. She was one of the most analytical people to ever walk the face of the earth and could read people like reading a road map.

"I'm leavin' Medicine Bow," Troy said, softly.

"Well, honey, it's about time."

"I'm goin' to Denver," he ignored her lack of surprise.

"Do you have a job? And are you goin' alone?"

"Yes, ma'am, we do have a job." He fidgeted, "I'm goin' with Billy Ray Lockett."

"Oh good Lord," Lola clasped her hands together. She knew Billy Ray up until the time he turned twelve and the Lockett family moved away from Medicine Bow. He was a handful at that time. She heard that Billy Ray and his cousin had spent some time in jail.

"We're drivin' to Denver in his cousin Larry Lover's Cadillac. Their grandfather has a cabin in the mountains outside the city."

"Give me strength." Lola looked up to the stain-glass window high in the vaulted ceiling, "Misery does enjoy company."

"We plan on leavin' right away."

Lola turned toward him, "Sometimes problems have a way of following a person."

"I feel like I need to move, to do something, even if it is all wrong." He looked Lola directly in her eyes. "Being sick the way I've been has made me question a lot of things about life. I don't want to embarrass my family anymore."

Before Lola could respond, she was interrupted, "Ma, I'm about ready to catch one of them greasy old pigs," Delphia yelled through the front door of the church before running away.

"You have always had an inquisitive mind, but I want you to remember that what is essential in life is often invisible to the eye. I'll be praying for you." Lola placed her arm around Troy and gave him a quick hug. "Now, I'm goin' out into the heat and enjoy the fair."

Lola stepped from the darkness of the church into the bright sunlight with an uneasy feeling in her belly. She had a bad feeling about Troy leaving as she watched Sam Blake with a large group of kids crowded around him in the vacant lot between the church and the Youngs' home.

"Come on, Sam, get them lined up." Manuel Ortiz was struggling to keep five small pigs within the confines of a wire fence situated about fifty yards away from Sam. "The television crew is going to get here shortly, and we'll have a heck of a mess if they see these kids chasin' pigs all over town."

"To hell with them," Sam's voice echoed off the church. "If they don't like what we do in our own town, they can all go to hell." He motioned the mass of children to their starting position. "Come on, y'all, make it fair." He subconsciously looked down Road 10 leading into town to see if there might be a cloud of dust from the television crew. A year ago, the Dallas newspapers had a field day portraying him as being cruel to animals. He held out his massive arms, trying to keep the anxious kids from jumping the start. His pants were covered with dust and grease making it difficult to recognize him as one of the richest men in Texas.

"Come on, Sam," Manuel yelled.

"Just one second. Drew Fudderman!" Sam screamed at a large man at the end of the line of kids. "You aren't planning on chasin' the pigs, are you?"

"No, su." Even though everyone knew chasing the pigs was his intention just as he had the previous year where he was cheered on by the onlookers.

"Go on, step back," Sam waved his arm at Drew.

"I'm movin'." Drew stared at Sam with his beady eyes as he moved his huge three-hundred-pound body away from the line of kids. He wished he had arrived at the festival an hour earlier so he could have talked to Sam about any employment opportunities.

"I'm goin' to count to three and say go. Remember the pig has to be carried across the finish line for it to be yours." Sam held up his right arm. "One, two, three, go," he lowered his arm.

Manuel pulled the fence away, releasing the pigs. The five pigs didn't move until Jesse Dodge, who was much faster than the other kids, jumped into the midst of them, grabbing the first pig he came to by the leg. The other four pigs shrieked and ran in opposite directions. A couple of seconds later two screaming children jumped on Jesse's pig, knocking the animal from his grasp. The chase was on. The kids were running all over town chasing the pigs.

"Look there," Sam slapped his knee, "here comes Delphia with one."

"I caught me a pig, Ma." Delphia, covered in grease from head to toe, held onto the slippery animal as she came across the finish line and handed the pig to Manuel. He placed the pig into a pen in the back of his pickup.

"You shore did," Lola patted her greasy daughter on the top of her head. "I hope Jesse does too, or we will be hearing about this for a long time."

Monty Camp, Sam's hired hand, Earl's boy, was the next greasy tike to tote a pig to the finish line. Renaldo Ortiz, Manuel's grandson, came next, followed by Trey Camp, Monty's older brother.

Everyone was clapping and cheering as Jesse, exhausted and covered with grease, even more so than the other children, pulled the final and largest pig toward the yelling crowd. He was one hundred feet away, but his arms ached and he had a cramp in the calf of his right leg. He leaned over to lie on top of the pig to rest. The pig's mouth was wide open. Jesse could see its pink tongue. The animal wasn't breathing very hard. He placed his arms around the slippery animal and lifted with all his strength. The pig squirted out of his arms and landed a couple of feet away. Another boy, a boy from out of town, picked up the pig and easily carried it to the finish line. Jesse fell to his knees and slammed his fist to the ground.

"I caught a pig and Jesse didn't," chanted Delphia in a loud screeching voice. "I caught a pig and Jesse didn't," she yelled in a lower voice as she danced around in a circle. "I caught a pig and Jesse didn't," she sang in as low a voice as she could make, getting down on one knee and pointing toward her brother.

"Leave that boy alone," yelled Lola. "He's goin' to whup the tar out of you. Now go wipe the grease off your face."

Sam and Manuel both laughed and congratulated each other on another pig chase—um, contest without protestors interfering and everyone having a great time. All the townspeople joined in the laughter.

"Oh my goodness. Will you look there." Sam stopped shaking Manuel's hand and turned toward the Youngs' house.

All the people turned to see what Sam was looking at. Rebecca and Sara Young were walking arm in arm toward them. Both mom and daughter were dressed in black slacks with white blouses. Rebecca was slightly taller than her mother, but both possessed the same high cheekbones and shoulder-length auburn hair. Sara was naturally beautiful, and it was hard to tell if she was wearing any makeup. Rebecca was wearing a slight amount of eye shadow and a little lip-gloss. She easily could be mistaken as a fashion model from New York City.

"Oh my gosh," Sara stared at all the dirty children, "you all are one big mess."

"But we did have fun," Sam moved toward Sara, looking her straight in the eyes.

"Sam Blake, you are just as dirty as the children," Sara smiled at him.

"Y'all missed one of our best contests." Sam could smell the lotion and perfume on Sara. "Where is Uncle Martin?"

"He's not coming out in this heat until it's time to pitch horseshoes." Sara kept an arm's length from Sam.

Sam stood with his mouth open, much the same as the pig was doing moments earlier. His infatuation with Sara was a commonly known fact by the citizenry of Medicine Bow. The amount of money and time he invested in the town was due to his amorous feelings toward her. On occasion, he had asked her to drive to Dallas for a dinner and a movie, but any type of romantic involvement never evolved. Mostly because Sam would turn to mush in the presence of Sara. He could make split-second multimillion dollar decisions about land developments and negotiate deals with the shrewdest of oil men, but when he was around Sara Young, his knees would shake and the breath would leave his lungs.

"I caught a pig," Delphia interrupted with a loud booming voice. "And Jesse didn't, because he couldn't carry it across the finish line."

"Oh Jesse, after all the practice we had with speed running, and you still missed catching a pig." Rebecca rolled her big brown eyes toward the sky.

Rebecca never took losing slightly. She was the fastest high school girl in Texas at both the eight hundred meters and fifteen hundred meters. It was very unusual for a girl from the smallest classification in Texas high school athletics, basically a girl from a small country school, to be so successful, not only in Texas but on a national level. Her remarkable success as a runner was the only reason the television crew was on its way to town.

"Sara," Sam watched as the crowd headed toward the grassy area of the open field to begin the egg-tossing game, "you look very nice this morning."

"Thank you, Sam, you look a bit on the dirty side."

Sam looked at his grease-covered pants, "I'm fixin' to go clean up."

"Come be my partner in throwing the eggs," Sara moved closer to him.

"No, no, no," Sam moved back. Setting up and helping Manuel run the pig chasing contest was the extent of his involvement with the fair, and he never took part in any of the other contests or games.

"Now, I won't take no for an answer." Sara took hold of his dirty hand and led him to the wire basket of eggs. She picked the smallest egg and examined it for cracks.

Sam looked like a child who had been scolded, even though he was six feet three inches tall and weighed two hundred fifty pounds. He stepped in line with the contestants opposite of Sara, who was only ten feet away.

"Troy, I want to toss an egg with Luther." Lola motioned to Troy who was standing in the doorway of the church. "You still owe this town some reparation. You be the judge and we will call it even."

Luther Barnes had been Lola's partner for the past twenty years. He was seventy-seven years old, and everyone in town, except Lola and Sara, called him Square Shoulders, because the top of his shoulders came up to be level with his large ears. He and Lola usually won the contest. The thick skin on his calloused hands was in stark contrast to the pillow soft hands of Lola.

"Hey, Twoy. I can help ya be the judge." Drew Fudderman picked up the wire basket with three remaining eggs and cradled it in his massive arms.

"You can help, Drew, but don't get in the way." Troy had always been kind and patient with the oversized country boy, even when they had attended elementary school together and everyone else made fun of Drew. Troy remained steadfast in being his friend.

"All right. Everyone throw yore egg." Troy's order came before everyone was ready. The eggs flashed through the air in several different waves as each contestant lobbed their egg.

Ethel Camp, who didn't have an athletic bone in her body, was the only one to drop an egg.

"Jesus Jehoash fat, Ethel!" her husband Earl threw his cap to the ground. "Playing catch with five children over the past twelve years, and you can't catch the egg once."

Ethel gave Earl a lethal look as she stepped away from the line into the shade of the church. Earl didn't say another word.

"Step back, Drew." Troy noticed Drew moving closer to the contestants. "And put the basket of eggs down."

"I don't want somebody to step on um."

"Nobody is gonna step on um. Now put um down."

"Okay," he placed the basket on the ground.

"Everybody step back one pace," Troy motioned with his arms.

"Sam, you need to move back a little mo," Drew waved Sam back.

Sam glared at him, "Keep your eyes on the egg," he yelled to Sara as he tossed the egg.

"Don't worry about me," Sara easily caught the egg.

"Step back," Troy motioned the contestants back, noticing that three more people had dropped their eggs.

"You need to move back a little mo, Sam." Drew stepped directly in front of Sam and scratched a straight line in the dirt with his finger. "You need to stay even with the west of the people."

There were a few snickers from everyone because of the derision Drew was bestowing on the rich and highly respected Sam Blake. Sam simply moved back.

Sara tossed her egg the twenty feet to Sam, who cradled it in both hands. Lola threw her egg high into the air over Square Shoulders' head, but he took a quick step back and jumped high enough to snare the egg with one hand.

"Luther, you ought to try out for the Dallas Cowboy's next year," yelled Lola, joining everyone in laughter.

Remarkably, five more contestants dropped their eggs, leaving only three pairs of contestants. In past years, after so few tosses, only two or three eggs would have been dropped. The excruciating heat was making it more fun to be a spectator drinking a cold cup of lemonade in the shade than standing in the hot sun.

Troy was taking his job as judge very seriously. Noticing something odd happening with Monty Camp and his cousin Jimmy Troy decided to keep an eye on them. "Move back a step and throw when you are ready," he yelled.

Drew kept a close eye on Sam.

Sara and Lola easily caught their eggs, but Monty dropped his, yet it didn't break. He picked it off the ground, wiped it off and stepped in line as though nothing happened.

"Monty Camp, bring me that egg," Troy pointed at Monty.

The thin, red-haired boy looked at his cousin for support as he shook his head and moved toward Troy. He handed Troy the egg and stared at his large feet.

Troy took the egg and threw it to the ground. It cracked but didn't splatter. "Just as I thought. A hardboiled egg, you little pip-squeaks are disqualified."

"That's bad to cheat," Drew shook his finger in Monty's face. "Don't eva do that again."

"Well, well, well, we uh sowwee," yelled Monty, mocking Drew.

Troy grabbed Monty by the shoulder and spun him around. "Cheating is one thing, but disrespecting Drew is another thing. It's just plain mean. I won't have it, and if I ever hear it again, I'll whup you good."

"It's okay, Troy. They got the message," yelled Sara.

Troy glared at Monty.

"I'm sorry, Drew." Monty looked at the physically imposing farm boy.

"That's okay." Drew's outlook on life had never been fazed by how he was treated by others. His carefree and jovial disposition made him a pleasure to be around. Those closest to him knew he was neither dimwitted nor stupid; on the contrary, he was quite intelligent. He simply could not pronounce his r's. "Let's finish this contest. I want to see how fa Sam can toss an egg."

"Take two steps back this time," Troy was wanting the contest over, regretting that he had left the cool confines of the church.

Rebecca stepped into the playing area, carrying two cups of lemonade and handed one to her mother and the other to Lola. "Be careful not to wipe your hands on your white blouse." Rebecca remained precariously close to her mother.

"Stand back, honey, so I don't hit you when I throw the egg. Hold our drinks while we throw." Sara and Lola handed their drinks back to Rebecca.

"Throw the eggs," Troy's command was more intense than he had anticipated.

Sam and Square Shoulders both made shaky catches. All the spectators were very much engaged in the contest and applauded.

"Take two more steps back, and throw when ready," barked Troy.

Square Shoulders threw his egg at a perfect arc toward Lola. She made an easy catch as the egg fell gently into her soft hands.

Sam, who had been throwing the egg underhanded, decided for no particular reason to throw the egg over-handed, like a baseball. Although he had not thrown a baseball for over thirty years, he reared back and heaved the egg. All Sara saw was a shiny white object flying through the bright sky before it hit her directly between the eyes, hard enough to make her take three steps backwards. The egg splattered the front of her blouse, with the remainder of the yolk and shell hitting the front of Rebecca's white blouse. Surprised, Rebecca hunched over, taking several steps to the side, throwing the two drinks in the air and stepping into the wire basket with the remaining eggs, before landing on the seat of her pants.

Sam felt his heart jump into his throat as Lola moved to Sara's aid, and Rebecca jumped up from her fall, rubbing her right knee.

"I reckon that throw was a might bit hard. Sorry." Sam moved slowly to where Sara was wiping the egg from her clothing, unsure if he should try to wipe some of the gooey mess from the front of her blouse or let well enough alone.

"It's not your fault, Sam." Sara held her blouse away from her body, allowing the egg to dry, "Are you all right, Rebecca?"

"I'm okay," Rebecca continued to rub her knee.

"Well, we better go change," Sara rubbed her forehead.

Sam watched the mother and daughter walk toward their home. His feelings for Sara were genuine, and there was no other person he would rather share his fortune with. In business, he had always surrounded himself with highly qualified advisors and staff who he could delegate decisions to, but this personal matter was one he would have to handle himself.

Maliki and Tanya

"The people of Medicine Bow were really unique," Tanya stretched her arms over her head. "The first time I went there I thought they were backwards."

"I don't think the people there were backward, but they were different."

"They were only forty miles from Dallas, but thousands of miles away culturally."

Maliki could not help but notice her breasts as she held her arms higher and higher as she leaned back in the chair. He tried to look directly in her eyes.

"They were so accepting of one another, but I found the chasing pigs contest to be repulsive." She lowered her arms and cocked her head to look at Maliki. Men's peripheral vision was something she was well aware of.

"That's what makes this story so intriguing," Maliki stood up. "Shall we continue, or do you want to take a break?"

"I would like to get a little more comfortable before we continue. If it's all right with you."

"Certainly," Maliki watched as Tanya walked toward her bedroom. No doubt about it she was still very attractive. It hadn't dawned on him that there might be some uncomfortable situations while being alone with the woman whom his grandmother had insisted on helping with writing their story.

The smell of lotion was the first indicator that Tanya was back. Back she was, wearing red silk pajamas. She had been gone for only fifteen minutes, but had obviously refreshed her makeup and combed her hair. She moved to the kitchen and poured another glass of wine. "Okay, all ready." She put the wine next to her writing tablet, clapped her hands together, and sat down at the table.

Maliki opened another bottle of water and sat opposite of her. "This next part is where you are first mentioned in any of the writings. I think you will find it interesting how you were perceived by the townspeople."

"It was interesting to hear of the events that transpired prior to my arrival." Tanya took a sip of wine, "I pretty much know what the people of Medicine Bow thought about me."

Medicine Bow, Texas

News reporter Tanya Springfield, along with her cameraman Bob, stood outside the channel twelve news van parked on the side of the crossroads of County Road 10 and Interstate 35. She was whining with a greater fury than usual as the sun beat down on her jet-black hair.

"Bob, we are not driving down that ridiculous dirt road if there is even a slight hint of rain." She fanned herself with the notes she had prepared for the interview with Rebecca.

Tanya covered the animal cruelty story about the pig chasing contest held in Medicine Bow the previous year. She, along with several animal activists, refused to leave the town until they were assured the contest would no longer take place. They pestered the townspeople until several of the older members of the town agreed to reconsider taking part in the contest. Considered was a word Tanya and her friends scoffed at. They informed Uncle Martin and Square Shoulders that they shouldn't consider anything but should agree to stop the contest. The group suggested an alternative of having the town's children chase after greased balloons. Sam sat idly by as the argument continued until it started to rain. Road 10 becomes impassable when wet. It doesn't matter if a person has a four-wheel-drive vehicle, the angle of the road caused any vehicle to slide into the ditch.

The animal activists, along with Tanya and her cameraman, were stranded in the town where they were unwelcome guests. Square Shoulders, even though the strangers thought of him as quite peculiar, agreed to allow them to stay in the domino parlor behind the mechanic shop. Sam was very polite and made sure there was enough food and blankets for everybody.

Tanya was infatuated with Sam for being so kind, despite the animosity forged between them over the pig-chasing contest. She had taken extra care to choose her wardrobe for this particular journey to Medicine Bow.

"It's not supposed to rain," said Bob. "Let's get in the truck and drive to this little hole in the ground and get this interview over with. I want to spend some time with my family tonight."

Tanya opened the van door and lifted herself in, causing her short skirt to raise high enough to expose the top of the stocking on her right leg. Tom Young, driving his new Ford F-

150 pickup truck, pulled alongside the van just in time to see Tanya's well-formed leg sticking out. He had seen Tanya many times on television, but never from this perspective. She really had nice legs.

Tanya turned and stared at the handsome stranger, wondering why he was stopping.

"How y'all doin?" Tom turned down the radio in his truck. "I'm Tom Young, I reckon you are here to interview my sister Rebecca."

"Yes, we are," she glared at him, "but I'm not going down that road if there is even a chance of rain."

"It's not gonna rain. There's only that one tiny cloud." Tom pointed to the sky. "You can follow me to town, if you like."

"All right, let's go, "Tanya slammed the door to the van.

***

Bob pulled into the parking area adjacent to the church as the curious townspeople gathered around to see which celebrity would exit the vehicle to interview Rebecca.

Tanya was busy inside the van primping her hair, staring into a small compact mirror. She knew Sam would be at the interview, because he was the one who set it up. She wanted her appearance to be immaculate.

"What planet did we just land on?" Bob's mouth fell wide open as he gazed out the dark tinted window.

Outside the van, Delphia folded her hands over her eyes and tried to look in the dark back window, leaving a large grease smudge mark. Everyone else waited at arm's length, gawking.

"Don't worry, Bob, they're harmless." Tanya smacked her lips together and closed her compact mirror.

"Look at them two guys over there. They're covered with grease," Bob held his hands up.

"It's more likely oil they're covered with." Tanya opened the front door. "That's Sam Blake."

"Miss Springfield," Sam greeted the young reporter as she walked by everyone else.

"Well, well, Mr. Blake," Tanya smiled flirtatiously, "it is a pleasure to see you again."

"Miss Springfield, the pleasure is all mine." Sam had forgotten just how beautiful she was.

"I see you all have gone to great pains to make a good impression on the people of Texas." Tanya could not believe how disheveled the children were. "You do realize this interview will be recorded?"

"Us folks from Medicine Bow are prone to having a good time, and sometimes we get a little dirty in our quest." Sam removed his large hat and ran his fingers through his graying hair. "We don't want to represent something we aren't."

"Well, I didn't expect suits and ties," Tanya looked at the people surrounding her, "but the children look pretty bad."

Sam felt confident if Tanya had not yet figured out that the children were so dirty because of the pig chase—um, contest—then the secret was most likely safe.

"Miss Springfield," Delphia held her filthy hand out to the spotlessly dressed news lady.

Tanya jerked so as not to be touched by the dirty little girl. "Can I help you, young lady?"

"I caught me a pig. And Jesse didn't." She smiled, showing all her teeth, hunching her shoulders and staring straight at Tanya, waiting for her congratulations.

"What?"

"I caught a pig, and Mr. Ortiz gave me twenty dollars for it." Delphia held up a dirty twenty-dollar bill.

Tanya turned toward Sam. "Why, you cad. You're still holding that disgusting contest."

Sam glared at Delphia.

"I think I'll go get Becca," she turned and ran toward the Youngs' house.

"Mr. Blake, I can't believe you continue to abuse these animals even after you promised to cease."

"No, ma'am, I never promised anything."

"Well, I was under the impression the contest would not be held anymore, but obviously you continue to abuse pigs."

"Ma'am, I would prefer we discuss this at another time."

"That we will," Tanya made an about-face and walked to the van.

***

"Rebecca. Rebecca. They want you to be on television," Delphia screamed at the top of her lungs as she ran up the two steps onto the wooden porch of the Youngs' home.

Troy opened the screen door to the house, allowing Delphia to run past him into the large living room where Rebecca was holding a bag of ice on her mother's forehead. Tom and Uncle Martin sat quietly watching.

"Come on, Rebecca." Delphia grabbed Rebecca by the arm and pulled. "The television woman is here. And boy is she ever pretty."

Rebecca jerked her arm out of the strong grasp of her friend. "Don't grab me like that, Delphia. You're gonna get grease on my clean blouse, and I don't have another one to change into."

"I just want to let you know they are here." Delphia moved in front of Sara and held her hands down by her side.

"They followed Tom in, so we all know they are here. We would all appreciate it if you could be a little quieter," said Uncle Martin.

Delphia stood silently as Rebecca removed the bag of ice from Sara's head revealing a bluish, marble-sized knot directly between her eyes. "Oh my gosh," Delphia whispered, staring directly at Sara's blemish.

"Is it that bad?" Sara asked in a low voice.

"It's bad," Delphia answered in a hushed voice, "and that Miss Springfield is so pretty."

"Oh goodness," Sara put her hand up to feel the bump. "Why don't you all go out and meet Miss Springfield and I'll freshen up and be out in a moment."

Tom and Rebecca pulled Uncle Martin from his recliner as Delphia opened the screen door and the three of them followed her outside. Troy remained behind.

"Ma, I need to tell you something," Troy stared wide eyed at her.

Sara was pleased with how he had conducted himself over the past month, since his court appearance, and she knew for a fact he had been taking his medication, because she dispensed it to him every morning, up until two days ago. She suspected he hadn't taken it the past two days.

"Can it wait until tonight?" She stared into a small mirror at the large welt on her forehead.

"I'm leavin' for Colorado this afternoon. Billy Ray and Larry are on their way."

"I'm not gonna tell you what to do anymore," she stared into his glassy eyes.

"Okay," he was caught off guard by his mother's indifference. "I'm all packed, and we'll most likely leave while Rebecca is doing her interview."

"Please call and let me know when you arrive in Colorado."

"I can do that."

"You be careful, Troy." She felt a twinge of pain in her stomach, "I have to get ready for this interview."

***

Sara smiled as she approached Tanya and Rebecca, who were seated in chairs in front of a camera mounted on a tripod under the decreasing shade of the church. She had straightened her makeup and combed her hair before leaving the house, but she was still self-conscious of the bump on her head.

"Ma, do you remember Miss Springfield?" asked Rebecca.

"Of course I do." Sara noticed Tanya's shapely, nylon-covered legs. "How are you, Miss Springfield?"

"I'm exquisite. Thank you," replied Tanya. "Rebecca was telling me about your accident. Mr. Blake is just a little boy at heart." Tanya batted her eyes at Sam and flipped her hair back.

"Let me look at that head," Sam placed his hand on Sara's chin and raised her head.

"Sam, it's okay." She allowed him to feel the bump.

"That little bump will be gone tomorrow." Sam smiled at Sara, happy that she allowed him to inspect her injury.

"I would like to start with Rebecca and me seated by the church," Tanya sat straight in her chair.

"Okay." Rebecca also sat up straight as Sara moved to the side.

"Hello, everyone, welcome to the *Tanya Springfield Show*." Tanya was very relaxed as she spoke into the camera. "Today I am located deep in the heart of Texas in the little town of Medicine Bow. I am here to talk with this town's hero, Rebecca

Young, who also happens to be one of Texas's finest high school athletes. Welcome to the show, Rebecca."

"Thank you," Rebecca was glad to have the first words come out of her mouth without a mistake. "It's a privilege to have you all here in our town."

"It's unusual for someone from such a small community to have so much success in the track and field arena." Tanya glanced at her notes located at her feet. "Your times in both the 800 meters and 1500 meters races were the fastest in the state last year, regardless of classification."

"I don't guess you need to have a lot of people around you to be able to run fast."

"I guess not," Tanya smiled at Rebecca before facing the camera. "I should clarify to our audience that Rebecca is not only a high school state champion, but she is highly respected on the national track and field scene."

Rebecca continued to smile into the camera, remaining silent, waiting for a specific question.

"Last year I saw you in a newspaper clip wearing a tee shirt with the number 4:15. What do these numbers mean?"

"If I can run four minutes and fifteen seconds in the 1500 meters this next year, it will make me the fastest schoolgirl ever at that distance." Rebecca was somewhat surprised the well-known celebrity had seen her in the newspaper.

"What is your fastest time to date?"

"Four minutes and twenty-one seconds."

"That is fast."

"I can go faster."

"I understand you have a big race coming up next week." Tanya turned slightly toward Rebecca. "You're going to California."

"Oh yes, we already have our travel plans." Rebecca remained composed even though she noticed several filthy children making faces into the camera behind Tanya. "My mother, Lola, Uncle Martin, Luther, Delphia, Jesse, and Monty are driving to San Diego the middle of next week. I'm flying out Wednesday so I can be ready for the race on Friday."

"I understand this is a special race." Tanya squirmed in her hard chair. "Most high school athletes are running cross-country at this time, but you will be running the 1500 meters at the meet in California. How did this all happen?"

"It is unusual to run 1500 meters at any meet during the fall, and most girls at this meet will be running five kilometers. But there is a runner by the name of Tabitha Read who I beat when I was a freshman, and she was a senior here in Texas. It was the only race she lost during her high school career, and now she is running in California and has made a direct challenge to me to race her."

"And I take it you want to race her again?"

"Very much so," the excitement was evident in Rebecca's voice. "Tabitha, along with her coach, made the arrangements. It will be at Qualcomm Stadium in San Diego in conjunction with some sort of automobile swap meet and a college cross-country meet."

"Well, I'm sure our audience will be very interested in learning the results of the race." Tanya glanced at the children. "I didn't see a track in town, where do you train?"

"I run on the open road and through the fields. I also go to Dallas once a week to train with my personal coach."

"Stop the camera," Tanya jerked around. "Will someone please get these grease-splattered little brats out from behind me."

"They are not little brats," Rebecca barked at the surprised Tanya.

"Bob, put the camera on rollers." Tanya had been snapped at much worse during her career of interviewing the public, so she didn't take Rebecca's remark to heart. "Let's shoot the next part of the interview as we walk through the town."

Bob pulled the camera to the middle of the road.

"Rebecca. What type of social life do you have?" Tanya walked slowly down the road holding the microphone in front of Rebecca.

"Sometimes we travel into Dallas to eat and watch a movie. Most of the time we entertain ourselves." Rebecca walked at a slow pace next to Tanya. "The harvest festival here today is something special."

"To the right is the town's general store." Tanya pointed to the faded wood structure. "Do you ever have an urge to shop or hang out at a mall?"

"I like to shop in malls. I never enjoyed spending too much time in them."

"How about dining at a nice restaurant?"

"Sometimes I like getting dressed up and going to a nice restaurant. But a buffet is just as good."

"What about plays and dances?" Tanya seemed to be trying to coax Rebecca into telling everyone how dreary life in the small town must be. "You have to travel such a long distance to experience any type of culture."

Rebecca could see many of the town people following alongside, listening to the two speaking. She could tell by the smile on her mother's face that she knew her daughter was about to set the big city reporter straight.

"This town is so beautiful." Rebecca stopped and looked directly at Tanya. "I become not only inspired but motivated every morning when I wake up to the quiet sun creeping over the hilltops. I never seem to tire as I run through the fields, fearing nothing, knowing I am a special person to have this magnificent place to myself."

"You sound very confident. With the race next weekend in San Diego, do you think you will have the same passion for this small community after you experience big city luxuries?" Tanya raised her eyebrow as she waited for the answer.

"After you eat filet mignon and attend the *Phantom of the Opera*, are you happier than I am eating a bologna sandwich and watching the stars, while telling ghost stories to the children of this town? Happiness is happiness."

"That is so true. Why don't we sit down and meet some of the members of this incredible community who make you so happy?" Tanya pointed at Bob. "Cut it there. Let's film the final segment with members of the family in front of the church." Tanya was surprised at the tenacity and fire she found in Rebecca. She was very impressed with the young girl's maturity in answering her prying questions. But even more so than that she was impressed with her resolve in sticking with her true feelings.

"I'd really rather not be filmed." Sara put her arm around her daughter's waist as they walked toward the church. "You are doing so well. I don't want to embarrass you."

"Don't be silly." Rebecca sat down in a metal chair and patted the one next to her.

Sara eased into the chair, noticing a brown 1978 Cadillac Seville parked in front of Uncle Martin's home. She didn't say a word as Troy and his two friends got in the car and sped out of town.

Tanya primped her makeup before sitting next to Rebecca. "Let's have the brothers stand behind us." She took another quick look at her face and closed the compact.

"Tom is the only brother here," Sara smiled at Tanya. "Troy had to leave."

"What?" Rebecca asked her mother.

"Okay, he can stand behind us." Tanya noticed the bump on Sara's head stood out a little more than it had previously, as Tom moved in behind Rebecca.

"Welcome back to the *Tanya Springfield Show*. Joining us is running sensation Rebecca Young's mother, Sara, and her older brother Tom." Tanya turned sideways and looked at Sara. "I know you all are proud of Rebecca, but can you tell everyone what makes this young lady so special?"

"Besides being a very genuinely good person, she has something wired in her that makes her hate losing." Sara came across extremely confident and articulate. She could see Sam standing off to the side in front of the large group of townspeople watching the interview. "I believe no matter how successful she becomes she will always have her feet planted firmly on the ground."

"Well said," Tanya nodded toward Sara. "Has Rebecca always been a good athlete?"

"She always loved to run. We moved to Medicine Bow when she was a toddler just learning to walk. When we arrived here after a long drive from Missouri, she jumped out of the car and began running." Sara smiled at her daughter.

"But why do you think she is so successful as a runner?" asked Tanya. "Why is she so good?"

"She always loved inspirational quotes. Any reference to hard work, persistence, determination, or focusing was taken to heart by Rebecca." Sara leaned forward in her chair and smiled at Tanya. "She loves running and works hard at it."

"Tom," Tanya stood up and turned to Tom, holding the microphone in front of him. "Why do you think your sister is so successful as a runner?"

"She hates to lose," Tom stared into the beautiful reporter's eyes.

"Rebecca. Is that true?" Tanya sat back down.

"Yes. I love running and hate to lose."

"I know you lost your father at a very early age." Tanya looked at Sara rather than at Rebecca. "Was he a good athlete?"

"He was a very good high school football player. He would have been very proud of Rebecca." Sara felt the blood rush to her face. "He lost his life in a car accident when the boys were only two and Rebecca a baby."

"I'm sure he would be extremely proud of you." Tanya turned to Rebecca, noticing Delphia slowly moving closer, almost to being in the camera shot. "The future looks very bright, and I'm sure all of Texas is proud of you."

"I can tell ya why Becca is so special." Delphia jumped in front of Tanya before the reporter had time to protest. "Becca is the sweetest girl on the face of God's green earth. She loved me even when I was a God-awful, ugly baby. She loves me even if I have some faults, and I love her too. She taught me how to run fast, and I ran fast today and caught myself a pig annnnd Jesse didn't." Delphia crossed her arms and smiled into the camera.

Tanya dropped her hands and let her mouth fall open. "Well, Rebecca, it looks as though you have a lot of support in your hometown." Tanya looked directly into the camera. "That wraps it up from our visit with running sensation Rebecca Young and the good people of Medicine Bow."

Tanya shook hands with each member of the Young family and walked to the van as Bob stored his camera and tools. "Sam," she yelled loudly across the field, "could I have a moment with you?"

The large greasy millionaire walked to the van. "Ma'am, what can I do you for?"

"Oh, about twenty-five cents." Tanya winked. "Are you planning on attending the children's benefit in Dallas tomorrow evening?"

Sam knew she knew that of course he would be there. "No, I haven't made specific plans on attending."

"I would very much like to share a table with you." She handed him a purple business card. "I really am concerned about your persistence in continuing the absurd treatment of animals."

"I'll call you in the morning." Sam stared at the business card as Tanya slipped into the van and disappeared down the dusty country road. He was surprised at the crude sense of humor Tanya had displayed but was more concerned with the cold stare he was receiving from Sara as she walked with Rebecca toward their house.

Maliki and Tanya

"Oh my gosh." Tanya held a hand over her eyes. "I can't believe someone documented my telling Sam Blake I would do him for twenty-five cents."

"That tidbit of information came from Grandmother's diary. I'm sure at some point Sam had to explain himself to grandmother and he told her everything you said."

"It's a wonder we became such good friends." Tanya clasped her hands behind her head stretching her shoulders.

"Were you trying to snag Sam Blake?" Malaki stared at Tanya only five feet away with her breasts rising high in the air as if she were posing for him.

"I suppose if he were pursuing me he would have found very little resistance." Tanya let her arms fall to her side. "But more than all that I really found Medicine Bow to be very intriguing. It was such a different world from my life in the big city less than an hour away."

"Could you live there?"

"God no!" Tanya walked over to fill her wine glass. "Actually, at nighttime, I was frightened."

"Really."

"You grew up there. You wouldn't understand." Tanya tipped the wine bottle toward Maliki. "Do you want wine?"

Maliki's alcohol consumption had consisted of a couple beers, a sip of Jack Daniels, and no wine. Her standing in red silk pajamas and bright red lipstick holding a bottle of wine would make for a very successful advertisement. "Actually, I think I will try a glass."

"Okay." Tanya filled the glass almost to the brim and handed it to the handsome athlete. "That was interesting information about Troy leaving during the interview, something I never knew."

"That was the beginning of the journey that would change Medicine Bow for many years to come. We have it all right here."

"Good, I always knew Medicine Bow was an intriguing place to live but have wondered of the circumstances that took place." Tanya leaned over the table and adjusted the microphone. "He really was in as secure a situation as he could have wanted."

"It's all right here why he left." Maliki got a glimpse down the front of Tanya's pajama top. He wasn't sure, but he thought the very top button, now unfastened, was buttoned moments earlier.

"Shall we keep going?" Tanya smiled at him.

"Sure," Maliki took a large drink of wine.

Chapter Two

Amarillo, Texas

Explaining to his family and friends the need to leave the safe confines of Medicine Bow would have been futile for Troy. He was dying there. The very fact that Medicine Bow was such a safe and secure sanctuary to live made it necessary for him to leave. He needed to feel alive, to find adventure and experience a journey away from the safe haven and protection of the small-town community. The beginning of his venture brought him, Billy Ray, and Larry Lover to a truck stop restaurant in Amarillo, Texas.

"It's almost nine o'clock, and it's still got to be ninety degrees outside," Troy bellyached as he followed his friends inside the truck stop.

"How far are we from Denver?" Billy Ray asked as they followed the waitress to their table.

"About eight hours." Larry had made the trip to his grandfather's cabin near Winter Park high in the Colorado Rocky Mountains back when he was still in high school.

"Is the job in Denver really worth driving all this way?" Troy's desire to get away from home had been so great that he never got all the details about the job they were headed for.

"To be honest with you, I don't know," Larry leaned back in the booth. "Do you remember Jason Cook, the dude who bartended at Fritz's? He and I became pretty good friends before he moved to Denver last month to run a pizza place for his uncle. He's a pretty standup guy, and he told me he would give us a job if we would come to Denver."

"All three of us?" asked Troy.

"I told him there would be the three of us."

"How much will he pay?"

"That's the problem. It's only nine dollars an hour and most likely we all won't be working at the same time." Larry didn't seem very enthused about the job anymore and seemed to have something else on his mind.

"That's not very much money," said Troy.

All three boys watched the waitress walk by.

"There is another option I didn't tell y'all about." Larry leaned over the table and lowered his voice. "I met a biker at a party in Dallas last week, and I told him we were heading to Denver to take on a job. He seemed really interested in the fact we were heading to Colorado. He told me to give a friend of his a call when we hit Amarillo, and he might have work that would make us change our minds about the pizza job."

"What kind of work?" asked Billy Ray.

"I don't know. He only gave me a telephone number to call. The thing is, I don't know anything about it."

"I bet it's selling either crack or crank," said Billy Ray.

"I asked, and he said it wasn't anything to do with drugs. I was wasted, but I know he said it had nothing to do with drugs. He knew I worked on the oil rigs." Larry held his chin up higher, "Maybe it is something to do with physical work, like construction."

All three waited silently as the waitress served their meals.

"I reckon it wouldn't hurt for me to call." Larry smiled at the waitress. He was far from being handsome. His large ears rose high on the side of his oblong face and his lips were extraordinarily thick, yet he had an uncanny knack for attracting women. "I'll give him a call after we eat."

"Sounds good." Troy began eating his burger.

"Troy, what's this I hear about yore ma and Sam Blake having eyes for each other? Hell, man, Sam ain't got any kids. If yore ma married him, you could be in a lot of money. Ole Sam has to be one of the ten richest men in Texas." Larry took a large bite of his sandwich.

"I don't know what my ma has on her mind." It was obvious to Larry that Troy was annoyed by his bravado in talking about his mother.

"Don't get me wrong, but yore ma is one fine lady." Larry grabbed the check from the table and stood up. "I'm gonna call this number from the payphone."

"Use your cell," said Billy Ray.

"I don't want them to know it's me."

"That don't sound good," said Billy Ray, watching Larry walk away. "Something tells me I'm gonna end up back in the big house."

Larry talked on the phone for almost ten minutes. When he finished and approached the table, it was obvious from the smile on his face that there was going to be a change in their travel plans. "Man, this sounds too good to be true. They are having a party at a farmhouse outside the city this Friday night."

"What city?" asked Troy.

"Amarillo." Larry held his hand up, "Listen, we can meet with some people who, if everything goes right, plan to offer us a job that could pay up to ten thousand dollars for less than a month's work."

Billy Ray and Troy looked at each other.

"I know it will cost us the job in Denver, but we can't pass this up." Larry was too excited to care what the other two thought. "Let's just hang here in Amarillo until Friday and meet these people. If we have any doubts at all, we walk away."

"Count me in," said Billy Ray, "but we best call Jason in Denver and give him an excuse just in case this is a wild goose chase."

"I'll call him and tell him the car broke down." Larry pulled out his cell phone, "Are you in, Troy?"

"Hell, yes. I don't feel like driving eight more hours to make pizzas." Troy was more than in. He was excited to be on to a new adventure. It would be a quest to the unknown where he wouldn't have to kowtow to a conventional boss or have to play by someone else's rules. His spirit was free.

Maliki and Tanya

"So, they stayed in Amarillo," Tanya turned off the microphone.

"Yep," Maliki moved his finger around the brim of the empty wine glass.

"It was always obvious that Troy was a free spirit." She stood up and stretched, "It seems so many of his problems were blamed on his illness."

Maliki was a little light-headed after drinking the glass of wine. He was beginning to enjoy watching Tanya every time she reached her arms around her back to stretch. "Troy really was a free spirit who was seeking adventure."

"Well, I never thought of Troy doing the things he did because he was a free spirit. But I guess it makes sense." Tanya walked to the wine cabinet, "I am going to have another glass of wine, how about you?"

"Are you trying to get me drunk?" Maliki looked down at the next notebook labeled Sam.

"Of course not," Tanya winked at him, "how about some Cabernet?"

"I'll drink whatever your drinking." He opened the notebook and sat back down at the table. "You know, the next week while Troy, Billy Ray, and Larry were waiting in Amarillo was pretty active for everyone in Medicine Bow."

"That's when Rebecca went to California to race." Tanya filled both glasses with the Cabernet wine.

"Yes," Maliki accepted the glass of wine. "It's also when you met Sam at the fund-raiser."

"Oh, yes."

"It will be interesting to see if you remember the night the same way Sam did."

"Yes, it will," Tanya took a tiny sip of wine.

Dallas, Texas

Sam Blake noticed a glitter in Tanya's dark eyes as she sat across the dinner table fiddling with her napkin. Two crystal champagne glasses sparkled from the flame of a single candle in the middle of the pale blue tablecloth. After clearing away the dirty dinner dishes, the busboy placed a small vase with six yellow roses next to the candle.

"Please leave the water," said Sam cordially, placing a twenty-dollar bill into the young man's hand.

"Sam, I would like to thank you for honoring me with your presence tonight." Tanya placed her napkin into the busboy's cart of dirty dishes. "Everyone is looking at me with a hint of jealousy in their eyes."

"Thank you, Tanya, but I believe it is the other way around." Sam was uncomfortable, to say the least. Not because he was unaccustomed to dining at high-priced, sophisticated establishments, but because he didn't want to be considered an item with the beautiful Tanya Springfield. It must have cost her a pretty penny to secure a table for only two. When she asked him to accompany her to the benefit, he rationalized it would be a good time to straighten out any ill-will she might hold against him because of the incident with the pigs. He made it clear that she was to arrange for her own transportation to and from the evening's events, and that there was a good chance he would have to leave early.

"I can't believe a man who was covered with grease only a day ago could clean up so nicely."

"I was tickled you asked me to the affair tonight so we can discuss a compromise regarding the goings on in my community."

"I hope our time tonight is more than just an opportunity to discuss pigs." She leaned back in her chair and placed the wine cup to her red lips. "However, I do feel that greasing and chasing innocent pigs is an inexorable and disgusting thing to do."

"I truly understand how a woman of fine upbringing from the city would look at the chasing of these pigs as being mean-spirited." Sam took a large drink of water, "It is a contest that has been a part of the community for more than a hundred years. I remember catching a pig at the fair when I was just ten years old."

"Good Lord, Sam." Tanya placed her glass of champagne on the table but continued to look Sam directly in his eyes. Change comes very slowly to a man like him, but for the life of her she could not understand the thrill he received from the insidious contest. "Sam, if you continue to persist with this contest, the animal activists and press are going to make you out to be a scoundrel."

"They won't know if you don't tell them."

"I held the understanding there would be no more chasing of pigs."

"I'm sorry about the miscommunication," Sam smiled. "Let's take a break from this discussion. I see the governor is making his rounds."

"Sam," the governor patted Sam hard on the back. "I'm glad you could take time from your busy schedule to attend this worthy event."

"Governor," Sam turned and shook his hand. "You are lookin' well."

"Ms. Springfield, are you tryin' to hook Texas's most notorious bachelor?" the governor winked.

"No, sir, I'm just trying to come to a compromise with Mr. Blake on a very sensitive issue," Tanya winked back at the governor.

"If you can come to any sort of compromise with Mr. Blake, I would consider that to be a remarkable task," stated the governor.

"Sir," a young photographer pointed his camera toward the red-nosed governor. "Can I get a picture with you between Ms. Springfield and Mr. Blake?"

"I would be pleased to be immortalized with these two fine people."

The governor leaned down as the light from the camera flashed. He placed his hand on Tanya's shoulder and said, "Y'all enjoy yore evening. Sam, I'll talk with you later."

"That was interesting." Tanya leaned forward in her chair and posed for Sam as she watched the governor move to the next table of guests.

"I suppose I should explain myself." Sam pulled his chair in closer to the table. "I had planned to attend this function before we talked last night. I plan on meeting with the governor in a few minutes."

"I think I liked you better when I thought you were a man without character," Tanya forged a disappointed look. "Now that we have two centerpieces at our table, I'll sit here quietly thinking of the opening lines for my story about the vicious animal mauler of Medicine Bow."

"I never once intended using you for anything but a dinner companion this evening. In truth, I find you to be both beautiful and exciting. Like all men, I have a weakness for beautiful women. But you are also very intelligent, so I figured that spending this time together would not only make for an exciting evening, but also give me a chance to share with you a proposal I have come up with concerning the pigs in the contest at our harvest festival."

Tanya placed her perfectly manicured hand on top of Sam's large hand. She was a little infuriated that only one set of pictures had been taken, because she had given fifty dollars to two separate photographers. She knew this was a special occasion, and she had a limited amount of time with the rich Texan. "Sam, I wish to be your friend. At the same time, I am an animal lover."

"I'm ready to make a deal with you."

"I am a bit surprised that I am about to have Sam Blake give me his word of honor." Tanya tipped her head.

"Without going into the graphic details about the fate of domesticated animals, I will take it for granted that you realize most pigs will eventually be butchered and eaten." Sam tipped his head emulating Tanya's gesture, "Am I correct?"

She nodded.

"I am willing to make an agreement with you this evening. If you agree with what I propose, then five lucky pigs, the one's chosen to be a part of our contest, will in return for their contribution to our festivities, be given a life of luxury." There was not a hint of a smile on Sam's face. "I will hire a caretaker to massage and pamper them. They will have all the corn and apples they can eat, along with monthly visits to the veterinarian."

"What in the world."

"All I ask is that you come to my assistance if ever I should be questioned by any outside group concerning this contest."

"Are you being serious with me?"

"Serious as the day is long."

It was a well-known fact throughout Texas that Sam was exceedingly extravagant. Tanya was caught off guard by his bizarre proposal. The idea of having pigs pampered in such a way was remarkably odd to say the least, even by Sam Blake's standards. Most of her friends were animal lovers, some to the point of being activists. They would certainly scoff at such a peculiar offer, yet the idea held a certain appeal to her.

"Sam, I really don't know what to say."

"I hope you will agree. And if you do agree, I will hold you to your word."

"Oh, Sam. I can't believe you have come up with such an extraordinary proposal." Tanya breathed deeply through her mouth. "I will agree if the apples you give the pigs are candied."

"Agreed," Sam placed his hand across the table.

"I can't believe I just negotiated a deal to give five pigs a life which will most likely be better than mine." Tanya placed her small hand in his. "I envisioned a much different evening."

"It truly has been an enjoyable dinner, but I need to attend to some business." Sam stood and wiped his hands with his napkin. "I appreciate your company as well as your candor this evening."

Tanya slumped down in her chair, watching silently as he made his way out of the dining hall.

Maliki and Tanya

"So you made an agreement with Sam Blake to have pigs pampered." Maliki gulped the last drink from his glass of wine. "That's really all that happened that night, wasn't it?"

"Yes," Tanya took in a deep breath. The wine was making her a little giddy. "Sam never had anything but business on his mind."

"How about you?"

"What are you insinuating, Maliki?"

"Tanya," he smiled at her, speaking with a hint of derision. "Did you have more than business on your mind?"

"What do you think?" She walked to the wine bar, never taking her eyes off Maliki. She seized the bottle of Cabernet and moved perilously close to the handsome athlete as she filled his empty glass. He could smell the shampoo in her hair as she lightly brushed him after filling his glass. "Well, what do you think?"

"I really, really don't know what I think about your intentions with Sam." He watched her slip back around the table, noticing the bounce in her breasts under the loose-fitting, pajama top.

"Good answer," she sat down and took a sip of wine.

"You did have a reputation as …" He hesitated, knowing he better pick his words carefully. "As the most eligible woman in Dallas."

"Isn't it amazing how we can refer to a male as the most eligible bachelor and it sounds so manly, but a woman on her own, dating several men, comes across as a floozy."

"I didn't mean to suggest in any way that you are anything but a lady." Maliki truly meant what he said.

"I know you didn't." She decided to let him off the hook. "Actually, I was in a high-profile job at that time, and I liked being in the company of powerful men such as Sam Blake and the governor. Sam definitely had eyes for your grandmother and not me."

"Common sense told me, with you and my grandmother becoming such good friends, that there was never anything between you and Sam."

"Only friends," she relaxed. "I found Sam to be an amazing man despite the contest he continued to hold. He is and has always been very environmentally friendly and a wonderful conservationist of the lands he holds."

"After your and Sam's date … meeting," Maliki caught himself. "Sam headed back to Texas and then to California."

Van Horn, Texas

"Knock it off, you big-eared buffoon."

Sara glanced into the rearview mirror to see Jesse, Delphia, and Monty sitting quietly while Uncle Martin and Square Shoulders argued in the far backseat of the van.

"You've always been a farmer," said Square Shoulders.

"Most of my life, but not always," retaliated Uncle Martin.

"Yore nothing but a used up old sod buster." Square Shoulders looked out the window, not even giving Uncle Martin the courtesy of looking him in the eyes.

"You know damn well that I worked for three years in Houston dealing with top secret issues for the space industry."

"Maybe as a janitor."

"I was an engineer dealing with top secret, classified information."

"Bullshit, tell us all one classified secret you know." Square Shoulders continued to look out the window.

"That would finally give me a reason to shoot ya and put yore crinkly, old ass out of its misery." Uncle Martin winked at the three curious children who were turned in their seats watching the old men argue. All three laughed. They had seen the two men banter back and forth many times before.

"Knock off the language back there." Lola turned from her passenger seat in the front to give the men a menacing look. She knew it was just a part of their nature to pettifog.

"How about if I ask Sara to stop this van and I whip yore ass?" Square Shoulders finally turned toward Uncle Martin.

"Don't let these grey hairs fool ya. I could whup you when we were young, and I can whup you now."

"Lordy, Lordy, Lordy, this is going to be a long trip." Lola put both hands to her ears.

Sara concentrated on driving. California was by far the longest distance they had ever driven to watch Rebecca run. She knew Uncle Martin and Square Shoulders were the oldest of friends and understood they were simply letting off steam. She also knew it was going to be a long trip if she didn't stop soon to allow her passengers to stretch. She drove up the off ramp toward some much-needed coffee, but only for Lola and herself. She wasn't going to allow the old men any more caffeine.

"You all can get something here, if you like." Lola handed Jesse a ten-dollar bill. He snatched it from her hand and ran toward the gas station entrance, closely followed by Monty and Delphia.

"We do have sandwiches, so don't get too much," Sara yelled to the children.

"Can you please get yore big male ass out?" Square Shoulders yelled at Uncle Martin who was having difficulty getting out of the backseat. "You look like a big old water buffalo trying to climb out of here."

"You know I have arthritis in my back. Give me a break." Martin made it out the van door and stood up straight to stretch. He had put on a few pounds over the past couple of years, so being called a water buffalo didn't sit well with him.

"Could you grab me a cappuccino?" Sara asked Lola as she began fueling the van. "Get us a newspaper too."

The smell of popcorn filled the inside of the service station. Delphia, holding a bag of peanut M&M's, Jesse with a bag of potato chips, and Monty with two quarts of Gatorade prepared to pay the cashier. Lola held a newspaper under her arm as she finished filling a second large cup of coffee.

"I'm thinking about buying that bag of orange slices," said Uncle Martin to no one in particular, eyeing a single bag of sugar-coated orange slices hanging from a wire candy holder.

Square Shoulders reached up and seized the bag of candy from the rack before Martin could make his move. "I love these candies. They'll last me all the way to California."

Martin grabbed the bag and yanked as hard as he could, ripping the bag, scattering pieces of candy across the floor. The young cashier who had a pierced nose and purple hair watched with her mouth wide open as both men put their hands up like two nineteenth-century boxers.

"Uncle Martin!" yelled Sara, stepping through the door into the station. "Luther! I can't believe you two would act in such a manner in public. Now both of you get outside and don't get in the van until I get there."

The young cashier was much calmer about the episode than Sara anticipated she would be. "There's several bags of them orange candies on the bottom of the rack if y'all want them," she said. "They're two for a dollar."

"I don't think they deserve any candy." Sara placed her credit card on the counter.

"I understand. My grandpa is ornery as the day is long." The cashier took the receipt. "Y'all have a safe trip."

Sara raised her eyebrows and walked out the door. Uncle Martin and Square Shoulders were waiting with the three children standing between them. Lola was in the front seat reading the paper.

"Jesse, would you mind sitting in the way back with Uncle Martin?" Sara asked as she neared the van.

"No, ma'am," answered Jesse.

"Luther, you can sit in the middle, opposite Martin, with Delphia and Monty." Sara glared at the two men, letting them know she was fed up with their behavior. "Now let's get going."

"Umm, umm, umm. Look here," said Lola, holding the newspaper so Sara could see it.

Sara fastened her seat belt and glanced at the newspaper. There was a picture of Sam in a tuxedo sitting across the table from a very photogenic Tanya Springfield, with the smiling governor of the state of Texas posing between them.

"It says millionaire Sam Blake was wooing more than the governor at the children's fund-raising dinner last night as he dined with beautiful Dallas news lady Tanya Springfield," Lola read.

"Well. Mr. Blake certainly gets around." Sara spun the tires as she reentered the highway.

San Diego, California

The parking lot at Qualcomm Stadium was filled with antique automobiles. Uncle Martin and Square Shoulders were the best of friends as they moved toward a 1957 Chevy.

"Rebecca's race is about three hours away, so you all can spend a little time out here if you like." Sara carried a small backpack in her arms as she spoke to Uncle Martin.

"Maybe we can walk around a bit." Uncle Martin turned to Square Shoulders who nodded in approval.

"We'll be on the side of the finish line." Sara walked toward the large stadium followed by Lola and the kids.

The infield of the stadium was full of athletes stretching and running in preparation for the events of the day to begin. Most were college athletes getting ready for the cross-country meet to begin. There was to be four different levels of competition with runners starting and finishing in the stadium, but most of the race would be run outside around the perimeter of the stadium. Rebecca's special 1500-meter race would be held after the final cross-country contestant crossed the finish line.

"This is perfect running weather, nice and cool." Sara set her backpack down on a seat and looked out over the large stadium at the thousands and thousands of empty seats. "At least we won't have to worry about finding a place to sit."

"This is wonderful," said Lola.

"I'm so glad you made this trip with me." Sara put her arm over her best friend's shoulder. "I don't remember ever watching a track meet without you."

"Watching Tom and Rebecca run over the years has been a true blessing." Lola sat down in her seat.

Sara couldn't help but feel a twinge of guilt in the fact that Troy had never fulfilled his potential as a runner. She knew the same opportunities available to Rebecca and Tom had been given to Troy, yet he never could take advantage of them. What made her sad was that Troy always considered himself to be as accomplished an athlete as his siblings, but he never understood the time and commitment the other two made in realizing their success.

"Ma, we're going to climb to the top of the stadium," said Jesse.

"I'm going too." Delphia looked to her mother for support in her tagging along with the older boys.

"Y'all take Delphia and keep an eye on her."

"She's such a pest and always threatens to tattle on me even when I don't do anything wrong."

"Take her anyway. Monty, help watch her."

"Yes, ma'am." Monty peeked at Lola through his red hair as the wind blew it over his eyes.

The first wave of cross-country runners came across the finish line as Uncle Martin and Square Shoulders made their way up the steep steps to where Sara and Lola were sitting. They were taking their time laughing and conversing with each other.

"I am glad to see you two enjoying each other's company." Sara smiled at the two men as they approached her.

"We may argue some, but I do like this old coot," said Square Shoulders.

"Arguing with him is like wrestling with a pig in the mud. Pretty soon you realize that the pig enjoys it." Martin slapped Square Shoulders on the back.

"There's Rebecca," Lola pointed to the track.

When Rebecca entered the stadium, she instantaneously looked into the stands for her family. She waved several times as she approached the track and yelled to her mother, "How was your trip?"

"It was eventful, honey. How are you feeling?"

"All right, but my right knee is a little sore." Rebecca rubbed the outside edge of her knee. "Brenda put some liniment on it, and I'm sure it will be fine after I warm up."

"It's probably from sleeping on a different bed." Sara didn't seem too concerned.

"Hi, everyone," Rebecca gave a short wave to the rest of the group.

The three kids came running down from the top of the stadium toward the lower railing with Delphia leading the way. "Yore gonna run like the wind today." Delphia stared admiringly at Rebecca.

"I'll bet you lap the rest of them girls," said Jesse.

"Yeah, you'll win easy." Monty noticed how Rebecca was touching her right leg. "Does yore leg hurt?"

"A little, but I'll be okay." A big smile came across her face as she looked behind the boys. "There's Sam."

"Are ya ready to run?" Sam walked to the railing in front of Rebecca.

"I'm ready, but a little nervous."

"That's usually a good sign." Sam pulled something from his coat pocket and handed it through the railing. "I brought you a good luck charm."

When Rebecca was a little girl Sam often referred to her as a little butterfly because she was always on the run and constantly moving. She and Sam had a special connection. He enjoyed telling her stories as she sat listening and looking at him with her big saucer eyes, melting his heart.

"Thank you, Sam, I love it." She clutched a bright red and yellow butterfly fashioned from twenty-four karat gold and outlined with small diamonds. "I'll see you after the race." She ran to the middle of the track and waved to her mother in the stands.

Sam turned and looked up to where the rest of the group was sitting. He could see the surprised look on Sara's face as he made his way up the stairs.

"Did ya bring me something, Sam?" asked Delphia.

"Yeah, a twenty-dollar bill if ya bring me back a Coke."

"That's not a good gift," Delphia shrugged.

"Girl, if you know what's good for you, you had better change your attitude." Lola glared at Delphia. "Sorry about that, Sam."

"Lola, no need to apologize." Sam looked at Sara, "Sara, how are you today?"

"Sam," she gave him the cold shoulder.

"How are ya doin,' Sam?" asked Uncle Martin.

Sam sat down next to Sara, "I've been on the run for the past forty-eight hours, and I'm plumb tuckered."

"Hmmmmm," Sara turned her back to Sam.

"I'll go help the kids with the drinks," said Lola.

Sam turned toward Sara and took a deep breath. "I have something I would like to talk with you about."

"Does it concern Miss Springfield?"

"Of course not," he hesitated. "If you think I have some amorous feelings toward Tanya Springfield, you are greatly mistaken."

"Am I mistaken about the picture of you and her at the dinner the other night?" She turned to face him. "I know we never had any formal agreement between us, but I ... you know what I mean."

"I understand, that's why I came here to ask you to do something for me."

"What would you like for me to do?"

"The biggest mistake I've made involving you … us, is that I never tell you how I feel. I've never been afraid to take a chance, never with anybody but you."

"Sam, I was embarrassed." She knew Sam was speaking from his heart and that he wouldn't have come all the way to California if he wasn't hooked on her.

"I want you to know that I think you are the greatest woman in the world. I know I should have told you this on several occasions, but I just didn't."

"We have only dated a few times. But it is humiliating to have a beautiful woman like Tanya Springfield come to my home and see her walk away with a man I think highly of," Sara brushed her finger over his hand.

Sam had never met a woman who enticed him the way Sara did. Her natural physical beauty along with her gentle approach to something as simple as touching his hand made his heartbeat double.

"I have a difficult time talking to you," said Sam, "because I don't want to say the wrong thing."

"You can tell me anything."

He looked at her chiseled profile and smelled her perfume. He almost lost his composure.

"I want you to go somewhere with me on Sunday." His voice was very firm.

"But we won't be home by then."

"I made seven reservations on the same flight Rebecca is on this evening," said Sam. "You can leave the van at the airport; Stanley has arranged for a driver to get it back home. I'd fly you on my private plane, but I have to go to Sacramento this evening, and I'm sure you would rather spend this time with Rebecca."

"Where would we go and for how long?"

"New York City, two nights."

"Sam, I need more time. I have no clothes."

"You only need bring your personal items. I need you to trust me."

Sara looked at him without a hint of suspicion. Countless times she had wished for Sam to take her away.

"Well?" Sam waited for her response.

"We're going to have a very happy group of Texans when they find out about these plans. That was one heck of a long drive," she leaned over and hugged Sam.

"Here's the drinks." Lola gave no indication that she had heard much of the conversation, but she knew she needed to interrupt. "Rebecca is coming to the line for her race."

***

Rebecca was focused as she stepped up to the starting line. She had been running competitively for over ten years, but this was by far the biggest and most important race of her life, so far. Besides aiming for a fast time, she really wanted to beat Tabitha Read. Tabitha had insulted her on more than one occasion, albeit subtle tidbits of scorn splattered throughout her many interviews with the press. Most recently she had called her a farm girl with an attitude.

Rebecca made eye contact with Tabitha as she positioned herself on the right side of her dainty rival. There were six other runners in the race, but everyone knew the race would be won by either Tabitha or Rebecca. Rebecca planned on running in the footsteps of Tabitha and fly past her with two hundred meters left in the race. Tabitha had already met the Olympic qualifying time for the 1500 meters but wanted to make a statement to everyone that she was the fastest woman's middle-distance runner in the United States.

The gun sounded, and Rebecca's start was quick, fast enough she needed to slow to allow Tabitha room to run in front of her. Tabitha was notorious for her fast pace, and she usually won from start to finish, enjoying it when she could humiliate her opponents by beating them badly. But today she was startled by the quickness of Rebecca and had to sprint to the first curve to secure the spot as the front runner. Rebecca relaxed and ran closely behind with the rest of the runners following.

Rebecca's legs felt very strong, strong enough she could easily have blown by Tabitha. But Coach Joan knew that Tabitha would never let an opponent take the lead, that patience would give Rebecca the best chance of winning the race. The race seemed to crawl at a snail's pace. She heard coach Joan yell, "one oh five," yet it didn't feel as though she had run the first four hundred meters in a minute and five seconds.

Rebecca and Tabitha were fifteen meters in front of the nearest competitors as they approached eight hundred meters. The pace picked up and now was blistering, yet Rebecca felt stronger than she had ever felt at this point of a race. Tabitha kept pressing, trying to break away from her relentless pursuer.

The race was taking place in a flash. Rebecca's concentration was so great she couldn't hear the cheering and screaming from her family and friends. She was breathing hard and could feel a slight tightening in her upper right thigh as she began the final lap well ahead of the other competitors, but two meters behind Tabitha.

Rebecca's hair, tied into a ponytail, began to fluctuate from one side of her face to the other as she began to make her move around Tabitha. The tightening in her upper thigh had moved down to her knee and was becoming painful. She lengthened her stride as they approached the final curve. Tabitha hung tight to the inside of the track as Rebecca ran to her outside with a slight irregularity in her gait.

Entering the backstretch, both girls were in full-out sprint. Rebecca was still a body length behind, gaining ever so slightly with each stride. Both girls running with heads steady, focusing, with determined looks on their faces, finally lunging forward at the finish line. Both girls were sure they had broken the tape.

Rebecca hopped several steps past the finish line and clutched her right knee. Tabitha trotted to her side and placed her arm around her shoulder, breathing hard and saying nothing. Rebecca straightened and gave her a quick hug.

"Nice run." Coach Joan put her arm around Rebecca's waist and helped her walk to the infield. She noticed moisture in Rebecca's eyes. "What's wrong with your leg?"

"I pulled something in my thigh or knee," she was relying heavily on her coach to walk. "Did I win?"

"I couldn't tell, the judges are trying to make the decision." Joan motioned to a trainer, "We need to get you to the trainer's tent. I don't want you walking on the leg."

Coach Joan had coached Rebecca for nearly ten years and in that time had never seen her cry. She knew that her star athlete was in much more pain than she was letting on. She helped her stand as two trainers made their way toward them with a stretcher.

Rebecca observed the group from Medicine Bow in the stands watching her being carried to the trainer's tent. Sara made her way to the tent and entered right after Rebecca and the attendants.

"Are you okay?" Sara put her hand to her daughter's flushed cheek.

"I think so, it doesn't hurt at all now."

"Everyone's really worried about you. I'm so proud of you."

"It was so nice having everyone here," Rebecca stood up. "I think I broke the tape before Tabitha, but it is so funny because I'm really not positive I did."

"No matter the result, you ran a great race. I'll bet really fast too."

Coach Joan stepped into the tent. She walked over to the ice chest and grabbed a bottle of water. She said nothing, which caused Rebecca to feel she had lost the race.

"Well, did we win?"

"You ran it in 4:16.08."

"Did we win?" Rebecca put her hand on her knee, not because it hurt, but because had it not been so painful down the backstretch, she would have run the race fast enough to break the high school girls all-time record in the 1500 meters.

"According to the judges," Coach Joan smiled, "you won."

"Yes!" Rebecca threw her arms around her mother.

"I saw the photo and honestly could not tell if it was your forehead or your bangs that broke the tape, but it doesn't matter because your body was definitely there before her."

Both Joan and Rebecca chuckled. They had spent hours discussing hair styles over the past years. Joan had always wanted Rebecca to cut her hair shorter, but Rebecca refused to cut her beautiful tresses.

"We're flying back with you all this evening," Sara interrupted the private joke.

"You are?" Rebecca was surprised to the point of leaving her mouth open.

"All of us, I'll tell you all about it on the flight home."

"Good, that means I can take the kids out for a picnic the day after tomorrow. I was worried we wouldn't be able to do our annual picnic before school started."

"I don't think that's a good idea," said Joan. "You need to rest your leg."

"I'll just walk the kinks out," Rebecca had a big smile on her face.

Joan knew that the future was limitless for her special, once in a lifetime athlete, and she wanted to make sure she did everything in her power to facilitate and promote her chances for success. She also knew that Rebecca's priorities were firmly grounded, that she enjoyed life, and would never miss a chance at spending time in the country with her friends.

"I'm sure everyone is waiting to hear how you are doing. And if you won the race." Sara hugged her daughter, "Let's get going and you can tell them yourself."

Maliki and Tanya

"My God, Aunt Rebecca was a great runner." Maliki shook his head.

"I remember the sportscaster at our news station was completely blown away when he heard how fast she ran that race." Tanya turned off her microphone. "He was certain that she would set a new record for schoolgirls sometime during her upcoming senior year."

"Grandmother told me she received many letters from colleges trying to recruit her and that everyone felt the Olympics was a certainty."

"She had such a bright future at a very young age." Tanya stood up and looked Maliki directly in his eyes. "Much like someone else we know."

"I can guarantee I would not be even close to the runner I am without Aunt Rebecca's help." Maliki smiled as he watched Tanya pull out her compact and apply a light coating of bright red lipstick. "Did you know that Grandmother was upset about the picture of you and Sam?"

"No, I didn't," Tanya rubbed her lips together. "It is a little unnerving to hear how troubled she was about the picture."

"Did you know Sam asked Sara … Grandmother, to New York City?"

"I had no idea." Tanya stood up from the table and walked to the large picture window and looked out into the darkness. "But nothing Sam Blake did would surprise me."

Maliki walked over next to her, "Let's step out on the deck."

"It's freezing."

"We'll only be out for a minute." He opened the sliding glass doors and stepped out onto the large deck. Tanya slowly followed him into the frigid outdoors.

"I need to grab my coat," Tanya folded her arms.

"We'll go back in a second," Maliki put his arm around her. He very much wanted her to see the stars on such a clear night. "Look at the sky."

"Oh," Tanya took in a deep breath as she looked at the bright sky full of sparkling stars, "it's beautiful."

"Are you frightened?" Maliki lowered his head to look her in the eyes.

"No," she brushed her cheek lightly on his shoulder, "not with you here."

Maliki took pleasure in the moment of holding the older woman. He enjoyed her softness, in contrast to the domineering and forceful demeanor she had earlier revealed. He was surprised that the powerful Tanya Springfield would show him her submissive side.

"I love this," Maliki looked to the heavens.

"It really is dazzling," Tanya snuggled closer.

"I come out here every night." He felt her shiver. He didn't say another word but turned and slid open the glass door, allowing her to walk into the warmth of his home.

Tanya took pleasure in Maliki's boyish, country charm. She excused herself and walked to her bedroom.

Maliki poured himself another glass of wine. He moved to the kitchen and pulled out a small tray of cold cuts and placed them on the countertop. His mind was racing as he folded up a piece of turkey and shoved it in his mouth. He watched as Tanya came back in and walked straight to the wine bar.

"Are you hungry?" Maliki asked as she prepared to open another bottle of wine. "I have lots of food."

"I'm fine," she poured her wine. "Maybe later."

Maliki set a small plate of lunchmeat on the table next to his full glass of wine. He removed the notebook labeled Troy. The smell of Eternity perfume preceded Tanya as she approached the table.

"Right after Rebecca's race in California is when things started changing for Troy," said Maliki.

"This will be intriguing." Tanya set up the microphone. "It's a time I know hardly anything about."

"It's really the beginning of his troubles." Maliki opened the notebook.

Farmhouse outside Amarillo, Texas

This might be the biggest mistake of my life, Troy thought as he watched two large bikers approach the car. Smoke filled the air from a large fire burning a half mile away, illuminating the night. Larry Lover rolled down the front window in order to talk with the menacing men.

"How y'all doin'?" Larry asked anxiously. "We're here to see Bodine."

The dirty biker stepped back and spoke into his radio.

"Tell them Bodine from the Palace asked us to meet him here," Larry said.

The biker waited until a reply came over the radio. He leaned into the car to inspect the occupants. He smiled, showing his blackened teeth before confirming the right of passage. "Go on in. Bodine says to park in the field on the north side of the house. Y'all have a good time."

Larry drove his car past the two-story farmhouse and parked on a grass-covered field. Five bikers and three scantily clad women were sitting on the wooden porch. Several more bikers and half-naked women were yelling and dancing around a fifty-gallon barrel in the middle of a huge bonfire burning in the front yard. The smell of the burning chemicals filled the clean air.

Troy could feel the blood rushing through his body as he followed his friends toward the melee. He couldn't remember ever feeling as good as he did then. The feeling of rapture brought about a feeling of confidence that he never could have felt with the use of his medication. He could become the life of the party on his own wit and persona without the aid of any medication.

"Are y'all ready to party?" asked Bodine. He held out his hand to Larry.

Larry cackled with an uncharacteristic phoniness as he held his hand out to the large man.

"Glad y'all could make it," said Bodine, examining the three men through his beady, grey eyes.

"These are my friends Billy Ray and Troy Young," said Larry. "Is everything still cool with the job?"

"Oh yeah. Y'all are gonna meet the man tonight. His name is Mr. King."

"We still talking ten grand?" asked Larry.

"If you impress Mr. King and he thinks you can do the job without any snags, he'll pay at least ten thousand dollars." Bodine confidently smiled at the three.

"Does he have the money?" asked Billy Ray.

"Oh yeah, the money will be no problem." Bodine turned toward the group partying in front of the house. "Now, there are several girls from the club out there waiting to partee. Y'all have some fun and I'll let you know when Mr. King is ready to meet."

"Grab yourselves a beer," said a grubby biker, opening a door to large white refrigerator on the porch of the farmhouse.

"Take good care of these fellas, Pig Pen." Bodine slapped the back of the disheveled biker as he walked through the screen door into the house.

"Will do," Pig Pen handed each of the boys a tall can of beer.

It took three drinks of beer before the alcohol hit Troy, like a mule kicking him in the head. Although the loud music had been playing all along, it now felt as if each beat of every sound was thumping in his chest. He jumped off the porch and began dancing around the fire. He was dancing faster than the music, stopping only long enough to down the rest of his beer in one long drink. He tossed the aluminum beer can into the mixture of chemicals burning in a fifty-gallon barrel.

"Don't do that," yelled a biker who was standing next to the fire with his arm around a pretty blond-haired woman.

"No problemo." Troy pulled the blond lady from the biker's grasp and began to dance with her. The biker pulled her back to his side. Troy leaped back on the porch, opening the refrigerator and grabbing another beer.

"Oh crap," said Billy Ray. He knew from past experiences that his friend was in a state of excitement far higher than anything the party could offer.

"What's going on, have you lost yore mind?" Larry was stunned as he watched Troy strutting in front of the bikers, completely out of control. He had been forewarned by Billy Ray that Troy had problems, but this was ridiculous.

"I'm just partying with these dudes," Troy took another drink of beer.

"They're gonna kick the hell out of you," Larry held his hand up. "And us."

"I'm not afraid of anything or anybody." Troy pointed his right finger at the stunned bikers.

"Y'all are about to get yore asses kicked from here to El Paso and back." Pig Pen stood on the edge of the porch.

Troy momentarily stopped to look at Pig Pen. There was something strange about the large biker. His eyes were clear and focused. The other bikers were ready to fight, but Pig Pen was willing to negotiate. Something didn't add up.

Troy raised his beer over his head and yelled, "I am the toastmaster from Medicine Bow. I want to raise a toast to all my new friends here tonight. I hope for only friendship, prosperity, and happiness for y'all." He stopped to look at the bikers, many unsure of the aggressive nature he displayed and others actually standing with their drinks raised high. Maybe he had found a new niche for his life, that of a toastmaster.

Billy Ray and Larry were standing by the front door of the farmhouse, hoping for protection from the well-dressed men right inside the screen door.

Bodine opened the door and said, "Mr. King is ready to meet."

"Come on, Troy, we need to go inside," yelled Larry, relieved by the timing of Bodine.

"The toastmaster will be back momentarily." Troy bowed and walked to the front door.

A small man who appeared to be in his fifties with dark, thinning hair was sitting at a small kitchen table, smoking a cigarette. He sat silently looking through his cold, dark eyes as the three friends made their way into the kitchen. Behind him stood two men dressed in polo shirts and leisure slacks.

Larry and Billy Ray were terrified. The mannerisms and the obvious authority Mike King possessed frightened them. They stood silently avoiding eye contact with the powerful man.

"I'm not afraid of any of this," bellowed Troy, stepping to the center of the kitchen with his hands to his side and his chin held high. He placed the empty beer can on the table.

"These are the men I told you about," said Bodine, staring threateningly at Troy.

Mike King looked at the three without smiling or changing his expression. "You recently got out of prison. Is that right?" he asked.

Troy thought he noticed a small flicker of light in the eyes of Mike King before they turned cold and dark again. He suspected the danger facing his friends and him was real and life-threatening, but it wasn't going to stop him from impressing his future employer.

Before Troy could say another word, Larry answered, "Billy Ray and I robbed a little nickel and dime store and spent almost two years in jail."

Troy's lungs were filled with smoke and his mouth was dry from his excursion dancing around the fire. He took a deep breath and said, "I was at Bellvidere for a couple of months. Damn, I could use another beer."

Mike King turned to Bodine and asked, "What is Bellvidere?"

"A psychiatric hospital."

"You were in a mental institution." Mike King made his statement with enough spit and slobber coming out his mouth to make him resemble a rabid dog. "One of you pimple-assed little pissants informed us you were all ex-convicts."

"It was me," answered Larry in an act of true bravery. "I'll vouch for Troy."

Mr. King looked at the floor, shaking his head harder than a normal person would think necessary. "If I want something done right, I have to do it myself." He looked menacingly at Bodine.

It was the first time Bodine had come face to face with the notorious man, so rather than make any excuse, the large biker simply took a couple steps backwards.

"What about your families? Will they worry about you being gone for an extended period of time?" Mr. King focused on the three workers. "You won't be able to have any contact with them for over five weeks."

"No," answered both Larry and Billy Ray.

"No," answered Troy, knowing full well that it wasn't the case. He knew he should remain silent, but there was something churning inside him which made it distressingly necessary to impress Mr. King. "Sir, we can handle anything you have in mind for us. Start a business. Set up books. Anything. Let's have a toast."

"What the hell is he talking about?" Mr. King asked nobody in particular.

"I'm starting my own business. I'll charge twenty dollars per toast," Troy continued. "Don't worry. You don't owe me anything for the toast to those assholes outside."

"Enough, Troy," warned Billy Ray.

"Young man, you shouldn't drink if you can't handle the liquor. Now, let's get to business." Mr. King didn't say so, but he was mildly impressed with the machismo of Troy. "I'm going to give each of you one thousand dollars as down payment for the work you will be performing. By accepting the money, you will be giving me your word of honor that you will speak to no person about the job or anyone you have met here tonight. If you perform your job to our satisfaction, you will each receive an additional nine thousand dollars."

Each boy was handed one thousand dollars, all in twenties. Billy Ray looked at Larry confirming they had heard the powerful man state that they would each receive ten thousand dollars, not ten thousand in total.

Troy held the money tightly in his right hand. "A toast to Mr. King."

Larry hit Troy hard on his arm and yelled, "Shut yore mouth."

Mr. King ignored both boys. "You are to leave for Denver immediately after this meeting. Do not call anyone. Get in your car and drive. When you arrive in the metro area, you are to go to the suburban city of Aurora, where you will be staying in an apartment for the next three days." He paused, noticing Troy was trying to speak. "Are you listening?"

He hadn't heard a word he said, but he knew Larry was paying attention.

"On Monday you will leave the apartment complex and take a bus to downtown Denver where you are to wait on the northeast corner of Broadway and Colfax. Two men driving a white construction van will pick you up at exactly four p.m. The work you are to perform will be physical, so take advantage of the next days to rest. All questions about your job are to be directed to those contacts in Denver. Follow these directions, and I'm sure our dealings will be cordial and profitable."

"Boss," Troy interrupted.

Mr. King glared at Troy. "You talk too much and don't listen enough. That could be a problem."

"Shut up, Troy." Larry was sure Troy was going to get them killed. "We'll make sure it's not a problem."

"I highly recommend you do so." Mr. King gave a serious look to Bodine. "Give them the address to the apartment."

"It's easy to find this place." Bodine handed Larry an envelope with a set of Colorado license plates. "Put these on your car when you get to Aurora."

A middle-aged man dressed in black slacks and a white shirt entered the front door of the house and walked over to Mr. King and said in a low voice, "We have a dilemma outside."

"What's the problem?" asked Mr. King.

"The biker Pig Pen, he's been walking around to the back of the house and making telephone calls. I think he might be reporting to someone."

"Gentlemen, this meeting is over." Mike King moved quickly toward the back door. He hesitated at the door and looked at the three boys. "I want you to leave for Denver. Now."

The three boys walked through the smoke-filled air toward Larry's Cadillac. The loud and boisterous party continued behind them.

"Are you sure y'all want to leave? Hell, we could stay here and party for a while," said Troy.

"Shut up and get in." Larry had heard enough from Troy.

"I'm serious about being a toastmaster," spouted Troy as he climbed into the back of the Cadillac.

"That is the stupidest thing I have ever heard," snarled Larry, turning on the ignition. "I don't want to hear another word about you being a toastmaster."

"It's just an idea I can't get out of my head."

"All right, Troy. I've had it with you." Billy Ray turned around in his seat and confronted his friend. "I know damn well you haven't been taking your medication. Get the bottle out and take a pill."

"I'm doin' fine without it," Troy said as he leaned back in the seat.

"Now, Troy! We ain't takin' off until you do." Billy Ray turned to Larry. "Don't leave."

"All right." Troy opened his knapsack and took out the bottle of medication. He hesitated before popping a pill in his mouth.

"Put those pills somewhere close by." Billy Ray glared at Troy. "You are going to take your medication. Do you understand?"

"I reckon." He returned the medication to the knapsack.

"You put our lives in danger tonight, and I know how you get when you don't take that stuff." Billy Ray continued to glare at Troy. "Is everything cool between us?"

"It's good." He hadn't been taking his medication, so it was hard to be mad at Billy for stating the obvious. Even though his mother was sure he had been taking the lithium, it had been three weeks since he had taken his last tablet.

"I'll drive a couple of hours, and one of y'all can take over." Larry broke the ice as he drove away from the farmhouse.

All three remained quiet as they began travelling toward Colorado. They all shared the same euphoria of having been paid a thousand dollars each, but at the same time they had uneasy thoughts about the mysterious job they were headed toward.

Maliki and Tanya

"So that's how they met Mike King." Tanya turned off her microphone. "He was a really bad person."

"They didn't know." Maliki scratched his head. "They thought they had finally gotten a lucky break in life."

"What a contrast, at this time, what was happening to Troy compared to Rebecca's accomplishments," said Tanya.

"Rebecca was finding fame while Troy was covertly seeking his riches."

"I found it interesting how brazen Troy was in such a dangerous situation with the bikers. Do you think he was naturally fearless, or do you think it was because of his sickness?" asked Tanya.

"I don't think he was afraid of anything in life - but life itself."

"What in the world do you mean?"

"He didn't want an ordinary life," Maliki paused. "It frightened him to think he would have a nine to five job with two kids. He wanted excitement and adventure."

"That makes sense." Tanya made her routine stretch where she arched her back, bringing her arms to her side, holding her shoulder blades back, as she looked to the ceiling.

Maliki couldn't help but stare.

"Gosh, it has to be getting late," she relaxed.

"It's almost midnight." He looked at his watch.

"Shall we stop for the night, or keep going?" Tanya walked to the wine bar and filled her empty wine glass with water from the sink.

"Let's keep going." Maliki watched Tanya make her way back to the table. Her body was slender and athletic. He remembered how nice she had felt when he placed his arm around her earlier on the deck. Recalling the moment brought about a twinge of excitement to his brain.

"I'm not tired at all," said Tanya.

Maliki stared at her for a moment and opened the notebook labeled Sara and Rebecca.

Medicine Bow, Texas

It's a perfect morning, there isn't a cloud in the sky, Rebecca thought as she laid a checkered red and white picnic basket onto the wooden floor of the porch. She sat down next to Uncle Martin on the cherry wood swing he had designed and made himself.

"Do you want to come with us?" Rebecca asked.

"You'd probably have to carry me," answered Uncle Martin, staring down the street toward the church. "It looks like you have a small army coming this way."

Jesse Dodge was leading a group of five enthusiastic kids, walking in formation toward the Youngs' house. They had all run home after church to change clothes. The afternoon picnics were a tradition, which Rebecca enjoyed and looked forward to with the same amount of eagerness as the children. She almost cancelled the trip because of the injury to her leg from the race, but now she was glad she hadn't changed plans. Besides, a person was allowed only a few chances in life to indulge and have a couple pieces of Lola's angel food cake with chocolate fudge frosting.

"Where y'all going today?" asked Uncle Martin, gently rocking.

"To the creek above pit hill."

"That's where Danny Tucker shot me in the ass. I was walking in front of him when he tripped on a piece of driftwood and shot me right in the butt with his twenty-two rifle."

"Oh Martin, are you still telling that story." Sara stepped out the front door onto the porch. Her makeup was done perfect.

"You look great," said Rebecca.

"Thank you. Lola and Ethel are taking me to the airport to meet Sam, so I won't be home when you get back."

"You're gonna have a great time." Rebecca hopped off the rocker and hugged her mother, noticing how good she smelled. "Are you going to see a show?"

"Sam's making all the plans and reservations."

"I'll bet he has some plans for you," said Uncle Martin, swinging faster.

"Get your mind out of the gutter," Sara frowned at Martin.

"I won't be able to call because the cell phone doesn't work at the creek. So I'll tell you now that I hope you have fun." Rebecca picked up the picnic basket and hurried toward the anxious kids. "Trey, did you bring the water?"

"It's in my backpack," said Trey.

"Jesse, you carry the picnic basket first, then Monty and I'll carry it last," delegated Rebecca.

"What about Delphia and Crystal? They're big enough to carry the basket," stated Jesse. He hadn't forgiven his sister for catching a pig at the harvest festival and mocking him for his failure to catch one.

"When we get to the creek, Delphia and Crystal can lay the blankets out and set up the picnic lunch," said Rebecca, walking in front of the boys with the two girls close by her side.

Jesse, Monty, and Trey had all been on the excursions several times with Rebecca over the past three years, but this was the first time they noticed how truly beautiful their guide was. Rebecca was wearing a tank top and baggy red shorts. All three boys were blatantly looking at the back of her long tan legs as they walked through a field of sagebrush and cactus.

"We always have to feed them boys," said Delphia, looking back at the three boys.

"Everybody needs to do their part, that way we can all have fun without one person having to do all the work," stated Rebecca.

"You're so smart, Rebecca." Delphia leaned closer to Rebecca and whispered, "Jesse's been real mean to me since I caught that dirty, old, greasy pig."

"Let's just enjoy ourselves. Stop for a second. Does everyone have sunblock?" Rebecca untied her waist packet and placed it on the ground. She bent over, taking the opportunity to stretch her hamstring muscles, reaching in to get the suntan lotion. "Monty, make sure you put some of this on." She turned in time to see all three boys look away.

"Rebecca! Them boys are looking at your butt," yelled Delphia.

Trey held his mouth wide open, Monty's face was flushed bright red, and Jesse glared at Delphia.

"Monty, cover your face with the lotion." Rebecca tossed the sunblock to the embarrassed mop-headed boy. "You all know the way, so you lead us."

"I saw them, I saw them lookin'," whispered Delphia.

"Let's just drop it."

"Look, there's the Fuddermans' house." Jesse pointed toward a rickety old shack about a half mile off the trail.

"The poor ole Fuddermans ought to build themselves a new house," said Monty.

"Why don't they build them a new one?" asked Delphia.

"I reckon they don't want to," answered Rebecca, knowing that most of the people in Medicine Bow had asked the same question at one time or another. The Fudderman family had lived on the same quarter section of land for over one hundred fifty years, and each generation lived in the same lean-to shack, surrounded by several log corrals. Not one single soul of the Fuddermans ancestry did anything to improve the living conditions of their land.

"Rebecca. Do you think there is something wrong with Drew Fudderman?" asked Monty.

"I don't. Drew is very intelligent. His appearance and the way he talks sometimes makes people think differently of him. It's a good lesson to learn that you can't always judge a person by their looks."

"I like Drew," said Crystal.

"So do I," said Rebecca, motioning for the boys to move in front of her. "Let's get going. We have nearly two miles before we make pit hill and another mile to the river."

The cliffs around pit hill were created when the Texas highway department excavated sand to be used as aggregate in cement for the highways. Manuel Ortiz owned the land and sold thousands of truckloads of sand. The end result was a large pit with sand cliffs, some of them forty feet high. Tom and Troy had brought Rebecca to the area on several occasions to traverse the cliffs. She enjoyed spending long afternoons climbing and sliding down the sand walls.

"Can we climb the walls?" Jesse asked, staring at the high walls.

"No. We can come back here another time. We need to keep going so we have more time at the river," answered Rebecca.

The beach area of the river was a place where the fine sand of the creek made a buffer between the grass pasture and the water. There were several trees where they found shade to place their blanket and picnic lunch.

"Take your shoes off," Rebecca instructed Delphia and Crystal. "We have to watch where we walk because there are small branches under the water and they really hurt when you step on them."

The three boys remained back, biding their time to allow the girls time to get into the water. They patiently watched the girls wade their way into the middle of the shallow stream.

"I have the matches," said Trey.

"Here's a good one." Jesse put a foot-long piece of dry driftwood to his lips and sucked air through the porous branch.

"Let me go first," yelled Monty.

"Quiet." Jesse handed the wood to Monty and looked over his shoulder toward Rebecca.

Trey placed the flame of the match to the end of the long branch as Monty sucked hard on the other end. When the smoke finally hit Monty's lungs, he pulled his mouth away and leaned over coughing. Trey seized the piece of wood from his brother and took a quick toke of smoke before handing it to Jesse. They continued to watch the girls move farther away as they shared the piece of wood.

"Be careful not to step into the quicksand," said Rebecca, smiling at the girls.

"What?" yelled Crystal with her eyes wide open.

"She's just kidding," said Delphia, stopping to let Rebecca go first.

"If you fall into the quicksand, make sure you lie on your stomach and swim out," Rebecca continued teasing the girls.

"I don't know if I like this river." Crystal grabbed hold of Rebecca's arm.

"I'm just joking with you." Rebecca allowed Delphia to take hold of her other arm. "Besides, you should know better. We were out here last summer."

"I liked it when Troy came last year," said Delphia. "He really teased us."

"He liked it too." Rebecca turned to look at the boys. "Let's go back. We can go a little farther downstream after lunch."

Crystal spread the small blanket on the ground while Delphia reached inside the picnic basket and pulled out the sandwiches, chips, apples, and angel food cake. The three boys sat watching, waiting for their reward for carrying the supplies.

"It smells like somethings burning," Rebecca looked in all directions.

"I don't smell anything," said Jesse.

"Me either," said Trey.

"I don't smell smoke," concurred Monty.

The girls began distributing the food, and when Delphia handed Monty his sandwich, she noticed a distinct odor of smoke. She remembered the boys talking the previous year about how driftwood could be smoked. So that memory, along with her intuitive ability in putting two and two together, meant trouble for the boys.

"Rebecca," Delphia whispered. "I think Monty has been smoking wood."

"Monty Camp! Have you been smoking driftwood?" Rebecca stared at the scared mop-haired boy.

"Well." He wasn't sure if he should rat on the other two boys.

"Look me in the eyes and tell me the truth." Rebecca moved closer.

"Yes," he looked down.

"Do you know what that smoke does to your body?"

"Yes."

"Don't patronize me, Monty Camp." Rebecca was uncharacteristically upset. "I can't believe you would come up here to smoke wood."

"I'm sorry," he looked her in the eyes, "I really am."

It finally dawned on Rebecca that he wouldn't have smoked the wood by himself. She turned to Jesse and Trey. "Did you all smoke too?"

"Yes," answered both.

Rebecca stared at the boys for several seconds while they fidgeted with their food. Loyalty was an important aspect of her life, a characteristic she sometimes took for granted.

"You all shouldn't have let Monty take the blame alone." Rebecca spoke in a much calmer manner. "I better never catch you smoking again."

"We won't," said Jesse, looking down and jerking his head back up to look directly at Rebecca.

"Okay. I believe you." Rebecca looked at Monty who was still frightened. "Let's eat and enjoy our time here."

Delphia sat on the opposite side of Rebecca to eat her lunch, knowing she would be protected from the onslaught of rage that would eventually come her way. She sat extraordinarily close.

"You best not tattle on the boys anymore." Rebecca gave Delphia a stern look.

"Rebecca, is it okay if we go and throw the Frisbee around?" Monty asked.

"Of course," answered Rebecca. "The girls and I are going to hike downstream."

Rebecca walked toward Monty as he searched for the Frisbee in the backpack. She put her arm around his neck and gave him a firm hug. He felt relieved in having her soft cheek brush his freckled face. He pulled away and followed the other boys toward the pasture above the creek. The girls removed their shoes and headed to the creek.

"Rebecca, why did you give Monty a hug?" Delphia asked as the three girls began wading in the shallow water.

"Because I could tell he got the message and wanted to let him know it was time to look forward."

"But he was smoking."

"I know. But I didn't want to ruin our day of fun. We only have so many days when we can be together to enjoy each other. I have control over whether we have fun or not, and I chose fun." Rebecca cupped water in her hand and splashed the two girls.

"This is fun," yelled Delphia, splashing Rebecca.

Monty, Trey, and Jesse were competing to see who could throw the Frisbee the farthest. Monty threw first and ran to spot where the Frisbee hit by pushing a small branch into the ground. He tossed the Frisbee back to Jesse. Jesse in turn reared back and threw the aerodynamic piece of plastic as hard as he could. The Frisbee went way right and slid under a thicket of weeds.

"That doesn't count," yelled Monty, running to retrieve the plastic disk. "It has to go straight."

"Yes, it counts." Jesse began counting his steps as he walked toward the Frisbee.

"No, it doesn't, Jesse. It has to go straight." Monty carefully reached into the bristly weeds in search of the toy.

"All right." Jesse stopped only a few feet from Monty.

Had Monty not been so adamant in denying Jesse his toss, he might have heard the rattling of the snake, warning him to stay away. He was staring at Jesse as he reached into the weeds groping for the Frisbee. The snake struck before he could move a muscle, with its white fangs sinking into his skinny wrist. Monty recoiled with all his strength, pulling the snake with him and hurling it high into the air.

"Oh Lord! Did he bite you?" Jesse screamed in disbelief, slowly approaching his friend.

Monty stood holding his bloody wrist as his brother came running.

"Sit down, Monty. Sit down," yelled Trey, placing his arm on his shoulder. "I have to get Rebecca."

"Push down on it and make it bleed," yelled Jesse.

"It got me good," moaned Monty.

His arm was feeling numb as he pushed more blood from the two puncture wounds. He was feeling woozy, so he laid his head into the grass field.

Jesse put his hand on his friend's head. "Hang on, Monty. Here comes Rebecca."

"Did the fangs go all the way in?" asked Rebecca before she got close enough to see all the blood.

"Yeah. It got him," yelled Jesse.

"Oh Lord," said Rebecca. Looking the half mile back to the river where her shoes were. "I have to get help."

"Is he okay?" asked Trey, who had purposefully taken his time walking with Delphia and Crystal so he wouldn't have to see his brother suffering.

"No. He's hurt bad. Crystal, give me the ribbon from your hair." Rebecca motioned to the young girl.

Crystal began to cry as she removed her ribbon and handed it to Rebecca. Rebecca placed it over the two puncture holes and said, "Hold this tight to those wounds if he starts bleeding bad. You don't have to keep it there unless he's really bleeding. Make sure to keep his arm down low below his heart. I have to run to the Ortizes' and get help."

Rebecca was going to have to run through the field barefooted rather than run the half mile back and get her shoes. She could feel the hard ground on her bare feet as she began her journey toward the Ortizes' ranch. She could see the trees surrounding the ranch and they didn't look that far away, but she knew it was at least three miles.

Monty's lips were turning blue and his face was a pasty white. Delphia held his head in her lap. Crystal was on her knees sobbing, holding her brother's hand.

"Rebecca will get ya help." Delphia ran her hand through Monty's bushy red hair.

"Let me see if it stopped bleeding," Jesse removed the cloth ribbon from the wound. A small amount of blood was still flowing. What was more worrisome than the bleeding was his shallow breathing. He was obviously in distress.

Rebecca was running as hard as she had ever run, running in full stride but remembering her speed would come from running correctly. It wasn't a time to lose concentration. Whether Monty lived or died could hinge on a matter of seconds. The hard crust from the sun-baked dirt was cutting into the bottom of her feet, every step was agonizing. She thought of the sad look on Monty's face when she had earlier scolded him. The vision of his freckled face in great pain caused her to lose concentration. She looked down too late to avoid stepping on a sharp rock. She felt a dull pain as the rock placed a small puncture wound in her foot. She hopped a couple of steps and continued running. The injury to the bottom of her foot was deadened to pain, but a tightening in her right knee caused her to hop rather than run.

***

"Manuel," Esther Ortiz yelled to her husband. "Look."

Manuel Ortiz was dressed in slacks and a polo shirt but was still helping his hired hand check the fluids in his new Ford F150 pickup truck. He wiped his hands off and threw the rag to the side before looking toward his wife.

"Yes, what is it?"

"Isn't that Rebecca?" Esther pointed down their driveway.

Manuel knew it was Rebecca, and he could tell by the way she was struggling that she was in trouble. "Drop the hood, Lloyd," he jumped into the front of his truck.

"Mr. Ortiz, we need help. Monty Camp was bit by a rattlesnake," Rebecca leaned over at the waist.

"Where's he at?"

"In a field by the creek, about three miles down."

"Get in," Manuel opened the door and allowed Rebecca to get into the backseat of the crew cab. He drove while talking on his radio. "Esther. Call 911 and tell them Monty Camp was bit by a rattlesnake and we need a helicopter. Have them come to the ranch."

Manuel sped through his pasture toward the children.

***

Monty lay motionless in Delphia's arms. His face was white as a ghost.

"Is he breathing?" asked Manuel, jumping out the front door of his truck.

"He's still breathing," Delphia answered with tears streaming down her face.

Manuel picked up Monty from Delphia's arms and carried him to the truck. They all loaded into the truck and sped over the rough field to the Ortiz's ranch.

"Esther, are they sending a helicopter?" Manuel opened the door and lifted Monty out. He placed him on the tailgate of the truck.

"It will be here shortly."

Manuel pulled the ribbon away from the injury. Monty's arm was swollen and the two puncture wounds were turning purple. Esther was already prepared and began to wash the wound with warm water and soap. When she was finished, she sat next to him and held his arm under his body. It wasn't the first rattlesnake bite she had doctored.

"Rebecca," Esther yelled, "your uncle is on his way with Earl."

"Let me look at that foot." Manuel leaned over Rebecca and inspected her foot. He had seen many serious wounds from his time on the ranch, and he knew a little soap and water along with a clean bandage would fix the punctured foot.

Rebecca wasn't worried about her foot. Her knee caused her concern. The injury wasn't a sprain, it was something more severe, something she had never experienced before.

Uncle Martin and Earl, in Earl's old rickety pickup truck, came to a screeching halt next to Manuel's truck. The helicopter flew over their heads.

"Are ya all right, son?" Earl rushed to Monty's side. "Good Lord, we have to get him to the hospital."

Manuel and his hired hand raised the boy between their arms and rushed him toward the helicopter. Earl held his son's arm as they ran to the paramedics. The nurse wasted no time in strapping Monty to a gurney inside the helicopter and waving the pilot to take off.

"I'll give you a ride to the hospital," Manuel yelled to Earl over the noise of the helicopter.

Delphia watched as Esther placed a large bandage on the bottom of Rebecca's foot. She placed her arm over her shoulder and said, "You saved Monty. Becca, you ran fast enough to save him."

"We need to call yore mother," Uncle Martin said to Rebecca.

The ache in her leg was now a pain covering the entire right side of her body. She groaned as she sat on the tailgate of Manuel's truck.

"I need to call Sara," Uncle Martin repeated.

"I don't want to bother her." Rebecca grimaced. "This is one time I don't want to bother her."

"She will be real upset with me if I don't let her know." Uncle Martin shook his head and rubbed his chin.

"Please! Don't ruin her trip. We can set up the appointment with Doctor Doyle."

"I'll call him when we get home." Martin still wasn't convinced. "But if the Doc tells me yore leg is seriously injured, I will call Sara."

"That's a deal."

"Let's go home." Martin opened the door to Earl's truck. "You kids hop in the back of this old junk heap."

New York, New York

It was nearly ten o'clock when Sam opened the door to the penthouse suite at the exclusive Plaza Hotel. The room smelled of fresh roses and the plush carpet felt as though it were an inch thick. A bottle of champagne waited in an ice bucket next to the oversized bed. On the bed lay three evening gowns, one black, one red, and one white.

Sara was speechless as she slowly walked throughout the room. She stepped out onto the balcony and took in a deep breath of air. She moved back inside and ran her fingers along the white marble walls. "Not a speck of dust." She smiled at Sam and picked up the white dress and said, "For me."

"I hope you like them. I have a feeling Stanley had Jackie do the shopping." Sam relaxed on the chestnut leather sofa and placed his hat on the marble table next to it. He was enjoying watching Sara's exhilaration.

"This is fabulous, Sam." Sara had been energized ever since they left Texas.

"If you want a different dress, we will have time to shop tomorrow."

"They're perfect." She removed her dark grey jacket and slipped her shoes off. She sat next to Sam and placed her hand on his shoulder. "Are ya tired?"

"I 'spose so. I was up late last night."

"Oh Sam, this is marvelous." She startled him as she jumped up from the couch and scampered toward the bottle of champagne. Sam just watched with a smile on his face.

"Sara."

"Let's have a drink." She didn't hear him as she placed two crystal glasses on the marble countertop.

Sam sighed. He reached inside his inner coat pocket and retrieved a small box. A smile came across his face as he cradled the box, waiting for Sara to fill the glasses with champagne.

"Sara," Sam stood as she approached, "I have something I want to ask you."

Sara's mind was still racing as she waited for him to explain himself. She didn't have time to think of what he had on his mind before he set the glasses down and held out the box in the palm of his hand.

"I hope I'm not being presumptuous. Will you be my wife?"

The breath exited Sara's lungs. She looked at Sam to make sure it wasn't some kind of prank. With all the strength she could afford, she reached out and accepted the package. She sashayed toward the bed where she sat down, took a deep breath, and opened the box. The ring inside the box had one large diamond surrounded by several smaller ones.

"Sara, I think about you all the time." Sam moved to the bed.

Tears were flowing down from her eyes.

"Well?" Sam asked.

She arose from the bed and swung her arms around his neck. He was still waiting for an answer. She released her hug and gently ran a finger below her eyes, wiping away some of the tears.

Sam held her tight with both arms clasped around her waist, looking directly into her eyes.

"Sam Blake. I can't think of anything in the world that would make me prouder than to be your wife."

It was Sam's turn to have his breath taken away. He had always been very confident in his life's choices but never had been so sure of something as he was of his love for Sara.

"Shall we have a toast?" Sara asked.

"Absolutely." Sam allowed her to slip from his arms. He accepted the glass of champagne from her.

"To the happiest day of my life." She lightly touched his glass with hers.

"Only to this point." He took a sip.

They both slowly sipped their glasses of champagne. Sam could tell there was something on her mind as she remained quiet.

"Sara. Is there something wrong?" he asked.

"Why did you propose so quickly?" She clarified her question. "I mean tonight."

Sam pondered the question. "We're spending two nights alone, something we've never done before. I just want to give you a little time to think about being married to me before you tell everyone back home. If for some reason you want to change your mind … it will be easier this way."

"Sam, I've known you long enough to know I will not change my mind. I really appreciate you thinking in such a way." Sara took Sam's glass from his hand and placed both glasses on the nightstand. She leaned over and kissed him on his lips. It was by far the most sensuous kiss they had ever shared.

Sam pulled her close and they kissed for several minutes before she pulled from his grasp. She grabbed her night bag and excused herself into the bathroom. She sat down on the side of the bathtub deep in thought. Lola had warned her not to have sex on this trip. Her advice had not come from a religious point of view. Lola made sure Sara was straight on knowing that her advice was woman to woman advice, not that of her pastor.

Sam sat quietly playing with the remote control to the television. He waited fifteen minutes before yelling, "Sara. Is everything all right?"

There was no answer, but before he could yell again, she stepped into the bedroom wearing a short white robe. She slowly walked toward him and just before she reached him, she dropped the robe. She was wearing a black negligee open at her midriff.

Sam's pulse rose to a dangerous level. "You do know I have another room?" he asked.

"I was with you when we registered."

Sam stared at her. The symmetrical lines of her body were perfect. The skin at every point of her body was taut without a blemish. Her long legs were muscular, and her breasts defied gravity. Her full lips were light pink and there was a slight bit of makeup around her beautiful blue eyes. Her auburn hair hung low to her shoulders. She was gorgeous.

"I will never allow you to be bored," she sat next to him on the bed. "Tonight I just want us to get better acquainted. We can sleep in separate beds. Okay?"

"Okay," Sam wasn't entirely sure what she meant as he leaned down to kiss her. He moved a hand to the back of her head and brought his lips to her waiting mouth. He had never kissed anyone with so much passion. They kissed for several minutes before the stimulating effect of her scantily clad body rubbing next to him, along with the smell of her perfume, caused him to lean back and gasp for air. He could feel the wetness from her tear-filled eyes on the side of his cheek as he rolled over, allowing her to straddle him. She leaned back and laid both her hands on his chest. He decided to take a chance and boldly slipped the strap from her gown, exposing her right breast. She not only didn't resist but reached up and lowered the other strap. He gently touched her breasts before placing his arm around her and bringing her mouth to his for the most intense kiss he had ever experienced.

"Tomorrow will be an incredible day." Sara sat up and placed her hand on his heart, staring him in the eyes. "I doubt I will sleep a wink tonight."

"Thanks for accepting my proposal." He placed his hand over hers. "And thanks for thinking of me in this way."

"I love you, Sam Blake." She leaned over and kissed him slowly on the mouth. It had been a long time since she told a man she loved him.

"I love you too." He placed his right hand on the back of her head and gently stroked her neck.

"You make me feel so good." She sat up on the bed and straightened her negligee.

"We need to set a date for the wedding." Sam smiled as he looked at her smeared lipstick and disheveled hair. "You are so beautiful."

"How about Valentine's Day?"

"Valentine's Day it is." He continued watching her.

"Can I ask you a question?"

"Of course."

"Do you have any problem with sleeping in separate beds tonight?"

"No," Sam was taken off guard by the question.

"I know it seems silly." There was no sign of distress on her face. "I really want this night to be special."

"It is the most special night of my life." He looked at the top half of her breasts barely covered by the negligee.

"I hope all I did was appropriate."

"It all was very appropriate." His thoughts were on how firm her body felt in his arms only moments ago. Her actions were more than appropriate, they were perfect. He very much preferred a lady, in bed and otherwise.

"We do have two more nights here." Sara stood up from the bed.

Sam was unsure what she meant by her remark of being there two more days. He put his hat on his head before looking at Sara and walking out the door toward his room.

Sara was sure her desire would have gotten the best of her had Lola not been so adamant about her not having sex on the first night together with Sam. As she sat on the edge of the bed looking at her magnificent ring, she was glad she had heeded her good friend's advice.

***

The restaurant at the Plaza sat open at the entrance to the hotel, surrounded by marble columns. Bright flowers in vases decorated each table as waiters, dressed in light blue jackets, moved quickly from table to table delivering coffee and breakfast to the early morning patrons.

"This establishment has a sentimental place in my heart, and this is the first time I've been back since I was here with my dad." Sam leaned back in his chair and watched Sara stare blindly at the sparkling diamond ring on her petite finger. "Daddy would bring me here every time we came to New York City. He loved to take in breakfast and watch the people coming and going in such a rush. We would sit right here and he would tell me stories. He was fifty-two years old when I was born, and his father, my granddaddy, was fifty-three when he had my father. So, I never knew my granddaddy."

"I know so little about your family." Sara looked Sam in the eyes to let him know she was clinging to every word he was saying.

"It's one of the reasons I wanted to come here to reminisce." Sam's expression was one of contentment. "Daddy died almost twenty years ago, and Mother passed twelve years ago."

"I remember your mother's funeral." Sara placed her hand over Sam's large hand.

"My daddy would have loved you, Sara. He was a big, mean, rough Texas man, but he could be, at the same time, the most tender and kind person alive. He held a great fondness in his heart for both honesty and beauty. There was not a man on this earth he did not respect, but at the same time he had few friends. His closest friend was Manuel Ortiz's father Robert. The two of them inherited a great deal of land from their families and both invested wisely." Sam placed his hand over Sara's. "Now, my mother was a city woman. She was raised in Chicago, but her only sister lived here in Manhattan. That is why we spent so much time here."

"And your dad enjoyed his time here?"

"Very much so."

"It's just that New York City is pretty much the opposite of Medicine Bow."

"Daddy liked getting dressed up in his country attire and wearing his Stetson and going out on the town."

"Kind of like you, Sam."

"Now, the only relatives I have known were my Aunt Doreen, my mother's sister, and her daughter Dodie who lived in a penthouse here in Manhattan." Sam was upbeat by the attention Sara was giving him. "Daddy was a very wealthy man when he met my mother, and they never made any sort of agreement concerning money. The only thing he did was give Aunt Doreen a million dollars, immediately after he married my mother."

"Why in the world would he give her so much money?"

"He could be quite outlandish in his behavior, and he never backed down from making a tough decision. He told my mother on the night they were married that he would never allow money to come between her and her sister. The best way he figured to do so was to make money a non-issue." Sam smiled. "And it never was."

Sara removed her hand from Sam's. "Sam, I have always had pretty much everything I needed. I can't say for sure that I won't allow money to affect my behavior."

"I never realized how much money Daddy had until I reached the age of twenty-eight. He wanted to make sure I understood the power of wealth. He told me on several occasions the story of King Solomon. Like I said before, he loved the biggest and largest of everything, so he often referred to the richest man of all times. He made it very clear that old King Solomon could never find happiness in wealth alone."

Sara imagined Sam's father speaking to him as they sat in the large restaurant in one of the largest cities in the world.

"I want you to know there will be no prenuptial agreement of any sort." Sam stared her straight in the eyes. "What I own, you also own."

"Sam, I haven't even thought about any of this." The fast pace of the two days was electrifying to Sara. "Everything is happening so quickly."

"I know I can never take the place of your children's father." Sam's expression was poised. "I will help them as much as I can."

"Sam, you always have."

"Hopefully I can help them find how wonderful life can be and not be a burden of any kind."

"You know Rebecca absolutely adores you, and Tom has the utmost respect for you. With Troy ... that's something we can work on." Sara knew Troy would have a difficult time accepting her marriage to Sam.

"This family is something I will take very seriously." He noticed how deep in thought Sara had become.

"There is something I would like to ask you."

"Anything."

"You're fifty years old and have no children of your own." She cleared her throat. "Do you want a child?"

"I would very much like to have a child of my own." His answer was straightforward. "But only if you are comfortable in having another baby."

"This is something I would have laughed at a day ago." Sara sat up straight in her chair, "I need time to think about it."

"Fair enough," said Sam. "We do have tickets to a Broadway show tonight."

Sam's cell phone rang. Jackie and Stanley were the only two people with his number, and they would call only in case of an emergency. He looked at Sara as he answered.

"I'm sorry to bother ya, Sam, but I received a call from Sara's Uncle Martin, and he needs to speak with her." Stanley hesitated, "Apparently, Rebecca has seriously injured her leg."

"I'll let her know," Sam answered calmly.

"There's something else," said Stanley. "I received a call from Ed Dodd at the Dallas FBI office who asked if I knew of any young men from Medicine Bow who might have been in Amarillo over the past week."

"What did they do?" Sam asked.

"They were at a party where an FBI informant disappeared. The car they were in was registered to Larry Lover and one of the boys referred to himself as the toastmaster from Medicine Bow."

"Call Ed back and get all the information you can from him."

"He did say it is a life-or-death situation."

"I'll call ya back." Sam closed his phone.

"What is it, Sam?"

"You need to call Martin." He handed her his cell phone, "Rebecca injured her leg."

Sara's face was white as a ghost as she dialed Uncle Martin's phone number. When it came to her children, she would always suspect the worst.

"Uncle Martin," she said into the phone.

"I was waitin' for yore call."

"What's going on with Rebecca?"

"She hurt her leg yesterday, and we took her to see Doc Doyle this morning. His X-ray showed some sort of spot or bump and he wants her to see a specialist immediately," said Uncle Martin. "She wouldn't call you because she didn't want to spoil yore trip."

"Let me talk to her."

"She's stayin' at Lola's." Uncle Martin was feeling guilty about not calling right after Rebecca injured her leg. "She hurt herself running for help after Monty Camp got bit by a rattlesnake."

"Is he all right?"

"He'll live."

"I'm going to talk with Sam, and I'll call you back as soon as I know what I'm doing." Sara handed the phone back to Sam.

"Sara," said Sam sternly. "There is something else I need to tell you."

"Yes," she expected his message to be about their upcoming marriage.

"Troy could be in a great deal of trouble."

Sara sat quietly. She was still thinking about Uncle Martin's remark about a spot on Rebecca's knee.

"One of my good friends who works with the FBI called today inquiring about Troy and Larry Lover."

"Is Troy in trouble with the FBI?" She asked the question like she already knew the answer.

"He was at a party where something happened to an FBI informant. His life could be in danger."

"Oh Sam." Sara felt terrible that her problems had ruined a very sentimental moment in Sam's life; a time that would be hard to capture again. "I'm so sorry."

"There's nothing to be sorry about." Sam motioned toward the waiter. "We have a problem, and we're gonna take care of it."

"Thank you." It was not Sara's nature to be overly emotional, but she could feel tears rushing to the corners of her eyes. "For everything."

Sam noticed the dampness in her eyes. "I promise we will come back to this same hotel after we are married and everything will be perfect again."

Chapter Three

Maliki and Tanya

"What terrible timing for Sara." Tanya pushed her chair back and stretched out her legs. She was wondering if Sam and Sara would have become intimate that evening had they remained in New York City. Of course, she didn't want to bring up the touchy subject with Maliki about his grandmother's sex life, so she sidestepped the subject. "They left New York that afternoon."

"Yeah, they were in Texas early evening." Maliki shuffled through some papers on the table. "We have some of Aunt Rebecca's early medical reports."

"Do you think they would have left if they would have had only one crisis to deal with?"

"I don't know." Maliki paused for a moment. "Maybe if it had only been Troy's problems they would have stayed."

"Interesting," Tanya stood up.

"Grandmother was used to problems with Troy."

"You don't feel she liked Rebecca better?"

"Mothers and daughters probably bond better than mothers and sons." Maliki wondered what Tanya's point was, "Does it make any difference?"

"For this story." Tanya fidgeted with her wine glass. "I think it does."

"How?"

"Well," she sat back down, "It was probably lucky for Troy."

"Wow, how so for Troy?"

"Obviously, she was going to take care of Rebecca." She hesitated, "Troy was a troublemaker and she had already invested all the emotional capital in him that she was going to."

"I guess he was a troublemaker." Maliki held his hands palms up. "But how does that make him lucky?"

"Because of Sam Blake." She raised her eyebrow. "Sara turned over the problem of Troy to Sam. And believe me, Sam can handle problems."

Maliki wasn't sure how to take her confidence in knowing that Sam could handle problems. Nevertheless, she was correct in that Troy was fortunate to have Sam looking out for him. He yawned.

"Shall we go to bed?" Tanya asked, out of the blue.

"What?" Maliki's expression was priceless.

"Shall we quit for the night." Tanya was enjoying his discomfort. "You know. Get some sleep, some shut-eye."

"Let's do. We actually got a lot further than I thought we would tonight."

"Tomorrow is Friday, so we should be able to get through everything by Monday." Tanya stood up and stretched. "I need to be in Dallas by Monday night."

"That shouldn't be a problem."

"I would like to take you out to dinner either tomorrow night or Saturday."

"That would be nice." Maliki imagined Tanya to be a very alluring dinner partner. "There are some awesome places to dine in Aspen."

"It's a date." Tanya moved around the table and hugged Maliki and whispered in his ear, "Good night."

"Good night." Maliki watched as she made her way to her bedroom.

****

He had all the notes organized and coffee brewing by the time Tanya returned to the living room the next morning. She was wearing baggy sweatpants and a large neck Texas sweatshirt.

"Did you sleep well?" asked Maliki.

"Incredible," Tanya took in a deep breath, "I slept like a baby."

"There's cereal for breakfast."

"I'll grab a cup of coffee. I'd like to get started quickly this morning." Tanya placed her recorder at the center of the large table.

"All right, we should be able to cover a lot this morning." Troy watched Tanya pour her coffee. "We are to the part where Grandmother and Sam came back to Medicine Bow after cutting their stay short in New York City."

Medicine Bow, Texas

"Are you sure Troy is one of the boys involved in this fiasco?" Sam had a distinct way of standing with his arms to his side, with his shoulders forward. Whenever somebody rankled him he would posture himself in such a way. His father had displayed the same pose when he was threatened.

"There is no mistake, Sam," said Stanley. "The FBI informant was found murdered in a field near the farmhouse outside Amarillo where the boys were spotted. Apparently, they were meeting some crime head by the name of Mike King."

"Do they have pictures of Troy at the farmhouse?"

"No. The informant who used the name Pig Pen was killed after the party, but he called in the license plate number from Larry's Cadillac before he was identified. He made it clear in his call that the boys were in grave danger." Stanley handed Sam three pages from the FBI headquarters. "I've never heard Ed so shaken."

The office Sam worked from was far different than the offices in other large ranches. It was equipped with all the latest high-tech equipment and was staffed with five accountants, two secretaries, and two-part time security guards. Several off-duty police officers from local counties were hired to patrol the large ranch. But Stanley and Sam's personal secretary Jackie Renner were the only ones who worked shoulder to shoulder with Sam.

Sam looked upon Stanley as a member of the family rather than as an employee. Stanley worked for Sam's father helping secure and build the Blake fortune. He was a true Texan from the top of his grey head, past his pot belly, to the tip of his wing-tipped cowboy boots. He was born on the plains of the Texas panhandle to parents who were fourth generation Texans. His father named him Stonewall Jackson Jones. He changed it to Stanley when he turned eighteen. Loyalty and precision in his judgment in handling the Blake fortune made him a very rich man in his own right. He had a stockpile of important people in high places who made any information he forwarded to Sam highly accurate. There was no question Troy was in big trouble.

"I also have some information from the Dallas vice squad where this fella Pig Pen worked for the past three years," Stanley continued. "They know that some type of scam or theft is going down in Colorado sometime in the near future. The word is that anyone who accepts money for the job from Mike King would be signing their death warrant. Whatever it is this Mike King is up to, he didn't want to use any of the bikers or their friends because he plans to kill them when he's finished with them."

"We best find him soon. I'll let Sara know how important it is we get in touch with him," Sam said. "What do we know about Mike King?"

"Mike King is an alias. Everyone is tight lipped about his identity. Something tells me nobody really knows who this guy is."

"Jackie," Sam looked at the FBI papers, "get me the governor on the phone."

"Will do," said Jackie. "Sara's on the line now."

"Sara." Sam cradled the phone to his ear. "How's Rebecca?"

"She's holding up better than I am. We're waiting for the specialist now."

"I didn't think ya were gonna be able to see him for a week."

"He looked at the X-rays and told us to come in today." It was apparent that Sara didn't want to discuss the reasons at great length. "I'm sitting here with Rebecca along with Lola and Delphia."

"You'll have to fill me in later." Sam hesitated for a moment, "Sara, it's very important we contact Troy as soon as we can." He spoke in a calm manner, yet he wasted no words in explaining the danger Troy faced. He made clear the importance of collecting the telephone numbers and addresses she had used over the past years to correspond with either Billy or Larry.

"Sam," Jackie interrupted. "The governor is on line one and he's in a hurry. Tanya Springfield is on line three, and Drew Fudderman is on line four."

"Governor, I have a problem I hope y'all can help me with." Sam's deportment became more professional. "It's concerning the incident in Amarillo last Sunday."

The governor was silent for a moment before his reply. "Sam, it's a very sensitive issue, with federal implications."

"Yes, sir, I do understand. But one of the young men from Medicine Bow is tangled up in the mess, and I believe his life is in jeopardy."

"Yes, sir." The governor never offered anything without being asked.

"I need any information you have on a man named Mike King. Also, any mention if a young man by the name of Troy Young was at the house."

"Sam, I'll do my best." The line went dead.

"Jackie, tell Ms. Springfield and the Fudderman boy I can't speak with them now." Sam leaned back in his office chair. "See if you can get ahold of Tom Young."

Jackie flicked the bangs of her red hair as she twirled around in her office chair. She was a perfectionist who blossomed during hard times. "Tom Young's on line one," she yelled.

"Tom, how are ya, son?" Sam's tone was more cordial than usual.

"Fine, thank you, sir," said Tom.

"We're trying to get in touch with Troy."

"Ma told me. I've tried calling him on his cell. I even tried calling Larry and Billy Ray's folks, and they haven't a clue as to their whereabouts. Both of their moms told me they couldn't care less if they saw them again."

"Tham boys have seen nothing but trouble their entire lives." Sam sucked in a deep breath, "Do you have any ideas on how we can find them?"

"I know Billy Ray and Larry have the same granddaddy who lives in the Dallas area. He might have a notion to where they are."

"Do you know his name?"

"I believe it's Lockett." Tom paused. "Billy Ray told Troy they could spend some time in his cabin in the mountains."

"Tom, would you mind going to Denver?" Sam asked. "We are going to need someone there to check out any leads."

"I reckon so."

"I'll have Stanley make the arrangements. Ya need to leave immediately." Sam thought for a moment. "Would ya mind if Drew Fudderman tagged along for some company?"

"I suppose it wouldn't hurt to have him go along." Tom had always liked Drew.

"I'll make the arrangements."

"Sam," said Tom softly, "Ma told me about your plans to marry her."

"I hope you approve."

"My ma deserves only the best," said Tom firmly. "I'm happy for the both of you."

"I'm very fortunate to have your mother in my life." Sam felt some relief in Tom's approval. "I'll have Stanley make the preparations in Denver for y'all."

"I'll start packing." Tom hung up the phone.

"Jackie, get Drew Fudderman on the phone."

"He never hung up. He's on line four," said Jackie with a snicker.

"Drew, I understand you are trying to get a job." Sam spoke quickly.

"Sam, you know I have been asking fo a job fo a long time."

"Would you be willing to travel to Denver with Tom Young?"

"To Denva."

"Yeah, Denver."

"When would we go?"

"Tonight."

"Tonight."

"I'll have a car over to pick you up in an hour."

"An houa."

"Dammit, Drew! Quit repeating everything I say."

"Okay."

"Another thing," Sam hesitated for a moment. "I need someone to take care of a few pigs, on a permanent basis."

"Some pigs. On a pemanent basis."

"Yes, five pigs." Sam wasn't about to discuss the agreement he held with Tanya with Drew. "Y'all have some pens out there, don't you?"

"We have lots of cowwals."

"If you can turn one of the corrals into a pig pen, I'll have five pigs for you to take care of," said Sam. "Now, these are special pigs that will require special care. Is it gonna be all right with yore daddy?"

"We can handle five pigs in ow sleep."

"Now dammit, Drew, y'all can't eat these pigs." Sam might have to hire another full-time employee to keep an eye on the Fudderman family.

"We won't."

"Manuel Ortiz will bring the pigs by tomorrow. I want you to tell yore daddy to call me this evening so I can give him the directions on how to take care of these pigs."

"Okay."

"You need to get ready to leave now. You need enough clothes for a week."

"A week."

"A week." Sam shouted into the phone.

"How much ya gonna pay me?"

"Dammit, Drew, I don't know. Now get packin'." Sam hung up the phone and sat at his desk in silence. All he could hope for was that Tom would find his brother before Troy found more trouble than even he could get him out of.

Dallas, Texas

The sterile white walls of the waiting room at the AIM Oncology clinic were anything but soothing to Sara as she sat alongside Rebecca. They had been waiting nearly two hours, after the technician finished her MRI, for Dr. Meersman who was running late. Lola sat patiently in a small chair, clinging to her purse, every now and then glancing at a magazine.

Rebecca was trying to page through a magazine with Delphia hugging her right arm. She would pull her arm away from her admiring little friend to only have it grabbed again.

"Coach Joan and I are still planning on going to Fredericksburg on Saturday." Rebecca turned to Sara.

"Let's wait and see what the doctor says," Sara said.

"I really enjoy running the hills there." Rebecca was interrupted by a young nurse.

"The doctor will see you now."

"Thank God," Lola said. "Delphia and I will be waiting right here for y'all."

Sara walked behind Rebecca into a small room and sat in a chair situated to the side of a hospital table. Rebecca was wearing white shorts and waited a few minutes before hopping onto the examination table. The doctor entered holding X-rays in his right hand.

"Hello," He extended his left hand toward Rebecca.

"Hello," Rebecca said, apprehensively extending her hand.

Sara and Rebecca made eye contact with each other. It was obvious they were both amused with the appearance of the doctor. His long grey hair was sticking out in all directions, and his eyes were bulging from their sockets. But his demeanor was anything but comedic as he set the X-rays on the table.

"Young lady, we have a problem." He moved very close to Rebecca.

Rebecca could feel her heart beating faster and faster.

"What we have is an osteosarcoma, a tumor on the proximal tibia." He picked up the X-ray and held it so Rebecca could see the image. Sara stood so she could also see the pictures. He pointed at a small dark spot. "I knew what we were dealing with when I saw the X-rays from your family physician, but I wanted to verify with the MRI."

"What are we talking about?" Sara tried to keep her composure.

"What can we do about it?" Rebecca asked.

The doctor looked into Rebecca's eyes. He had seen the same frightened look many times before, but where he usually found tears, he found none in Rebecca's eyes. He knew about the athletic prowess of the strong young lady, but he also knew it was his job to save her life.

"We have some very difficult decisions to make over the next couple of days." The doctor tossed the X-rays onto a chair. "This is a very tricky disease and must be handled quickly and with the greatest of care."

"Doctor." Sara wasn't ready to accept his diagnosis. "Are you sure this is osteo …"

"Osteosarcoma," said Doctor Meersman. "I'm as certain as I can be. It is one of the most common types of bone cancer, and I have dealt with it many times. Certainly, we must perform several tests before continuing with any form of treatment."

"Cancer," gasped Sara.

Doctor Meersman, even without further tests, was certain of his diagnosis of the tumor. He wished he were wrong, but he knew he wasn't. "Osteosarcoma is a cancer."

"What can we do to get rid of it?" Rebecca asked tersely.

"It depends on whether the cancer is localized. But you have to realize that this small tumor can affect the entire body." The doctor paused to take note of Rebecca's reaction to his thoughts on the disease. Many patients were in shock from hearing for the first time that they have something as life-threatening as cancer growing in their bodies, and they tuned out everything said during the initial diagnosis. Rebecca was listening intently. "If it is localized, I don't believe radiation alone will eradicate the tumor. But we must perform a complete bone scan and check to make sure there are no deposits in the lungs. Somewhere along the line, surgery will most likely need to be performed."

"Will I be able to run again?"

"I understand you are very determined, so I would never rule anything out." Doctor Meersman wavered. One of his greatest traits was that he always said what he thought, sometimes being honest to the point of being considered insensitive. "But my first inclination is to tell you that you will not be able to run, at least not competitively."

"Not competitively." Rebecca acted as though she didn't understand him.

"If the cancer is localized to the tibia, we can treat it with a limb-sparing procedure."

"It can't possibly be that bad," Rebecca screamed and vaulted off the table. "It doesn't bother me at all. I'm sure I will be able to run."

Doctor Meersman remained calm. He had witnessed many different reactions to such a diagnosis, and Rebecca's delayed response was nothing out of the ordinary.

"Doctor," said Sara, "we need to get a second opinion."

"I understand." The doctor stood up. "We have several names of specialists on file, but this needs to be addressed immediately."

"I don't mean to question your professionalism." Sara knew better than to burn any bridges. "I owe it to Rebecca to be as sure as possible before making any decisions."

"Again, I totally understand." The doctor looked at Rebecca's pretty face. "Doctor Larson would be my choice of doctors if I were diagnosed with this disease."

"Thank you," said Sara.

"If you do choose Doctor Larson, I would like to be present during her examination. It is important that the doctor who performs the initial biopsy be the one who performs the surgery."

"Okay, we need some time to absorb all this." Sara felt disconcerted with the doctor referring to surgery as though it was a certainty. As they left the examining room, she knew she needed to remain strong for the sake of both herself and Rebecca.

Denver, Colorado

Tom had always been self-conscious regarding his appearance, but he never felt more awkward as he filled out the paperwork in preparation for Drew and his hotel room. Not because he failed to dress appropriately, but because his partner was dressed more for farm work than for appearing in public. The well-manicured hand of the pretty receptionist waited only a few inches from his hand, while Drew leaned over his shoulder watching every letter he spelled.

"Drew, could you move back a little?" Tom shook his shoulder and smiled at the receptionist.

"Just want to make sho you don't make any mistakes," said Drew, continuing to look over Tom's shoulder. "Sam's payin' me to help you."

"I'm capable of handling this myself." Tom continued to force his smile toward the hostess who appeared to have a smile permanently engraved on her face.

"Tom, do I need to give you any money?" Drew reached into the pocket of his bib overhauls and pulled out a worn billfold.

"It's all taken care of." Tom glared at Drew, knowing he shouldn't be so upset with his friend for simply being himself. Drew was dressed in an old tee shirt covered with bib overalls, not even new bibs but a pair of old, patched ones. It was embarrassing riding on the airplane, but not nearly as uncomfortable as being with him in the ritzy Brown Palace

Hotel in downtown Denver, Colorado. Tom was sure the pretty hostess was going to tell them they needed to change clothes or leave.

"Here are your keys." The pretty girl handed him the keys. "The elevator is to your right."

Tom snatched his suitcase and walked quickly toward the elevator with Drew following closely behind with his tattered duffle bag.

"This is nice," said Drew, stepping into the room behind Tom. "Sam did us nice."

"Drew. Sit down." Tom pointed at a chair. "Do you have any good clothes?"

"I got my Sunday outfit." Drew remained standing.

"Get the damn things out and let me look at um." Tom kicked Drew's garment bag.

Drew slowly opened his bag and pulled out a white dress shirt and a pair of black slacks. He reached deeper into the bag and retrieved a black pair of socks and dress shoes.

"Why in the hell didn't you wear these clothes today?"

"I wanted to be comfotable while we wu on the plane."

"From now on, Drew, I want you to dress like it is Sunday morning. If you need any new clothes, I'll buy you some."

"Okay." Drew opened the large curtains and looked out the window. He looked down toward the busy street below. "Do ya think we can find Twoy?"

"I expect to." Tom began unpacking his suitcase.

"It sho is a big city."

"We can only do our best." Tom began hanging his clothes in the closet. He felt badly for belittling Drew about his appearance, but he knew they were going to be in the city for quite some time, and he would have much more to worry about than his friend's appearance.

"Ya want to get somethin' to eat?" Drew asked.

"What ya want to eat?"

"How about steak?" Drew pulled out a wad of hundred-dollar bills. "I got plenty of money."

"Put it away, Drew. Stanley gave me one of the Blake Enterprise credit cards."

"Then we can eat what we want."

"I reckon." Tom pulled out his cell phone. "Sam will call as soon as he has any information for us."

"You know, Tom. I hope Twoy stands up to those two guys."

"You mean Billy Ray and Larry?"

"Yeah, the last time I saw them, befo they left Medicine Bow, they were awful to me."

"They just never took time to know you."

"I was happy when they left." Drew sat down on the edge of the bed. "Twoy was always nice to me. I think he was Ben's best fwend."

"How is Ben?" Tom asked.

"He's in the Navy."

"He's been in the Navy ever since he left high school." Tom pulled a polo shirt over his head.

"He's mighty impotant to the Navy."

The last time Tom saw Drew's older brother Ben, he made it clear that he couldn't discuss any aspects of his duties in the Navy because everything he was involved with was top secret. He showed Tom some of the letters he had written home to his father during the time he was overseas. Several sentences and words were cut from the pages of the letters. He said the intelligence department had to censor everything he did for national security reasons. Ben had abruptly left, telling Tom he needed to catch a helicopter that was scheduled to pick him up at their farm. Tom was skeptical, to say the least, about the tall stories Ben told him, but he didn't want to tell Drew how he felt.

"Ben shore has seen a lot of places," said Tom.

"You know, maybe Ben can help us."

"Maybe," Tom knew it wouldn't hurt to appease Drew in regard to his brother's fables. "I'm gonna take a shower, and then we can go get something to eat."

"Okay, Tom." Drew pulled a pillow out from under the covers on his bed and turned the television on.

Tom could hear his telephone ringing over the noise in the shower. He turned off the water and jumped from the shower and wrapped a towel around himself. By the time he exited the bathroom, Drew was already deep in a conversation with Sam.

"Sam, this hotel is mighty nice." Drew turned his back to Tom.

"Put Tom on." Sam knew he would quickly become exasperated with Drew if he continued talking with him.

"Okay, Sam. Did you get the pigs to the faam?" Drew turned to watch Tom quickly dressing.

"Yes, we did. The pigs are in capable hands with yore daddy. Now dammit, put Tom on the phone."

"Okay, Sam. Now, I don't mean to dwell on this too much, but have you decided on how much you ah gonna pay me fo mindin' the pigs?"

"Fifty dollars each per week, if you don't eat them. Now put Tom on."

Drew handed the phone to Tom.

"Hello, Sam." Tom sat down on his bed.

"Son, I want to tell ya right off. There is some bad news about Rebecca." Sam's voice sounded tired. "The specialist they went to this afternoon told Rebecca that she has a cancerous tumor in her leg."

"It's that serious?" Tom didn't know how to respond.

"Sara is planning on getting a second opinion, so we won't know for sure just how serious it is until they have another doctor examine her. She said she will call you this evening."

"Should I come back home?"

"It would be better if you waited, at least a couple of days. We found out that the Lockett boys' granddaddy has a cabin outside the town of Winter Park. It's about an hour and half outside of Denver, up in the mountains."

"Do you want us to drive up there?"

"Stanley and I debated on whether to have y'all go or to get in touch with the police department there." Sam hesitated, "We think it would be better for you to contact Troy."

"We'll leave the first thing in the morning."

"Tom, you make sure and let Troy know that he is in a hell of a lot of danger. The FBI boys in Dallas are telling us that they plan on killing Troy and his friends when they are finished with them."

"I'll keep tryin' to reach him on his phone."

"We know Larry Lover has been using a cell phone, but it isn't registered in his name."

"Hopefully Troy will call Ma."

"Sara thinks he will." Sam took in a deep breath. "The more we learn about Mike King, the more worried I am about Troy."

"It's a hell of a mess." Tom thought about telling Sam how much he appreciated his help, but the tone of Sam's voice was very businesslike, so he decided to forego the sentiments.

"Yes, it is, and your Ma is going to have all she can handle in taking care of Rebecca. Make sure to keep us informed tomorrow."

"I'll talk to you then." Tom hung up the phone.

"We goin' to the mountains?" Drew asked.

"Yeah, we need to check and see if Troy is at Billy Ray's grandfather's cabin."

"I ain't neva been to the mountains."

"Neither have I," said Tom. "We best get us a quick bite to eat and get to bed so we can get an early start in the morning."

"We'll find him, Tom."

Tom realized that Sam was right as rain in having Drew make the trip with him. Even though the large country boy was like a fish out of water in the city, he was still a comfort to have around.

Aurora, Colorado

"I can't believe I lost to you again." Larry picked up his black king and laid it over onto the half-empty chessboard. "How much do I owe ya now?"

"That's double or nothing seven straight times." Troy stood up from the small table and stretched. "Sixteen thousand eight hundred dollars."

"If I ever come across that much money, I'll give it to ya," Larry said sarcastically, pushing the chessboard to the middle of the table.

"I'll give ya another chance at double or nothing."

"Not at chess, ya won't."

"What do y'all think of us takin' in a little nightlife tonight?" Billy Ray sat on the edge of the couch in the middle of the small room flipping through channels on the television. "Nothing against y'all, but I'm sick and tired of being cramped in this damn apartment. Tonight could be our last chance for a while to get out and check things out."

"Hell yeah." Larry stood up from the table. "Let's check us out some Colorado women."

"I'm gonna take a shower first," Troy said, walking to the room he was sharing with Billy Ray. It would have been much more convenient for the boys had Mike King rented a three-bedroom apartment. Troy's relationship with Billy Ray was far closer than the one he shared with Larry, even though he had met Larry first, so it almost went without saying that Billy and Troy would be bunk mates. Billy Ray had always watched over Troy, and for the past five days at the apartment he had made sure his friend took his medication. It was just a charade, with Troy only pretending to take the tablets in his presence. Billy had forgotten that when Troy took his tablets he would become extremely lethargic, and Troy was hiding his energized feeling very well as they prepared to go out on the town.

The dance club was much louder than any of the boys had envisioned, with everyone moving at a frantic pace. The fact they were defying the orders of Mike King never entered their minds as they made their way through the maze of people in the club.

"Let's stand over there." Larry pointed to a railing at the side of the dance floor. "Y'all get us a spot, and I'll grab us some beers."

Troy followed behind Billy as he pushed his way to the railing, and Larry feathered off toward the bar. Troy was looking at all the attractive women dancing with their partners, but he could only see them as a mass of humanity bundled together. The feeling of being excluded was a warning signal, one he had in the past ignored.

"Good Lord. Have ya ever seen so many beautiful ladies?" Larry handed Billy Ray a beer and set a Coke down on the wooden rail in front of Troy.

"I have to get out of here, y'all," Troy said, glancing over his shoulder at two girls dancing right behind him. He turned and made eye contact with the pretty blond only an arm's length away from him.

"We can't leave now," Larry said.

"I have to." Troy looked as if he were about to have a panic attack. "I know the address. I'll take a taxi."

"All right, man, I'm gonna have some fun." Larry leaned around Troy and pointed at the blond girl. "Would ya like to dance?"

"Sure." The blond girl continued making eye contact with Troy as she followed Larry to the dance floor.

"Are ya all right, Troy?" Billy Ray asked.

"I need to get the hell out of here."

"What's wrong?"

"I feel like I'm gonna have one of those nights … you know. And I don't want to ruin what we have going here." Troy stepped away from the wood rail.

"Can you make it back to the apartment?" Billy Ray was looking around his friend at the girl dancing behind him.

"Yeah. I'll be fine." Troy looked past Billy Ray at the mass of people and hurriedly made his way to the door.

Billy Ray watched his friend make his way out of the club before asking the girl to dance.

Rocky Mountains, Colorado

Drew was squeezing the dashboard to the rental car as Tom maneuvered the four-wheel-drive vehicle around the hairpin curves of Berthoud Pass. The concierge at the Brown Palace warned him about the treacherous mountain pass, but driving on the slippery road as it rose higher and higher into the clouds was much more frightening than he had anticipated. Large snowflakes were beginning to fall. His knuckles were beginning to turn white as he grasped the steering wheel, keeping his eyes on the wet pavement, never allowing them to wander to the steep precipice only a couple of feet from the wheels of his car.

"This sho is a beautiful place," said Drew, "but I'll be glad when we get off this mountain."

"Not half as glad as I'll be." Tom kept both hands glued to the steering wheel. "It looks like this is the top."

"I ain't neva seen snow." Drew opened his window and put his hand outside. "That is cold."

"It's a lot different up here, a lot different from the thick Texas air." Tom's eyes were the size of saucers as he began the decent down the mountain.

The slow descent down the mountain led them to the small ski town of Winter Park. They drove carefully to the western edge of town where they searched for a small logger's road that would lead them to the Locketts' cabin. The temperature was well below freezing and there was over five inches of snow on the ground as they drove onto the gravel road.

"The cabin isn't very far down this road."

"I hope we don't get stuck." Drew watched the windshield wipers push away the heavy snowflakes as they fell and stuck to the window.

"We best hurry." Tom drove carefully through the tall pine trees lining the road, "I sure hope Troy is here. If not, it's been a hell of a drive for nothing."

"That's it," Drew yelled, pointing toward a small wood sign with the name Lockett burnt on it. The sign blended in with the pine trees, and Tom would have missed it had it not been for Drew's keen eye.

"No cars." Tom drove up the driveway and parked in front of the cabin.

Drew walked up the wooden steps to the porch of the log cabin and pounded on the door. Tom moved to a window and looked in past the tattered curtains. There were no lights on, and the moss rock fireplace was unlit.

"Nobody's here," Tom said.

"It's all locked up." Drew jiggled the doorknob.

"Damn." Tom pulled out his cell phone and tried to make a call before slamming it shut and putting it back in his pocket. "It doesn't work up here."

"It's awful cold up hea, Tom." Drew pulled the collar of his light jacket tight around his thick neck as the large flakes of snow covered his head.

"It shore is." Tom looked to the side of the cabin where a small stream meandered down the mountain. On the other side of the stream was a forest with thousands of pine trees covered with snow. "But it is beautiful."

"Let's go to town and get something to eat," said Drew.

"Nothin' we can do here." Tom looked one last time at the cabin before getting in the vehicle. Drew sat silently as Tom drove carefully down the logger's road through the ever-increasing snowfall.

Tom couldn't help but wonder if he might be a complete fool for searching so frantically for his brother. After all, most of the time when Troy found himself in trouble, it was because of something he had created for himself. Troy's imagination often worked overtime, and his ability to convince everyone that his ideas were real was unmatched. He induced people to his way of thinking because he actually believed his lies. Such as the time he convinced Uncle Martin and Square Shoulders that there was gold in the sand pit. He went so far as to say he had taken several pounds of the ore to Lubbock, where a professor at Texas Tech confirmed it was real gold. When it was found that there was only sand in the pit, everyone was so embarrassed that little was said about Troy's shenanigans. Now, with the cancer Rebecca was facing, Tom would rather be by her side, but he knew that by finding Troy he would be taking a great deal of pressure off his mother's shoulders.

Maliki and Tanya

"I'm not entirely sure if I understand why Sam wanted to find Troy so badly." Tanya placed a finger on her lip and momentarily thought about her statement. "I mean, Troy seemed to have caused a lot of problems in Medicine Bow."

"Grandma." Maliki never hesitated in his answer. "Sam knew that Grandma held a special place in her heart for Troy. He also held information from Stanley that Troy was in extreme danger. The fact Troy had no father around to help also played a part."

Tanya shrugged her shoulders, suggesting that she would have left Troy to fend for himself.

"My life would have been much different had Sam not been so persistent. He wanted to allow Grandma the time to take care of Rebecca."

"True," Tanya nodded. "Knowing Sam Blake, I'm sure the deeper he got into Troy's problems, the more determined he became."

"Exactly," stated Maliki.

"It's strange how much people's actions affect other people." Tanya hesitated in thought. "I wonder if Troy would have returned to Texas if he knew his sister was in trouble?"

Maliki leaned back in his chair and pondered the question.

"I don't think he would have," Tanya answered for him.

"You're probably right," stated Maliki. "In Troy's mind, he knew he wasn't a supportive person."

"I think he was selfish." Tanya waited to see if she was offending Maliki by insulting his biological father.

"Not only selfish, but he despised the idea of family," offered Maliki.

"Interesting," said Tanya, "I probably should hear more before making judgement."

Chapter Four

Denver, Colorado

The cold breeze cut through Troy's light blue jacket, causing him to shiver. His tanned face was flushed, and his eyes were watering as he, along with Larry and Billy Ray, waited at the corner of Colfax and Broadway. They were downtown, in the mile-high city of Denver, Colorado, just a few blocks from the Brown Palace Hotel. They were following, to the letter, the instructions given to them by their new employer, Mike King. The bus from Aurora was on time, and they were able to walk to the intersection with fifteen minutes to spare.

"I hope they hurry before I freeze to death." Troy held his arms to his chest.

"It must not be that cold. All these people are in short sleeves." Larry shivered as he pointed toward several businessmen moving about.

"Either they are touched in the head or used to this weather." Troy put his hand to his red nose.

A large white van with the words "Explorer Construction" came to a screeching stop near the curb. The sliding door of the van flew open as the three boys stepped back.

"Get in, assholes, before a cop comes along," a dark-haired Italian man yelled.

Larry gazed in, saw it was filled with a variety of tools, and understood that the dilapidated vehicle was their ride. He climbed into the back, followed by Billy Ray and Troy, who sat on the handles of several shovels. The driver squealed the tires as he pulled into traffic, shaking his head as he looked at the other dark-haired man sitting next to him.

"You were right, we should have handpicked these guys ourselves," said the Italian man.

"You never have listened to me, Vinny," said the large man in the passenger seat.

"You three dickheads were told to meet us on the northeast corner, not the northwest corner," Vinny yelled, looking at the three passengers through his rearview mirror.

"This is the first time we've been here, we weren't sure about our directions," Larry said, staring into Vinny's eyes.

"From now on, you shit for brains, look at the mountains and know that you are looking west. Try and figure the other directions from there." Vinny turned in his seat and eyeballed his passengers.

"Sorry," Larry said.

"No more mistakes. I wanted to turn on Broadway and take Seventeenth," Vinny said.

The shock absorbers of the van were worn to the point of being useless. The twenty-minute ride was uncomfortable for the three boys riding in the back as they traveled through the lower income neighborhood. Vinny pushed a garage door opener as he drove up a long driveway toward a ranch-style house. He parked inside an empty garage.

"Each of you take a pair of gloves." Vinny turned in his seat. "Come on, let's go. We need to unload the tools."

Troy exited the van and noticed several pieces of plywood piled at the front of the garage, with a large gas-powered posthole digger in front of them. He was about to ask what the posthole digger was to be used for but noticed Vinny giving him a serious look. Instead, he pulled two shovels and a pick from the van and followed everyone inside the house and down to the basement. They continued unloading until the van was empty.

"Is that everything?" Vinny asked, watching Larry push the final wheelbarrow down the concrete steps into the basement.

"That's it," Larry said, enduring the musky smell of the basement.

"Okay, here's a list of the tools. When you are finished, I want every piece of equipment on this list accounted for. Capisce?" Vinny looked at each boy, noticing they all seemed confused. "Capisce means do you understand."

"We capisce," Larry said, feeling more at ease with Vinny.

"Listen very carefully to what I am about to tell you. You are going to knock a hole through this concrete foundation, right here." Vinny pulled a loose piece of siding from the wall, exposing the concrete foundation. "The opening needs to be four feet by four feet in size. After you have made the opening, you will dig a tunnel, also four feet by four feet, to a drainage culvert, approximately one hundred ten feet from this wall."

"That's all we need to do?" Larry asked.

"That's it," Vinny answered. "You may hit some hard dirt, and that is where the gas-powered posthole digger can be used."

"We each get paid ten thousand dollars," Troy reiterated.

"Yeah," Vinny's expression was one of surprise. "If that is what you agreed to."

"When will we get the money?" Larry asked, having not noticed the startled expression on Vinny's face.

"I'll have to find out." Vinny regained his composure, "It will be right after the job is finished."

The full basement of the house was partially finished with cheap wood paneling on the walls and worn shag carpet covering the floor. The fireplace brick had a black smoke stain above the firebox and a slight odor of smoke filled the room. The house had been used as a rental for a long time.

"Where should we put the dirt?" asked Larry.

"This is very important." Vinny eyeballed each of the boys. "All the dirt is to remain in the house. You can start filling these rooms and take it upstairs if need be. It can go everywhere but in the master bedroom."

"It's going to make a big mess," Troy understated the obvious.

"I don't give a damn about this house." Vinny raised his voice, "You just do what you're told to do. None of you are to leave this house while working on this tunnel. I'm going to take you out to show you where you are digging to. After that, you are going to be here until the morning of October, 28. Do you understand?" Vinny asked.

"Yes," Larry answered. "Are y'all gonna stay here?"

"Hell no. We won't be back until the night of the twenty-seventh. That's when we will pick up the tools. Do you understand that we need to have all the tools in the garage on the twenty-seventh?" Vinny wanted to be clear with the boys what was expected of them.

"We understand," said Larry.

"Okay, here are the rules. You cannot leave this house after we leave." Vinny paused. "You cannot have any contact with family or friends until the job is finished. The television is to be watched down here in the basement, we have already covered all the windows so no nosey neighbors can look inside. Tony is covering the upstairs windows with plywood."

"What if someone comes to the door?" Larry asked.

"Don't answer it."

"Okay," Larry shrugged his shoulders.

"You need to dig a little over three feet per day to meet our deadline. If for some reason you can't make the deadline, I want to know at least two days ahead of time. Any questions?" Vinny asked.

"What about food?" Larry asked.

"The refrigerator and pantry are full of food."

"Can I ask what the tunnel is going to be used for?" Larry asked.

"You can, but I won't tell you. You had to have realized we aren't going to pay you thirty thousand dollars for a few weeks work for selling Girl Scout cookies. This is something that has been well thought out and planned for over two years. The less you know, the better for everyone."

"What happens if we have a problem?" Larry asked.

"Use this phone to call this number." Vinny handed Larry a cell phone and a piece of paper. "The only time you can get a hold of anyone will be at seven o'clock in the morning. Make sure you keep the phone charged, because I don't want you using any other phones."

"That should be no problem," Larry was feeling more comfortable with the situation.

"Everybody upstairs." Vinny followed the three boys up the stairs to the kitchen. He placed a piece of paper and pencil on the counter next to the sink and walked to the back door.

"Are y'all sure you don't want us to put some of the dirt in the backyard?" Troy asked, looking over Vinny's shoulder into the small yard, surrounded by a six-foot privacy fence.

Vinny turned and looked at Troy for a moment. Mike King had warned him that Troy was a potential problem. "I ought to put a bullet in your little pea brain right now. I know you are going to foul us up some way."

"Don't worry about Troy. He's just trying to think of ways for us to do y'all a better job," Larry interjected, wishing Troy would be more like Billy Ray and keep his mouth shut.

"We don't need no heroes. You go along with the program, and do exactly as I say, or you and your friends will have more trouble than you can bargain for." Vinny stared coldly into Troy's eyes, "Do you capisce?"

"Yes, sir," Troy answered.

Billy Ray nodded toward Vinny. He was happy that Troy was being somewhat civil. Nevertheless, Troy's behavior was a little peculiar, and he knew he needed to question his friend about whether he was taking his medication. If Vinny were to witness Troy in a manic state, the Italian would certainly be forced to shoot all three of them.

"Okay, let's get down to business." Vinny sketched some lines on the piece of paper on the counter and pointed at them with the pencil. "This is Pleasant Street, the street in front of the house, to the west. If you look out the back door, Olive Street is the street you can see between the brown house and the blue house on the other side of the privacy fence. The culvert, where you are digging to, is parallel with Olive Street. You are going to dig in a straight line to the culvert. Do you see what I am talking about?"

"I understand, but how do we know if we are going in the right direction?" Larry asked.

"You have about a forty-foot span to work with between the two houses. It's shorter if you stay closer to the blue house but not disastrous if you don't. We've surveyed the height of the culvert from the basement floor and know that it is fifty-five inches lower than the floor. Now that is to the center. So, if you take a ten-foot two by four, and keep it level, you can measure the low end, making sure to drop five inches every ten feet. You have everything you need downstairs."

"No problem." Larry had always been very mechanically minded, and his smile let everyone know he knew exactly how to dig the tunnel.

"No problem," echoed Troy.

"When you get to the culvert, you're going to cut a hole in the side of it, using the abrasive metal cutting blade on the cut-off saw." Vinny was feeling good about Larry's ability to, at least, comprehend the job. He had doubts about Troy, but it was too late to find new workers.

"Let's get back in the van and I'll show you where we are going to meet after this is all over." Vinny opened the door from the kitchen to the garage.

The garage was filled with smoke from the cigarette Tony was smoking as he waited, leaning lazily with one arm on the van. Tony watched the three young men climb into the van, never making eye contact with any of them, before sliding the door closed and climbing into the front seat.

Vinny drove southward on Pleasant Street two blocks to Forty-Eighth Avenue, turning east across Olive Street, one more block to Nome Street, where he made a U-turn and parked on Forty-Eighth Street in front of Wood Park.

"Look across the park to the opening in the side of the hill." Vinny pointed toward a small opening about one hundred yards from where they sat. The culvert, covered by a metal grate, was protruding from the side of the hill. "That's where the culvert ends. It dumps into that small stream. Do you see it?"

"Yeah," Larry said. "What about the grate?"

"We'll take care of it when we come back to get the tools."

"How far will we have to crawl through the culvert?" Troy asked.

"Over a hundred yards," Vinny answered.

"That's a long way to crawl," Troy said.

"It's bigger in there than it looks. Plus, you'll be carrying some packages." Vinny waited for a reaction. When he didn't get one, he continued, "There will be a black car sitting in the parking lot directly above the culvert opening. I want Larry to go to the car and take the keys from under the floor mat and open the trunk. Troy and Billy are to hand the bags to Larry as quickly as possible, and Larry is to place the bags in the trunk. After the bags are secure, all three of you are to get into the backseat of the car and wait for us. Capisce?"

"Yeah, we understand. How long will we have to wait?" Larry asked.

"As long as it takes. Probably about ten minutes." Vinny drove slowly to the parking lot. "Here's where the car will be."

There was a drop-off over a three-foot brick retaining wall and another three-foot drop-down over a grassy knoll to the culvert from the parking lot. They would have to hand the package up about six feet, so whatever they were going to remove from the house would not weigh very much.

"We chose this house because it sits so deep into the lot, that way you don't need to dig as far to the culvert." Vinny drove the van into the garage, leaving the door open behind him. "Are there any questions?"

All three looked at each other and shook their heads.

"Okay, hop out. If you have any problems, you have my number." Vinny waited until the three boys were clear of the van before backing out.

"I think we can handle this," Larry said. "Don't y'all?"

"Oh yeah," said Billy Ray. "I'm wondering just how hard it will be to dig."

"Only one way to find out," said Troy. "We best get started."

Medicine Bow, Texas

Sara embraced her third cup of coffee as she looked out the window at Delphia tossing a softball back and forth with Chrystal. Everyone was wasting time as they waited to leave for Rebecca's doctor appointment in Dallas. Even though she was staring out the window, Sara's mind was on the mental state of Rebecca. Her daughter had spent the entire morning in her room by herself. It was disconcerting to Sara, because isolation was something Troy had always done and was something not inherently a part of Rebecca's makeup. The diagnosis by the new doctor would be a judgment they would have to abide by, and the anticipation of her diagnosis was overwhelming.

***

Rebecca lay in her queen-size bed gazing at the ceiling. God had given her a talent and the enthusiasm to enjoy it. She had worked very hard to develop her skills and was now faced with the possibility it could all be over. There was still some pain in the knee but much less severe than a week ago, and most of the swelling had gone down. Rebecca was sure these were signs that the knee was healing itself, but there was a constant notion in her head that Dr. Meersman was right and she would need surgery.

"Rebecca," Sara knocked gently on her bedroom door, "would you like something to eat before we leave?"

"I'll be right out." Rebecca sat up in her bed.

Sara worked on making several sandwiches as she continued looking out the window. Uncle Martin was now tossing the softball back and forth with the girls. He motioned Delphia to run toward the kitchen window so he could toss her the ball.

"Delphia," Sara yelled out the window, "tell Uncle Martin to come in and have a sandwich."

"Okay," Delphia turned and ran toward Uncle Martin.

"Uncle Martin is going to pull a muscle if he isn't careful," Rebecca said, looking out the window over her mother's shoulder.

"Remember when he used to chase you?" Sara was happy to see Rebecca somewhat upbeat.

"He always played with us." Rebecca sat down at the table and began to eat a sandwich.

"Are you ready to go?" Sara sat down next to Rebecca.

"Yes," Rebecca lowered her head.

"Honey," Sara placed her hand on Rebecca's arm, "we need to talk."

"I know I haven't been very nice to be around."

"Under the circumstances, I think you have handled yourself very well."

"I just don't know what I'm going to do if this doctor comes up with the same diagnosis." Rebecca turned her chair to face her mother.

"If she does come up with the same conclusion as Dr. Meersman, then we will find the best treatment possible."

"I'm trying to be strong." The tears were flowing from Rebecca's eyes.

"You are strong." Sara tried to keep from crying but seeing the distress in her daughter was breaking her heart, and she began to sob.

"Whatever happens," Rebecca sat up straight, "I want to handle it better than I did this last week."

"There is no doubt in my mind that you will," Sara dabbed her eyes with a napkin. Ever since Rebecca had started elementary school, it was a prevalent opinion of all her teachers that she was far more mature for her age than any student they had taught. Sara found Rebecca's perception during difficult times something she had always took for granted, but now she needed to be strong for her daughter.

"I've been thinking a lot about Troy." The tears in Rebecca's eyes were drying. "He must have been so miserable. I wish I would have taken more time to help him."

"I've been trying to think of what to say to you all morning long." Sara smiled for the first time that morning, "I just needed to let you speak."

"I hear there's a sandwich in here for me." Uncle Martin slapped his hands together as he entered the kitchen.

Delphia followed close behind the old man, tossing a softball from hand to hand.

"Sit down here, Delphia." Sara placed her sandwich onto the table. "You can have this sandwich. I'm going to get freshened up."

"Becca. Are ya scared?" Delphia sat down at the table.

"A little."

"Ma told me that a body can be consumed by fear." Delphia stared intently at Rebecca. "I know no fear could consume you, Becca."

"Eat yore sandwich, young lady," Uncle Martin said. "Give us a little peace."

"I just want Becca to know I love her."

"You'll have plenty of time to tell her you love her on the drive to Dallas," said Uncle Martin. "Yore Ma is gonna be here any second. So eat."

"What are you gonna do today?" Rebecca asked Uncle Martin.

"I'm just gonna piddle around and wait to hear from y'all."

"Why don't you come along?"

"Ohh, I best wait here." He knew it would be pure torture to travel with the four women.

"Well, I don't blame you." Rebecca stood up and gave Uncle Martin a strong hug. "Ma will call and let you know how things go."

"No matter what happens," Uncle Martin spoke in a soft voice, "we'll help ya get through it."

"I know you will." Rebecca released her hug as Lola entered the house.

"Are we ready to go?" asked Lola.

"Let's go," said Rebecca.

Dallas, Texas

The doctor posed to give Rebecca the second opinion was a petite woman in her mid-fifties with short brown hair. She was in direct physical contrast to Dr. Meersman, who towered over the tiny doctor as she extended her hand toward Rebecca.

"Rebecca, I'm Doctor Larson."

"Hello, Rebecca." Dr. Meersman stood to the side of Dr. Larson.

"Hello," Rebecca shook Dr. Larson's hand and then Dr. Meersman's. "Dr. Larson, this is my mother Sara Young."

"My pleasure," Dr. Larson said with a frown on her face, "can we sit for a moment?"

"Rebecca, Sara." Doctor Meersman motioned toward two chairs in the examining room. "We have had a chance to discuss your case in quite some detail."

Rebecca sat down next to her mother. Her first impression of the new doctor was one of uncertainty. She liked her appearance but wasn't exactly thrilled with the scowl on her face.

"I believe the initial diagnosis of osteosarcoma is correct." Dr. Larson was brutally honest as she looked Rebecca straight in the eyes. "The type of treatment that you will require is something Dr. Meersman and I disagree upon."

Rebecca held her hand to her mouth as she listened, breathing her warm breath into her palm.

"It's the reason I wanted Dr. Larson to give the second opinion," Dr. Meersman continued. "On many things, we are as different as night and day."

Rebecca turned toward her mother, unable to respond to what the doctors were saying.

"You will be the ones who have to make the decisions on what treatment you receive." Dr. Larson removed one of the X-rays from a folder and held it in front of Rebecca and Sara. "We will try to be as specific as we can about the challenges you are facing."

Rebecca removed her hand from her mouth and sat quietly, staring at the two doctors whose judgement would have an enormous impact on her life. Dr. Meersman's hair was sticking out even further than the last time they met, and his eyes seemed to bug out extra far as he spoke.

"We have both looked at the MRI but would like to have another MRI and a CT scan before the biopsy," said Dr. Meersman. "We need to find out how far the mass has spread."

"What kind of treatment are we looking at?" Sara asked.

"I can't answer that question until after the tests," answered Dr. Larson, turning to look at Dr. Meersman.

"This is where we differ." Dr. Meersman moved next to Rebecca and placed his hand on top of hers. "This disease is something we must give our utmost attention. If we don't, it could kill you."

"Okay," Rebecca was breathing hard.

"Now I know how important running is to you, but I also know that your life is invaluable." He stared directly into her eyes. "I can't tell you exactly how radical the surgery will need to be in order to rid your body of this disease. I can only say that you will need to have surgery performed. I repeat, surgery must be performed."

"Are you talking about an amputation?" Sara looked straight at Dr. Meersman.

"I don't know. I can only tell you that if we can kill this thing with a leg-saving procedure, that is what we will do." Dr. Meersman let go of Rebecca's hand and turned to Dr. Larson. "It's time for Rebecca to make her decision."

"It's best you choose your doctor before the biopsy and bone scan," Doctor Larson said.

"How can we make this decision?" Sara's voice cracked. "We still don't have enough information."

"I understand it is difficult," said Doctor Larson. "The one single difference that distinguishes me from Doctor Meersman is that I am much more conservative in my approach to handling this disease. I understand that Rebecca has a wonderful future ahead of her as an athlete, but in a nutshell, Doctor Meersman is much more likely to perform limb sparing surgery than I am."

"With the information we have now, do you think the leg should be amputated?" Sara asked.

"Most likely." Doctor Larson clenched her teeth. "I know it sounds harsh at this time, and if I am your choice as the doctor to proceed, of course I will do all I can to save the leg."

Sara sat with her hand over her mouth.

"We need to decide," Rebecca said.

"You should decide before the biopsy is performed." Dr. Meersman ran his hand through his bushy hair. "The biopsy should be performed by the doctor who performs the surgery."

Sara remained silent. She had checked the credentials of the doctors and knew they both were at the top of their field.

Rebecca considered the tired, bulging eyes of Dr. Meersman. She turned and looked at her mother and noticed how terribly tired she appeared.

"It is best if you decide as soon as possible," said Dr. Larson.

"Dr. Meersman, I want you to do the surgery." Rebecca made the difficult choice without consulting her mother. "Nothing against you, Doctor Larson."

"It's okay." Dr. Larson placed her hand on Rebecca's hand and said, "I do insist on one thing. Even if Doctor Meersman decides on a limb-sparing surgery, I would like for you to have preoperative chemotherapy."

Both Sara and Rebecca looked at Doctor Meersman.

"It is something we can discuss." Doctor Meersman gave Doctor Larson an agitated glance before turning back to Rebecca. "Young lady, let's get you scheduled for these tests."

Sara noticed the tension that materialized between the two doctors when Dr. Larson mentioned chemotherapy. She was beginning to worry that the two doctors were one in the same and that Rebecca wasn't getting a choice in caregivers, so she was somewhat comforted by the strained looks the two were giving each other.

"I need to get back to work." Dr. Larson patted Rebecca's hand and turned to the door. "I'm sure Dr. Meersman will take great care of you."

"Dr. Meersman," Sara watched Dr. Larson close the door on her way out, "can I ask you something?"

"Certainly."

"I couldn't help but notice the tension between you and Dr. Larson when she brought up the subject of chemotherapy. Is there something we should know about all this?"

"Great question," Dr. Meersman clasped his hands together and sat next to Rebecca. "I am …" he hesitated. "Some doctors feel that I am somewhat unorthodox … untraditional, you might say, in the way I take care of my patients."

"Should we be concerned with this approach?" Sara was concerned.

"No, Dr. Larson and I have had several heated discussions over the use of chemotherapy for patients who all are much older than Rebecca." Dr. Meersman's voice was very comforting. "I believe that every individual is different, and therefore every treatment plan is different. The issue of quality of life is something Dr. Larson and I discuss, very courteously, and I believe you misread the look I gave her when she mentioned chemo."

"Will chemotherapy be a part of Rebecca's treatment?"

"Most likely."

"Thank you for the explanation." Sara was impressed with the warmth and honesty of the doctor, but she was still worried. She was going to have to lean on Sam Blake once more to make sure Rebecca would get the best treatment possible.

Aurora, Colorado

"I knocked a hole through. I can see dirt." Billy Ray leaned on the sledgehammer he had just finished swinging with fury. The cheap carpet in the basement of the house they were destroying was covered with dust.

"Let me swing for a while." Troy swung the sledgehammer with the same amount Sof ferocity as his friend had moments earlier. Dust was caked to his shirtless body as his biceps bulged each time he contacted the concrete wall. He hit the wall repeatedly with the sound of a dull thud resonating through the small room. Billy Ray and Larry watched with astonishment as he hammered the wall until a small crack formed, and then a football-size piece of concrete fell to the carpet.

Larry reached in with a pry bar and broke loose another small piece of concrete. "There's the rebar." He sat the pry bar down and grabbed the sledgehammer. He tapped the rebar with the sledge and listened to the ringing of the metal, a much different sound than they had heard when they hit only concrete. "We can loosen the concrete by hitting the rebar. We'll have this concrete out in no time."

Troy could feel his heart thumping against his chest as he sat down to catch his breath. "Good Lord, this feels good," he said.

"Why don't we finish knocking out the concrete, then call it a day?" Larry took the sledge from Troy and prepared to strike the wall.

"That sounds good. I'm getting awful hungry." Billy shoveled several small pieces of concrete off the carpet and into the wheelbarrow.

"Come on, y'all. We can have several feet of dirt dug out of this thing by tonight if we keep going," Troy yelled at his friends.

Billy Ray stopped shoveling and looked closely at Troy. He wondered if he had reneged on his promise to take his medication. It had been three mornings since he had witnessed him taking his capsule of lithium.

"Come on, y'all. We can't stop now."

"Man, are you taking your medication?" Billy moved close enough to consider his friend's glossed over eyes.

"I'm just hyped. Don't worry, I'm taking all I need." Troy turned his head away Billy's intrusive look.

"It's ten o'clock. We've done enough for one day." Larry set the sledgehammer down. "We don't need to burn ourselves out."

The cold air from the open refrigerator was refreshing to Troy as he looked over Billy's shoulder into the fully stocked icebox.

"At least we are going to eat well," said Billy.

Troy changed into a pair of khaki shorts while Billy prepared sandwiches. Larry, using a pry bar, knocked a section of dirt from the hole onto the carpet.

"The dirt's pretty soft," said Larry.

"No matter what it takes, we'll get it done." Billy took a bite from his sandwich.

"I have a question." Troy sat down on the floor holding his plate of food in his dirty hands. "What is Vinny going to bring back with him?"

"Maybe drugs," Billy shrugged his shoulders.

"Someone is going to be chasin' them." Troy sat his plate in front of him. "I can't imagine why else they would need this tunnel. Did you see the eyes on the one dude?"

"You mean Tony?" asked Larry.

"Yeah, he wouldn't look ya straight in the eye. I don't trust anyone who can't look me straight in the eyes." Troy took a bite from his sandwich.

"We best take some precautions after they pay us," interjected Billy.

"I still wonder why we're digging this tunnel." Troy pushed his plate to the side and lay down on the dirty carpet.

"Well, we will have plenty of time to think about it." Larry tossed his paper plate into the trash container and sat down on his cot. "We need to get started early in the morning, so I'm gonna crash."

"Whatever it is they have, it's gonna be worth a lot of money." Troy continued, "I'm sure we're not gonna ruin this house for nothing."

"I doubt they care," said Billy. "It looks like a rental."

"I guess we're the reason folks renting things should make background checks," said Troy.

"I guess," Billy picked up his cot. "Something tells me you're gonna yap all night, so I'm gonna sleep in the other room."

"Larry." Troy sat down on his cot.

"Yeah."

"What do you figure these fellas are up to?"

"I told ya I don't know."

"They said they would have several bags with them when they get here. Do ya reckon they are jewel thieves?"

"They wouldn't need more than one bag for jewels." Larry placed his pillow over his head. "Go to sleep."

"I'm gonna do some traveling with my money. I have a terrible urge to see the world." Troy spoke to the ceiling. "I may try to become a track coach. I did help Rebecca with her form running when she was little. I don't mean to brag, but I did help her."

Larry pulled the pillow tighter around his ears as Troy talked into the night.

Medicine Bow, Texas

Sara spent more time at the Blake ranch over the past week than she had since she moved to Medicine Bow sixteen years ago. But this was the first time Rebecca had joined her. Sara assumed that when she married Sam, they would move into the large ranch house and her children would consider it home. Seeing Rebecca move around the house as though she had always lived there made Sara happy.

Rebecca looked comfortable sitting at Sam's large oak desk, with Sam looking over her shoulder, resting one arm on the back of the leather office chair, while holding a cup of coffee. Rebecca was exceptionally adept at handling computers, yet she allowed Sam the courtesy of showing her how to navigate his supercomputer.

"Just push enter," said Sam, taking a sip of coffee and pushing his chest out.

"All right," said Rebecca, smiling to herself.

"Sam," said Jackie, poking her head into the office holding a piece of paper. "This fax just arrived."

Sam handed the paper to Sara.

"That was quick." Sara accepted the paper from Sam and gave Jackie a look that only another woman would notice. Jackie could have given Sara the fax without going through Sam.

Sara had called Dr. Meersman earlier that morning asking about the specifics of Rebecca's disease. Rather than try to explain over the telephone what was taking place with the tumor in Rebecca's knee, the doctor offered to send her the information.

"Doctor Meersman says the tumor extends proximally into the epiphysis," said Sara, reading from the piece of paper as she moved closer to Sam and Rebecca.

"I wonder what the epiphysis is," said Rebecca.

"I have no idea," said Sam, sipping his coffee.

"Look it up," said Sara.

"Already doing it." Rebecca typed quickly on the keyboard.

"He says the tumor does not involve the knee joint. He writes 'good news' next to it," Sara continued to read.

"Good." Sam nodded his head.

"The tumor is localized," read Sara. "Nothing in the lungs."

"The epiphysis is the end of the long bone." Rebecca probed below her knee as she read from the computer. "Proximal is the part closest to the place of origin."

"That is where it hurts." Rebecca swung around in the office chair and pointed to her knee.

"Why couldn't he have just said right below the knee instead of all this technical hogwash," Sam asked.

"Doctor Meersman writes that with the limb-sparing procedure there is a greater risk of a recurrence of the disease." Sara looked at Sam and Rebecca. "He sure has mentioned this point a lot."

"I reckon he wants you to understand," said Sam.

"I guess," replied Sara. "He also says there will be some loss of muscle strength and possibly loss of joint motion."

Rebecca quietly listened to her mother. Doctor Meersman had made it clear that the surgery would hinder her ability to run, but she still could not accept this. She had always been able to defeat adversity. Her strength would allow her to overcome this life-threatening threat, and she would continue in her quest to become a world-class runner. The doctor could state definitively that she would not be able to run after the surgery. But she would continue to not believe him.

"The doctor wants to operate in two weeks," Sara's words broke Rebecca's train of thought.

"Rebecca, you haven't ever flown in my jet, have you?" Sam moved so he could look Rebecca directly in her eyes. "Why don't we take a little trip a couple of days before you go into the hospital?"

"Where would we go?" asked Rebecca.

"Nowhere in particular."

"It sounds exciting," Rebecca smiled.

"That's a wonderful idea." Sara placed her arm around Sam's waist.

"Getting away always changes one's perspective," stated Sam.

"I'm going to stay positive," said Rebecca.

"That is something all of us plan on doing." Sara smiled and placed her head on Sam's shoulder.

Aurora, Colorado

"Hold the tape tight," Larry yelled from deep inside the tunnel.

Billy held the end of the one-hundred-foot tape tight to the jagged concrete in the basement of the house they were demolishing. Dirt was piled almost ceiling height around him, to the point they would soon have to carry it upstairs.

"How far are we?" Billy yelled into the cavern.

"A little over seventy feet," Larry's voice echoed back.

"Why don't y'all come on out and have lunch?" Billy could tell by the reflection of the light on the side of the cave that his two friends were already making their way toward him.

Both made their way out of the hole and brushed the soil from their jeans. Their faces were dark with dirt.

"Damn. It seems like we've been digging for forever." Larry had scolded his two friends over the past week for whining and complaining, but he was so tired he had to vent.

"We're only two thirds there," stated Billy.

"We have twelve days left to finish." Larry lay flat on his back.

"I've never been so tired in my life." Troy sat in the large pile of dirt.

"We're gonna have to start taking the dirt upstairs pretty soon." Billy sat down next to Troy. "I'll take over digging after lunch."

"That'll work. I'm gonna have to check the elevation again, so I'll help in the tunnel," said Larry.

The procedure they used in digging the tunnel came about by trial and error. The most efficient plan was to have one person pick the dirt loose onto a small piece of plywood and shovel it into a wagon attached to a long rope. The second person would push the wagon as the third person pulled the rope. Everyone kept busy, but being the person on the outside pulling the rope was by far the cleanest and easiest of the jobs. They had used the auger a couple of times to break up spots where the dirt was exceptionally hard. The vibration caused the dirt from the top of the tunnel to fall, bringing about the fear of the tunnel collapsing. So, before using the auger, they would brace the sides and top with plywood.

"Y'all know we're about out of lunchmeat," said Larry.

"I'm gonna buy me the thickest steak in Texas when we finish this job," said Billy. "Whose phone is ringing?"

"It's not mine," said Troy. "I never charged the battery."

"It's mine." Larry had borrowed a girlfriend's telephone before they left Texas and never returned it. He moved toward his cot and answered the phone.

Billy and Troy moved closer to Larry, making sure not to miss anything he might say.

"Hello. Yeah, Vinny. No problem. We're over seventy feet. Okay, we'll have everything in the garage." Larry folded his phone and set it on the cot.

"What did he want?" Billy asked.

"He wants to make sure we will have the tunnel finished." Larry had a concerned look on his face. "He reminded me that we're supposed to put everything in the garage when we finish."

"I'm gonna get back to work." Troy threw his half-eaten sandwich into the garbage can. He took his flashlight and shined it down the narrow tunnel. It seemed to become smaller each time he entered it, yet he continued to cross the threshold of the opening and made his way through the cavern with the musky smell of freshly moved dirt filling his nostrils. The smell reminded him of the fields of Texas, but the cool temperature told him otherwise. For a moment, he became anxious, momentarily fearing the tunnel might collapse, but it was only fleeting as he arrived at the end. Adrenaline took the place of fear. He pointed the flashlight toward the wall of dirt and knelt with one knee forward and began chopping with the pick. Larry had cut the handle of the pick down so they could get a full swing. The dirt fell onto a small piece of plywood, and he used a shortened flat shovel to put it into the wagon to be pulled out of the cave.

After filling the wagon, Troy sat down on his butt and leaned against the dirt wall. He could see Larry crawling toward him, blocking the small dot of light at the end of the tunnel.

Larry had carved a small shelf on the side of the cave where he placed the ten-foot two-by-four and level. He took the two-by-four and placed it on the floor and put the level on it.

"Still going downhill," he said, looking at the bubble of the level.

Troy allowed Larry to push the wagon several feet before continuing with the pick. The first few swings produced hard pieces of clay, but the third strike sank into soft soil. He wasn't sure if he should be happy or if he should be a little skeptical of the change. Nevertheless, he continued to knock the soft dirt away from the wall until he heard a loud clank. He had hit concrete with the pick.

"What was that?" Larry had heard the noise even though he was nearing the tunnel opening.

"I think I hit concrete." Troy climbed into the large hole he had produced and pushed the dirt away from the concrete. "It looks like the foundation to a house."

"Are you sure?" Larry yelled down the tunnel.

Troy climbed closer to the concrete and cleared more dirt away. He pushed at the dirt with the handle of the pick and the entire ceiling of the cave gave way, collapsing on top of him. He couldn't breathe. The soft dirt covered him completely. In a fit of panic, he shook his head and shoulders as hard as he could possibly shake them. The dirt siphoned away from his face, falling to the floor of the cave below. He could see light about two feet above. He freed his right arm and began pushing the dirt down away from his torso. There was no way to go down. He squirmed until enough dirt was shaken from his body that he could reach up and grab the bottom of a blue piece of siding and pull himself up out of the cave. He was in the backyard of the blue house they had been using as a guide for the tunnel. He walked to the back corner of the house and peeked around the corner. There was a covered courtyard with a large glass patio door to the back of the house. He stepped onto the patio and looked through the doors. There didn't seem to be anyone home. He moved quickly along the back of the house to a gate on the far side where he exited and walked as casually as possible around the block. The door opened before he reached the front porch.

"Good Lord, man, I thought you were dead." Larry's hair was matted with dirt. "I shore was happy to see your feet move up."

"There's a big hole in them peoples' backyard." Troy moved to the upstairs kitchen door and looked out. "The people who live there are gone."

"We have to get it covered," said Larry. "We can use some plywood from downstairs."

Billy climbed a mound of dirt that was covering the floor and grabbed the top of the 4x8 piece of thick plywood and yanked. The plywood fell on top of the dirt. "Do we need the whole sheet?" he yelled up the stairs.

"Yeah, it's a big hole," yelled Billy.

Troy opened the back door and allowed Larry and Billy to carry the sheet into the backyard. He scaled the six-foot-high wood fence and jumped into the neighbor's backyard. He quickly moved to the patio doors and looked inside the house. He easily slid the door open and stepped inside. All the lights were off, and it seemed nobody was home. He stepped back outside and closed the door.

Larry and Billy placed one end of the plywood on top of the fence and pushed it into the backyard.

"I need a shovel and one of y'all to come help me," said Troy, peeking through a crack in the fence.

Larry climbed over the fence and looked around the dirty yard. "Are ya sure nobody is in the house?"

"The back door's open and I looked in."

"There might be someone sleeping."

"I don't think so," Troy began pulling the plywood toward the hole, "look for yourself."

Larry pulled the sliding glass door open and stepped inside. He vanished for a couple of minutes. Troy had the plywood ready to place over the hole as Larry retreated from the house.

"Nobody home," said Larry. "There is a car in the garage."

"We need to cover this before they do get home," Troy replied.

Larry jumped into the hole and began shoveling dirt onto the grass above. He was creating a large pile of dirt but continued digging until he had cleared the dirt out of the way of the tunnel.

"You're getting a big pile up here," yelled Troy into the ever-deepening hole.

"We can spread it out. The grass up there isn't very good anyway," stated Larry. "It's a lot easier throwing the dirt up there than it is pulling it down the tunnel."

"I reckon," said Troy, looking down at Larry, who was a good seven feet down inside the hole. "Maybe we should dig some of the tunnel and put the dirt up here. There's an old flower box at the back of the yard where we can throw some of it."

"Tell Billy to bring some buckets and we can dig several feet of this tunnel real quick." Larry's face was covered with dirt, "I'm already hitting hard clay."

The boys worked at a frantic pace, taking turns digging in the hole and handing five-gallon buckets of dirt out of it and spreading the dirt around the flower garden at the back of the yard. Larry figured they had pushed their luck as far as possible with the notion the neighbors could come home at any time. He crawled out of the hole and said, "Let's cover this up."

Billy methodically carved a ledge around the hole large enough for the plywood to fit neatly down below the dirt line. They pushed the plywood into place and covered it with soil. It was hardly noticeable in the unkempt yard.

All three were exhausted by the time they reached the basement of their house. The hard work was finally taking a toll. The misfortune of the cave collapsing had turned out to be a blessing. In the short time they were in the neighbor's yard, they had progressed the tunnel a full eight feet.

Seattle, Washington

Mike King sat in his plush office, comfortably leaning back in a leather chair, talking on the phone to Vinny. A view of the Space Needle was framed in the picture window directly in front of him.

"I want to make damn sure everything is taken care of," he said into his phone. "No errors. Stick with the plan all the way to the finish. You know how important this money is to both of us."

"Everything is as it should be," assured Vinny.

"Ending of the three boys' contracts?"

"Yes," Vinny knew exactly what his boss meant, "all taken care of."

"I'm going home this evening. I take it you have everything under control."

"There will be no reason to bother you." Vinny knew the finicky nature of his boss was one where he needed to be precise in his answers. "It will all be over with by the time you return."

"I'll speak with you then." He hung up the phone.

Anytime Mike King spoke on the telephone, his discussions were short. Besides, there were several business items he needed to take care of before making his way across the border to the tranquility and sanity waiting for him in the countryside outside of Vancouver, Canada. He was an American citizen, but his wife was from Canada. His legitimate business, at least on paper, was a perfect facade for a heartless sociopath to fly under the radar. To be able to handle millions of dollars under the guise of being not only a successful businessman, but also a very generous one.

His business consisted of buying and selling used bowling alley equipment. As technology progressed in bowling paraphernalia, many owners of bowling alleys upgraded to the more modern equipment. Mike King bought the obsolete equipment. His reputation for paying top dollar was well known, and therefore MTAR Bowling Equipment was well established. After buying the old equipment, selling it was irrelevant; in fact, many of the metal recycling businesses and landfills in the area were full of bowling pins and other bowling accessories. If the company was looked at closely, or maybe not close but logically, it would be found that nobody wanted any of his archaic product.

Mike King's analytical abilities were off the chart. His crime syndicate was where all his money originated. Any endeavor pursued by his thieves was well thought out and meticulously planned. MTAR Bowling Equipment was simply a place to launder the money and give Mike King a solid reputation in the eyes of the community and his family. Ironically, Vinny and the other bandits were all employees of the company who received W-2s each year and filed their taxes as such. The company accountant, along with several other legitimate employees, were oblivious to the crime factor of the business. Mike King kept track of all paperwork and handed them over to the accountant for proper filing and documentation.

Aurora, Colorado

For the first time in Troy's life, he felt claustrophobic. It was necessary to put a bend in the tunnel after the ceiling collapsed, making it difficult to see the light at the other end. The smell of dirt was making him nauseous, and the hard work was giving him a headache. The good news was that he expected to hit the drainage pipe with every swing of the pick.

He was on his knees digging with a fury that was frightening.

Pulling the wagon full of dirt out of the tunnel was now the most difficult task. It was a two-man job handled by Billy and Larry. Billy's muscles bulged from his body as he worked shirtless outside the tunnel pulling the rope attached to the wagon. Larry pushed and guided it. They would dump the dirt from the wagon, and Billy would spread the soil throughout the house. Larry then had the arduous task of pulling the wagon back through the tunnel.

"Do ya want to get out of here for a bit?" Larry yelled over the wagon as he approached Troy.

"No, man." Troy shoveled the loose dirt into the wagon. "I know I'm almost there."

The boys had been working for over twelve hours. Larry's body ached as he jerked on the rope and, when it tightened, began pushing the wagon toward the light at the end.

"I think Troy might be losing his mind," said Larry when he came close enough to Billy to be heard. "He's talking to himself."

"Oh man," said Billy. "I don't think he's been taking his meds. I just hope he doesn't go off the deep end until we finish with this job."

"I'm exhausted." Larry watched Billy dump the wagon load of dirt. "Troy won't rest, so I guess we best suck it up and keep going."

Troy could be heard whooping and hollering at the other end of the tunnel.

"Tell him to be quiet," said Billy. "Someone's gonna hear him."

Troy was sitting with his back to the cold dirt on the side of the tunnel laughing, holding the pick in the air in such a way it frightened Larry.

"Troy," said Larry. "Are you all right?"

"Look, man." Troy placed the point of the pick into a small hole at the end of the tunnel and clanked it against concrete. "The pipe isn't metal but concrete. There are no more than three or four more loads left to push out of here. If we were to start right now, it would be about ten thousand dollars a load."

Larry was relieved to find Troy's euphoria warranted as he crumbled to the ground next to him. "Let's sit here a moment and enjoy ourselves."

"I can't believe we finished. I can't believe it," said Troy.

"Why don't you get out of here and get something to drink." Larry wanted Troy out of his way. "Tell Billy to bring the cut-off saw down here so I can cut a hole in this pipe. We ain't pushin' another load of dirt out of this hole. I'll throw the rest of the dirt into the drain."

Troy looked down the long, murky passageway he had helped create. His arms were weak and felt as though they couldn't hold his weight as he began to crawl down the tunnel to the opening leading to the basement of the house. As he struggled to crawl the length of the tunnel, he knew the hard work was over and he had only two more nights before he could celebrate.

Fort Worth, Texas

The nervous tension Sara was experiencing was becoming greater and greater as the date of the operation approached. Sam insisted on taking the trip in his private jet that he had promised Rebecca. The operation would be performed in little more than seventy-two hours, and Sara was at her wits' end. The past three weeks of chemotherapy had been physically hard on Rebecca, making her sick for the best part of the treatment. Her hallowed appearance deteriorated on a daily basis.

Sara's opinion on the trip being a good idea had changed along with Rebecca's appearance. She wanted to cancel or at least postpone the trip. She tried to tell Sam that it would be prudent to keep Rebecca close to home before the operation. He would have none of that and told her he would drag her to the airport if necessary. He knew deep in his heart it would be helpful to get Rebecca's mind off the surgery. His plan was to fly to Denver for two days and back to Dallas where Rebecca would be admitted to the hospital.

Sara finally agreed.

"Jerry, how's the weather in Denver?" asked Sam.

"It's clear." Jerry stood back from the cockpit door as his three passengers entered the airplane. "A bit cold."

"This plane is a lot bigger than I expected." Rebecca stepped around Jerry, crowding close enough to him to smell his cologne, before moving toward the back of the plane.

"It's a twelve-passenger aircraft." Jerry looked closely at Rebecca as she passed.

"Jerry, this is Sara's daughter Rebecca." Sam crouched so as not to knock his hat off on the low ceiling.

"Pleased to meet you." Jerry's face was deeply tanned and enhanced his white teeth as he smiled at the beautiful young woman. When he heard he was flying Sara's daughter today, he had hoped she would be attractive. He wasn't disappointed.

"Nice to meet you." Rebecca smiled back at him as she sat in a cushioned leather seat.

"You all will find most everything on the craft has been modernized," said Jerry, "but the galley is my pride and joy."

"Jerry has been my pilot for a little over a year now," said Sam. "He has done a magnificent job of taking care of the plane."

"What kind of plane is it?" asked Rebecca.

"It's a Hawker/Raytheon." Jerry opened the door to the kitchen. "The galley is full. Please help yourselves to refreshments."

"We have individual computer ports at each seat." Sam pointed to a computer screen. "Jerry changed the size of the screens from five and a half inches to seven inches."

"Come here." Jerry took hold of Rebecca's soft hand, gently coaxing her from the cushy seat. He led her to the cockpit where he pointed at the pilot's seat. "We have a couple of minutes before we take off. I'll show you some of the instruments."

"Wow, this is awesome." Rebecca clasped her hands to her chest as she looked at the instrument panel in front of her. "I can't imagine what it looks like when we are a couple of miles in the air."

"It really is beautiful."

"Do you know what all these buttons are for?" Rebecca looked at the display panel.

"Every one of them." Airplanes were Jerry's passion. "We don't have time right now for me to explain all the systems involved with this aircraft, but maybe we can meet at another time and I will explain it all to you."

"I would like that," Rebecca smiled at Jerry.

"I just wanted to let you see what it is like in the pilot's seat, but now I need all passengers to return to their seats and we will get ready to depart to Denver." Jerry held his hand for Rebecca to take hold of. He followed her back to her seat.

In the deep recesses of Sara's mind, she couldn't help but wonder how this cancer would affect her daughter's relationships. Rebecca's smile was heartwarming to her as they approached.

"Have you been a pilot for very long?" asked Sara. She had met him on her trip to New York and wondered how old the youthful pilot was at that time, but they were in such a hurry they never had a chance to talk. Now that he was obviously infatuated with her seventeen-year-old daughter, she was going to make sure and get all the details about him from Sam.

"I flew for the government before getting my commercial license about five years ago," Jerry stated very politely.

"He came highly recommended," said Sam, "and I have found him to be a better catch than anticipated. Stanley thinks he is the finest pilot on the face of the earth."

"Thank you, sir." Jerry took in a deep breath, "I believe it's about time to depart."

Rebecca watched the short but very muscular pilot make his way to the cockpit, moving with ease into the pilot seat. She was sure there was more to him than was being disclosed at their first meeting. Anyway, the clandestine mystery man would make for a wonderful fantasy.

"Buckle up, honey," instructed Sara, sitting a couple of seats back from her daughter.

"With flight preparation and all, it'll only take us about an hour and half to get to Denver," said Sam. "Shall we put a movie on?"

"I think I'll just enjoy the flight," said Rebecca, leaning back into her seat.

"I think I'll enjoy it too." Sara pulled Sam's hand to her cheek and looked him directly in the eyes and whispered, "Thank you."

Denver, Colorado

"There's Tom and Drew," yelled Rebecca, walking in front of Sam and Sara as they entered the lobby of the Brown Palace Hotel in downtown Denver.

"Hi, sis." Tom placed his arms around Rebecca and hugged her tightly.

"You look tired," said Sara.

"I shouldn't be. We haven't done much of anything but wait." Tom kept his arm around his little sister's shoulder.

"Hopefully Stanley will have some information this afternoon about the fella who hired the boys," said Sam. "He told me that he has some leads he's been following."

"If anybody can find out about him, it's Stanley." Tom removed his arm from around Rebecca's shoulder. "How was y'all's trip?"

"It was fabulous," replied Sara. "The sunlight on the snow-covered peaks was breathtaking."

"The weathermen here say they are getting more snow in the mountains than they have had in a long time. If you want to have your breath taken away, ya ought to try driving on those peaks," laughed Tom.

"Hello, Drew," said Rebecca, holding her hand out. "This is as quiet as I have ever seen you."

"Tom told me not to hawass Sam."

"I just want you to be on your best behavior," corrected Tom.

"Well, you look very nice," said Rebecca, noticing the white shirt and black pants Drew was wearing.

"Thank you, Becca. Tom wants me to wea my best clothes when we go out to eat."

"Dammit, Drew," Tom gave him a malicious look. "Stop makin' it sound like I'm looking after you like a mother hen."

Drew ignored Tom's comment and looked at Sam. "Sam, how's my daddy doin' with the pigs?"

"I haven't had a chance to talk with him," answered Sam.

"I talked to him last night." Drew moved uncomfortably close to Sam. "He said they ah doing just fine. He ain't had any notion of eating even one of them."

"That's great." Sam took a step back from Drew. "I need to make a quick call."

"Ah we gonna eat now?" Drew moved along with Sam. "We been waitin' fo y'all to eat."

"If you let me make this call we can find somewhere to eat." Sam gave Drew a decisive look.

Sam's demeanor toward Drew was often one of impatience, but in reality, he actually enjoyed the straightforward manner of the backward country boy. He watched Drew turn toward the others as he spoke on his phone with Stanley. He knew that by ten o'clock Stanley was to receive information about the boys from Medicine Bow from either Mike King himself or someone very close to him. Stanley had solved some of the mystery about Mike King, and the more he learned, the more concerned he became for the safety of Troy.

"Stanley," Sam spoke into his cell phone. "Have ya heard anything yet?"

"First thing, Sam, the FBI arrested a biker last night for the murder of Agent Miller. That's the FBI informant named Pig Pen who was at the party," said Stanley.

"That's good."

"Not really. Something tells me they have the wrong fella, and even if they don't, I doubt he'll talk," answered Stanley. "Having someone collared will take the heat off Mike King, and we lose some of our lap dogs."

"How much information do you have on this fella?"

"Not a hell of a lot. I know Mike King is an alias and the people who know him are either very loyal or scared to death of him." Stanley paused. "A lot of people who come into contact with him disappear."

"Any idea where he's from?"

"One source I spoke with thought he spoke with an accent like someone from Minnesota. But that's a long shot," said Stanley. "Sam, I think it's gonna take a lot of time and money to expose this rascal."

"Time is something we don't have."

"I have a meeting in about an hour with a character by the name of Bodine," stated Stanley. "Everyone I've talked with in regard to the party at the farm in Amarillo tosses out his name."

"You be careful," warned Sam. "Make sure and have someone tag along with you."

"Aaron is going with me." Stanley didn't say so, but he wished Jerry was in Texas to help watch his back. "I'll call you after the meeting."

"I'll be waiting."

Sara could see the worried look on Sam's face as he approached the group. "Is everything all right?"

"Nothing new," Sam smiled at her.

"I hope you don't mind eating Chinese food," said Sara, placing an arm around Sam's large waist. "Drew went to ask the girl at the front desk about Chinese restaurants."

"He's stuck on that girl," said Tom. "He asks her a question every time we walk by the front desk."

"She probably likes the attention," returned Sara.

"Rebecca, are you okay with Chinese food?" asked Sam.

"It was my choice." Rebecca moved to the other side of Sam and put her arm around his waist.

"It doesn't make a bit of difference where we eat." Sam put his arms around the shoulders of mother and daughter and pulled them close.

"We need to go to the Sixteenth Street Mall. It's close enough we can walk." Drew approached the others holding a piece of paper with directions. He walked to the exit and opened the door. "It sho is cold out hea."

"It'll be a nice, brisk walk," said Sara.

Rebecca and Sara let go of Sam only long enough to make their way through the exit. They took hold of him again as they made their way through the corridors of downtown Denver. It was a day of good humor, laughter, food, and shopping. They stopped at the curiosity shops scattered along the long outdoor mall, mostly for warmth, but Sam would usually reward the shopkeeper by purchasing some trivial item. Sam enjoyed the time of leisure where he could laugh and relax.

Sam's phone rang.

"Stanley." Sam stopped in his tracks and turned toward the window front of a building to shield himself from the cold, bitter wind.

"The boys are gonna be killed at the end of the job." Stanley didn't waste any words. "This Bodine character was at the farmhouse where they met Mike King."

"Did he tell ya who this Mike King is?"

"I don't think he knows," said Stanley. "Actually, I don't think he knows much."

"Can he contact Troy?" Sam pulled the collar of his coat tighter around his neck.

"No, he's at the bottom layer of this mess. But he does know that Mike King has something planned in Denver," said Stanley. "He figured whatever they planned would have already taken place."

"How does he know they plan to kill the boys?" Sam was talking as quietly as possible into the phone.

"He met Larry Lover at the strip club he works at." Stanley hesitated, "Somehow another customer had been searching for men without family ties to do some sort of hard work. Larry fit the bill."

"He wanted someone without family ties."

"Bodine is scared to death of these people. He wishes he hadn't gone to the farmhouse that night," said Stanley. "While he was there, he heard the fella he met at the strip club say that our boys would never see another day once they finished the job."

"Did he actually see Mike King?"

"I don't know, he supplied the strippers for the party. But he seemed terribly frightened about that night, and somehow I feel he might have seen Mike King's face."

"What in the hell do you think is going on here?"

"I don't know, Sam. All I know is that Troy is in serious trouble."

"Stanley, I want ya to call Ed and give him all this information." Sam watched the rest of the group make their way into a coffee shop. "I'm plannin' on stayin' in Dallas so we can be close to the hospital."

"I figured you would," Stanley said. "Tell Rebecca I'm thinking about her."

"I'll do that. I'm about to freeze to death so I'll talk with ya when I get back." Sam closed his phone.

Tom was hoping Sam would offer to take him and Drew back to Texas with them on the airplane that evening, but no such luck. Sam wanted them to stay in Denver with orders to keep trying to call Troy's cell phone. Denver was such a large city, Tom couldn't help but be skeptical about the importance of his staying behind. Nevertheless, he shook Sam's hand and hugged his mother and sister before they entered the taxi for their journey back home.

Maliki and Tanya

"So, Sam knew that Mike King was very dangerous before Troy did." Tanya stood up from the table.

"Sam had so many connections, but it was still frustrating to him and Stanley that they couldn't find Troy." Maliki looked at his watch. "Wow, time really flew by today."

"It sure did. It's already dinnertime."

"I want to take you into Aspen for dinner one night," Maliki stated. "Would you like to go tonight or tomorrow?"

"How about if we make reservations for everyone from Medicine Bow when they get here. It would be nice to talk over dinner." Tanya was totally relaxed. "Let's have a light dinner. I told Sara I would call her sometime tonight and let her know how everything is going."

"Sure." Maliki felt very comfortable with Tanya. He wondered what she and his grandmother would discuss but didn't ask.

"Looks like Rebecca had eyes for Jerry from the moment they met," stated Tanya.

"Aunt Rebecca was mature for her age, but she was still only seventeen years old."

"Oh to be seventeen again," said Tanya, stepping into the kitchen.

"Would you really want to be seventeen again?" Maliki followed her.

"Yeah." Tanya thought for a moment. "If I know what I know now."

The more acquainted Maliki became with Tanya, the more captivated he became. She had a beauty about her that came from her self-confidence and honesty that really charmed him.

Aurora, Colorado

The Channel Thirty-One newscast had just started when the sound from the garage door resonated from above. Larry was halfway up the stairs before the second rap could be heard on the garage door into the kitchen. He moved quickly as Billy and Troy sat statuesque with the cards from a three-handed rummy game still in hand. They had been anticipating the arrival of Vinny for several hours. Larry unlocked the door from the kitchen to the garage. Vinny moved quickly through the door followed by two men Larry had never seen before. Bags under Vinny's deep, dark eyes were sagging to his cheekbone. All three men were wearing black leather gloves as they quickly moved past Larry and down the stairs to the basement. Without saying a word, Vinny shined a light into the tunnel. "This looks more like three by three than four by four," said Vinny.

"No, it's pretty close to four by four," returned Larry. "It's not that hard to crawl through."

"It's too late to do anything about it now." Vinny glared at Billy and Troy still holding the cards in hand. "Go load the tools."

Billy and Troy remained quiet as they followed Larry upstairs.

"Take the light and check out the tunnel." Vinny handed the flashlight to one of the men and watched as they made their way without question into the opening.

Vinny's sidekick Tony sat quietly in the front seat of the van, never making eye contact with the boys as they loaded the tools.

The two unknown men came up from the basement and brushed the dirt from their pants.

"It'll work," said the shorter of the two as they both made their way into the back of the van.

"Someone has been trying to contact Mr. King in regards to your whereabouts," said Vinny as he closed the side door to the van. "You can contact your family the day after tomorrow, so don't blow it now. With all the hard work you have done, don't blow it."

"Everything's cool," said Larry. "We haven't talked with anyone."

"That's the way it needs to remain," said Vinny.

"Vinny." Larry moved beside the driver's door as Vinny got in the front seat. "Are we gonna get the rest of our money tomorrow?"

"Yeah, tomorrow." Vinny closed the door and rolled down the window. "Pack your clothes and take them to the end of the tunnel tonight. These two will be here at approximately ten o'clock in the morning. They are going to be in a hurry."

"Are you gonna be with them?" asked Larry, pushing the garage door opener.

"No, Tony will," Vinny answered. He turned and looked out the back window as he gunned the engine. He wasn't planning on being within a hundred miles of the metro area tomorrow.

The boys stood in the garage and watched the van pull out into the cold night.

"He shore wasn't very friendly," said Billy as the three made their way into the dirt-filled basement.

"He looked worried." Troy noticed a concerned look on Larry's face. "What are you thinkin' so hard about?"

"I was just thinking." Larry took in a deep breath, "Is Tony gonna give us our money?"

"Do you think we're the fall guys?" asked Billy.

"I really didn't think so until now," answered Larry. "The way Vinny acted when I asked him about our money just doesn't seem right."

"I got the same feeling," said Billy.

"I don't know. I'm so damned tired I can't think." Larry lay down on the covers he used for a makeshift bed. "Maybe our viewpoint will improve with a good night's sleep."

Troy listened to Larry and Billy debate the possibilities that might await them in the morning. His body was exhausted, yet his mind was telling him otherwise. He had been having difficulty sleeping ever since he arrived at the house. He knew tonight would be no different. Deep down inside he recognized the symptoms, yet being in a strange environment helped him rationalize his sleeplessness as being a symptom of the unfamiliar surroundings. Tonight he wasn't about to lie awake on a pile of dirt in the cold basement.

"If y'all want to pack your bags, I'll take them to the end of the tunnel," said Billy.

Troy removed his only clean pair of pants and shirt before stripping down to his underpants and placing his dirty clothes into his duffel bag. "I'm gonna take a shower," he said.

"Here's mine." Larry placed his bag next to the tunnel. "I'm gonna crash."

"I'll get these in the tunnel," said Billy, "and I'm gonna do the same."

By the time Troy returned from the shower, Billy and Larry were sleeping. He had considered telling them about his plans for the evening but knew they would never allow him to leave the house. He quietly opened the door and stepped outside into the cold and made his way down the dimly lit street.

***

Troy flashed his driver's license at the burly bouncer before making his way through a vociferous crowd of young people toward the dance floor of the upscale nightclub. He had walked nearly a mile to the Stop N Go gas station and called for a cab. The cab driver never hesitated when asked about the best place to go in Denver to meet young ladies. The driver told him his dress was appropriate, yet he was still self-conscious about wearing a white western shirt and black wrangler jeans that had been in his suitcase since he left Texas. He figured he would only be there a couple of hours and have a couple of beers before heading back to the cold, dank house. Troy couldn't keep his eyes off a small girl with wavy blond hair as she danced erotically only a few feet away as he sipped on a Coors Light beer. She noticed his interest and moved close enough to bump him with her hip.

"Hi, cowboy." She turned her back to her dance partner.

"Hi, gorgeous," Troy yelled over the loud music.

"You going to dance with me tonight?" She acted like she was a long-lost friend.

"I shore hope so." Troy was conscious of her partner dancing alone. "Maybe in a bit."

"What's your name?"

"Troy."

"I like the sparkle in your eye, Troy. I'm Mary Margaret." She began dancing again but looked back over her shoulder. "We're sitting over there," she pointed to an empty table. "Come and have a drink with us."

When Mary finished dancing, she sat down next to a girl dressed in baggy gym clothes. The girl had on no makeup and her hair was in a loose ponytail. Troy watched as the girl stood to allow Mary access to a seat next to her. The baggy pants she wore made her rear end protrude from her backside. Troy thought for a moment she looked like a donkey.

Troy waited a few songs before sliding his way through the crowd, holding on to his bottle of beer. He was feeling very confident as he made his way toward Mary.

"What's happening, Mary?" Troy leaned over the table preparing to ask the pretty girl to dance.

"Hey, dude," Mary's eyes were glazed and it was obvious she remembered him but not his name. She smiled when the guy she had been dancing with grabbed her hand and pulled her toward the dance floor.

"Have a seat." The girl in the baggy workout clothes pointed toward the empty chair Mary had just vacated. "I'm Rosie."

"I'm Troy."

"I know." She leaned close and put her mouth close to Troy's ear. "I just arrived and was standing at the bar when you told Mary your name."

"I'm sorry, I didn't notice you."

"That's all right. Mary twisted my arm and talked me into coming here tonight. I was working out at the recreation center and she insisted I come here without changing." She continued to talk with her mouth only inches from Troy's ear and her hand touching his muscular bicep. "So here I am, embarrassed to get up."

Troy noticed that for a girl who had just worked out she smelled very good. There was something sensual about every movement she made. He made small talk with her and eventually ended up with her gently rubbing the rock-hard muscles of his upper back. He shifted his position so he could stare into her pretty eyes before leaning forward and kissing her on her naturally full lips. They continued to kiss for a couple of minutes, mindless of their surroundings.

Rosie broke the embrace and looked directly into Troy's eyes before saying, "I'm going to go home and change clothes."

"You don't need to change." Troy felt as if a jolt of electricity was flowing through his body.

"I live real close." Rosie broke her grip on him and downed the last of her rum and coke before giving him a quick kiss on the lips. "Don't leave."

"Wouldn't dream of it." Troy could see Mary on the dance floor right in front of him, but it was Rosie's lustful gaze as she moved from the club that enticed him to stay.

Troy sat alone for the next thirty minutes, drinking excessively. Every now and then he would stand up and dance alone to the music. He was debating with himself if he should go to the dance floor and cut in on the guy dancing with Mary. The more alcohol he consumed, the more boisterous he became. He would sit down and then suddenly stand up and do a double step, holler, and spin around before sitting down again. Every time the waitress came near he would dance in front of her. Finally, she became so exasperated with his harassment that she walked over to the security men watching the door and complained.

"To hell with y'all," Troy said under his breath as he gave the security men a spiteful look before sitting back down.

"Did Rosie leave?" asked Mary, reaching across the table to grab her margarita.

"She'll be back shortly." Troy stood up in a gentlemanly gesture, cradling his bottle of beer. "She went home to change clothes."

"We're going to have fun tonight." Mary bumped her hip into Troy's hip before quickly putting her drink on the table and moving back to the dance floor.

Troy watched Mary dance until his eyes spotted the black stockings and white fishnet blouse worn by Rosie as she walked seductively toward him.

"I'm back," Rosie understated as she stood before Troy. She had the flattest stomach and fullest breasts he had ever seen, all situated at eye level in front of him. Her blond hair was pulled to one side and her lips were bright pink with a gloss finish. She was gorgeous.

"Sit down." Troy stood up to allow her to move back to her original chair. "I'll order you a drink."

Rosie was obviously infatuated with Troy, and he was grateful that such a beautiful lady was paying so much attention to him. They were two people coming together by way of fate with very different backgrounds and needs, only comparable in their dread of the mundane.

Troy's brain began to gyrate in his head as he sat next to Rosie.

"You are the most gorgeous, beautiful woman I have ever seen. I can't believe how lucky I am tonight," Troy yelled over the loud music. "You are the reason poetry was invented. If I could paint I would make a fortune painting your portrait."

"Do you always talk this much?" Rosie placed her hand over his mouth.

"Only when I have something to say." He climbed up on top of the table and hollered as loud as he could, "Everybody. I want to make a toast."

"Troy." Rosie held her hand over her mouth as she watched several people stop and take notice of Troy.

"A toast." Troy pulled a handful of twenty-dollar bills from his pocket and held them over his head. "Tonight I have found a piece of heaven."

"Please, Troy." Rosie was turning a bright shade of red.

Troy motioned to the cocktail waitress he had annoyed earlier. She hesitantly moved toward him with a sneer on her face. He tossed several hundred dollars on her tray. Holding his arms wide, he yelled, "I want to buy everyone a drink. I want to make a toast."

The waitress looked at him with disbelief.

"I ain't been to all corners of this great round planet we live on, but I would bet a million dollars to a pickle there ain't a prettier girl in the world than the girl I'm with tonight."

"This is so embarrassing." Rosie looked at the crowd who were laughing and holding their drinks up. She began to laugh.

"My toast … If I had a choice, I would rather have one hour being in your company than live one hundred years without knowing you. I toast your beauty." He chugged his beer, threw the bottle in the air and watched it break on the dance floor. He looked down at Rosie.

Rosie looked at him somewhat bewildered, unsure if the toast made sense, but she understood the intent was thoughtful.

Out of the corner of her eye she could see the large bouncers approaching the table.

"Troy, get off the table," she warned. "They are going to throw you out of here."

"Gentlemen," Troy nodded to the large men.

The smaller of the two, an African American man weighing about three hundred fifty pounds, grabbed Troy by the seat of his pants and pulled him off the table. The larger bouncer, a graying white man standing six feet eight and weighing in excess of four hundred pounds, caught Troy by the legs and began carrying him toward the door.

"Don't come back," said the smaller man, pushing Troy out the door into the cold night.

"Y'all have a fine night." Troy turned toward the men and straightened the collar to his shirt. He took a step toward the giants as Rosie pushed her way around them.

"Troy, are you all right?"

"I reckon they don't have a sense of humor." Troy was feeling very tired but smiled as the beautiful girl put her arms around him.

"That was nice what you said about me." She placed her arms around his neck and kissed him on the lips.

The taste of her lipstick and smell of her perfume were intoxicating. Her warm breath being cooled by the freezing air ricocheted off the side of his face as she relinquished the kiss and looked at him through her seductive eyes. He moved his hands along her back and pulled her breasts into his chest.

"Let's go," said Rosie, noticing the gawking security guards standing in the door of the nightclub, obviously enjoying the show. "Where are you parked?"

"I didn't drive." Troy remembered the reality of his situation, "I came in a taxi."

"I can give you a ride." Rosie noticed him hesitate, "Come on. I won't bite you."

Troy followed her to a bright red Mustang. He waited as she unlocked the doors, wondering if he should tell her the truth about his situation. Possibly he could just go with her and never again set foot in the frigid house. Deep down he knew what waited for him in only a few hours was not going to be good.

"Rosie," Troy moved into the passenger seat of the car. "I can't stay with you tonight. I have an important appointment tomorrow."

"It must be important." Her smile was dazzling.

"Believe me, it is. But I want to see you when it's over."

"When what's over?"

"I can't tell ya." He couldn't believe his luck. He finally met the girl of his dreams and he was most likely losing her forever. "At least not tonight."

"Okay, I'll give you a ride home." She started the car, "Where do you live?"

"Texas." He was too tired to elaborate. "I'm stayin' at a place in North Aurora. I'd appreciate it if you could take me to Colorado Boulevard and Colfax, and I can take a cab."

"I hardly drank anything." She held her foot on the brake. "I'll give you a ride."

"That's all right." He didn't want her involved.

"Okay. I'll take you to a Holiday Inn and we can call a cab. You can wait in my car until it comes." Rosie spun out of the parking lot.

The taste of lipstick lingered in Troy's mouth as he leaned back in the car seat. He blatantly stared at the stunning body of the girl he had met only hours before. His eyes moved to her beautiful face that was framed by her slightly disheveled hair. He was totally captivated by her as she pulled into the parking lot of a Holiday Inn.

She handed him her cell phone. "Just dial all sevens."

"Let's talk for a while." He sat the phone above the dashboard.

"Do you want to go to my place?"

"No." He was extremely tired and his words were becoming indistinct, but he wanted to spend as much time with her as possible. "Let's talk a little before I call."

She turned off the engine and turned to face him. He turned toward her and they kissed.

"Rosie," said Troy, placing his hand on her thigh.

"Don't talk." She kissed him on the side of his neck. She needed to not be alone just as much as he did. Both their hearts were beating furiously as she reached down and unbuckled his belt. He raised up and pulled down his jeans as she completely removed her skirt. He fell deep into the seat as she straddled him, pushing her knees into the cushions on each side of his powerful legs. He reached inside her blouse and under her bra as she snapped the buttons to his shirt. They stared passionately into each other's eyes as they made love in the front seat of the compact car.

***

"Troy. Wake up." Rosie leaned inside the passenger door and pulled on Troy's arm. "The taxi is here."

"All right." His jeans were wrapped around his ankles. "I can't move."

"Come on. I can help you." She reached into the car and put her hands around his head and pulled him to her abdomen. "Come on now, you have to help."

He kissed her on the belly button.

"Troy." She pulled hard and he fell head-first onto the cold pavement.

"I couldn't help it. You are so beautiful." He lay flat on the cold ground with his pants still around his ankles.

The taxi driver stepped from the cab and helped Rosie lift him to his feet and pull up his pants.

"Let's get him in the back of my cab," said the driver as if it were an everyday occurrence to pick up a fare with his pants around his ankles.

"Troy." Rosie leaned into the backseat of the taxi. "I paid the driver, and I'm going to place a card with my telephone number in your wallet." She showed him a card and placed it in his wallet, then put the wallet in the front pocket of his jeans.

"Thank you," he whimpered.

"You make sure to call me, all right? I mean it, Troy, I expect you to call me."

"I will," his words were barely audible.

Rosie watched the cab drive away. No matter how bizarre her experience with Troy had been over the past couple of hours, she felt in the pit of her stomach that all was right with the world. At least at that moment it was.

Maliki and Tanya

"So, you were conceived in the front seat of a red mustang." Tanya folded her arms over her chest and smiled at Maliki. "Interesting that your mother would be so blatantly honest."

Maliki gave her a confused look. "Wasn't Mom. The last part came from Troy."

"I never really thought about it, but I guess it really isn't that important to know where your conception took place."

Maliki stared at Tanya, noticing that her face was somewhat flushed. He was surprised at how comfortable he felt in discussing the intimacy that occurred between his mother and father, yet Tanya seemed somewhat embarrassed. For a slight moment, he thought that maybe the rosy color of her face wasn't from embarrassment. He quickly changed the subject.

"Troy's life would have been much different had the bouncers called the police and had him hauled off to jail rather than toss him out of the club."

"That's how life works. Unknowingly, little occurrences in people's lives often have large consequences."

"Nonetheless Troy found himself back at the cold house."

"How about we stop for the night? I do want to call your grandmother."

"Sounds good. We can pick it up from here tomorrow." Maliki watched Tanya make her way to her bedroom. He wondered what sort of relationship he might have with the beautiful woman in the future. Halfway through their time together, he was still extremely mystified with her.

Chapter Five

Denver, Colorado

Rex Parker parked the white van two blocks from the Federal Bank on the side of Seventeenth Avenue. He looked as though he were any tourist enjoying downtown Denver. He was sporting dark designer sunglasses, a thin mustache, and a neatly trimmed beard as he stepped out of the van and opened the utility door. He handed his associate, Jimmy Marsh, a large canvas bag filled with more bags. Jimmy adjusted his fake beard and pulled his Bronco's cap over his eyes as he followed Rex two blocks to the side entrance of the bank. They had rehearsed the plan over the past year to the point they were very relaxed as they entered the bank. Everything was situated as they had anticipated. The only real important issue was that all three guards were accounted for; they didn't want to get shot in the back.

Rex began his criminal career with a bang, unlike other wayward young men who had found mischief stealing pop bottles and progressively worked their way up the ladder of social misfits; he was an honor student who had never been arrested. On his eighteenth birthday, he and one of his buddies walked into a bank in Baltimore, Maryland, and robbed it. He found the feeling of exhilaration from taking the money to be addictive, so he robbed three more banks that week. He spent the money traveling back and forth to Florida, living a life of luxury, but he was a rookie and was soon identified by the authorities. The police began to put pressure on his ailing mother, and Rex, being somewhat of a mama's boy, turned himself in. He received three years at the Federal Correction Institute in Jefferson County, on the southwestern edge of the Denver metro area. He experienced an easy three years where he was neither rehabilitated nor punished. All his incarceration accomplished was to introduce him to the beauty of Colorado and to Jimmy. Having tasted the luxuries money could buy, he became seduced by the pleasures an entry level job could not provide. He made a promise to himself that he would be well prepared before he robbed another bank. Along came Vinny

Barrows, who offered him and Jimmy a well-thought-out plan and a million-dollar payday.

It was déjà vu as the bright lights of the bank corridor brought back the feeling of elation he had experienced as an eighteen-year-old, but it was the smell, unnoticed by all the customers, the smell of cleanliness found where fresh new money was abundant, that really excited him. He sucked in a deep breath and signaled to Jimmy that he was about to approach the guards. Jimmy held the canvas bags over his shoulder as he prepared to begin.

Jimmy's hands were shaking as he moved to the front of the line of people waiting for the next available teller. He was a phony. His reputation was greater than his abilities. He and two of his friends were involved in a fight at a park in the Bronx where a well-known thug was killed. His loudmouth friends told everyone how Jimmy had killed the guy. Everyone was afraid of him, but his time of truth had arrived and he was shivering like a frightened child.

The old guard sitting at the security desk showed his coffee-stained teeth as Rex approached. He knew there was something wrong, but Rex was upon him before he could take action.

"I have enough explosives strapped to my body to blow this entire city block off the face of the earth." Rex pulled the front of his jacket open far enough to show the guard the explosives taped to his body. "I want you to stand up, without pushing any buttons, and walk to the side of your desk, then place your weapon on it."

The old man kept his eyes glued to Rex as he followed orders.

"Now, call the other guards over here." Rex looked in the direction of the two young guards totally unaware of what was happening. "Motion to them to come to your station. Don't call them on the radio."

"Bill," the old guard motioned to the closer of the guards, "tell Hank. I need you both at my desk."

The old guard nodded his head toward Rex as the two guards approached. Rex opened his jacket.

"I want both of you to place your weapons and radios on the desk." They both did as told. "Now call the president of the bank and tell him you need to speak with him immediately."

Rex was becoming nervous as the guard made the call. He knew that with this call the police would now become an issue.

President McDonald walked toward the guard station, running his hand through his grey hair, sensing that something was out of the ordinary.

"Hello, sir." Rex showed him the explosives. "I need you to do exactly as I ask. Do you understand?"

"Yes," replied the visibly startled president.

"We are going to let your customers leave the bank." Rex took Mr. McDonald by the arm. "My partner is going to tell them to exit, and then I want you to lock all the doors. Do you understand?"

"Yes."

Rex motioned to Jimmy.

"The bank is now closed." Jimmy moved in front of the waiting customers. "All customers need to exit now."

President McDonald hesitated. Rex grabbed him by his tie and pulled his face close to his and yelled, "If you want to keep innocent people from coming into this situation, you need to lock the doors. Lock the front door first."

The president put his hand out to the old guard who handed him his keys. He moved to the front door and locked it.

"I want all customers to this door." Rex pointed to the back door.

"Everyone, please exit here." President McDonald had regained his composure and was guiding the customers toward the back entrance.

"If you do everything I tell you to do, when I tell you to do it, not one of your employees will be harmed." Rex led the president back toward the tellers. "All of you will live to be very old and have a great story to tell your grandchildren. If you cross me, I will blow this building to kingdom come. Do you understand me?"

"Yes," answered the president, "completely."

Jimmy began pulling several small bags from the large bag he had been carrying and laid them at the feet of the president.

Rex kicked the bags and said, "I want you to take these bags and place ten million dollars in them. If there are any explosive devices in the bag with the money or if I find the money to be traceable, we will shoot you. Understand?"

"Yes."

"This is one time in your life where you don't want to be a hero. Just do as I say and leave the rest to the law."

The police began to gather outside the front door as President McDonald carried the bags toward the safe, with Jimmy following close behind.

Rex turned to the old guard and said, "Use your cell phone and call the police. Tell them to stay away from the bank. Make it crystal clear to them that explosives are involved. Do not tell them anything else except about the explosives."

The guard did as he was told. "This is Broderick from the guard station inside the Community Bank. I need to talk with the commander in charge of the police force outside the bank." He hung up the phone.

"What the fuck." Rex gave him a malicious look.

"The commander of the police is going to call," said the old guard as the phone rang.

"This is Captain Thomas. Who am I speaking with?" The voice coming from the phone was very loud.

"This is Broderick, the head guard on duty inside the bank." Broderick watched Rex step closer. "I am to tell you the men robbing the bank are covered with explosives. You are to keep a safe distance from the bank."

"How many robbers are in the bank?" Captain Thomas asked.

Broderick hung up the phone.

Rex waited patiently as President McDonald, carrying several duffle bags, followed by Jimmy, also carrying bags, came out of the vault. They placed the bags at his feet.

"Okay. Open the bags and dump the money on the floor," said Rex. "Don't worry, we have all day."

The president again ran his right hand through his grey hair, realizing how fortunate he was to have heeded the advice of the crook. He had thought about placing an explosive pack of money in the duffle bag but at the last moment left it behind.

He emptied the money on the floor. Rex meticulously inspected each packet of money.

"Pack them up." Rex pointed to the two younger guards. "Which one of you wants to find a little excitement and maybe get some paid time off from this lousy job of yours?"

Both guards worked at packing the money into the duffle bags, eyes down, saying nothing.

"All right! I'll make the choice. You." Rex pointed to the guard with black hair and a mustache. "What's your name?"

"Travis."

"Okay Travis, you are going to make the little trip along with Mr. McDonald. Don't worry; if you do as I say, you will not be harmed. "

Both the young guard and President McDonald were visibly shaken.

"Old-timer," Rex looked at Broderick, "get me the police back on your phone."

"This is Captain Thomas." The loud voice could be heard over the phone.

"The man inside wants me to relay a message to you."

"First tell him Chief Randal is in charge, and he is in direct contact with the mayor."

Broderick looked at Rex. "Police Chief Randal is now in charge. Along with the mayor."

Rex couldn't believe how well the plan was working; just like clockwork, the city officials were lining up. "Tell them in one hour I want a Lear jet, completely fueled, waiting for me at the Front Range Airport on the other side of Denver International Airport. Tell them I have enough explosives to blow the building apart."

Broderick relayed the message.

"Mr. McDonald, you are leading the way, then me, followed by Travis, and my associate brings up the rear. We will each carry two bags, and you two will carry three. I am going to tie a rope through all our belt buckles to make sure neither of you decide to bolt. Broderick, I want you to call the police chief and tell him if they shoot either one of us the explosives will detonate." Rex looked at the old guard. "Call now. Tell them all we want to do is get to the airport. We will not negotiate until we are at the Front Range Airport."

Broderick made the call as Jimmy slipped the thin rope through the belt loop of each man's trousers.

"Unlock the door." Rex picked up two bags and moved next to Broderick and held out his hand. "Give me your cell phone."

The cold air greeted the four men as they made their way outside the bank onto the quiet sidewalk. Although the police were visible at every corner of every building, they walked unchallenged the two blocks to the parked van. They placed the money into the back of the van. Jimmy pulled the rope through the belt loops and pushed Travis into the backseat. Rex opened the front passenger door and motioned Mr. McDonald inside, where he fastened the seat belt around him before moving to the driver's seat. Both hostages cooperated as instructed.

With some difficulty, Rex pushed the redial button on Broderick's phone with his heavily gloved index finger. "Chief Randal," he spoke into the phone.

"Yes," the chief of police hesitated.

"I just want to make sure you know that all we want to do right now is get to the Front Range Airport. I will then release a hostage." Rex spoke quickly as he looked down the empty street. Two police cruisers came into view and slowly maneuvered to block the street. "I don't want to see a helicopter over us, and I don't want to be stopped for any reason. No negotiating about any of this."

There was silence on the other end, so Rex closed the phone.

Front Range Airport is situated about five miles east of Denver International Airport, isolated on the prairie of the eastern Colorado high plains. The highway to the airport spans an area where there are no buildings and very few people. The isolation of the airport was the main reason for picking Denver for the heist. The police would never jeopardize the welfare of thousands of people in the city when they could negotiate the situation on a vacant country road.

"Looks like they want to keep us from leaving." Jimmy looked out the front window of the van from the backseat.

"They'll move." Rex drove the van toward the two police cars blocking the street. He slowed to a crawl as he came within twenty feet of the cruisers and then inched forward. The cruisers relinquished and moved back, allowing him to proceed. He turned onto Seventeenth Street and drove the speed limit. He handed the cell phone to Mr. McDonald.

"Hit redial." Mr. McDonald did as told. "Don't say anything when they answer and hold the phone toward me."

The bank president silently cooperated, waiting for instructions as Chief Randal answered the phone. Rex released his foot from the accelerator and then pressed down again, making the van come to a complete stop before jerking forward. He continued this jerking motion with the van two more times before yelling loudly into the phone, "This van isn't going to make it to the airport."

Rex could hear the chief of police speaking on the other phone.

"I want to know if there is an airplane waiting for us at the airport?" Rex yelled into the phone.

"Who am I speaking with?" asked the police chief.

"None of your fucking business," Rex yelled even louder into the phone.

"Okay," said Chief Randal, annoyingly. "Everything has been arranged for at the airport, but I want one of the hostages released immediately."

"That's not going to happen until we are at the airport, and I see the plane." Rex continued to make the van jerk. "I am having mechanical problems with this van and need you to get me another vehicle."

Chief Randal and Captain Thomas were following in a convoy of police cars no more than a half block behind and were aware of the van's problem.

"I don't want any police officers within a quarter mile of this van." Rex spoke with authority into the phone as he pulled onto Pleasant Avenue. "I want another vehicle to replace this one within fifteen minutes. Capisce?"

Aurora, Colorado

"Just sit tight," said Larry. "Whatever is gonna happen is gonna happen."

"Something doesn't feel right. Let's get the hell out of here," Troy muttered, speaking as if he was in a trance. "I think this place is gonna collapse."

"Come on, Troy, don't lose it now, we're almost finished here." Larry was pacing back and forth from the kitchen table to the living room window which was covered with plywood. The house was cold and damp with dirt in every room, but it was the basement that the boys now found unbearable to spend even one more minute wallowing on the giant mounds of dirt.

The boys could hear the ubiquitous sound of sirens in the distance before they heard the garage door open. Then Larry's cell phone rang.

"Hello." Larry was sure it would be either Vinny or Tony.

Billy and Troy could tell by the surprised look on Larry's face that the caller was not Vinny.

"It's yore brother." Larry handed the phone to Troy and looked toward the door connecting the kitchen to the garage. "We have to hurry."

"Tom." Troy's voice was barely audible.

"Troy, where are you?" Tom yelled into the phone.

"At a house in Colorado."

"Who's with ya?" Tom could tell from Troy's voice that he was on a downward spiral. He had witnessed it several times before, but never at a time when his brother was at such great risk.

"Billy and Larry." Troy's voice was even more faint. "We been digging."

"Troy, put Larry back on the phone."

Troy handed the phone to Larry.

"Larry, listen to me carefully," Tom yelled into the phone. "Y'all's lives are in danger. Whatever you are doing, the people you are involved with plan to kill ya when you're finished."

"How do you know?" Larry wondered if Tom might be as psychotic as Troy.

"Sam Blake's connections. We got this cell phone number from a biker named Bodine." Tom was talking loud and quickly but would have been more frantic had he known the actual situation with Rex already in the garage of the house. "If y'all were at a party outside Amarillo with a biker called Pig Pen, then ya better skedaddle. They done killed Pig Pen."

"Come on, Larry, hang up the phone. They're in the garage," screamed Billy, opening the door from the kitchen to the cold garage.

"Tom, I can't talk anymore. They're here." Larry closed his phone.

"Wait, Larry. Who's there?" Tom screamed into the phone.

Larry pushed the button to silence his phone and placed it into the front pocket of his jeans just as Rex stepped into the kitchen, followed by Jimmy pushing two blindfolded and frightened men.

"Each of you grab two bags and go out the tunnel," ordered Rex. "Hurry."

Troy was queasy and light-headed as Larry handed him two large duffel bags. He felt as though his mind was floating outside his body.

"Come on, Troy, we are right behind you," screamed Larry.

Rex led the two hostages into the back bedroom while Jimmy watched the three young men carry the heavy bags down the basement stairs.

"I ain't going back in that tunnel," Troy mumbled.

"Listen, Troy, if you don't go now they are gonna put a bullet in each of our heads." The frantic tone of Larry's voice didn't affect Troy. "Pick the bags up and go."

Larry moved in front of Troy and pushed his two bags into the dark tunnel and crawled in behind them. Troy waited in front of Billy and stared at Larry in a catatonic state. Larry reached out and grabbed Troy by the collar of his shirt and jerked him into the cave, pulling his shirt halfway up his back.

"Move it, Troy." Billy struggled to maneuver Troy's two bags along with the two bags he was in charge of into the tunnel. "These damn bags are heavy."

"This is a matter of life and death," said Larry angrily. "Now follow me."

Larry hurriedly pushed the two bags in front of him and continued pulling Troy by the collar as they made their way down the tunnel. Billy grappled with the four remaining bags, following closely behind.

"Good Lord,' said Larry. They were making good time but he was becoming fatigued and he was about to tell Billy to leave the bags when he came to the crook in the tunnel where the ceiling had collapsed. He noticed a small flicker of light from behind the wood barrier covering the opening. He reached up, and using all the strength he could muster, moved the plywood barrier slightly to the side. He crawled up a little higher to get a better angle and pushed with all his might. He moved the plywood far enough to create a two-foot opening, large enough for them to escape. He poked his head out the opening and looked into the yard. Sirens blared in the distance, but everything else was painstakingly calm.

"What are ya doin?" Billy looked around Troy and yelled as Larry pulled himself out of the tunnel.

"Tom was on the phone. He said Sam Blake got wind that these fellas are gonna kill us. I believe him." Larry spoke as quietly as he could. "Hand me the bags."

"They're definitely gonna kill us if we take these."

"These bags may be the only thing to keep us alive." He moved the plywood another foot to make the opening large enough for the bags.

Billy pressed against the hard clay of the tunnel and squeezed around Troy. Although not completely certain he was doing the correct thing, he handed the six bags through the opening to Larry.

"Hurry up," said Larry anxiously, looking toward the house they had just left across the neighbor's empty backyard.

Billy looked nervously back down the tunnel to see any sign of Rex or Jimmy.

Larry took two of the bags and moved toward the corner of the neighbor's home. The commotion from the other side of the block was becoming louder, and he could hear a helicopter hovering from the south. He quickly moved to the back of the house. The patio door was still unlocked. Without bothering to check to see if anyone was home, he slid the door open and placed the two bags on a tile floor. He crouched down and made his way to the north side of the house where Billy was pulling Troy from the hole.

"Take Troy inside the house," Larry spoke softly. "I'm gonna cover this hole."

Billy all but carried Troy to the still open patio doors and disposed of him on the floor inside. To his relief, by the time he returned, Larry had pulled the plywood back over the hole and was covering it with dirt.

"I'm glad we took the time to make this wood fit." whispered Larry to Billy, who immediately began helping him push dirt on the wood. "Make sure we cover it completely."

"Go ahead and get the bags in the house," Billy said. "I'll finish covering this."

"Be quick. They could be coming down the tunnel at any time." Larry picked up two more bags and made his way to the house.

Larry entered the vacant home just in time to see Troy exit through the kitchen into the garage.

"Troy," yelled Larry, as he followed after his sleepwalking friend.

By the time Larry reached the garage door, Troy had already climbed into the backseat of the neighbors' Suburban.

"Troy," Larry yelled.

Troy lay motionless.

Larry opened the front door to the vehicle and checked the ignition, no keys. He looked above the visor, but still no luck. He went back into the kitchen, and there to the side of the refrigerator was a peg board with each key labeled: front door, back door, F-150, Escort, and Suburban. He grabbed the key.

Billy slowly closed the patio doors behind him, laid the remaining two duffle bags down, and held his finger to his lips as he made eye contact with Larry. He moved to the side of the glass doors and pointed out. Two police officers were at the back fence peeking through the pickets into the backyard of the house that had the hostages.

"I have the key to the car in the garage," Larry held up the key.

"Where's Troy?" Billy whispered.

"In the garage."

Billy moved the six bags into the kitchen out of the view of the police officers should they look through the patio door. Larry began placing them into the back of the Suburban.

The doorbell rang.

"Oh crap," said Larry. "That has to be the police."

"We have to answer it," said Billy.

"Wait here. I'll do it." Larry brushed as much dirt off his jeans as he possibly could.

Larry looked out the peephole in the front door, and sure enough it was a uniformed police officer impatiently pushing the doorbell. He opened the door far enough to stick his head out.

"We need you to vacate this house immediately." The officer spoke as soon as the door opened.

"A police emergency. We need everyone out. Now!"

"Okay." Larry shut the front door.

Larry tossed the keys to Billy as he entered the garage. "Let's go."

Billy backed the Suburban into the street. They drove unnoticed out of the neighborhood.

"Good God, Larry. What have we just done?" asked Billy, unable to register the fast pace of the events that had just transpired.

"We can't think about that now. We need to get the hell out of the city as fast as we can. Let's take this to the Cadillac and ditch it somewhere." Larry noticed Troy sitting up in the backseat staring blankly ahead. "Troy, you need to get it together."

"I'm tired," muttered Troy.

"He's gonna fall asleep and we'll never be able to wake him," said Billy. "Believe me, I've seen him this way before."

"Let's get to Gramps's cabin."

Denver, Colorado

Tom tried calling Larry's number several times without success as he pranced back and forth in the hotel room at the Brown Palace. He had not connected all the commotion, happening several stories down and only blocks from where he and Drew waited, with the trouble his brother was facing, until he looked at the television screen.

"Turn it up Drew," said Tom.

The special report on the screen showed the police activity taking place in the eastern suburb of Aurora. Tom listened to the reporter confirm that there were two hostages still being held at the house before picking up his cell phone and dialing Sam.

"Hello," answered Sam.

"Sam, have ya heard about the mess we have going on here?" Tom hurriedly asked.

"No. what's going on?" Sam sounded tired. "We're here at the hospital with Rebecca."

"There's been a robbery right here within a few blocks of this hotel," said Tom. "I talked with Troy about an hour ago, and he told me he was in some house where he had been digging."

"What makes you think it has to do with the robbery?"

"Troy sounded really down, like he hadn't been taking his medication, so he handed the phone to Larry Lover. Larry sounded really scared, and he told me he was waiting for someone and then he hung up on me." Tom's voice quivered.

"Did he say who they were waiting for?"

"He didn't say. I reckon it was the robbers," answered Tom. "I did get a chance to tell Larry that they were likely to be killed if they hung around."

"So they do know the situation is life-threatening," replied Sam.

"I didn't have much time, but I believe they know," countered Tom. "This news is on all the channels. I'm watching it now, and the house is surrounded by the police."

"That might be the best thing for the boys," sighed Sam.

"Might be," Tom hesitated. "I'm thinking Troy and his friends dug them a way out of that house."

"You and Drew stay right where you are at," said Sam. "I'll have Stanley pass on this information to Ed Dodd."

"Sam," Tom's voice softened, "have they operated on Rebecca's knee?"

"Not yet, there's been a delay," answered Sam. "As soon as I know more, I'll let ya know."

Winter Park, Colorado

Large flakes of snow hit the windshield of the brown Cadillac Seville parked along Highway 40 just outside the small mountain town of Winter Park, Colorado. The engine idled quietly. Larry and Billy were sitting inside the warm confines of the automobile wondering how they were going to be able to traverse through the snow drifts covering the logger's road that twisted and turned over the next couple of miles, coming within yards of their grandfather's cabin. Troy slept in the backseat.

"We have to find a snowmobile," Larry finally interjected, putting the car into reverse and backing onto the highway. "It's the only way we can get to the cabin."

"What are we gonna do with the car?" asked Billy.

"We'll figure something out." Larry drove cautiously on the highway back toward Winter Park. The roads were well plowed but still very slippery. He pulled into the parking lot of a gas station and stepped out of the car into the cold mountain air. He pulled the collar of his light jacket tight around his neck to keep the large flakes of snow from hitting his bare chest as he walked across the cement driveway into the convenience store. A grey-haired man in his sixties, dressed in a dark blue shirt sporting the station's logo, was leaning with his elbows on the counter next to the cash machine. He looked up from the magazine he was reading and continued to chew on a toothpick. Larry poured two cups of cappuccino.

"Shore is cold out there," said Larry, placing the coffee onto the counter.

"Yep. This could be a record-setting storm." The man punched the keyboard of the cash register.

"The snowflakes shore are big."

"That usually means a short and sweet snowstorm, but the way the weatherman is talking, we are in for a really bad one." The man looked up at Larry. "That'll be three dollars."

Larry handed him a five-dollar bill and asked, "Do you happen to know where I can rent a snowmobile for a few days?"

The man looked at Larry for a brief moment before putting the money into the cash register. He laid the change on the glass counter.

"There are a couple of places to rent snowmobiles," said the man, looking more anxious now. "But, if you want to buy a good used one, I can help you with that."

"I shore might be interested."

"It's worth at least nine hundred dollars."

"I need it right now."

"Let me call my wife. We just live right down the way." The man moved quickly toward the phone and dialed the numbers. "Mary. I have a guy standing here who's interested in buying the Arctic Cat. Would you go out and fire it up? I'm sending him down right now."

"I don't have a trailer," said the old man.

"There's enough snow that I can just drive it."

"Where you going?"

"To a cabin a couple miles north of here," lied Larry, becoming paranoid.

"I know a guy who has a trailer if you're interested," said the old man.

"That's not necessary." Larry knew the fewer people involved the better.

"All right. Just take a right turn on the street in front of the station, and I'm the third house on the left. You'll see the big metal garage."

Larry could see Billy through the front window of the station, running toward the store.

"Thanks, we'll head that way now." Larry stepped out into the snowstorm, holding the two steaming cups of coffee.

"Man, we need to get going," yelled Billy. "Troy is starting to freak out."

"We gotta get out of here," screamed Troy as Billy and Larry settled into the car.

"I found us a snowmobile. We'll be to the cabin shortly." Larry handed his cup of coffee back to Troy.

"Come on, y'all, let's go to California." Troy pushed the coffee away and laid his head back on the seat.

"I've seen him like this before. He's gonna crash and sleep for days," carped Billy, holding both cups of cappuccino in his hands. "I should have noticed … he hasn't hardly ate a bite the last two days. He needs his medication."

"Let's git to the cabin and then handle this problem," said Larry, driving away from the gas station.

"It ain't got nothin' to do with my sickness," mumbled Troy, barely coherent. "We just need to keep movin'."

"That's what we're fixin' to do," said Larry.

The roofs of the houses they passed were covered with snow. The third house on the left was a blue, two-story, Tudor-style home with a large metal building at the end of the driveway. An old lady bundled in a large overcoat was hunched over at the front of the garage as Larry made his way up the driveway.

"I'll be right back," said Larry, stepping from the car into the blowing snow.

"Come on in," said the old woman through a scarf around her face, holding open the door on the side of the garage. "I'm Mary, Melvin's wife."

Warm air from an overhead heater was sucked outside through the open door as Larry entered. The building looked larger from the inside than it did from the outside. There was an old pickup truck with the engine hanging from a cherry picker parked in the far corner of the shop. The smell of gas fumes was ever apparent from the snowmobile idling by the overhead garage door.

"Thank you, ma'am." Larry shook the snow from his hair. "Nice shop."

"Melvin is a very talented mechanic and business has been good, so we decided to put up this building a couple of years ago." Mary placed her hand on the seat of the running snowmobile. "The engine started right up."

"Man, this thing is huge." Larry sat in the large seat.

"I think it's the biggest of its kind."

"Why do you only want nine hundred dollars?"

"We're getting too old to get out and drive it anymore. The grandkids never seem to make it up here during the winter." Mary bit her upper lip and then proceeded to explain. "Melvin wants more room for the shop."

"My grandfather showed me how to drive his snowmobile, but it's been a while. I may need some help in how to operate this thing." Larry had driven a combine from the time he was ten years old, and he knew if left alone he would eventually figure out how to drive the snowmobile.

Mary quickly showed him the basics of operating the perfectly tuned machine.

"I definitely want to buy it," shouted Larry as he revved up the engine. "I was wondering, ma'am, if yore husband would be willing to work on my car while we are up in the hills?"

"You better ask him yourself." Mary gave him a curious look as she handed him a brown manila envelope. "Here's the title."

"Thank you." Larry turned off the engine and stepped away from the snowmobile.

"Have you been listening to the news about the robbery in Denver?"

"No." He was taken off guard by the fact that the news had already reached the small community. "We've been listening to music."

"Well, some guys robbed a bank in Denver and took the bank president and one of the guards hostage. The police just went inside the house they were holding out and lo and behold the robbers had already escaped." Mary was excited to have someone to share the tale with.

"We'll have to turn on the news." Larry quickly opened the side door, allowing the cold wind to fill the room. "Hopefully yore husband will agree to work on the car, and I will come back and exchange it for the snowmobile."

"I'll wait for Melvin to call."

"Thank you, ma'am." Larry hurried through the blowing snow toward the car.

"You might reconsider going out tonight," Mary yelled toward Larry as she pulled her coat tight around her neck. "I think it's going to get worse."

Dallas, Texas

Rebecca repositioned herself as she tried to find a comfortable spot on the hard gurney. The nurse had already moved the bed to a better angle to read and brought her an extra pillow. She had been waiting for over an hour and there was still no intravenous needle in her arm.

"Rebecca," the nurse peeked through the curtain surrounding her, "Doctor Meersman is here."

"How are you holding up?" The doctor moved closely to the side of the bed.

"Okay," she turned toward him, "I want to get this over with."

"It's going to be a little longer." He took hold of Rebecca's hand and looked at her through his large protruding eyes. "I want to consult one more time with Doctor Larson."

"How much more time?" asked Rebecca.

"I'm going to meet with Doctor Larson right now." He opened the curtain and signaled to the nurse. "We are going to move you to a more comfortable bed."

"Doctor Meersman, how much longer?" Rebecca's voice was loud.

"I'll be back within the hour." He moved toward the exit. "Your mother will be here shortly."

Rebecca waited for her mother in a small room with a door, unsure if the delayed operation was good news or bad news. There was no pain in her knee. She had told herself countless times that running was creating discipline that would help her focus when dealing with adversity. Now, facing uncertainty and the idea of never running competitively, she was frightened. This was a real-life predicament with the severity of the problem already having been decided within the confines of her leg. Being alone for this short time allowed her to wonder whether she should hope for the best, or prepare for the worst, or if it mattered at all.

Winter Park, Colorado

Larry turned off the radio as he parked outside the filling station. He placed his head on the steering wheel. After thinking for a moment, he turned the car off and handed the keys to Billy. "Get the money out of the trunk," his voice was energized, "and find all the clothes we have left."

"We're lucky we left some clothes in the car. Most of our clothes are still at that house. most likely with the police now." Billy opened the car door and moved to the trunk.

Troy was sound asleep in the backseat, cuddled in a fetal position.

"Maybe you have the right idea," said Larry, staring at Troy. "I wish I could sleep through all this."

Billy opened the front door of the car and placed a bag on the seat next to Larry. "We still have four suitcases back there and quite a few sweaters."

Larry pulled the drawstring and opened the bag of money.

"Look at this." Billy picked up a handful of one-hundred-dollar bills.

"It seems like there should be bands around these bills," stated Larry.

"Only a few of them have the bank wrappings still on them and the rest are loose," replied Billy.

"Good Lord. I'll bet there is over a million dollars in this bag alone." Larry reached in and took ten bills and placed them in his billfold.

"I'll put my clothes on first, and then it's going to get interesting trying to dress Troy," Billy Ray said.

"I bet we can put all six bags of money in our three suitcases." Larry opened the car door. "I'll go buy the snowmobile and be right back."

Melvin looked up from the small television set on the counter and watched Larry approaching. He wondered what had been so important to have the young man sit in the cold for so long before coming in to make the paper exchange. He was a curious man by nature. The snow was covering the license plate to their car, but he deduced from Larry's accent that he was from Texas. There were many people from Texas who had snow cabins and came into his station. He was pretty sure Larry was going to offer him less than the nine hundred dollars he was asking. He mentally prepared to accept eight hundred fifty dollars. Being so late at night, he figured he could accept a check. He doubted they would have nine hundred in cash.

"It looks like the snow is lightening up," said Larry as he approached Melvin. "You shore were right about the large flakes."

Larry handed him the large brown envelope.

"I need to sign a couple of papers." Melvin opened the envelope and pulled out the paper.

"I'm going to grab a few supplies to take up to the cabin." Larry surveyed the various items on the shelves. "We don't have anything to eat up there."

"How do you want to pay for the snowmobile?" Melvin looked cross-eyed at Larry.

"Cold hard cash."

"That is something I do accept." A smile came across the old man's face. He had turned on the news because Mary had told him about the robbery in Denver. The idea that Larry had anything to do with it was far from his mind. Even if he did suspect the young man, he wouldn't have given a damn. He kept his nose to the grindstone and meticulously filled out the paperwork.

"Mary told me you were a pretty damn good mechanic." Larry laid several food items out in front of Melvin.

"I suppose I am."

"Would ya mind tuning up my Seville while we're at our cabin?" Larry felt comfortable asking the old man. "I'll pay ya whatever ya ask."

"Well, I'm pretty busy this week." Melvin meticulously signed the title and slowly made out a bill of sale.

"We're gonna be at the cabin for at least five days." Larry was surprised at Melvin's hesitancy in taking the job. "No hurry at all."

"I guess that will work." Melvin handed Larry the papers. "I'll call Mary and have her open the garage door. Just drive it up by the snowmobile."

"Thank you, sir."

"Just give me an extra twenty for the food."

Larry counted out ten one-hundred-dollar bills. He didn't have a twenty. "I'll give you eighty extra as a down payment on the tune-up."

"That'll work." Melvin picked up the hundred-dollar bills, still less than skeptical. In fact, he figured Larry to be a rich Texan here only to enjoy beautiful Colorado. "You be careful driving in these mountains at night. Things have a tendency of sneaking up on you."

"Will do," Larry nodded.

"Don't let Mary talk your leg off about that robbery in Denver."

"Yeah, she was telling us about the robbers being gone from the house."

"Oh no, that's old. They just found them."

"They did?"

"Both shot dead. In a park a couple blocks away from the house." Melvin's voice was more excited than distressed.

Larry's heart felt like it came to his throat.

Melvin didn't notice the distress on Larry's face as he watched him leave the station.

Larry ran across the slick driveway to the car. He brushed the snow from his hair as he opened the front door. He could hear the radio.

"Good Lord, Larry," Billy yelled as Larry entered the front seat. "I just heard on the radio that Vinny killed them two fellas."

"The old man just told me." Larry let out a deep breath, "Let's get out of here."

"I'll be glad to get up to Gramps's cabin." Billy looked out the car window at the heavy snow. "We best take Troy to the cabin first. We're gonna have to take the car with us after we pick up the snowmobile. I put all of Troy's clothes on him, and I fit all the money into our suitcases. I reckon it was a blessing we left most of our clothes back at that house."

"I reckon," said Larry.

The large overhead door was open. Mary was waiting just inside the door with the Arctic Cat idling quietly next to her.

"I was about to pull it out of the garage," she said to Larry as he stepped out of the car.

"Thank you, ma'am," said Larry. "We need to use the car to pick up some supplies and will bring it back in about an hour. If that's all right."

"I was going to run down to the market," Mary looked at him suspiciously.

"I can leave the car over yonder." Larry pointed to an area of the driveway partially covered by the overhang of the garage. "I can leave the keys in it."

"That will be fine." She pulled her scarf tight around her neck, making it evident she didn't want to stand out in the cold any longer. Larry was glad she didn't mention the robbery.

Larry settled into the seat of the large snowmobile. He gunned the engine and accelerated onto the snow-covered street. Billy followed close behind, slowly steering the Cadillac down the slippery highway to the logger's road leading to their grandfather's cabin.

Larry drove the snowmobile about twenty feet up the logger's road and stepped into knee-deep snow as he made his way back to the well-plowed highway where Billy waited with the window down.

"Damn, it's cold out," said Larry. "I'll take Troy and one suitcase. There ain't no place to park the car here, so you're gonna have to drive around until I get back."

"Yore gonna have to tie him to you," said Billy, looking both ways down the highway before getting out of the car and opening the back door.

"Take his belt off and loop it through mine," said Larry.

The wet snow was sticking to the tops of the boys' heads as Billy helped Troy onto the back of the snowmobile.

"Come on, Troy. You have to hold on." Billy held his semiconscious friend by his massive shoulders and shook him hard.

"Y'all need to let me sleep," mumbled Troy as his eyes rolled back in their sockets.

"Troy," Larry yelled loudly. "You have to hold on or you're gonna fall off."

"I can take the small bag with me this trip." Larry motioned to Billy to hand him the smallest suitcase.

"Are ya sure ya want to take a bag? Keepin' Troy on the back of that machine is gonna be a job in itself." Billy held the suitcase at his side.

"I reckon you're right. We need to make three trips anyway." Larry revved the snowmobile engine and sped down the snow-covered road.

The ride to the cabin, under most any other circumstance, would have been fun. Larry handled the snowmobile easily over the treacherous road as Troy held onto the back of his shirt, balancing on the backseat until they pulled up the driveway to the cabin.

"Come on, Troy, you have to stay awake a little longer," said Larry, pulling away from Troy's grasp and sliding off the snowmobile.

Larry walked bowlegged to the front porch where he reached under a flat piece of moss rock, partially covered with snow, and retrieved the key to the cabin's front door. He stepped into the front room and onto the red sandstone floor. It was as cold inside as it was on the outside. He was happy to see several logs on the hearth of the large moss rock fireplace. He went back outside and placed his arm around Troy's waist and towed him inside where he placed him on the couch situated in front of the fireplace.

"There ya go." Larry lifted his friend's legs up onto the couch. His hands were numb from the cold as he removed his gloves. He pulled the screen to both sides of the firebox and reached up and pulled the metal damper down. He threw several pieces of kindling onto the large metal grate. His grandfather had always allowed him to start the fire when he came to the cabin as a child. He felt a great calmness overtake his body as he reached up and took a box of matches off the top of the mantle. He lit the kindling. It took only seconds for the flames to become high enough to place a log on the fire.

"That feels so good," Larry said to himself as he looked at his friend sleeping soundly. "Damn, Troy, you are a mess."

The glow from the fire filled the room as Larry removed Troy's wet coat. He then took a quilt from off the bed in the back bedroom and covered his friend. He knelt in front of the fire and held his hands to the warmth, wishing he could lie down and rest. Time was of the essence, so he placed three large logs on the fire and pulled the screen shut. He grit his teeth as he put his gloves over his dry hands and made his way back into the dark, snowy night.

Dallas, Texas

The television set in the waiting room at the hospital was set on a local channel, which had not picked up on the robbery in Denver. Sam was somewhat relieved that the news of the situation transpiring in Denver was not being reported locally in Texas. Sam had not discussed his earlier telephone conversation with Tom.

The operation had been scheduled for nine o'clock, almost two hours earlier. The entire town of Medicine Bow had turned Rebecca's operation into an opportunity to spend time together in Dallas. Last night when Sam, Sara, and Rebecca arrived at the hospital, many of the townsfolk of Medicine Bow, along with several members of Rebecca's track team from Grant High School, greeted them. Rebecca was thrilled to tears from the outpouring of support and love. Most of the people from Medicine Bow spent the night at a hotel in Dallas, allowing them to show up at the hospital early that morning.

Sara made sure she thanked each of her friends for being by her side. She was trying to be strong, but by the time she left Rebecca in the hands of the doctors, she was exhausted. The bright walls of the hospital seemed to heighten her mental fatigue. The entire setting contrasted with the wide open and natural beauty of the country. Rebecca had worked so hard and held such a good attitude that it broke her mother's heart to see her subjected to such uncertainty at this early age. Realization that a team of doctors were preparing to cut into her beautiful daughter's leg was becoming unbearable.

"I'm worried about Rebecca," sobbed Delphia, clutching Sara's arm.

"They will take care of her," said Sara, hugging the frightened little girl. "The doctors are going to help Rebecca."

"They are going to ruin her leg," shouted Delphia.

"Come here, child." Lola grabbed Delphia around her midsection and pulled her onto her lap. "You have to sit here and be civil or I will take you back to the hotel room. Sara has enough on her mind that she doesn't need to listen to your worries."

"Oh God," Sara lowered her head into her hands.

"Sara, we are all here with you." Sam knelt in front of Sara and placed his hand gently on the side of her face.

"Sam, I'm so worried, I don't know what to do." Her hands were trembling.

"That's why we're all here. To help you and Rebecca." Sam stood up, hovering over her. "Let's go for a little walk and see if we can't find out why there's such a hold up. I never was much for sittin' and waitin'."

"No, Sam. I think we better wait here in case the doctor comes to talk with us."

"Let's go talk with the doctor." Sam reached out and grabbed Sara's hands and pulled her to her feet.

"Delphia, how about you and I go and do a little exploring," said Uncle Martin, standing in front of Lola. "Maybe Sam can find out more about what's going on by the time we get back."

"I want to wait here." Delphia placed her face deep into her mother's shoulder.

"Oh, go with him." Lola pulled Delphia to her feet.

Delphia glared at her mother as she moved slowly toward Uncle Martin. "We best be goin' to explore something and not just walkin' around."

"I was thinking' we could go look at the book depository."

"What?" Delphia curled her lip and opened wide her mouth.

"You know, where President Kennedy was shot from," said Uncle Martin. "Anybody who wants to go is welcome."

"I reckon that would be exploring." Delphia walked over and took Uncle Martin's hand.

Several kids gathered next to Uncle Martin, all relieved to be leaving the depressed atmosphere that had developed in the hospital waiting room.

"Well, let's see what we can find out," said Sam to Sara.

"Lead the way, Sam." Sara followed Sam into a large corridor.

There was no hesitation in Sam's gait as he walked straight toward the nurse's station outside the operating room. The clanking sound from the heels of his boots echoed off the solid walls of the hallway as he approached two nurses at the station.

"Howdy, Helen," said Sam to the closest nurse, reading the name off her nametag.

"Hello."

"Helen, could you possibly get us in touch with Doctor Meersman? He is scheduled to operate on Rebecca Young." Sam stood up tall.

"Rebecca is still in pre-op," said the blond nurse behind Helen.

"She was scheduled for surgery two hours ago," said Sara.

"Let me see if I can get one of the doctors to talk with you," said the blond nurse, smiling at Sara as she made her way through a set of double doors.

"I just don't understand why there is such a delay," said Sara, more to herself than to anyone else.

"Doctor Meersman is a wonderful physician, I'm sure he has his reasons," said Helen, holding up a finger as she answered the telephone. "I'll send them right down." Helen hung up the phone and pointed down the corridor. "Go through the set of doors and take the second left. Doctor Meersman will be there."

"Thank you," said Sam as his telephone rang. Caller ID showed Tom's cell phone number. "You go ahead Sara. I best take this call."

"All right," said Sara hesitantly before walking through the doors.

"Tom." Sam moved several feet from the nurse's station.

"Sam. Have y'all been watching the news?" Tom's voice was distressed. "Have ya heard anything about Troy?"

"We haven't heard anything."

"The police entered the house where Troy was diggin', and just like I thought everyone was gone, except for the two hostages." Tom swallowed hard. "They found the two robbers dead outside the house."

"Are ya sure Troy was in this house?"

"I'm positive." Tom paused. "I'm worried as hell about Troy."

"You did tell him he was in danger?" Sam asked, acclimating himself to the dilemma.

"I told Larry. I've been tryin' to call back, but he won't answer."

"Well, keep tryin," said Sam.

"How's Rebecca?" Tom's voice softened.

"They haven't operated yet," Sam's voice was harsh. "Yore mother's meeting with the doctor right now."

"I thought they were goin' to operate hours ago."

"I don't know what the problem is, but I'm fixin' to find out," said Sam.

"Okay, Sam. I'll call ya back in a few hours." Tom closed his phone.

Sam leaned against the smooth masonry of the hospital corridor, placing the sole of his boot to the wall, and dialed Stanley's number. It was a hell of a fix surrounding him, but he knew he shouldn't burden Sara with any more problems than the one she was facing with Rebecca. As soon as he was absolutely sure of the circumstances of Troy's involvement with the happenings in Denver, he would inform her.

"Stanley," said Sam into his phone as soon as he heard Stanley open his phone. "Have ya heard anything about what's happening in Colorado?"

"I'm watchin' it on CNN right now," said Stanley. "I relayed the news ya gave me this morning to Ed Dodd. But that's the last I talked with him."

"So ya don't know anything new?"

"Only that the two robbers are dead," said Stanley. "If the boys are involved with this one, they shore fell into a dangerous mess."

"Call Ed Dodd back and see if he has anything more."

"I'll do that," said Stanley. "How's Rebecca? Jackie has been waitin' by the phone for you to call with an update."

"We're about to find out why they haven't operated yet."

"If it ain't one mess it's another," said Stanley. "Let us know whenever ya find out."

"I will do that." Sam took in a deep breath as he closed his phone.

****

Sam could tell there was something terribly wrong when he entered the pre-op area through the double doors. Sara was standing between Doctor Meersman, who was dressed in blue scrubs, and Doctor Larson. Sara reached her arm out toward Sam as he approached her.

"Doctor Meersman has changed his mind about trying to save Rebecca's leg," blurted Sara with trembling lips.

"Why?" Sam looked flabbergasted as he stared into the bloodshot, bulging eyes of the doctor. "Doctor, why have you changed yore mind?"

"Mr. Blake, I spent last night, the entire night, going over the CT scan and MRI of Rebecca's tumor." Doctor Meersman shuffled his feet. "I came to the conclusion that I am not completely confident about leaving the leg. This change of heart is completely new to me. Something I have never done before."

"Have ya noticed something different that wasn't there two weeks ago?" Sam asked in a nonthreatening yet querying manner.

"No," answered Doctor Meersman. "It has been a borderline decision whether or not to save the leg from the very beginning."

"Why in the hell didn't you make that decision before now?"

"Mr. Blake, it is partly due to your methodical efforts to make sure I was doing my job," said the doctor, now looking back and forth at Sara and Sam. "Doctor Pint at the Mayo Clinic phoned me yesterday afternoon, and Doctor Polivka at Johns Hopkins notified me later in the evening with their opinions on the CTs and MRI you had sent them. These men made it clear to me that it would be prudent, and most likely be their decisions had Rebecca been their patient, to rid her body of the cancer by removing her leg."

"Doctor Meersman called me this morning to discuss his decision," interjected Doctor Larson. "I totally agree with his current decision."

Sam had made it Jackie's full-time duty to check Doctor Meersman's credentials and history in respect to handling patients with the same bone cancer as Rebecca. Apparently, she had done a very thorough job of making sure the doctor was making the best decisions for the well-being of Rebecca.

"We need to postpone the operation," said Sara.

"No," exclaimed Doctor Larson.

"That would be a terrible mistake," cried Doctor Meersman frantically.

"But if we aren't sure, we …"

"Mrs. Young, we are sure about the tumor in your daughter's leg," interrupted Doctor Meersman. "The fact that her lungs are clean is … it's mind-boggling to me; especially with the size of the tumor."

"We both agree that the operation should be performed immediately," said Doctor Larson.

"Sam." Sara looked to Sam with a look of helplessness.

"We need to include Rebecca in this conversation," said Sam. "Have y'all talked with her about any of this?"

"No," said Doctor Meersman. "We should do it immediately; she has been waiting in limbo to long."

Rebecca was sitting in a chair, wearing a white gown, reading a magazine, when the entourage entered her room. She was starving, and oddly enough it was her hunger that was keeping her mind off the long wait.

"Rebecca." Sara rushed to her side and kissed her on the cheek.

"What's going on?" Rebecca could tell there was something drastically wrong.

Sara didn't wait for the doctors to respond. She took hold of Rebecca's hand and began to speak, "Honey, I have to tell you something." Sara squeezed her hand. "Doctor Meersman now feels it is necessary to remove your leg."

"What?" Rebecca had spent the morning and greater part of the afternoon imagining that the operation would be less radical than she originally thought it would be. The longer the doctor delayed the operation, the more optimistic she had become, even to the point where she had been daydreaming about winning the state championship this upcoming track season.

"Rebecca," said Doctor Meersman, taking his hair cover from his head, allowing his bushy hair to burst out. "I'm sorry. Terribly sorry. I should have made this decision before now."

"It's necessary to get rid of the cancer," said Sara.

"Listen," Doctor Meersman knelt down in front of Rebecca, "it has been wonderful being around you and getting to know you over the past few weeks. I love your smile and spirit. You have been blessed with a great gift. It would be the biggest mistake of my life to allow this cancer to spread to the rest of your body."

"It's not fair."

"This disease you have doesn't play fair," said Doctor Larson rather coldly.

"Can't you just take the tumor out?" Rebecca looked directly into Doctor Meersman's eyes as she wiped a small tear from her cheek.

"I could try. But if I left even a minute part of the tumor, it would cost you your life," said Doctor Meersman, placing his hand to her chin. "That leg is far from being the best part of you."

Rebecca's head felt like it weighed twice what it usually did. She lowered her eyes to the floor.

"We can have the operating room prepared for surgery by seven tomorrow morning," said Doctor Meersman, moving his hand to the side of Rebecca's face.

"What do you say, Rebecca?" asked Sara.

"If we have to, we have to."

"Why don't you put some clothes on and go out to the waiting room for a bit?" Doctor Meersman tried to look her in the eye. "I am sorry, Rebecca."

It came natural for Rebecca to put her arms around the doctor's neck and hug him. "Thank you for trying."

Maliki and Tanya

"Rebeca's surgery was part of a human-interest story that I had debated whether to cover and eventually decided not to. I thought it would be a simple repair of her knee and she would be back running in a few weeks," said Tanya. "It's fascinating now to hear the details of how the decision to remove her leg transpired."

"The turnaround in the severity of her disease was what made everything so devastating for everyone." Maliki leaned back in the chair. "The optimism of everyone in Medicine Bow was what made the decision to remove Aunt Rebecca's leg seem like such a great tragedy."

"Even for me," stated Tanya. "I heard about it the next morning from our sports anchor. He had gotten wind of it and called me immediately."

"I can't imagine how distressed Grandmother was."

"And Sam," said Tanya. "He still had the problem of Troy to deal with, and he had to inform Tom of Rebecca's ordeal."

The deeper they delved into the story, the more businesslike Tanya became. Maliki heard her speaking for over an hour to his grandmother in the early morning hours. Her attire and mood were now much more professional than when they first started.

"I heard you talking with Grandma this morning," replied Maliki. "Did she have any new perspectives?"

"Speaking with her allowed me to realize how well-prepared she was to handle adversity. Her life was always filled with uncertainty."

Maliki thought for a moment. "Uncertainty makes the world interesting."

"Wow, very philosophical." Tanya smiled.

Troy smiled back. He looked at her bright red lips and her blouse buttoned snuggly up to her neck. He thought she could be the perfect poster woman for ambiguity. "Let's keep going."

Rocky Mountains, Colorado

"There's the cabin," yelled Billy, pointing toward a driveway cut through a cluster of tall pine trees. Even though Larry had been there less than an hour earlier, he was so tired he would have driven right past the entrance had Billy not warned him. It had been a long tortuous journey to their grandfather's cabin from Winter Park after leaving the Cadillac at Marv's garage. Billy was holding a suitcase in one hand and holding onto Larry with the other. The strong wind was blowing snow, cutting through the layers of clothing they were wearing, frosting them to the bone.

Billy moved quickly to the fireplace and threw a log on the glowing coals of the once roaring fire. It felt warm inside the cabin, out of the wind, but with the fire down to embers, the temperature was hanging around freezing. Troy was curled on the sofa in the same position Larry had left him, sleeping like a baby.

"Oh God, does that feel good," said Larry, pulling his oversized gloves off and placing his hands palms forward toward the fire.

Billy shed his wet sweaters and shirts until he was down to only a thin, but dry, tee shirt. He placed another log on the roaring fire before picking up the suitcase and placing it on the small kitchen table. He unzipped it and let the top of the suitcase fall open. He had left only a couple pieces of clothing and filled the rest with money.

"How much money do ya suppose is here?" he asked Larry.

"Enough to keep us on the run for quite a while," answered Larry, walking to the kitchen sink and turning on the faucet. "Damn. The water's shut off."

"Gramps always shut the water off so the pipes won't freeze when he leaves for Texas in the fall. Ya have to go into the crawl space in the bedroom to turn it on." Billy pointed toward the back bedroom. He then opened a cabinet over the sink and reached up and felt around until he found a flashlight and an unopen package of batteries.

"Gramps has some candles and matches up there too," stated Larry.

Billy handed Larry the flashlight before reaching up and pulling several long candles and a large box of stick matches from the cabinet and placed them on the kitchen counter.

"Could you go down and turn on the water?" asked Larry. "I reckon I best go and pick up the other bags before I get too comfortable here."

"I'll do it," said Billy, holding up a can of chili. "I'll get us some dinner started."

"Good Lord, this has been a long day," Larry understated, removing his still wet gloves and looking at his red hands.

"I can't imagine a longer day," countered Billy.

"I'll be back shortly." Larry pulled the collar of his coat tight around his neck and adjusted his stocking cap before stepping into the cold night air.

The crawl space was thirty-six inches high covering an area twenty feet by thirty feet, accessible through a hole in the floor in the corner of the master bedroom. The opening was covered with a piece of plywood attached to the floor with two metal hinges. Billy crawled into the hole where it was cold enough for him to see his breath. He found the faucet and turned on the water and hurriedly crawled out of the cold underbody of the cabin.

Billy laid Troy's suitcase on top of his suitcase and opened it. Several packets of money fell to the floor. He had always wondered what it would feel like to be a millionaire, yet the sight of this money left a dead feeling in the pit of his stomach. He turned the suitcase over and emptied the contents onto the floor. There was only one of Troy's shirts along with a small overnight bag.

"Have ya any medicine left?" Billy muttered to himself as he unzipped the bag. "Yes!" he yelled. There was a container with pills surrounded by a toothbrush, toothpaste, deodorant, and a comb.

Troy sighed from the sofa loud enough for Billy to hear him.

"Troy," said Billy, shaking his friend.

Troy woke with a start, obviously disoriented. "What?" came Troy's veiled response.

"Ya need to take some medicine," Billy handed him a capsule of lithium.

Troy was breathing heavily, catatonically looking into the fire. He reached out and accepted his medication. "I need a drink of water," he muttered before placing the capsule in his mouth.

Billy walked to the kitchen sink and poured his friend a glass of water. He stopped for a moment to ponder the circumstances. The entire situation seemed to come barreling down on him. A lot of it was fatigue, but it was far more than that. The uncertainty of everything was too astounding to even think about.

Troy remained silent as he reached up to take the glass of water. He took several gulps.

"Troy. I know you are gonna sleep for a long time," Billy reached down and took the glass from his hand. "I want ya to eat something first and then get cleaned up."

"Okay," said Troy indifferently, standing up.

Billy walked him into the bathroom. He then went to the kitchen and opened a can of chili and put it in a pan. He carefully placed it in the coals at the side of the fire in the fireplace. He heard the howl of the snowmobile engine in the distance.

"Larry sure is pushing that machine," Billy said to himself before stepping to the door and looking outside. Large flakes of snow were still falling from the sky.

Larry, precariously holding onto the bags of money, barely made the turn into the cabin's driveway. He accelerated the engine, sliding the machine into the railing of the cabin's porch, coming to a sudden stop. He unbuckled his belt and pulled it through the back loops of his jeans, allowing the two bags to fall to the ground.

Billy stepped into the cold and grabbed the bags.

Larry followed Billy into the cabin and brushed the snow from his face. "We got to get the hell out of here," he yelled.

"What's wrong?" Billy could see that Larry's eyebrows were frozen white as they both moved toward the fire. He reached in and pulled the pan of chili out and set it on the hearth.

Larry hesitated for a moment as he warmed. "Tony and another fella were at the end of the road."

"Are they behind you?"

"No, they headed back toward town." Larry wiped the wetness from his face. "They realized they couldn't drive down the road, so they turned around."

"Let's not panic," said Billy nervously.

"They must have a pretty good notion we're here if they drove all the way up here in that storm."

"I can't believe they already found us. Are ya sure it was Tony?"

"Hell yes," said Larry. "I was lucky to be in the trees loading the bags when they drove up. Even though it's so dark, I recognized Tony when he stepped out of the car and looked down the road. He was wearing a black leather coat. I guarantee they will be giving us a visit soon."

"We are in one hell of a mess." Billy sat down on the sofa.

"Where's Troy?" asked Larry.

"He's in the bathroom. I just gave him a pill."

Larry sat down on the sofa and laid his head back on the soft cushion. He closed his eyes and remained silent as he contemplated the situation.

"What ya thinking?" asked Billy.

"I think we best hop on that snowmobile and make our way into town and turn ourselves over to the police."

Billy was relieved it was Larry who made the suggestion. But he knew he was the one that needed to come up with a logical plan to make everything work. Larry was too tired to think.

"Larry, I agree with ya. We have to turn ourselves in," stated Billy. "But all three of us can't ride on the snowmobile."

"We're gonna have to leave Troy here," Larry said softly.

"But if Tony finds a snowmobile and makes his way up here before we get back." Billy moved to the hearth so he could look directly at Larry. "He'll kill Troy."

"All three of us can't fit on the snowmobile."

"I was thinkin'," contemplated Billy. "Remember old man Brelsford's cabin?"

"On the other side of the creek?"

"Yea, it's only a couple hundred yards away," stated Billy. "We can stash Troy and the money there."

"We have to walk there," said Larry. "There's no road leading to his cabin. Man, Billy, I don't know if I can make it."

"Let's do it," Billy was excited. "If you can make one trip there carrying two suitcases, I'll do the rest."

"I reckon I can." Larry sat down on the sofa. "Just give me a minute."

Billy readied Troy for the journey to the neighbor's cabin as Larry rested. He carried the suitcases to the door and steadied Troy who was walking better than expected. Larry sucked in a deep breath and prepared to step back out into the cold darkness. He followed Billy and Troy, carrying two suitcases. The walk through the woods was slippery and precarious. Billy never hesitated in breaking the front window to the cabin before crawling into the living room. After opening the front door, he directed Troy to the back bedroom where he tucked him away for the night.

"I'm gonna go back to Gramps's cabin," said Larry, having placed the two suitcases on the floor. "I'm so tired I can hardly stand up."

"Go ahead. I need to write Troy a note, just in case the police don't make it here by the time he wakes up. His phone isn't charged, but we need to leave it with him anyway." Billy felt a surge of energy flow through his body. For the first time in a long time he felt he was doing the right thing. "Get some rest and we can get out of here by first light."

"That's only a few hours off." Larry stepped out the door, "I'll see ya at the cabin."

It was a sleepless night of twisting and turning in anticipation of giving themselves up to the authorities. Both Billy and Larry were happy to see a dull sliver of light appear behind the heavy clouds covering the valley to the east. The snow continued to fall as they made their way to the snowmobile for their final journey from their grandfather's cabin. The large snowflakes stuck to the boys like honey as they shivered in the excruciating cold. The seat of the snowmobile was covered with several inches of snow, which Larry brushed away before sitting in the driver's seat. Billy climbed on the back of the machine and held tight to the back of Larry's coat.

"Hang on." Larry spun the snowmobile around and gunned it down the driveway onto the snow-covered logger's road leading back to the main highway.

Snow was clinging to the top of Larry's stocking cap as he tipped his head to keep his eyes from being frozen. He was driving the snowmobile as fast as it would go, peeking over the frozen windshield. The snow intensified and the wind was blowing harder than it had been when he made his final trip the night before.

Billy never attempted to look around Larry who was sheltering him from the wind and snow. He felt as if he were floating through space, no longer hearing the sound of the engine or feeling the cold air pushing against his arms.

The snow-covered pine trees outlining the road all looked similar, making it seem as if they were sitting still, yet they were traveling at forty miles an hour. Larry had lost track of time and distance. He was tired of the cold and tired of running. The narrow road disappeared directly before his eyes as he flew over the first pile of snow left by the snowplow before hitting the highway. He was conscious of the change but too fatigued to respond.

The snowmobile crossed the highway less than a hundred yards in front of a large tanker truck carrying jet fuel. As it hit the wall of snow on the opposite side, it flew through the air into a grove of trees, hitting the trunk of a Ponderosa pine. Larry was crushed directly into the tree. Billy was hurled from the back and hit six feet higher on the same tree.

The truck driver slid to a stop and parked as far to the side of the road as possible and turned on his emergency lights. He called on his radio for help before climbing from his cab and walking to the site of the wreck. He checked Billy first for vital signs and then Larry. It was obvious both boys were dead.

Colorado State patrol officer Tom Millet was two miles east of Winter Park, having just come off Berthoud Pass when he received the radio call of a snowmobile accident with fatalities. With lights flashing and siren blaring, he drove through town and could reach the accident within fifteen minutes of the first report. He was the first policeman on scene and began his duty to confirm the death of the two victims. He parked his patrol car behind the large tanker truck on the shoulder of the highway and walked up to the driver-side door.

"It's pretty gruesome down there," said the portly truck driver, opening the door to his truck, but making it obvious he had no intention of exiting his vehicle.

Officer Millet stood on the embankment on the side of the road and looked toward the smashed snowmobile, approximately thirty feet into the woods off the highway. He could easily see the snowmobile and two bodies lying in the thick snow. He was wishing he had not been the first to respond as he began to slide down the shallow embankment toward the wreckage.

"Good God!" Officer Millet moaned when he saw the young man's head nearly severed at the neck. There was an eerie silence surrounding him as he reached down and pulled the wallet from the back pocket of Larry's jeans. "Lawrence Lover from Texas," he said to himself. "Let's see who your friend is." He stepped through a knee-high drift of snow where Billy lay with his head split open, leaving no doubt that he was dead. He reached behind the mangled body and removed his wallet. He had to walk sideways to make it up what had seemed like a slight hill on the way down but seemed like the side of a mountain as he slipped several times climbing up the embankment. When he finally reached the highway, he walked to his car and radioed in the identities of the dead men. The boys were now the responsibility of the coroner.

"I need you to fill out this form, if you would." Officer Millet handed the truck driver a clipboard with papers on it. "Just write down what you saw."

Officer Millet waited for about ten minutes when he heard sirens approaching in the distance. The snow was still heavy and the wind was beginning to pick up. He climbed out of his car and walked to the tanker truck.

"Are you finished with the form?" asked Officer Millet, holding onto his hat with one hand.

"They're filled out the best I know how," said the truck driver, sticking the clipboard out the window. "All I saw was a blur go by in front of me."

"It should be only a little longer and you can be on your way," said Officer Millet, noticing his fellow officers pulling their cars onto the shoulder of the road a few hundred feet past the accident scene. They didn't hesitate in stepping out of their vehicles to immediately monitor the traffic.

The fire engine from the Winter Park volunteer fire department came to a slow stop behind the police cruiser. Coroner Pete Lumpkins pulled his van with flashing lights in behind the fire truck. Officer Millet didn't want to talk with Coroner Lumpkins, even though they were casual friends, so he walked back toward his cruiser. But Coroner Lumpkins followed him to the car.

"Tom. Sheriff Hunker is en route to this scene. He wanted me to tell you he is bringing a snowmobile and wants you to go with him to a cabin a couple of miles down this road."

"Why in the hell doesn't he get one of his deputies to go with him?"

"That's what you get for living in a small town." The overweight coroner stood at the window of Officer Millet's car and looked at him through hollowed eyes. "Are you sure there were only two on the snowmobile?"

"As sure as I can be. I'm sure as hell not going to climb back down there."

"Apparently these two were involved with the bank robbery yesterday in Denver. They have another friend who should have been with them."

"Well, I hope they don't expect me to try and get to that cabin in this blizzard." Officer Millet pulled the collar of his coat around his neck. "I plan on finishing this report and going home."

"The sheriff wanted me to tell you he might need your aid. You can do what you like. I passed along the message." He turned and walked back toward his van, sliding on the slick pavement.

"Son of a bitch, it has to happen at the end of my shift." Officer Millet tossed his paperwork toward his briefcase and closed the car window. He could hear the sound of a snowmobile approaching in the distance. He put his hat on and stepped from his vehicle.

The driver of the snowmobile was wearing an orange jumpsuit and a dark blue ski mask. The words Sherriff Department were visible on the side of the snowmobile as

Sheriff Hunker released the throttle, sliding precariously close to the patrol car.

"Tom," said Sheriff Hunker, tipping his head down so the snow wouldn't blow in his eyes.

"Dave." Officer Millet and the sheriff were neighbors whose daughters were teammates on the Winter Park freshman basketball team.

"Is everything under control here?"

"Nothing more to do, both parties are deceased."

"The FBI boys are on their way. They think these two are connected with the robbery in Denver. The FBI notified us last night about the possibility of them coming up here to their grandfather's cabin." Sheriff Hunker stepped from the snowmobile and brushed the snow from his shoulder. "They want me to check the Lockett cabin. It's about two miles up this logger road. I was hoping you would ride along."

"Hell, Dave, I'm not dressed to be riding on the back of no snowmobile, especially in this damn blizzard."

"Molly and Andy are both over an hour away. I hate to go up there without any backup."

"Oh, all right." Officer Millet reached into the backseat of his cruiser and pulled out his leather jacket. He knew he would feel guilty for the rest of his life if he allowed his friend to go alone to the cabin and something awful happened to him.

Dallas, Texas

It was a little past ten o'clock in the morning and the doctors still hadn't started the operation. Sara and Sam had spent the entire night at the hospital, most of it comforting Rebecca, until she finally dozed off. The others from Medicine Bow had left for home when they learned the operation was postponed. They were expected to return later in the day.

Sam stood up from the uncomfortable chair where he had spent the last couple hours. The nurse had taken Rebecca to pre-op at exactly seven. He was about to walk down the hall to inquire about the progress of the operation when his phone rang.

"Sam, the news people here are reporting that two men were killed in a snowmobile accident outside Winter Park where

Billy's grandfather's cabin is," said Tom with a trembling voice. "They're saying the two fellas killed are part of the group who robbed the bank yesterday."

Tom's message caught Sam completely off guard. "Did they give any names?"

"All they are saying is that the accident may be related to the robbery," said Tom. "Sam, I'm about at my wits' end."

"You and Drew pack up and go to Denver International Airport. There will be two tickets on the next flight to Dallas on United Airlines. Catch a cab to the hospital."

"We're on our way." Tom sucked in a huge breath of relief.

Sam dialed Stanley's number.

"Sam, I reckon you already heard about the accident in the mountains," said Stanley.

"How do you know about it?"

"I just finished talking with Ed Dodd."

"Was one of them Troy?" Sam asked with his heart beating hard against his chest.

"He hasn't got positive identification yet." Stanley hesitated, "He knows the two dead are our boys."

"When did the accident happen?"

"Real early this morning," said Stanley. "Ed gave the Colorado authorities the information Tom gave us about the boys being in the house and that they might be heading to the Lockett cabin, so they were on the lookout for them."

"Call me as soon as you get any more information." Sam closed his phone and walked back into the waiting room and sat down.

"Was that Tom?" Sara asked.

"Yeah," said Sam, "he was checking in."

"What's wrong, Sam?" Sara could tell something was amiss from the distress on Sam's face.

"There was a robbery in Denver yesterday," Sam's smile was phony. "Tom thinks Troy had a part in helping the robbers escape."

"Why would Tom think such a thing?"

"He actually talked with Larry yesterday, and he's just speculating now."

"I don't understand why he would think Troy would be involved with a robbery." Sara was tightly holding her hands on her lap.

"It's just a guess on Tom's part at this time." Sam wasn't going to distress Sara until he was absolutely sure of the situation. He would then be blunt and straightforward with the information. "How about if I get us another cup of coffee."

"Sure," said Sara with a concerned look on her face.

"Mrs. Young," said Nurse Helen as she stepped inside the waiting room. "Doctor Meersman wanted me to inform you that they have started the operation."

Rocky Mountains, Colorado

The snow on the front porch of the Lockett cabin came to the top of Sheriff Hunker's boots as he waited next to the front door, gun in hand. Officer Millet stood quietly on the opposite side looking through the bottom corner of the living room window. The sheriff began tapping on the door with his gloved knuckles.

"Police. Police," shouted the sheriff.

There was no answer.

"Sheriff's department," he banged harder on the door.

Officer Millet tried shining his flashlight through the window, but the frost obstructed his view. He moved to the center of the window and tried scraping the snow, but also to no avail. The inside of the window had a thin layer of frost covering it.

The sheriff slowly turned the knob on the door, and to his surprise it opened. "I'll go first," he whispered. Moving quickly, he entered the cabin, followed closely by Officer Millet.

It was freezing cold inside, with a distinct smell of smoke. Both men remained quiet as they walked across the stone floor of the living room, guns at shoulder height. The sheriff pointed to the back bedroom, and both men eased toward the closed door. Standing to the side of the door, the sheriff eased it open. He stepped inside and rotated his gun a full one hundred eighty degrees before stepping all the way into the small room. Officer Millet remained at the bedroom door with his back to the sheriff.

"There ain't anyone here," stated Officer Millet, lowering his gun. "The fire's been out for a while."

"I imagine the boys decided to go back to town and a nice warm meal after they found out how cold it is up here," countered sheriff Hunker.

"I wonder why they didn't eat this." Officer Millet poked the pan of chili sitting on the hearth with his gun.

"Dave," a dispatch from the sheriff's radio interrupted the conversation. "The FBI are on their way to the Lockett cabin."

"When?"

"They should be there within ten minutes. They are on the logger's road now. You should hold your position until they arrive."

"We'll wait. Let them know the cabin is empty." The sheriff could tell Officer Millet was more than a little perturbed with having to wait, but there was nothing he could do. "The FBI agents must be from Denver. They're not afraid of a little snow."

"Boy oh boy," Officer Millet sat down on the sofa. "We can't even start a fire."

"No, we can't. This is a crime scene." The sheriff sat down next to officer Millet.

Sheriff Hunker held the door open for the two FBI agents, allowing them to step inside the cold cabin and shake the snow from their clothing.

"Sheriff, I'm agent Dodson and this is Agent Schroth," said the older of the two men.

"Sheriff Hunker and Officer Millet."

"Damn, it's cold in here," said Agent Dodson. "I take it you have searched the entire cabin."

"Yes. There are only four rooms," stated officer Millet.

"No basement?" asked Agent Dodson.

"Only a crawl space," answered the sheriff.

"Did you check it?"

Officer Millet looked at the sheriff and answered, "No."

"We'll do it." Agent Dodson looked at Agent Schroth.

"There's a trapdoor in the bedroom," Sheriff Hunker pointed to the bedroom.

Agent Schroth quickly moved to the door and opened the plywood covering. Agent Dodson waited at the entrance as the younger agent lowered himself into the shallow crawl space and shined his flashlight from wall to wall.

"Nothing here," yelled the agent.

Officer Millet reached down to help the FBI agent exit the crawl space. He dusted the dirt from his knees as he closed the door.

"I think we have done what we need to do tonight. Let's tape off the door and I'll get a crime team up here when the weather is more cooperative," said Agent Dodson. "It's got to be snowing about two inches every hour."

"What do you know about the men killed in the accident this morning?" asked Officer Millet. "Did they have anything to do with the robbery in Denver?"

"They were in on it." Agent Dodson pulled the ski cap over his ears, "Right now we don't know for sure how deep they were involved in the whole situation. We have some sources telling us that they were only there to dig the tunnel and probably unaware of the entire scheme. We still have a lot to learn."

"Do you suppose they might be running from more than just the authorities?" asked the sheriff.

"Don't know," Agent Dodson shook his head. "Obviously there is no money here, and neither of the men at the accident had more than a few dollars on them. We can get a lot of answers if we find the third boy from Texas."

"If he's still alive," Agent Schroth interjected.

"It will be a while before we understand the entire situation," said Agent Dodson. "I do know the people at the top of all this are very ruthless. So, to answer your question, Sheriff, they probably were running from more than the authorities."

Dallas, Texas

Thank God there were only two other couples in the waiting room, and both families were there in support of loved ones who were experiencing minor surgery. The group of people from Medicine Bow had shown up at the hospital and were taking up more than half of the area. The wait for news of Rebecca's surgery had already taken longer than anticipated, and everyone was becoming restless.

Delphia eagerly accepted a twenty-dollar bill from Sam, the third donation, in order to make a trek to buy refreshments. She ran out of the room right past Nurse Helen.

Sara's breath seemed to leave her body and the blood rushed from her head as the nurse approached, walking through the mass of people, with a concerned look on her face.

"Mrs. Young," said the nurse, "everything is fine, but I wanted to let you know the operation is taking a little longer than anticipated."

Sara held her hand to her mouth. She wasn't sure how to interpret the information. She had asked the doctor to keep her updated.

"I'm not sure how much longer it will take," the nurse stated. "Doctor Meersman is always very meticulous."

Sara remained quiet.

"Everything is okay, isn't it?" Sam asked.

"As far as I know everything is going fine." The nurse forced a smile.

"Are they finished with … have they taken the leg?" asked Sara.

"Yes." Helen frowned. "But she is still in the operating room."

"Can I see her?" Sara's face was bright red. "Right now."

"Just as soon as they finish," Nurse Helen gently touched Sara's shoulder before turning and walking away.

"It's going to be okay." Lola took hold of Sara's hand and moved to the chair next to her.

Sam's phone rang. Caller ID showed Stanley on the other end.

"Stanley," Sam answered, moving out into the hospital corridor.

"I just got off the phone with Ed," Stanley hesitated.

"Well." Sam's blood pressure rose to a dangerously high level.

"It was Billy Ray Locket and Larry Lover who passed in the accident."

"God dammit, Stanley, why did you hesitate, you almost gave me a heart attack." Sam shifted the phone from his right hand into his left. "What about Troy?"

"He's no place to be found," answered Stanley. "They don't know where he is."

"My God, had you told me Troy was dead," Sam shook his head. "I don't know how I would have broken the news to Sara. At least now we can wait for more information."

"Ed's been really good about keeping me informed."

"Keep me informed," said Sam, "and come right to the point next time."

Sam melted into the group standing around Sara and Lola.

"Oh, Lola. This is killing me." Sara leaned toward her friend, "I hope we never have to go through something like this again."

Lola squeezed hard on Sara's hand. "I want to say a prayer for Rebecca." Lola let go of Sara's hand and motioned for the others to gather closer.

It was amazing the calm that came over Sara as Lola prayed. As Lola finished the prayer, Sara looked up at all her friends and family holding hands in support of her and Rebecca. The tranquil and peaceful moment brought a smile to her face, even as tears stayed formed in her eyes.

The sound of high heel shoes clanging on the tile floor in the corridor outside the waiting room caused everyone to turn their heads toward the entrance door. The heavy smell of perfume flowed into the room along with Tanya Springfield.

Tanya was carrying a vase with an arrangement of red and yellow roses. She stopped at the entrance and stared in, surprised at having all the eyes of the people in the room glued to her. Without great charisma, she walked across the room and stood in front of Sara.

"These are for Rebecca." Tanya set the roses down on a table in front of Sara. "I'm so sorry."

"Thank you," Sara's voice had some uncertainty in it.

Tanya pulled a metal chair and placed it in front of Sara. She sat down. She took hold of Sara's hands and looked her directly in the eyes.

Sam moved to the back side of the waiting room.

"Thank you again," Sara said.

"Is everything going okay with the operation?" Tanya asked Sara.

"We don't know." Sara squeezed Tanya's hands.

"I want to tell you one thing," said Tanya. "Of all the people, young or old, who I have interviewed, throughout my career, Rebecca is the one who impressed me most."

"It's all so devastating." Sara tried to hold back the tears, but it was useless.

"I can't imagine." Tanya let go of Sara's hands to rummage through her purse to find a tissue. "Rebecca is very strong."

Sara sniffled and nodded her head in agreement.

"She's fallen a long way because she had a long way to fall. Very few people will ever be as successful at what they do during a full life as she has been in her young life." Tanya shuffled in her chair. "All the sports guys at the station are talking about Rebecca today. I just wanted to come down here and reinforce what you already know. Your daughter is a really special person."

Sara turned in her seat to better face Tanya. It took a lot of guts for the beautiful reporter to come into the stress-filled situation and try to comfort her. Especially since it had been only a few weeks earlier that she had felt like strangling her.

"Mrs. Young," Nurse Helen stood at the entrance door.

"Yes," Sara stood up.

"You can see Rebecca now."

Sara looked toward Sam, who moved to her side.

"Thank you for coming by," Sara leaned over and gave Tanya a quick hug.

"Good luck," whispered Tanya.

"Tell Becca that I'm out here." Delphia stepped in front of Sara.

"I'll tell her."

"We'll be waiting to hear from you." Lola threw her arms around Sara.

"We'll let everyone know."

Sara, followed by Sam, slowly entered the curtained cubicle in the recovery area where Rebecca lay on a small bed with tubes wandering from her body. Sara positioned herself to the side of the bed and leaned over to kiss her daughter on the forehead. Rebecca's eyes were opened but glazed.

"Rebecca," said Sara softly.

Rebecca tried to focus her eyes.

"It's Mom."

"Hi," she blinked several times.

"Sam's here too."

"Hi, sweetheart," Sam reached around Sara and gently rubbed Rebecca's hand.

"I'm so thirsty," said Rebecca.

"Sara." Doctor Meersman slid around Sam into the small cubicle next to the bed. He smiled at Rebecca. "I just missed you in the waiting room. Helen didn't give me enough time to clean up so I could tell you in person that everything went very well. The nurse will be in here shortly with something for Rebecca to drink and a snack."

"There are no problems?" Sara asked.

"Nothing out of the ordinary," Doctor Meersman motioned toward the hallway. "Can we step out for a minute?"

Doctor Meersman was still dressed in his scrubs, and his bulging eyes were slightly bloodshot. His grey hair was matted down from the hair net he used during the surgery, which actually made him look more professional than he did with his usual wild hairdo.

"Everything went just fine," the tired doctor nodded to both Sara and Sam. "Since you live so far from the hospital, I want to keep Rebecca here for a few days to monitor her for infection."

"Everything is all right?" Sara looked at the doctor, unsure if he was telling her everything.

"Yes," he shook his head up and down. "At this time, I am confident the cancer was isolated to the knee."

"Are ya sure, Doctor?" Sam asked.

"Mr. Blake, I am not totally sure about anything when it comes to this disease. But I want to assure you that I am doing everything in my power to make her better."

"Couldn't ask for anything more." Sam gave Sara a reassuring look.

The doctor shrugged his shoulders and looked at Sara. "Now all you need to do is work on the emotional and mental state of your daughter. I think that physically she will do just fine."

The thought that Rebecca was going to all right physically was comforting to Sara. She had always considered the physical strength of Rebecca to be her greatest attribute, but now that she thought about it, she realized that Rebecca was every bit as strong mentally as she was physically. Now all she had to do was be strong herself as she prepared to reenter the recovery unit. She was very happy to have Sam along for support.

Rocky Mountains, Colorado

Troy woke with a start. He pulled on the blanket wrapped around his shoulder, and even though it was extremely cold, he threw it to the floor. His surroundings were completely unfamiliar. Three suitcases were stacked next to the bed. He ignored them.

"Billy, Larry," he yelled as he made his way from the bed into the cold confines of the living room. "Where are y'all?"

He walked into the kitchen where he found his bottle of pills and a note. He picked up the note.

> *Troy,*
>
> *Take a pill. We will be back shortly, or someone will. You are at our grandfather's neighbor's cabin. Vinny's sidekick Tony is snooping around so we thought it would be safer. Take your pills.*
>
> *Billy*

Troy walked by a mirror on the bathroom door. He had seen sick coyotes that looked better than the image that pathetically stared back at him. His eyes were hollow and his face long and thin. How could he have changed so quickly? He had always been cautious about his appearance. He moved closer to the reflection and breathed a steady steam over the image in the mirror, wondering if he had the strength to overcome what he had become.

He moved away from the steam-covered mirror and walked shoeless over the cold stone floor into the kitchen. He opened a breakfast bar and hurriedly swallowed the contents. The food tasted good. He sat down at the table and consumed three more bars.

He walked to the front window and looked out at the snow coming down, creating a high drift that covered the entire front porch. He went to the bedroom and retrieved the sleeping bag he had been sleeping on and placed it on the floor in front of the fireplace in the living room. He grabbed a match off the mantle and twirled it in his fingers before placing a handful of kindling in the firebox and lighting it. He watched the flames consume the small wood before covering it with a large log. He sat down on the quilt and held his feet to the warm fire.

"How long have I been here?" he asked himself.

He looked through the cupboards in the kitchen where he found extra batteries for the flashlight and several packets of matches. He found a pair of snowshoes in the closet in the bedroom, along with sweaters, ski gloves, and hats. Stored under the bed was a sturdy sled. He was confused as to why Billy and Larry would leave him and not return. It was becoming obvious that there was something wrong. They were very loyal friends and would never abandon him.

Troy stood in front of the fire, feeling the heat on his face. The warmth made him feel very much alive. He contemplated for a long time before going to the kitchen table and opening the bottle and popping a pill into his mouth. He went into the bedroom and retrieved the suitcases and placed them at the front door. He opened the door and was greeted by a howling wind and blowing snow. He slammed it shut and moved to the living room where he covered his body with the warm sleeping bag and watched the fire burn to hot coals. He knew he had to leave the cabin, and this knowledge gave him a surge of energy.

Troy packed the three remaining boxes of cereal bars into one of the suitcases on top of the money. He went to the bedroom and put on sweaters from the closet. After struggling to get the fifth one over his shoulders, he decided anymore would completely restrict his movement.

He tied the suitcases to the large sled and placed the sleeping bag and a quilt over the luggage. He tucked his ears into a ski cap. He then put the snowshoes on before covering his hands with thick ski gloves. Snow blew into the cabin as he maneuvered out the front door and onto the high snow, pulling the sled behind him.

Medicine Bow, Texas

The second hand of the old Seth Thomas clock hanging on the wall in Rebecca's bedroom seemed to be moving in slow motion. Rebecca held a small butterfly pillow tightly to her chest as she watched the hand slowly move around the cylinder of the old-fashioned timepiece. Time had always been something she had been able to defeat, but now as she lay in her bed, it seemed as though it was methodically stalking her. She reached her hand below the comforter and guardedly felt the stump of her missing leg. She slowly rubbed the extremely sore remnant of what used to be a strong and muscular leg. There was only a stub existing in stark contrast to the beautiful leg only inches away. She massaged the top of her thigh, going lower and lower to the point where she could feel pain. She pushed on the soft tissue before jerking her hand away. She pushed with the palms of her hands on the soft mattress to place herself in an upright position with her back leaning on the soft leather headboard. Being bedridden since the operation had taken a toll on her once perfect body. She felt flabby, which brought her to think about something she rarely thought about before her illness, marriage and a family. The disheartening thought of how she would ever expose herself to anyone was too unbearable for her to envision. Thinking about this made her mind race.

A gentle knock on her bedroom door slowed down her thought process. She knew it was her mother.

"Yes," she whimpered.

"Are you awake?" Sara opened the door and cautiously entered the room. She had made the conscious decision to take care of her daughter rather than have a nurse come to the house.

"Yes."

"Are you okay?" Sara sat on the edge of the bed and placed her hand on the side of Rebecca's face before pulling a strand of matted hair away from her daughter's hot cheek.

"No," answered Rebecca.

Sara was at a loss for words.

"I need more Trazadone," Rebecca mumbled.

"How about a shower?"

"My leg hurts," Rebecca gritted her teeth as she spoke, "I don't want to get out of bed."

"I'll get you some Vicodin."

Rebecca tried to situate herself into a more comfortable position as she waited for her mother to return with the medication. She didn't even want to think about the long day that waited ahead.

"Here you go," Sara waited patiently holding a glass of water as Rebecca swallowed the pills. "Delphia wants to come over this morning and see you."

"I don't want to see anyone."

"It would make her so happy if you would talk with her for a few minutes."

"I only want to sleep." Rebecca slid down the bed and placed a pillow over her head.

"You can sleep a few more hours," Sara pulled the covers over her shoulders. "Maybe you will feel like talking later in the morning."

Sara sat on the bed and watched Rebecca fall asleep. It was painful to see her beautiful daughter suffer, but all she could do was hope that time would heal the anguish. Since the operation, the period just before daybreak had become the most difficult part of the day.

Sam had told her the night after Rebecca's surgery about Billy Ray Lockett and Larry Lover losing their lives in the snowmobile accident and the uncertainty of the whereabouts of Troy. The information at that time was easy for her to discount, to rationalize, in that it was one of those things out of her control. But as she sat on the bed, tired, somewhat relaxed, she worried about the safety of Troy.

Delphia showed up at the door to the Youngs' house at eight o'clock on the dot to take what she called her shift to watch over Rebecca. Sara, at first, thought that with Rebecca being in such a fragile condition, her daughter might say something to Delphia that could harm their relationship in the long term. The more she thought about it, she realized that Delphia was strong enough to endure anything Rebecca might say or do, and that Delphia was just the person to help Rebecca.

Delphia would open Rebecca's bedroom door every ten minutes to check on her sleeping patient. It was a little after ten when Rebecca finally woke from her deep sleep.

"Becca." Delphia slumped her shoulders and cautiously moved into the room.

Rebecca pulled herself up slightly onto a pillow. Her once beautiful auburn hair remained matted to the side of her face, and the room smelled as though she had been recuperating in it much longer than two days.

"I've come to be with ya today." Delphia fidgeted with the bob on top of her hair as she moved to the edge of the bed.

Rebecca moved her head to the side away from Delphia.

"You don't have to talk if ya don't want to." Delphia sat on the bed. "But if ya need anything at all, I'll go fetch it."

"I don't need anything." She continued to look away.

"I brought some lotion."

Rebecca moved her face deeper into the mattress. Her head was throbbing.

Delphia sat silently on the bed for a few moments before placing her hand on the white nightgown covering Rebecca's shoulder.

"I was just thinking about how you would take all us kids on Sunday afternoon picnics." Delphia climbed on the bed and leaned over the top of Rebecca so she could look her in the eyes.

Rebecca could feel the warm breath of Delphia on the side of her face as she listened to her friend speak.

"I was just thinkin' that maybe Uncle Martin could whittle you a leg out of a piece of wood."

Rebecca continued to listen with Delphia's face only inches from hers.

"Or maybe," Delphia rolled her eyes to the ceiling. "Old Henry down at the welding shop could take a piece of pipe and make a leg. I could take one of my old shoes and put it on the end."

Rebecca listened in amazement as her little friend discussed the possibilities available to allow her to walk again. The essence of Delphia eased the throbbing in her head.

"I don't know how we are going to attach the pipe," Delphia continued. "I suppose I could take one of Jesse's belts."

"Enough." Rebecca jerked her shoulders, causing Delphia to jump to the edge of the bed.

Delphia looked to the floor as she sat on the edge of the bed. It wasn't her intention to upset Rebecca.

"My God, girl, this isn't the tenth century."

"I just want to help ya walk again."

"I'm gonna walk again," whispered Rebecca, taking hold of Delphia's small hand. "They already have me a leg."

"They do?"

"It looks like a real leg."

"Will you be able to take us on picnics?"

"I suppose."

Delphia put a finger to her cheek. "Well, if Monty gets bit by a snake, I can run to Mr. Ortiz's house."

Rebecca stared for a long moment at Delphia's small hand before looking directly into her dark eyes. A sincere smile formed on her face for the first time since coming home from the hospital.

"A metal pipe?"

"I think the wood might have been better." Delphia hunched her shoulders and smiled.

"Maybe you could get a patch to go over my eye. Like a pirate."

Delphia giggled, "Yore too pretty to be a pirate."

Rebecca felt tears form in her eyes.

"Do ya want me to put some lotion on yore hands?" Delphia asked.

"I want to get cleaned up first." Rebecca continued to stare at Delphia. "Could you get Ma?"

"I'll tell her." Delphia opened the bedroom door. "Do you feel good enough to sit on the front porch?"

"I'll see."

"I can rub lotion and soften up those old corn cob hands of yours."

"That would be wonderful," said Rebecca.

***

Uncle Martin struggled to push his recliner through the front door and out onto the porch. Delphia was pulling with all her strength, but after several near accidents, where she was nearly smashed by the chair, Uncle Martin stopped pushing and stared at the girl.

"Dad gum it, Delphia. I'm gonna end up dropping this chair on top of you if you don't get out from under it."

"If you pull, I can push it out," suggested Delphia.

"All right. But stay out from under it."

Martin pulled on the top of the chair as Delphia, using all the strength in her legs, gave a tremendous push, lifting the chair out the door toward a surprised Uncle Martin. Martin fell back on the seat of his pants with the chair landing right in front of him.

"Good God, girl." Uncle Martin scurried to his feet.

"Sorry." Delphia rushed out the door onto the patio. "I don't know my own strength."

"You sure don't." The flustered old man brushed off his pants. "I can't believe yore strong enough to lift that chair all by yourself."

"I have real strong legs."

"I reckon." Uncle Martin shook his head. "Now use those strong legs to help me set this chair upright."

Delphia waited patiently until Sara finally helped Rebecca onto the porch and into the recliner after a much-needed shower and the administering of her pain medication. Sara placed a blanket over her daughter. Two bottles of lotion were set side by side on a metal chair next to the recliner.

"Here, give me yore hand."

Rebecca set her hand on the side cushion of the chair without saying a word as Delphia poured a liberal amount of lotion into the palm of her hand.

"I have two kinds of lotion." Delphia spread the lotion all the way up Rebecca's arm to her elbow. "But I like this one the best, because it smells so good."

"It does smell nice." Rebecca took a deep breath of fresh air. She relaxed her arm.

"I was just thinking," said Delphia, "you might be the best friend I will ever have."

"Forever is a long time."

"I know it is." Delphia showed all her teeth as she smiled.

"You are going to make lots of friends."

"None of them will be as good as you." Delphia picked up the metal chair and moved it to the opposite side of Rebecca. "Give me yore other hand."

Rebecca leaned back in the recliner. She stared out at the vast landscape where she had spent countless hours running and exploring. A small tear formed at the corner of her eye. It all looked so different now.

"Does that feel good?" Delphia stood up and wiped her hands on her pants. "It shore smells good."

"It feels good."

"Well, those old rough hands are a lot softer now."

"Do you know something, Delphia?" Rebecca whispered.

"What?"

Rebecca smiled. She wanted to tell Delphia that she was the essence of faith. That faith wasn't overbearing, but a quiet confidence that no matter how dire a situation, you have the belief that things will get better. Rebecca couldn't think of the way to put her reflective thoughts into words to tell her little friend, so she just smiled.

Rocky Mountains, Colorado

Walking with the snowshoes was far more awkward than Troy had anticipated, and the rigid shoes placed a lot of pressure on his lower legs. The more he practiced walking over the snow, the more comfortable he felt about his departure from the cabin. The sled glided easily behind and he felt confident he would be able to successfully take the suitcases of money with him. Lingering in his mind was the fact that it had been a long time since he had eaten a full meal.

The heavy snow had quit and the sun was shining on and off through a thin layer of clouds. The temperature remained well under freezing. Clothing-wise he had prepared well for his journey, putting on a coat over the layers of sweaters. The cold wasn't the most foreboding concern he faced. He could not remember even one small detail about his trip to the cabin with Billy and Larry. The dilemma of not knowing which way to go was the most daunting problem.

Ahead of him was what looked like a trail through the forest. Little did he know that a little over two hundred yards to the east of him, hidden by the trees, was the Lockett cabin and the logger's road leading back toward civilization. He began to pull the sled through the trees, down the miniscule trail, away from the town of Winter Park.

Fatigue was taking over his legs as he struggled to pull the sled farther and farther into the unfamiliar but extremely beautiful area. As he struggled to gain his breath, it became necessary to stop every few minutes, giving him a chance to survey the stunning landscape. The branches of pine trees strained to hold the bright snow that covered them. The sparkle from the sunlight reflecting off the ice crystals was magnificent. Troy looked on in amazement wondering what the area would look like in the summer. How it might smell.

He glanced back down the trail and figured he had traveled about three miles, almost all up an incline. He looked ahead and could tell that he would be going downhill for as far as he could see. He treaded forward, sometimes having to go at a snail's pace to keep the sled from hitting him in the backside. He could feel the cold beginning to creep through his layers of clothing. The temperature dropped as soon as the sun faded behind the mountain, even though it was still relatively early in the afternoon. He looked back and wondered if he should maybe retrace his tracks back to the cabin. He thought about it for several minutes and decided to continue in the same direction he had been going the entire day.

As darkness covered the area, the temperature plummeted. The brilliant coruscating stars were beginning to fill the heavens. It looked as if he could reach up and touch the crescent moon sitting high in the sky. The small amount of moonlight reflecting off the snow created enough illumination to allow him to see where he was walking. The trail narrowed and finally ended at the entrance to a small grove of trees two hundred feet ahead of what looked to be the top of a mountain.

Troy's breath surged ahead of him as he worked to pull the sled up the escalating incline. The bitter cold on his exposed face was painful and the burdensome sled was becoming heavier. He pulled until he could pull no longer and fell to the snow in exhaustion. Shivering, he laid his head back into the powdered snow and looked to the sky. Light snow began to float down as if each flake knew exactly the spot it was to land. He blew his breath upwards and lifted his gloved hand to catch several sparkling flakes. His body shook as he struggled to catch his breath.

The wind howled through the trees, making a sound of which Troy had never heard. The thought that he was going to freeze to death startled him enough to jerk to a sitting position. He tried to stand but was thwarted in his effort by the long, stiff snowshoes on his feet. He tried several times to stand before finally pushing hard on the side of the sled with his arms and rocking himself upright.

The wind was increasing, swirling the cold, powdered snow like it was sand in a desert. Troy shielded his numb face with his arm as he pulled with all his might up the steep incline, before turning his back to the wind and pulling the sled into the waiting forest at the top of the mountain. The trees were a welcome reprieve from the relentless wind. He pulled the sled next to a thick pine tree. He untied his snowshoes and kicked them to the side of the tree before shaking the snow from the heavy quilt and wrapping it around his shoulders. He placed the sleeping bag on the snow and sat on it. His entire body ached, and he was greatly fatigued as he pulled the quilt over his head. He remained under it for over an hour before poking his head out into the freezing wind. He opened the top suitcase and retrieved a candle and packet of matches, then pulled the three suitcases off the sled and laid them long ways next to each other. The cold was making his head throb as he poked his snowshoes into the deep snow on each side of the luggage. He tossed the quilt over the protruding snowshoes and suitcases and slid the sled over the edge of the it on the side of the snowshoes. He placed the makeshift tent so the howling wind blew from the sled side, making the loose end of the coverlet flop up and down. When he was sure the quilt was not going to be blown away, he climbed under and lay on the suitcases.

Troy realized it was going to be an uncomfortable night as he leaned in the shallow tent and removed his gloves. He lit a candle and held his left hand over the flame. The unsecured side of the make-shift tent blew wildly in the wind, allowing frigid air to invade inside. He wrapped the bottom half of the quilt around his feet and pushed the outside edge under his shoulder. It was still excruciatingly cold, but he did manage to fall asleep.

Peeking out from the cover he could see the sun shining through the trees from the valley below. He was high on a mountain, much higher than he originally thought. The cold air was bitter. Survival depended on movement, so he put on his gloves and pushed himself into a standing position. His legs were wobbly, and both had the same stinging sensation that wrapped from his hamstring to his kneecap. He reached down to retrieve a snowshoe, but fell to his knees, grimacing as great pain darted to his lower back.Although the quilt was wrapped tight around his head, Troy became aware of the sun through the trees below. He shed the coverlet from the top half of his body and sat up. He was high on a mountain, much higher than he originally thought, where the early morning sunlight could shine without impediment. The cold air was bitter, causing him to pull the quilt over his face. He knew survival depended on movement as he put his gloves back on his cold hands. He removed the quilt and pushed himself to a standing position. His legs were wobbly and both had the same stinging sensation that wrapped around the kneecap into his hamstring. He reached down to retrieve the snowshoes, but fell to his knees, grimacing as a great pain darted to his lower back.

The pain in Troy's lower back was excruciating. Nevertheless, he continued to put on the snowshoes and right the sled. He put the luggage and sleeping bag back on the sled and covered them with the quilt. He shook the snow off the tow rope and tied it around his waist. Leaning to one side he began to pull the sled through the trees.

Even though the mountain Troy had traversed the previous day rose high over the valley below, the treeless peaks to the south towered above the one he was on. The valley looked much more inviting, but the dark forest ahead looked impenetrable and frightening. His survival necessitated having to travel through the opaque wooded area.

The opening to the woods wasn't nearly as daunting from near as it appeared from the top of the mountain. The descent to the forest had been so severe that Troy found it necessary to allow the sled to slide down first as he braced his feet in the snow, sometimes sliding behind as if it were the sled in control of where, and how fast, they were going.

He was tired and his back ached as he continued on with the dull sun shining through the high clouds. Without any wind, the cold air felt thick and heavy on his body. Without stopping to survey the best route, he pulled the rope of the sled and began to traverse laterally through the trees.

Troy reached down and took a glove full of snow and placed it to his mouth. Something a true mountain man would never do. The dry snow stuck to his tongue, producing little if any moisture. He shook his glove off and blew a warm breath on his cold fingers. Inhaling an extra deep breath, he noticed something strange in the air. It was the smell of smoke.

There were more trees farther down the mountain, and several times he was forced to reverse his direction in order to maneuver the sled between the snow-covered branches. The soreness in his back was now only a part of the pain his body was suffering. Exhaustion and cold had altered his thought process. He was now traveling on instinct alone.

Plodding through the snow, Troy came upon a fallen tree covered with snow, much like the ones he had encountered on several occasions throughout the descent through the forest. This time he refused to turn around to avoid the obstacle. The long snowshoes gave him traction as he stepped on a branch and up onto the trunk of the tree. The sled easily slid over the frozen bark to sit precariously on top of the dead pine tree.

Troy examined the situation but made a bad choice and stepped onto a branch covered with snow. All he caught was air. He fell nearly five feet, jerking hard on the rope tied around his waist, bringing the sled down behind him. The sharp metal skid of the sled slammed hard on his right knee. He grimaced at the pain as he worked to untie the rope around his waist. When free, he rolled down the slope like a large snowball and hit hard at the base of a tree. He groaned in agony, unable to brush the snow from his body. All he could do was grit his teeth and wince in pain, too weary to move. The cold seemed to matter no more.

Medicine Bow, Texas

"I can't believe tomorrow is already Thanksgiving." Sara placed the coffeepot back on the burner, having just filled both Sam's and Tom's cups. She was happy. An emotion she hadn't felt for several days. Her happiness was because of the two men chatting at her kitchen table as if they were lifelong friends. She looked out the kitchen window at the church, but her mind was on her eldest son. Tom had been selfless in his search for his brother. And Sam, he had been indispensable and completely loyal in his support for her family. She needed to find time to tell him how she felt.

"It's been a long year," said Sam, removing his hat and setting it on the kitchen table. "This hot weather we're having doesn't help matters."

"If it's as dry as last year, we won't even have a crop this spring." Tom sat across the table from Sam.

"Y'all need to think about irrigating yore wheat." Sam wiped the sweat off his brow with the back of his hand.

"Irrigating cost money," said Tom.

"It also makes money," countered Sam.

"Haven't you and Uncle Martin had this conversation before?" Sara looked at the two men with a raised eyebrow.

"Only about a hundred times." Tom leaned back in his chair.

"Why don't ya do it?" asked Sam.

"I reckon it's because I'm not sure I want to plant wheat the rest of my life."

"Well," Sam hesitated and took a sip of coffee. "I guess that's as good a reason as any."

"I'm going to check on Rebecca." Sara put her coffee cup on the counter.

"Isn't Delphia with her?" asked Tom.

"She is. I just want to see how they are doing." Sara smiled as she left the room, knowing full well neither of the men even considered her real motive of allowing them time to bond.

"Sam," Tom waited until his mother was in the other room before he leaned forward and whispered, "have you read any of the tabloids?"

"I don't read that trash."

Tom picked up his coffee cup and remained silent.

"Well, what did they have to say?" Sam asked.

"They've been writing a lot about Troy." Tom liked the fact he had piqued Sam's interest. "And about you too."

"You can't believe any of that stuff. Hell, it hasn't been that long since the robbery. What do they do? Write this stuff beforehand?"

"I reckon I like it because they keep reporting on people who have seen him." Tom lowered his voice. "Where do you think Troy is?"

"I don't rightly know." Sam folded his arms across his massive chest. "What that boy does is very unpredictable."

"That's for shore." Tom walked to the kitchen counter and grabbed the coffeepot. He filled both his and Sam's cups. "Sometimes I feel like I don't know him at all."

"A lot of that has to do with his sickness."

"I can't count the times I had to walk away from him because I was so mad." Tom sat back down at the table.

"Well, he raised a lot of hell in this town." Sam leaned back in his chair. "But you know, Tom, the disease he has is as real as the one that took Rebecca's leg."

"It's always been all or nothing with Troy."

"That's why he is alive and kicking." Sam leaned forward and picked up his coffee cup. "That boy ain't gonna just fade away. When he goes, it will be with a bang."

"I was surprised that Ma never has said a word about Billy or Larry."

"None of us knew too much about the two boys," stated Sam.

"Ma's been really quiet about Troy."

"Sara's a smart lady. She knows there is little we can do now." Sam placed his hat on his head. "Stanley is keeping abreast of the situation. In fact, he is becoming infatuated with it."

"Wonder if Troy is dead?"

"One way or the other we will find him," Sam said with confidence.

Tom nodded his head in agreement. He had no doubt whatsoever in the truth of what Sam was telling him.

"So yore tired of planting wheat," Sam lightened up the subject. "What is it you have in mind?"

"I don't rightly know." Tom hadn't given it much thought that when Sam married Sara he would be his stepson. Six months ago, Sam would never have been interested in his future.

"Have you thought about college?"

"I'm too old for college."

"Good Lord, son, you're only twenty." Sam stood up from the table. "That's not even close to being too old."

"I reckon I need to do a little thinking about my future." Within thirty seconds of making this statement, Tom replied, "You know, Sam, I am a pretty good carpenter. I wouldn't mind doing something in the line of building homes."

"Well, that's a start. Think about that, and we can pursue it later." Sam looked out the kitchen door. "I'm gonna go find your mother."

Tom poured himself another cup of coffee. Not only was he unsure of what he was going to do for a livelihood, he wasn't sure what he was going to do for the rest of the day. Talking with Sam gave him a good feeling about his future. Anyone with Sam as a friend would be better off for it.

Rocky Mountains, Colorado

"Someone should shut up that damn dog." Pain shot through Troy's neck as he rolled his head from side to side. His eyes were closed, and he was having difficulty breathing. Five feet in front of him was a black chow in a defensive posture. The powerful shoulders of the animal would drive forward and her back legs would kick up snow each time she barked.

"Charlotte."

Troy was sure he was dreaming about the dog, but the voice he heard was real.

"Come here, girl." A large man with a white beard took hold of the dog's collar and struggled to pull her back. "What have you found?" The man cautiously moved toward Troy, who was half-covered in snow at the base of the tree. He pointed his shotgun in the air and leaned down, placing his face within inches of Troy's frostbit nose. Troy's eyes opened and twitched as they adapted to the light. He sucked in a rush of cold air to his lungs.

"I guess you're alive." The man disappeared without saying another word.

Troy had an odd reaction to the swift coming and leaving of the man; he didn't care. Lying idle, he was no longer in pain. But he knew he would have to come back to reality as he looked again into the face of the old stranger.

"I didn't leave you," said the old man as he took hold of Troy's coat and lifted him from the cold confines at the bottom of the Ponderosa pine tree. He hauled him like a sack of potatoes and placed him onto a thin piece of hard plastic. He took hold of a rope tied to the plastic sled and began to pull him down the mountain.

Troy remembered falling off the sled on several occasions as they made their way over the snow. Beyond that he didn't remember anything until he woke surrounded with warm blankets in a room filled with the aroma of fresh-cooked venison.

"Ya finally woke up."

Troy had a terrible itch on his nose, but when he tried to scratch it he couldn't move his arms because the blankets were wrapped so tight around his body. He wiggled trying to free his arms.

"Just lie back and relax." The coarse face of the old man appeared in front of him.

"How long have I been here?"

"Only a few hours."

Troy pulled his right hand out from the confines of the blanket and started to rub his sore nose. He found his nose to be covered with a heavy jelly substance.

"It's to help the frostbite."

"It hurts like hell."

"That's what frostbite does. It hurts," the old man stared at the side of his head. "You're lucky that it didn't get your ears; now that really hurts."

Troy tried to sit up, but his whole body ached, so he fell back onto the thin mattress.

"Ya hurt all over, don't ya?"

"Yes."

"That's what being half-frozen will do to ya."

"Just let me rest here for a spell and I'll be all right."

"Drink this."

Troy struggled to hold his head up high enough to receive the cup of fresh water.

"I'm going to help." The old man supported Troy's head until he finished drinking.

"Let's get rid of these blankets."

Troy grimaced in pain as the old man stripped away the blankets, revealing his emaciated body. He was dressed only in boxer shorts with his knee enveloped in a large ace bandage. He recoiled and reached for the blanket. "Hey."

"Don't look at me like I'm some sort of pervert. I've raised four boys that are old enough to be your father." The old man sat the blankets onto the fireplace hearth.

"I wasn't being rude. My whole-body hurts something awful."

"As I said, I can help. Now roll over on your stomach."

Troy's arms were barely strong enough to support him as he turned on the hard bed. His knee was throbbing and felt as if it had swollen to twice its size.

The old man placed a thin blanket, which had been warmed by the crackling fire, over Troy's worn and battered body. He placed a large hot water bottle on the blanket between Troy's shoulder blades and then placed another on the back of his legs.

"This water has herbs in it."

Troy painfully lifted his arms so they were folded over his head. The heat from the bottles was almost unbearable, but he said nothing.

"It'll pull the pain out." The old man patted Troy on his bony shoulder, "You'll feel better."

"Oooh." Troy lowered his arms and clenched the sides of the blanket. Being on his stomach was excruciating. When the old man removed the hot packs, a rush of cold air converged on his back. The stiffness in his shoulder had lessened, but the pain from his injured knee was piercing. He pushed the blanket to the floor and twisted over onto his back.

"My knee's killing me."

"I don't doubt that."

"Do you have some aspirin?"

"I've already given you six." The old man walked to a small cubbyhole and pulled out a bottle of ibuprofen. "I guess a couple more wouldn't hurt."

Troy sat up, allowing his left leg to drop off the side of the small bed. He slumped forward, grabbing his right leg with both hands. He grit his teeth as he noticed the ribs poking out from his side.

"I'll remove that wrap if you'll wait a minute." The old man held two pills in his open hand. "Take these."

Troy took the pain medication, then lay back and watched as the old man unraveled the bandage from his leg. His eyes almost popped out of his head when he finally saw the engorged mass of flesh that once had been his knee. From his lower calf all the way to his inner thigh had turned a color somewhere between black and dark purple. It had swollen so much that his kneecap had completely disappeared.

"It looks a lot worse than it is."

"I hope the hell it does." Troy fell back onto the bed.

"Ya did what you were supposed to." The old man chuckled. "Ya kept it elevated and iced for forty-eight hours."

"Is that how long I was out there?"

"I have no idea how long you were under that tree. It wasn't long enough for Ethel to eat ya."

"Who's Ethel?"

"It's the meanest, most cantankerous mountain lion you could ever meet." The old man's face hardened. "Just ask Charlotte. She's finally realized that it's best to leave that crazy cat alone."

Troy took a deep breath. The pain had lessened. "What's your name?"

"Steve, Steve Dalbey."

"Steve." Troy felt his own unkempt beard.

"I ain't always lived on this mountain."

"My name's Troy."

"Well, Happy Thanksgiving, Troy."

"It's already Thanksgiving?" Troy's teeth chattered.

"According to my calendar it is."

"This month disappeared on me."

"Time has a way of doing that."

Troy turned his head to look at his host. Steve spread a blanket across the mantle above the fireplace, before sliding a log on an already raging fire under a large, black, cast-iron pot. He was in continual motion around the small cabin.

"Let's get you under some covers." Steve tossed a blanket in the air and let it float down onto Troy's cold body.

The heavy smell of smoke covering the blanket caused Troy to shorten his breath, but the tremendous warmth allowed him to lie back in repose. He could hear Steve grinding roots and herbs on the wooden table behind him, followed by the sound of water being poured into a plastic water bottle.

"I'm going to raise your leg up."

Troy grimaced as Steve slid a pillow under his injured knee.

"This is going to hurt for a while." Steve placed the hot water bottle on the blanket covering his knee. "It'll make you heal a lot faster."

"Oooh," moaned Troy.

Steve remained by Troy's side until the pain subsided.

For the first time since they met, Troy took notice of his host. His skin was like a piece of old barn wood covered by a bushy, white beard. The deep wrinkles flowing from his hazel eyes seemed to flow naturally into his full head of gray hair.

"Do you want one of these?" Steve held up the bottle of lithium. "I imagine this is something you need to be taking."

Steve held a capsule in front of Troy. Troy waited several seconds before opening his mouth and accepting the medication.

Medicine Bow, Texas

Grave adversity and misfortune were adversaries of Stanley Jones; his entire life had been spent trying to divert tragic situations from happening to the Blake family. He now found himself face to face with one of the most difficult tasks he had ever undertaken, a meeting with the elusive Mike King.

Stanley was putting himself at great personal risk in undertaking the task of meeting Mike King privately, with no police involvement. Sara had received two letters from Mike King inquiring about the whereabouts of Troy and making veiled threats to the safety of the people of Medicine Bow. The first letter was ignored, but when the second one arrived, both Sam and Stanley figured they best take it seriously. Stanley would find the identity of Mike King.

"Stanley," said Sam, "I don't want you to take any unnecessary chances with this scoundrel."

"That son of a bitch has been making threats toward us long enough. And don't worry, I've dealt with worse than the likes of Mike King."

"We best get Ed involved."

"He's already involved. I want to talk face to face with this rascal before the FBI boys get him." Stanley reached into his shirt pocket and pulled out a small, tin box containing several rows of aspirin, neatly arranged on wax paper.

"You just took one of those aspirins not more than twenty minutes ago," said Sam, glaring at his old friend. "Do you have a headache?"

"No. I just feel better when I have aspirin in my system."

"You need to get in and see the doc." Sam suspected Stanley wasn't being honest with him, or with himself.

"I will," said Stanley, placing the aspirin into his shirt pocket. "I'm going to Denver tonight and on to Minneapolis tomorrow night. I want to see everything firsthand before I meet with this character."

"Maybe we can meet you in Denver tomorrow."

"That would be fine." Stanley placed his hat on his head and put on a light tan jacket. "I should be there by seven o'clock, so let me know your plans.

Sam knew that Stanley would never consult with a doctor unless he pressured him into doing so. He poked his head into Jackie's office. "Jackie, I need you to set an appointment with Dr. Bill for Stanley."

"For when?" Jackie knew better than to speculate about whether or not Stanley would actually go to the appointment. She learned a long time ago to go along with the program when it dealt with personal matters concerning the two men.

"Set it up for a week from Friday. That should give Stanley enough time to take care of the business at hand." Sam hesitated. "How would ya like to go with Stanley to Denver?"

"Sure, if you want me to," Jackie looked at Sam suspiciously.

"Where's Sara?" Sam ignored her quizzical gaze.

"In her room," answered Jackie.

Sara was splitting time between her home in Medicine Bow and time at the ranch. She felt very comfortable in her room at the ranch, which was much larger than the one she shared with her family at Uncle Martin's house. She was curled on top of the comforter to her unused bed deep in thought when she heard the knock on her door.

"Come in."

"Sorry to bother your nap." Sam walked to the bed and placed his large hand on the shoulder of his pretty fiancée. He could see how exhausted she was.

"I'm not really sleeping, just thinking."

"Wanted to let you know that Stanley has some leads concerning Troy."

"Sam, I know I should be able to handle this situation with more strength." Sara buried her face in Sam's arm. "I keep telling myself that I could have helped him." She paused. "I was so mean to him the night he left."

"Well." Sam sat on the bed unsure if he should tell her that she was more than patient with handling her tetchy son. "We're doing everything possible to find him."

"Oh Sam. I want to save hope that he will show up on the doorstep, but deep down in my soul I feel something terrible has happened to him. It's awful reading all those articles about how they are going to find his body when the snow thaws in the mountains." Sara swung her legs over the edge of the bed.

"You can't believe everything you read. Stanley is taking the disappearance of Troy as a personal challenge. If anyone can find out where he's at, it's Stanley."

"I need to let Stanley know how much I appreciate his help."

"I'm kind of worried about him," stated Sam.

"What's wrong?"

"He just doesn't look right. He's as pale as a ghost."

"Will he go in for a checkup?" Sara brought her hand up and gently rubbed the back of Sam's neck.

"We set an appointment, but I doubt that he'll go."

"He's a very tough old man."

"That he is." Sam stood up and put his hands out to help her to her feet. "Rebecca seems to be doing better."

"She is, Delphia is making her exercise."

"Are you up for a little trip?" He placed his arm around her waist and walked her to the door. "I want you to go on a little ride with me."

"Where?"

"Back to Denver."

"Sam." She turned and placed a hand on his bicep. "I have so much to do before Christmas. And now, Rebecca is insisting on changing her prosthesis before the Christmas party."

"It's only for the day."

"Of course I'll go," Sara tipped her head, "actually, it sounds like a really great idea."

"Stanley and Jackie are on the way there tonight, and we can meet them in the morning."

"Sam," she moved her hand down to clutch his. "I want to get married,"

"So do I," Sam was caught off guard by the suddenness of the remark.

"I mean now." She moved in front of him and placed her hands on the side of his face. "We don't have to wait until Valentine's Day … until everything is perfect to get married."

"There are a lot of preparations for a wedding."

"Lola could marry us now, and we can have a large wedding in February."

"Sara, I don't want to cheat you." He hugged her tight enough to feel her breasts on his chest. "I want you to have a wedding to remember."

"How could you possibly think that you have ever cheated me?" Sara could hear his heart beating through his barrel chest. "We need to get along with our lives."

"Why don't you start making the preparations?" He could fill the warmth of her breath on his chest. "We should be doing it now anyway."

"Sam, we're both adults." Sara stepped back so she could look in his eyes. "What I'm getting at, is if you …" She lowered her voice. "We can start sleeping in the same bed."

There was no doubt that Sam wanted to; in fact, it took all the discipline he could muster not to throw her over his shoulder and take her straight to his room and make passionate love to her right then. But her vulnerability made the choice an easy one. He stepped back and took both her hands in his.

"Let's wait," he whispered.

"I'll start planning."

The fact that they had been sleeping in separate beds was something that he had thought about many times over. He needed to keep the passion he felt under control because it could easily cloud his judgment. Patience was a virtue that would be rewarded with time.

Denver, Colorado

Light snow fell onto the limousine as it drove toward metropolitan Denver from Denver International Airport. The slow-moving traffic gave Sam a better perspective as to why the bank robbers used the desolate area in their ploy to fool the police.

"Mike King's men used the isolated location of the airport as a diversion for the bank robbery." Stanley sat across the seat from Sara and Sam in the back of the limousine. "He is a smart old polecat; I'll give him that."

"It's about the same distance away as the Dallas-Fort Worth airport, but there ain't a damn thing on the other side of this airport." Sam looked toward the east.

"And Mike King and his thieves knew that the police would move them out to this remote area rather than have a bomb go off in the city," said Stanley.

"Why did they need Troy?" asked Sara.

"They used the boys to dig the tunnel, nothing more or nothing less." Stanley looked out the tinted window of the limousine. "This is the neighborhood ... and right over there is the house where they dug the tunnel."

"We drove right by here when we came to Denver before Rebecca's operation," said Sara. "We were within a few blocks of Troy."

"We sure were," said Sam. "We drove by here twice, coming from the airport and again going back."

The limousine stopped in front of the house on Pleasant Street.

"Nobody lives here; apparently all the dirt from the tunnel was dumped inside," said Stanley.

"Let's step out and take a look around," said Sam, following Stanley.

"Why did they leave all the dirt inside?" asked Sara, walking up the front walk toward the house.

"I suppose they didn't want to rouse the neighbors' suspicion," said Stanley.

"All the windows are boarded up." Sara tried to peek through the front window.

"They didn't want the police to be able to look inside when they arrived with the hostages and money. It gave them time to make their way out the tunnel." Stanley walked to the gate at the privacy fence by the side of the house and pulled on the handle. "They locked this damn gate. I want to show y'all the house that the three boys escaped out of. You can see the roof if you stand back. It's the blue house with the white shingles."

Sam stood by silently, watching Sara stand with her right hand covering her mouth as she absorbed everything. He realized the therapeutic value of her seeing firsthand the house and location of Troy's dilemma. The neighborhood was one common to thousands of people, there was nothing special or extraordinary about it, and he hoped that allowing Sara to see the commonality of the area would allow her to hedge her fears.

"Jackie's meeting with a young lady who thought she may have met Troy at a night spot the night before the robbery." Stanley waited patiently as Sara stared at the house. "We're supposed to meet her in about an hour for an early lunch."

"Do you think it was Troy she met?" Sara walked toward the limousine.

"I don't know. But we are trying to be meticulous as possible in following the leads. She called the police to report she had encountered Troy." Stanley opened the door to the limousine, allowing Sam and Sara to enter. "The security men at the club identified a picture of Troy. They said he was thrown out because he stood on top of a table to give a toast. Apparently, he was pretty ornery."

***

Jackie was so engrossed in conversation with Rosie that she didn't notice Stanley, Sam, and Sara enter the Village Inn restaurant. She had been extracting information from the cordial young lady for more than thirty minutes, and she was happy to have had the time for the girl talk.

Rosie was shy at first, but she talked more discretely over the second cup of coffee about her chance meeting with Troy. She was unsure as to the motive of the powerful Texas group in having invited her to the late breakfast. She was tickled by the appearance of Sam and Stanley, both dressed in western wear sporting white cowboy hats as they moved toward the table.

"Hello," said Sara, noticing Rosie looking at her.

"Hi," said Rosie, fidgeting slightly in her chair.

"Y'all been here long?" asked Sam, holding his hand out to allow Sara access to the chair next to Rosie.

"Quite a while. We've had a nice talk," said Jackie, moving her purse for Stanley to sit next to her. "Rosie, this is Troy's mother Sara, Sam Blake, and Stanley Jones."

"Nice to meet you," said Sam.

"My pleasure to meet you, ma'am."

"Hello," said Rosie, feeling uneasy as she moved slightly to the side allowing Sara access to the chair next to her.

"Rosie was just telling me about the night she had with Troy at a local nightclub," said Jackie.

"Did you meet Troy only once?" asked Sara, wishing she were sitting across from the young lady so she could look her in the face.

"Yes," said Rosie, turning slightly toward Sara. "The night before the robbery."

"How did you meet?" asked Sara.

"He was looking at my friend Mary, and he came by the table where we were sitting and I asked him to sit down," said Rosie. "I thought he was very handsome."

"Did you talk long?" Sara smiled.

"Yes," Rosie was feeling a little nauseous.

"Did he indicate anything at all about what he was planning to do?" asked Sara.

"No," said Rosie, "I told the police everything."

"Why did they throw him out of the club?" asked Stanley.

"He was being loud." The queasiness in her stomach was increasing. "He was standing on a table giving me a toast."

A tall waitress, with her dark hair pulled back in a bun, distributed menus around the table. "What can I get you to drink?" she said.

"Coffee," said Sara.

"Coffee," said Sam.

"Yep," said Stanley.

"Just more water," said Rosie. "Excuse me."

She stood and quickly walked to the restroom.

"Did you find out anything?" asked Sam, feeling secure in his decision to have Jackie fly to Denver and talk with Rosie.

"Plenty," said Jackie. "This girl fell head over heels for Troy."

"They were only together for a few hours," said Sara.

"A lot happened in those few hours," said Jackie, looking over her shoulder to make sure Rosie was still in the restroom. "She went to the club to meet a friend and have one drink, but when she met Troy she knew she wanted to pursue him, so she went home and cleaned up. When she returned, Troy was pretty much out of control and had infuriated one of the waitresses. Troy was smitten by her new appearance and began to tell everybody in the bar how much he adored her. He was spending money like crazy, but the bouncers finally had enough of him and threw him out."

"Troy wasn't taking his medication," stated Sara.

"He was definitely manic at the club," said Jackie. "Rosie followed him to the parking lot and gave him a ride."

"Back to the house in Aurora?" asked Sara.

"No, they parked and waited for a cab," said Jackie. "Troy wouldn't allow her to go anywhere near the house. As they waited, he became very tired and she had a hard time getting him into the cab."

"That sounds like he was physically tired," said Sara. "He wouldn't come down from his manic state without having taken his medication for at least a week. If he was in a depressed state, he wouldn't have acted the way he did at the club."

"Something else," whispered Jackie, leaning over the table. "I think they might have been intimate."

"Did she say that?" gasped Sara.

"Not in so many words," said Jackie, sitting back in her chair.

"Hell, ya can't blame him for going after that pretty young gal," said Stanley, tipping his hat back on his head. "After seeing that house full of dirt and listening to this story, I was startin' to worry that Troy would rather dig than make love."

Sam laughed at his old friend before noticing the glare from Sara.

"Here she comes," said Sara, forcing a smile.

"Sorry," said Rosie, sitting next to Sara.

"Are you all right?" asked Sara.

"I'm okay."

"Why don't we order?" Sara opened a menu. "Maybe you just need some food."

"Mrs. Young," said Rosie, using a napkin to daub her flushed cheek. "Is Troy's sister recovering from her surgery?"

"Yes, she's doing fine." Sara leaned forward to better look into Rose's face. "How did you know about the operation?"

"I've read everything there is to read about Troy and the robbery."

"Have you talked to Troy since that night?" Sara wondered if she might know more than she was indicating.

"No," said Rosie. "But I haven't stopped thinking about him. Not even once."

"You really like him, don't you?" Sara placed the opened menu onto the table.

"I don't know him well enough to know the answer to that question."

As Sara looked at Rosie's profile, she realized that the young lady was older than she had initially thought. She also noticed what could only be described as a glow coming from her pretty pink face.

The waitress took the food orders, giving Sara a chance to think of more questions to ask Rosie. She could see why Troy was enamored by the young lady; not only was she beautiful, but she also had a very pleasant, quiet demeanor.

"Rosie, do you think Troy would try and get back in touch with you?" asked Sara, expecting Rosie to say no.

"I thought he might." Rosie placed her hand on her stomach. "I did give him my telephone number."

"Here, take a drink of water." Sara placed her hand on Rosie's shoulder and offered her the glass of water.

"Thank you," said Rosie, taking the glass.

"Would you like us to give you a ride home?" Sara felt a tremendous sense of compassion toward the young girl.

"I have my car outside."

"But are you feeling well enough to drive?" asked Sara, rubbing gently on her shoulder. "You must be coming down with the flu."

"Mrs. Young," Rosie sniffled as she turned to face Sara, "I'm pregnant."

"Oh," said Sara, not wanting to discuss something so personal.

"I'm not sure, but I think I am."

"You should see a doctor, honey," said Sara, placing her hand on Rosie's small hand. "I'm so sorry we bothered you today."

Jackie was about to remind Sara that Troy might have had sex with Rosie only a few weeks prior. But she realized it wasn't necessary when she saw the expression on Sara's face change from one of sympathy to one of shock as she realized it was her grandchild they were discussing.

"If I'm pregnant," said Rosie, looking directly at Sara, "it's Troy's baby, without any doubt whatsoever. It is Troy's baby."

Medicine Bow, Texas

Rebecca cherished Christmas. She loved it so much that even with her much changed life she couldn't focus on anything but the glitter and lights of the holiday. Having the Christmas Eve celebration at the Blake ranch made the holy day even more exceptional. The entire week prior to the celebration was reminiscent of five years earlier when the Youngs had spent Christmas at the large ranch where the anticipation was rewarded with the best Christmas of her life.

She had spent several days at the ranch after her surgery, so the fascination with the ritzy surroundings was dulled, but the bright lights that concealed all the buildings on the property were just as glorious as the first time she saw them. The oak trees lining the long driveway entering the ranch were covered with sparkling red lights that illuminated the area even in the midmorning sun. And this year Sam and Sara were welcoming all the people from Medicine Bow.

Rebecca had become so familiar with the ranch house that she felt as much a hostess as a guest in greeting the mass of visitors to Sam's lavish home. She would have been completely content with watching the people interact while sitting alone on the white leather couch in the oversized living room turned into a ballroom, had it not been for one thing. That was Sam's pilot Jerry. She noticed the handsome aviator the second he stepped into the foyer. She watched him until he made eye contact with her through the crowd of people, then she dropped her eyes. She ran her manicured fingers along the crease of her tan slacks, smoothing the fabric. The material looked natural covering both legs. She casually looked up and out of the corner of her eye, noticing Jerry make his way amongst the throng toward her.

"Hi," Jerry removed his nylon flight jacket. "Do you mind if I sit here?"

"No," Rebecca wanted to kick herself for speaking so delicately.

"How are you doing?" He set the jacket by his side and turned his beefy legs, pointing his knees toward her.

"Very well." She couldn't help but glance at his muscular arms and then up at the tight-fitting white polo shirt stretched over his chest adorning his deeply tanned face.

Whilst Rebecca was being somewhat judicious in her adulation of Jerry, his eyes were brazenly fixed directly on her chiseled nose.

"I brought you something," He handed her a small package.

"Did you have my name?"

"No, I have Delphia."

"We were only supposed to bring a gift for one person."

"I cheated," he held the package in front of her. "Come on, take it."

Rebecca rolled her eyes to the side, but nevertheless took the gift and slowly unwrapped it. "They're wonderful." She held two diamond earrings shaped like butterflies in the palm of her hand.

"Sam said you liked butterflies. I chose red because I thought the yellow ones might clash with your hair."

"I like them a lot." By instinct she opened her arms to offer him a hug.

Jerry accepted the opportunity. He moved the side of his face along her cheekbone, pushing her hair back, leaving his mouth next to her ear. He pulled his arms tight around her fragile body.

Rebecca could feel his warm breath on her ear. She rubbed his hard lower back.

He relinquished the hug. "I had them before you went into the hospital, but I never had the opportunity to give them to you."

"That's very nice." She could still feel the warmth of him on her chest.

"I found them at a shop in downtown Denver." Jerry flashed a smile, "The first time we met."

"You're so lucky. I mean, getting to fly all over the country."

"Yeah, it is a terrific job."

He was about to ask Rebecca if she wanted to go flying with him sometime when Delphia jumped on the couch next to him.

"You have my name," Delphia put a stranglehold on his left arm.

"Now how do you know that?" He lifted her with his powerful arm and pulled her into a chokehold on his lap.

"There's a list by the Christmas tree." She pulled out of his grasp and stood in front of him. "What did ya get me?"

"I'm not going to tell."

"Jesse said I'm lucky that you got me because you'll buy me something nice."

"Oh Delphia," Rebecca shook her head.

"Uncle Martin got Jesse," whispered Delphia.

"I'm sure Uncle Martin will get him something good." Rebecca placed her hands on her lap.

"Not as nice as good ole Jerry got me." Delphia grabbed hold of his arm again.

"I'll tell you what I got you." He winked at Rebecca as Delphia let go of his arm. "I whittled you a whistle."

"Ya did."

"Yep. It doesn't whistle very loud, but I made it with my own hands."

Delphia stared at him for a moment, and when he didn't laugh, she said, "Ma says that something made by someone is worth more than something bought." She hung her head. "I think Uncle Martin whittled Jesse something too."

"Well, Delphia, aren't you going to thank Jerry?" Rebecca winked back at Jerry.

"Y'all are foolin' me, aren't ya?" Delphia's smile was so big that you could see the red gums above her front teeth. "Ya are, aren't ya?"

"Yes, we are." Rebecca held her hand out to the small girl. "But it's not polite to ask what someone got you for Christmas."

"I hope you get something good for Christmas, Rebecca." She moved to Rebecca's side, "You deserve it."

"Look what Jerry gave me," Rebecca showed Delphia the earrings.

"Them are beautiful." Delphia ogled the earrings before standing and placing her hands on her sides. She stared spitefully at Jerry through her deep, dark eyes.

"I know. I know. I have your name." Jerry laughed at the way she was bending her neck to stare him down. "But I got those for Rebecca before I knew I had your name."

"Boy oh boy, I sure hope I get something as good as them earrings."

"Come on, Delphia, don't make Jerry feel bad."

"I'm just kiddin' you, Jerry." Delphia stared at the amused pilot before leaning over and whispering in Rebecca's ear, "Jerry shore is handsome."

Rebecca tensed.

"Is he your boyfriend?"

"Please, Delphia," Rebecca gave her a nasty look. "Why don't you go mingle?"

***

Sara wasn't nearly as excited as Rebecca about the Christmas Eve party. It wasn't that long ago she was pondering the idea of becoming a mother for the fourth time, but now she couldn't keep her mind off the news that she was going to become a grandmother. Even in his absence Troy brought turmoil to her life.

It had been a long week with the preparation for the dinner and the uncertainty of knowing whether or not Rosie was a gold digger, or the mother of her unborn grandchild. The stress was enough to wear out most anyone.

Again, Sam handled the problems with ease. He made it clear to Rosie that the baby would be checked for paternity, and it was a waste of time for her to try and fool anyone. And he, along with help from Dr. Meersman, was able to find Rebecca a leg, albeit one useless to walk on, that she could wear to the party.

It was hard to be despondent among the jovial crowd of people. Sam, Manuel, Stanley, and Ted were outside smoking cigars and laughing at the top of their lungs. Uncle Martin and Square Shoulders were entertaining a small group of people next to the Christmas tree. Everyone was cleaned up and primed to have fun. And, of course, Rebecca looked beautiful conversing with Jerry.

Chapter Six

Rocky Mountains, Colorado

Troy had never felt so good in his entire life. Over the past month he had been anything but babied by Steve. He was allowed two days of being bedridden before his host had him up and hauling water. As he mended, his chores increased to shoveling snow and chopping wood. His arms were stronger than they had ever been, and each day his knee felt a little better, allowing him to wander farther away from the cabin.

"Remember I will be leaving to visit my son in Phoenix tomorrow," stated Steve. "If you want to come along, you need to have everything packed and ready to go."

"I reckon I will be catching a ride with you, at least partway," said Troy. "I need to go up the mountain and get the rest of my stuff."

"Better pack everything today. We'll be leaving early in the morning." Steve held his twenty-gauge shotgun in his right hand. "You better take this with you if you're going up that mountain."

"I'll be fine."

"I'm not kidding about that cat," Steve set the gun by the front door, "she will attack you."

"If that ole cat wanted to eat me for lunch, it would have done it several days ago." Nevertheless, Troy picked up the shotgun. "I'm just goin' up to pick up the rest of my stuff."

"I thought you were there yesterday?" Steve pulled on his long beard.

"I was." Troy opened the door, allowing the frigid air inside. He didn't want to say more, he just needed to make sure he knew exactly where he was leaving his belongings.

Steve watched Troy, using his shotgun as a crutch, limp through the heavy snow. "Don't shoot yourself."

Troy just waved over the top of his head.

"Oh yeah. I forgot to tell ya. It's Christmas." Troy turned and looked at the old man standing in the log cabin with smoke billowing from the chimney. "It is?"

"Yep."

He was looking at a living Christmas card with the sunlight sparkling on the snow and the bearded old man perched in the backdrop. "Merry Christmas."

"Merry Christmas," Steve yelled back. He watched Troy until he disappeared into the woods.

The early morning cold caused crystals to form in the air, making it seem overcast even though the sun was shining. Troy made his way up the mountain in the cold haze, taking care not to shake the powdered snow from the low-hanging branches of the pine trees as he moved through the woods. Climbing the mountain was hard work. His lungs were burning as he trudged through the knee-deep snow. Approaching the outer edge of the trees, he could see the outcropping of rocks about three hundred yards up the steep slope. He stopped to rest, wishing he had brought his snowshoes. His knee ached, causing him to stop and rest every few steps. As he steadied himself on the steep slope, he felt a sudden surge of apprehension shoot through his body. It wasn't the pain or fatigue that was causing his uneasiness, because he could always make his way down the mountain to the cabin; it was a strange sensation that he was being watched. He carried the gun in both hands as he began making his way up the mountain through the deep snow. He pushed on until he reached the base of the rock formation he used as a reference point. He relaxed for a moment to look at the beautiful valley below him. A slight noise caused him to turn. He held the shotgun to his chest with both hands as he looked up and saw the large head of the cat blending into the rocks as it perched on a boulder about twenty feet above him.

Troy fell backwards into a snowdrift, landing softly on the seat of his pants. The lion sat patiently, looking at the startled man through slanted eyes as though he were asking, "What's wrong with you, Troy?"

Troy kept his eyes fixed on the cat as he sat in the snow, slowly pointing the shotgun upward. Large popcorn-sized flakes of snow fell from the sky, making it more difficult to keep his eyes on the dangerous cat above. He reached up and brushed the heavy snow from his eyes, causing the cat to snarl and show her teeth, as though she took the movement as an undisciplined sign of weakness.

Troy sucked in a breath of air through his nose, feeling the hair on both sides of his nostrils freeze as he filled his lungs with the cold air. He stared upwards at the beast, allowing the snow to accumulate on the whiskers of his face. The animal hunched her back and placed her front paws on the edge of the boulder, yet she remained balanced on the rock watching the snow consume her prey.

Troy finally had enough of the situation and stood up and shook the snow off his shoulders and head. As he looked up, the cat recoiled, sitting above him as if she were a patron watching a live play from the balcony.

"Well, go ahead." Troy held the shotgun in his left hand and placed his right arm straight out from his side. "My mother told me never to play with my food, and I'll be damned if I'll let you play with me before having me for dinner."

The cat growled, then disappeared.

Troy sat for a moment with the heavy fog from his breath filling the air as he looked in all directions, making sure the cat was not sneaking up on him. He moved cautiously around the rocks, with his head on a swivel and his finger on the trigger of the shotgun. He could see the sled directly in front of him, causing him to momentarily lose focus on the dangerous situation. As he stepped through the deep snow, out of the corner of his right eye he caught sight of the cat, but this time it was much larger and only about ten feet away. Troy turned and aimed the dark barrel of the shotgun at the cat. But he didn't fire. They stared at each other, looking close enough to see the moisture forming ice on the sides of their eyes.

"I don't want to shoot you." Troy held the sight on the cat's large head. "I just want to get my stuff, and I'll leave you alone."

The heavy breath of the mountain lion fell on the powdered snow in front of her as she sat twisting her neck and contemplating her options.

Troy held the shotgun to his shoulder with his right hand and made a snowball with his left hand. The powdered snow crumbled at first, but eventually his gloved hand gave warmth to melt the snow enough to make a snowball. He brought the snowball up and threw it with his left hand directly into the face of the cat, causing her to hunch her shoulders and growl loudly.

"Please, just go and leave me alone," Troy yelled, putting his left hand back up to steady the shotgun.

The cat turned her shoulders and shot off into the forest with such grace and speed that Troy lowered the gun and sat back into the heavy snow in disbelief. His heart was beating rapidly.

Washington State

Agent Dodd forwarded the news to Stanley that the search for Troy in the Colorado Mountains had been suspended. They hadn't found one fingerprint or any evidence concerning Troy in the Lockett cabin. He also stated that they had no reason to pursue Mike King regarding the crimes committed at the farmhouse in Amarillo or the robbery in Colorado. As far as they could tell, Mike King could be anyone. It was just a name.

A deserted area at the base of Mount Rainier would have been one of the last places Stanley would have suspected his destination would be on this dreary afternoon.

He drove cautiously through the wooded area in his rented Cadillac Seville, looking diligently for the road to cross over a small stream. He was to make a right-hand turn on an even smaller road when he traversed the stream. There, in a grassy meadow, he was to wait until he was contacted by the person who would transport him to the meeting.

As Stanley came to the stream, he reached for his phone and began punching in numbers, keeping the phone between his legs below the steering wheel. He wanted to be doubly sure his back was being covered. He was very anxious about meeting the man with as ruthless a reputation as any he had ever come across. He reasoned that the meeting would be one of obtaining information about Troy and nothing else. He wasn't interested in bringing justice to Mike King; as far as he could tell the authorities didn't have anything concrete to charge him with anyway. There was no reason to create a conflict with the disturbed man if it wasn't absolutely necessary.

"Jerry," said Stanley, looking straight ahead.

"Yes."

"Do you know where I'm at?"

"Yes," cracked Jerry. "Do you know where you're at?"

"Very funny," said Stanley, identifying the small road he was to turn onto. "Just keep close."

"I won't lose ya," said Jerry.

Stanley pulled to the side of the narrow gravel road, looking in all directions to see if he could see a sign of anybody at all. The area seemed completely uninhabited. He opened the car door and stepped out, checking his watch. He was fifteen minutes early. He waited patiently, noticing how breathtaking the view of Mount Rainier was, towering over the meadow. He finally heard the muffled sound of a small engine approaching from the woods in the distance. Two four-wheelers appeared at the end of the small gravel road and came quickly toward him. The helmeted drivers drove the contraptions onto the grass off the road and turned around in front of Stanley's car.

"Can you drive one of these?" asked the first driver, obviously a woman.

"I reckon I can," said Stanley. "I'd rather follow you in my car."

"You can't get where we're going in a car," said the woman, allowing the other driver to climb onto the back of her vehicle.

Stanley sat onto the seat of the four-wheeler and fidgeted with the controls. He revved the motor indicating to his guide that he was ready to proceed. He followed them as they drove through the meadow and into the woods, where they made a turn up a high embankment onto a plateau overlooking the area he had just come from. His car appeared as a tiny speck a couple miles away.

The driver of the four-wheeler allowed her passenger to climb off before stepping to the ground and taking her helmet off. Stanley remained seated, feeling a little exhilarated from the ride to the top of the foothill.

"Mr. Jones," the woman moved toward Stanley, "I'm Debe."

"Pleased to meet you, ma'am," said Stanley, rubbing his knee. "You can call me Stanley."

"Okay," said Debe, moving to Stanley's side. "First I have to check you for weapons. Is that okay?"

"It would be my pleasure to have you frisk me," said Stanley, holding his arms to his side as she ran her hands along the outside of his jacket and then along the inside of his legs.

"Careful, young lady," Stanley spread his legs wider, "you might find more than you bargained for."

His young escort only smiled, "Follow me."

Stanley followed Debe around a cropping of high rocks where they came to a large flat area with a man standing inside the opening of a large tent. Stanley proceeded toward the tent as Debe slowly moved to the far side of the campsite.

"Mr. King," said Stanley.

"Follow me," said the man, moving back into the tent.

Stanley was surprised at the amount of room inside. The high roof and extravagant furnishings was something he would have expected to find if he was visiting a sheik in ancient Persia, but not at the base of Mount Rainier. He was impressed, but wished he had some way of verifying that the man he was meeting with was actually Mike King.

"Wait there," said the man he had followed into the room, pointing toward a cushioned chair.

Stanley waited no more than a minute before a man, with his face covered with a ski mask, stepped into the room from a door in the back.

"Mr. Jones," he said. "I understand you wish to talk with me."

"Yes sir, if you're Mike King, I do," said Stanley.

"I'm Mike King." The man took a drink of water, not bothering to present Stanley with any refreshment. "So talk."

"What do y'all know about the whereabouts of Troy Young?" asked Stanley.

"Nothing," he took another drink.

"Do you know if he's dead or alive?"

"I think he's alive," said Mike King, placing his glass onto a coffee table.

"Why do you think he's alive?" asked Stanley.

"I have my sources, very reliable sources."

"Have y'all seen him?"

"No," said Mike King, placing his hand to the side of his head. "Not yet."

"Did those boys have anything more to do with the robbery than digging the tunnel?" asked Stanley.

"I don't know anything about a robbery."

"Bullshit," said Stanley, knowing it was time to get down to business. "You can be rude to me or anything else, but don't lie to me. I know you were the one who planned that robbery and so do the authorities."

"Well, Mr. Jones,' Mike King took a deep breath, "it seems you think you know all there is to know about me."

Stanley remained quiet, hoping the lout would give him some information he could rely on.

"I'm not the only one who would like to have a conversation with Mr. Young. If he is alive, and I'm confident he is, he will have to answer to Vinny Barrows and his colleagues."

"Is Vinny Barrows the person who robbed the bank?"

"I think Mr. Young might be sitting on a lot of money," said Mike King, ignoring Stanley's question. "A lot of money that isn't his."

"Whose money is it?"

"Mine and Vinny Barrows'."

"Why are you telling me this?" asked Stanley.

"I figure Troy will eventually call home," said Mike King. "When he does, it would certainly be to your benefit to have him contact me in reference to the money."

"If you will give me time to find Troy, without interference from you or Mr. Barrows, I will make sure you receive the money," said Stanley.

"I will make you that guarantee," said Mike King. "I will give you ten days to find him, but if we don't have the money by then, I will find him and make him wish he had died with his two friends."

"I'll hold you to your guarantee," said Stanley, wishing he could pull the ski mask off his arrogant host's head and shove it down his throat. "It would be a grave mistake for you to harm that boy in any way, so no matter what happens in the next ten days, you need to think of a different option in handling the situation."

"You know, I don't much like old men like you." Mike King threw his water bottle hard against the side of the tent. "So Stanley, don't be belligerent with me."

"Listen, you cheap hood," said Stanley, standing up. "You best leave that boy be."

"Sit down, Mr. Jones."

"I'm finished here," said Stanley.

"Sit down!" Mike King hit the coffee table, causing the glass to fly across the room. "You'll leave when I say you'll leave."

Stanley sat down.

"I told you not to be belligerent with me," said Mike King, standing up and pushing his chair onto its side. "I knew that boy was going to be a problem the first time I saw him, but let me tell you something, I know all about the little town of Medicine Bow, Texas, and I'll tell you, if I don't get my money back, the people of that little town will pay."

Stanley could hear several people moving outside of the tent.

"Do you understand?" asked Mike King.

"I do understand," said Stanley, noticing Mike King's head shaking uncontrollably.

"Now get your fat ass out of here before I bury you in that volcano outside, along with that fool who has been following you."

Stanley stood up and walked out the tent. Debe was waiting for him as he exited, already on the four-wheeler. She motioned for him to hop on the back of her machine. She drove quickly off the mountain with Stanley balancing himself with his hands on her back.

After Stanley stepped off the four-wheeler, Debe reached out to shake his hand. He hesitated for a moment before extending his hand. He was shocked when she pushed a small piece of paper into his palm. Before he could say a word, she sped off in a roar.

He nonchalantly sat down in his car and retrieved his cell phone.

"Dammit, Jerry, they saw ya out there," said Stanley into his phone.

"I don't think anybody saw me," replied Jerry.

"He just threatened to throw both our asses into the volcano."

"Bill and Clay would have stopped him," said Jerry. "At least they would have stopped him from throwing my ass into the volcano."

"You weren't alone?"

"No."

"Well, whoever they saw should have hid better." Stanley closed his phone and started the engine to the car. He drove to the pavement and pulled to the side of the highway. He was confident that he was not being followed. He unfolded the piece of paper and read: Jack Leclair. Vancouver Canada.

Medicine Bow

"I can't believe Sam wants to have a psychiatrist talk with us." Lola smoothed the final wave of fudge frosting onto the top of one of her delicious angle food cakes.

"That's what he told me last night," said Sara. "He left an open invitation to anyone in town that wants to come."

"Why would he do such a thing?"

"The more he's studied about bipolar disorder, the more he sympathizes with Troy." Sara sat down at the kitchen table. "He wants to help everyone understand why Troy caused so many problems over the years."

"But, a psychiatrist?" Lola had very little respect for the science of psychology.

"I think Sam is trying to help me cope with not knowing the whereabouts of Troy." Sara felt a twinge of guilt. "It's a positive way of saying that Troy is alive and when he comes back we will all better understand him."

"We do need to stay positive."

"That's so hard to do." Sara sighed.

"There's something deep in my soul that tells me he's still alive."

"Oh Lola, I try … when he missed Christmas, it was about all I could take. It is the one time of the year that he always enjoyed." She stood up and walked to the sink.

"There has to be a reason why he hasn't called ya." Lola rubbed a finger around the rim of the frosting bowl and placed it in her mouth. "That sickness must have him in its grip."

"I feel so terrible about the way I treated him before he left."

"There is not a thing in the world you can do about that now."

"That's true." Sara looked out the kitchen window. "You better hide the cake. Here comes Rebecca and Delphia with Jesse right behind them."

"It's a blessing that Rebecca is taking so much interest in helping Delphia practice running. Coaching children is that girl's calling." Lola placed a towel over the cake.

"They both help each other." Sara walked past Lola to the living room and opened the screen door. "Well, you three seem to be all smiles today."

"We were wondering if it would be all right to take the car to town this afternoon?" asked Rebecca. She walked into the kitchen with the help of her crutches.

"I suppose," said Sara, unsure if Rebecca was ready to drive to Dallas.

"Is that cake I smell?" asked Delphia.

"Don't even think about touching this cake." Lola raised the spatula up into a threatening position.

"Don't you be eating a bunch of that cake, girl, you're in training," said Rebecca.

"I'm hungry enough to eat the whole cake," said Jesse, following Delphia into the kitchen.

"Ya best leave it alone. I promised Uncle Martin and Tom I would bake them this cake for the carpentry work they did on our front door," said Lola.

"Can I borrow twenty dollars?" asked Delphia. "I need it for the movie."

"Have ya already spent yore Christmas money?"

"Yeah." Delphia gave her mother a sad look. "But I've been doing so good in school. I think I deserve a little reward."

"I need some too," said Jesse.

"You children are going ta drive me ta the poor house," said Lola, reaching for her purse.

"Are you sure you can drive all the way to Dallas?" Sara was cautious in the tone she used to ask the question.

"Of course I can," Rebecca shook her head in mock surprise that her mother would even ask the question. "I have no problem driving an automatic."

"What time is the movie you plan to see?" Sara wasn't about to argue with her daughter. In fact, she was happy to see Rebecca having the confidence to go out on her own.

"Two thirty," said Delphia.

"I'll treat you guys to lunch." Sara handed Rebecca two twenty-dollar bills. Rebecca's appetite hadn't returned since the operation, and she knew that giving her the money was a passive way to tell her to eat.

"Hello," Drew Fudderman knocked hard on the front door.

"Come in, Drew," Sara yelled from the kitchen.

"How doin'?" Drew placed a large basket on the table. The top of the basket was covered with a white cloth, but the smell of ham was palpably noticeable.

"What in the world do ya have there, boy?" asked Lola.

"I bwought y'all a ham." Drew yanked the towel off the basket displaying a beautiful brown ham.

"That's very nice of you, Drew," said Sara.

"It's kind of an advatisement fo me and Daddy's new company."

"You're starting a new company?" asked Sara.

"Fudderman Poak," Drew puffed out his chest. "Y'all can buy all the bacon, chops, and ham ya need at the Fudderman pig faum hea in Medicine Bow."

"What's the name of your company?" asked Rebecca.

"Fudderman Poak," answered Drew with a large smile on his face.

"How come you can pronounce the r's in Fudderman?" asked Rebecca.

"My ma made me say my name ova and ova again when I was little. I have always been able to say Drew Fudderman."

"If you can pronounce the r's in your name, then you can pronounce them in other words too." Rebecca sat down in a chair at the kitchen table.

"I don't know," Drew looked embarrassed.

"We'll do it for one hour every Sunday after church." Rebecca had no intention of embarrassing Drew, but she knew she could help him.

"Oh. I weckon."

"That's reckon, Drew." Delphia opened her mouth and shoved her tongue to the top of her mouth. "Rrrrrrreckon."

"Delphia." Lola gave her daughter a threatening look. "If you want to go to the movie this afternoon, you better mind your manners."

"Just tryin' to help, Ma." Delphia smiled at her mother.

"The first word we can work on is pork, so you will be able to pronounce your company's name," said Rebecca.

"Okay, I'll meet ya Sunday." Drew started to walk to the door. "I have to go out to Sam's wanch to take him some chops."

"Thank you for the ham," said Sara, watching Drew exit out the door.

North Las Vegas, Nevada

Bright light city could take any man's money, but the bedraggled young man, carrying a small bag of groceries, couldn't care less about the neon lights or the games of chance as he blended into the hodgepodge of miserable souls wandering aimlessly among the pawn shops and other dilapidated businesses of North Las Vegas. He scratched his dirty beard and ran his hand over his cowlicked hair as he opened the door to the Osage apartment building and made his way up the steep steps to room 223.

His stomach was too empty to growl as he placed the bag of groceries on a diminutive table. He peeled a green banana and began to eat, something he hadn't done in over three days. He heard a knock on the door as he swallowed a piece of the small, hard fruit.

"Frankie, come on, man, open up."

"What is it?" He opened the door only a couple of inches and peeked out.

"Hey, man, I'm having a little party in my room, and I was hoping you could livin' it up a little." The smell of whiskey trickled into the room through the half-opened door.

"I was just about ready to eat."

"Hell, I have a big bag of shrimp to cook. Come on now, we've been neighbors for a month, and I won't take no for an answer."

"I reckon I can come by for a bit." He was somewhat surprised at how much time had escaped him.

The inside of his neighbor's apartment smelled like a mixture of vegetable soup, fried shrimp, and cigarette smoke. It was impossible to tell if the stench was coming from the large pot-faced man sitting on the torn sofa or possibly the haggard-looking woman in the kitchen with the silly grin and glazed eyes. She was waving at him like a little baby who had just learned to wave bye-bye.

"This here is Frank," said his host to the man on the sofa. "This is my best friend Louis."

"How are ya?" What else could he say; he didn't even know the name of his host.

"Glad to meet you, man. Charley told me about you spotting him a hundred last week," said Louis.

"This here's my old lady, Jennifer." Charley placed his arm around the skinny waist of the lady at the kitchen door. "Ain't she pretty?"

"Ole goll." Jennifer began to stagger back and forth like a flagpole in a heavy wind.

"Proud to meet you, ma'am." The disheveled appearance of his three hosts should lend him to feel at ease with his own appearance, yet he was self-conscious of his scruffy beard and personal hygiene. He smelled.

"You men sit down and talk about whatever it is men talk about, and I'll finish making the food." Jennifer lit a cigarette and stared blankly at the boiling water in a large pot on the stove.

"Go ahead and sit in the easy chair, Frankie." Charley pointed toward a recliner with several tears in the fabric. "I'll grab some beers."

"Man, that loan made a big impression on Charley. Now days it's hard to find someone who cares enough about someone else to loan them money. We needed the business too. Most of the people we fix with social security cards are here illegally." Louis accepted a can of beer from Charley. "That was damn nice of you."

"It was no big deal." He didn't remember loaning the money to Charley.

"Man, you changed my outlook toward the world." Charley handed a can of beer to his new friend.

"He told everybody down at the shop about your kindness." Louis guzzled his beer.

"Where y'all work?" Troy opened his beer.

"Besides our little sideline, we bust tires at the Bellaire Service Center," said Charley with a trace of pride in his voice. "What do you do?"

"I'm a toastmaster." He surprised himself at how quick he answered the question.

"A toastmaster." Charley sat down on the edge of the sofa and looked at his guest as though he knew exactly what he was talking about. "Man, that would be an awesome job."

"What does a toastmaster do?" asked Louis, smashing his beer can in his large, grease-covered hands.

"I'm goin' to weddings and parties … uh … to make up toasts for folks on special occasions."

"People pay you to do that?" Louis looked at Troy with a confused look on his homely face.

"Oh hell yes." Charley seemed to know more about the occupation of a toastmaster than his guest. "People will pay big bucks for a good toastmaster."

"I just never heard of anyone doing that for a living." Louis stared at his smashed beer can.

"I bet you're a damn good toastmaster." Charley drank the last of his beer. "Did you ever think about becoming a eulogizer? Ya know, along with being a toastmaster."

"I don't believe I've ever heard of a eulogizer," said Troy.

"Me either." Louis looked more confused than ever.

"You know, when someone dies they always need someone to say nice things about them at their funeral," said Charley with a sparkle in his eyes.

"I think I need me another beer." Louis lifted his heavy frame from the sofa. "I ain't never heard of either of those occupations. Besides, who in their right mind would want a stranger to say nice things about them at their funeral?"

"It's just an idea," said Charley.

"A toastmaster is a positive person, you know, someone who brings out the best and brightest outlook for the future of the people they toast. I think a toastmaster might be the opposite of a eulogizer," said Troy, noticing Jennifer waving her arms.

"It's time to eat." Jennifer placed a large plate of breaded shrimp at the center of a piece of plywood situated on top of two truck tires. "Let me get the bowls."

Troy took his seat on a metal folding chair between Charley and Louis as Jennifer placed three bowls and a bottle of ketchup on the makeshift table. He was surprised that she had no soup to serve, only a plate full of overly cooked breaded shrimp. He wondered why she had the large pot of boiling water on the stove.

"I like a little ketchup with my shrimp." Charley shook the half-full bottle of ketchup.

"Don't be shy. Go ahead and dig in," said Jennifer.

The shrimp was surprisingly tasty. The three men ate for several minutes without talking as Jennifer waited at the kitchen door staring vacantly at the living room. "Frank, what part of the south are you from?" asked Charley, breaking the silence.

"Texas."

"I don't like to get personal with the people I do business with. You know the ID stuff?" Charley talked with his mouth full, having eaten an entire shrimp, including the tale, in one bite. "You seem to be different from anyone else I've fixed up."

Troy sat silently eating another shrimp. His past was a subject he would rather not discuss at this time; it was something he didn't want to even think about.

"Are your parents wealthy?" asked Charley.

Troy didn't answer. He noticed a small wooden bookshelf on the wall under the window. The books were of the nature he would never have thought to be read by a tire buster. He walked to the bookshelf and picked up a thick book, *Classics of Western Thought*, and began to thumb through it. It had been a long time since he had read a book or newspaper.

"I enjoy reading," said Charley. "You can borrow any of them, if you want."

"I'm surprised you like these sorts of books." Troy thumbed through the book.

"I have a college degree in psychology." Charley deposited another shrimp in his mouth, chewed it twice and swallowed. "I live the way I do because I choose to. You know, not too much stress. Hell, man, I don't want to become a rich bastard, maybe a little more money would help, but I never want to become a rich bastard."

"We don't care about being rich but would like to have enough money to buy a bar someday," stated Jennifer.

"My mother's not rich." Troy placed the book back on the shelf. "My father died when I was just a kid."

"I'm not tryin' to be a busybody." Charley stood and placed his hands on his midsection. "Hey Jen, could you get us another beer? I only want to be neighborly."

"No problem. I best git back to my room." Troy noticed several empty boxes stacked next to the bookshelf. "I was wondering if I could have a few of these boxes."

"You can have them all, if you want." Charley moved next to Troy. "I have some tape here too if you need to prepare something to mail."

"Thanks. I can shore use it." Troy placed the tape into one of the boxes and moved toward the door.

"It was nice meeting you," said Louis, looking out the window. "It's raining. We sure are having peculiar weather this year."

"Pleasure was mine," said Troy.

"We'll have to get together and hit the town one of these nights." Charley opened the door.

"We'll do that." Troy stepped through the door pulling the boxes behind him. He nodded his head toward Jennifer. "Ma'am."

"Nice meeting you, Frank."

"Y'all can call me Troy, that's my real name." He hesitated in the doorway. "Hey, Charley, don't worry about that hundred dollars. To be honest with you, I don't remember givin' it to you."

It had been a long time since Troy felt like doing something besides sleeping. He opened the door to the small closet at the back of his room and pulled out the suitcases of money and dumped them on his bed. He had spent thousands of dollars over the past month being a big shot, but it hadn't made a dent in the pile of bills. He stared at the sea of green covering the decrepit bed. He began carefully placing the bundles of cash into the boxes and taping them tightly shut. He filled all the boxes and left about two hundred thousand dollars on the bed.

It seemed like only yesterday that Billy and Larry had come by Uncle Martin's house in Larry's old Cadillac to take him away to become a part of the real world. Now, his most fervent concern, the one he needed to have an answer to first, was to the whereabouts of his two friends. His mind had played tricks on him, especially with the quickness of time, and he had expected Billy and Larry to find him. Now he realized how impossible it would be for anyone to know where he was.

"I need to call home." Troy was looking at the money, first smiling, and then laughing loudly. "Good God, I've lost my mind."

He opened his wallet, it was almost empty, only a slip of paper with the name Rosie and her telephone number. He placed two hundred-dollar bills in the wallet and put a blanket over the remaining money.

Rosie was the person who had been haunting him subconsciously over the past weeks. The one he had been yearning for, without realizing who he was missing. He looked at his cell phone sitting on the bed yet decided to be cautious in making the first contact with his previous life. Pulling a sock full of quarters from his dresser Troy emptied them into his pocket.

Light rain sprayed his face as he made his way to the payphone on the side of the convenience store. He dialed the telephone number.

"Hello," a soft voice answered after only two rings.

"Rosie," he shuffled his feet, "this is Troy Young."

There was a gasp on the other end of the line.

"Are you there?" asked Troy, feeling very uncomfortable about his decision to make the call.

"Yes, I'm here." She paused before speaking. "I'm just not certain who I'm speaking with."

"It's Troy Young, we met several weeks ago at the night club in Colorado. You gave me your telephone number."

"I know who Troy Young is."

"You sounded like you didn't remember me."

"Who is this? Really, who is this?"

"It's Troy. Why is that so hard for you to believe?"

"Troy's dead."

"Huh," for a moment Troy wondered if he might not be whom he thought.

"He's dead."

"Rosie, I have no idea why you would think such a thing, but I'm here just as big as life, still breathing and feeling better by the moment."

"Prove to me that you are who you say."

"I met you at a dance club in Colorado, for the life of me I can't remember the name of it, but we sat and talked while watching your friend Mary dance." Troy waited for her recognition of his facts.

"That's not good enough. You better tell me something nobody else would know, or I am going to hang up."

"I made a toast."

"Yes."

"It was for you." Troy was grasping for some fact.

"What happened when we left?"

"We made love." He knew he had found the clincher, "I kissed you on the belly button when I left."

"I can't believe this, all the newspapers have reported you to be dead in the mountains," said Rosie, excitedly. "Where are you?"

"I'm in Vegas. Why would the newspapers say I'm dead?"

"When the police couldn't find you they thought that you must have died and your body was covered by snow. After the snow stopped in the mountains, they searched for over a week for you." She paused. "I read everything there was about the bank robbery. It was big news for a couple of weeks, but it's dying down now. Everybody still wonders what happened to you, and where the money went."

"What about Billy and Larry? Were they arrested?"

Rosie did not answer, Troy waited patiently.

"Are you still there?" asked Troy.

"I'm here."

"What's the matter? Where are Billy and Larry?"

"They're dead."

"Dead!" Troy fell forward, placing his brow on the glass above the payphone. "Are you sure?"

"They died in a snowmobile crash." Rosie waited for a response from Troy. She didn't receive one. "I'm sorry, Troy, I thought you would have known. There has been so much written about the story over the past month."

Troy sniffled and turned to take notice if someone might be watching. "It never entered my mind that they might be dead." He sniffled again.

"I'm sorry, Troy." Having taken such an interest in the story over the past month because of her brief encounter with Troy, Rosie felt a strong kinship to him. "Your mother has been on television several times; she's been interviewed on all the talk shows."

"She has?"

"And your brother and sister." She hesitated again. "I have talked several times with your mother."

"Why?"

"You don't understand how big this story has been, not only here in Denver, but nationally. Pick up any *National Enquirer*, you'll find an article about the robbery. I know one thing too. Your family will never stop looking for you."

"I can't believe all this."

"Troy," Rosie hesitated for a moment, "I'm pregnant."

"You are."

"Yes, I'm pregnant with your child."

"My child."

"Yes, without a doubt, it's your child."

"I … I don't know what to say."

"I know the whole situation is a mess, but I would never lie to you about something like this," said Rosie.

"I want to see you again." Troy turned and placed his forehead to the cool glass of the telephone booth.

"I would like to see you too."

"Would you come to Vegas?" Troy's head was throbbing and he felt tired, not the usual sick fatigue he had been living with, but a normal tiredness.

"I … I don't know if I can get off work," she was caught off guard. "It would be better if you came back to Denver. You need to call your mother. If you come here, we can fly to Texas together."

"I can't leave, at least not right now." Troy looked out of the phone booth to the dilapidated area around him. "I can hardly believe everything you've told me."

"It's all true." She felt an excitement in the pit of her stomach, which reminded her she was ready for a life-changing event to take place. It was an opportunity to escape her humdrum daily existence. Without thinking logically about the outcome of her decision, she said, "I'll come."

"I'll go to the airport and get you a ticket tonight." Troy's voice was racing. It was the voice Rosie remembered from the night they had met. "Please, Rosie, don't tell anybody about coming here. It's important to me that I handle this situation on my own."

"Troy, I'll come, but I can't leave until Friday."

"A ticket for next Friday, early morning will be waitin' for you at the front desk of Frontier Airlines."

"Do you have a telephone number I can reach you at if there are any problems?"

"No." He wished he would have written Charley's telephone number down. "If they ask who purchased the ticket for you, tell them Frank Clark."

"I suppose I can go to the airport tomorrow night and pick up the ticket, that way I'll know for sure that I'm leaving on Friday." She hung up the phone, feeling as if her heart was in her throat.

Medicine Bow, Texas

"I know it's a long shot. But there's something about this girl that tells me she knows more than she's tellin'." Stanley placed his left hand onto the top of Sam's oak desk and took a sip from a cup. "Damn, this coffee is hot."

"What makes you think she would have any contact with Troy?" Sam leaned back in his chair and looked over the top of his reading glasses toward Stanley. "Hell, they only were together for a couple of hours. And besides, the FBI aren't very concerned about her."

"Call it a hunch."

"Are you sure you're not searching for a reason to take a jaunt to Vegas?"

"I reckon I might have a little itch to spend some time at the crap tables." Stanley puckered his mouth and sat the coffee cup on Sam's desk. "But damn it, Sam, there's something about this girl … if Troy's alive, he just might try and contact her. It's the only lead we have. The local fella in Denver followed her to the airport, and he sure enough thinks something's fishy about her accepting a ticket to Vegas on such short notice."

"You don't need my permission to go to Vegas."

"Something tells me that I won't be the only person following Miss Sievert onto that airplane. Mike King knows all about Troy's little rendezvous with her. Even though he told me he wouldn't interfere with our effort to find Troy for ten days, I don't trust him a bit."

"Why don't you have Jerry go with you?" Sam noticed how pale Stanley's complexion was. "Are you still taking aspirin?"

"They make me feel better." He didn't want to talk about his health. "I think I'll take this trip by myself."

"Sam," Jackie interrupted. "Drew Fudderman is at the front door."

"Tell him I'm busy."

"He has some more food for you," Jackie smiled and winked at Stanley.

"What in the hell does he have now?"

"I think it's more pork chops."

"Tell him to take them to the kitchen."

"Okay," Jackie walked out the door.

"Damn," Sam shook his head, "this is the third time this month he has brought me pork chops."

"Don't you have him doin' something for you?" Stanley sat down on the couch and tipped his hat forward. "Isn't he pamperin' some pigs?"

Sam dropped his hands to his side and stared at Stanley before quickly walking to the door. "Jackie, tell the Fudderman boy I want to talk with him."

Sam didn't say a word as he waited for Drew to enter the room. Stanley leaned back into the couch and waited with a big grin on his face.

"Drew." Sam started his questioning as soon as the large man walked through the door. "Y'all haven't butchered the pigs I've given you to watch, have you?"

"Well." Drew placed his hand on his chin and thought.

"What in the hell do you mean, well?"

"We might have accidentally butchaued one of the pwize pigs."

"How do you accidentally butcher a pig?"

"He got loose." Drew never wavered in his explanation. "And Daddy put him in the wong pen by accident. But we put back anotha pig that is just as good."

"I'm going to come out to your farm this afternoon and make sure you are taking care of the pigs in the manner we discussed."

"I think you'll be happy with us. But Sam, I think we should build a nice place fo us to keep the pigs. A place whea the special pigs can live out of the slop."

"There best be five pigs living in luxury on that farm." Sam's face was turning redder by the moment. "What in the hell do you mean where they can live out of the slop? They're supposed to be living in luxury now."

"They is, Sam." Drew placed his hand on Sam's right shoulder. "You can see how well Daddy and I have managed Fudderman Poak."

"I'll be out there this afternoon," Sam shook his head and motioned toward the door. "Now I have business to take care of."

"I'll see ya this aftanoon."

Las Vegas, Nevada

Troy held a bird's eye view of gate twelve from his seat at the five-card draw slot machine he was mindlessly placing dollar tokens into, when he noticed the airplane carrying Rosie pull up to the gate, a full ten minutes ahead of its scheduled time. The red light on top of the slot machine blinked a split second before the obnoxious noise began blaring. Four twos all in a row showed through the window of the machine.

"Hey man, that's four hundred bucks!" An old man patted Troy on his back.

"Oh shit." Troy pulled his Dallas Cowboy's cap lower over his eyes and brought his hand up to rub his closely shaved chin.

"Why in the hell can't I be lucky enough to hit a big payoff on the way home?" the old man whined to his wife. "I almost played that machine."

"It's going to take a few minutes to get your money," said the slot machine attendant, using her key to turn off the loathsome noise.

The passengers from the flight were beginning to depart the plane as Troy watched the attendant pull her key from the slot machine. "I'll be right back," she said, walking to her station in the middle of the concourse.

Troy waited by the machine watching the passengers exit the plane when he saw the slick black hair and unmistakable swagger of Vinny step to the side allowing the other passengers to move around him. Troy moved to the back of the slot machine, confident he had not been noticed.

"Come here," Troy motioned to the old man who had congratulated him.

"Me?" The old man pointed at himself and moved closer to Troy.

"Do you have a piece of paper and pen?" asked Troy.

"I believe my wife does." He looked back toward his wife. "Honey, do you have a pen and piece of paper?"

His wife reached into her purse and handed him the paper and pen.

"If you will do me a favor," Troy began writing, "I will tell the lady to pay you the money from the slot machine."

"Who do I have to kill?"

Troy looked back toward the people departing the airplane, but he could not locate Rosie. Vinny was still waiting in the same position, leaning against a pillar trying to look inconspicuous.

"All ya need to do is give this note to a young lady," said Troy, handing the note to the old man.

"I can handle that."

"There she is," Troy pointed toward Rosie as she stepped into the concourse through the tunnel from the airplane and stopped to look around. "The lady with the sunglasses and the scarf, carrying the blue knapsack."

"Just give her the note?" asked the old man.

"Do you see the man with the black hair and white shirt standing next to the column?"

"Yes."

"I don't want him to see you give her the note."

"All right, it'll be about five more minutes and we'll free up your money," said the attendant for the slot machines.

"Give the money to my father," Troy pointed to the old man with the note.

The old man winked at Troy and walked over to whisper into his wife's ear. His wife tottered to where Vinny was standing and began talking to the unsuspecting conman, as her husband slipped the note into Rosie's hand. The woman continued talking, something that seemed to come very natural for her.

Rosie opened the small piece of paper and read the note. She looked at the other passengers until she spotted Vinny who was impatiently listening to the lady tell him how her husband had just won four hundred dollars at a slot machine. She picked up her small carry-on bag, keeping one eye on Vinny, and slipped out of the concourse, unnoticed by the conman. She moved toward the lady's restroom. Once inside the restroom, she bit her lower lip and looked into the large mirror covering the full length of the bathroom wall. She ripped the note and tossed it into the wastebasket. For a moment, she contemplated buying a ticket back to Denver. "I hardly even know this guy," she said to herself, before taking a deep breath, moving into a stall and latching the door shut.

Troy waited outside the restroom, next to a payphone, one eye on the door and the other on Vinny, who was searching frantically. The diversion by the busybody had worked even better than anticipated.

Vinny walked within five feet of Troy, looking around urgently. When he couldn't locate his prey, he began jogging down the corridor away from the arrival gates, looking desperately for Rosie.

Troy opened his wallet and pulled out Charley's card and telephone number. He dialed the number and waited for an answer.

"Hello."

"Charley, this is Troy."

"Hey man, we were just talking about you."

"I was wondering if you could do me a big favor?"

"Shoot."

"I'm down at the airport, picking up a girlfriend … it's kind of a long story, but I'm having some trouble with a fella down here." Troy wasn't sure how to explain his dilemma. "I was wondering if you could come down here and give me a ride? I'll pay ya."

"No need for that. It's going to take me about forty-five minutes."

"That'll work. We'll be at the Southwest passenger check-in. Not at the passenger pick-up, but the check-in."

"I'll be there."

Troy hung up the phone and looked to see any sign of Rosie. He glanced down the corridor. No sign of Vinny. He stepped a couple of feet inside the women's restroom and yelled, "Rosie."

"Yes," she opened the stall door.

"It's me, Troy."

"Just one minute." She placed a tissue to her eyes and brushed her hair as she looked at herself in the mirror. She looked tired.

Troy lingered patiently at the entrance to the restroom, watching closely to make sure Vinny did not backtrack to the loading area. He didn't notice the silhouette of Stanley leaning against the wall only ten feet from where he waited.

"Troy." Stanley's voice was strong and steady even though he wasn't one hundred percent certain he was talking to Troy.

"Stanley." Troy stepped back in surprise.

"Son, we've been lookin' all over for you."

"How did ya know I was here?" Troy couldn't believe how old Stanley looked. His skin was the color of chalk.

"Your ma is worried sick about you." Stanley moved within an arm's length of Troy, ignoring his question. "Son, you look like hell."

"I've had a rough couple of months." Troy thought about telling Stanley he didn't look so hot but thought better of it. "I have a heap load of trouble right now that I need to smooth down before I burden my family again."

"We know all about your problems. But damn it, Troy, you shouldn't have left your ma hanging on the notion that you might be dead. That just ain't right."

"Stanley, I have some men after me who might harm my ma if they knew I was alive. I can't talk with ma just yet."

"Son, you ain't done anything so wrong that you can't face the music for it. And as far as those men … well, I already talked with Mike King about arranging a deal where he stays out of your life for good."

"Well, he must not have listened very well. He sent one of his men to follow Rosie on the airplane."

"Are you sure it's one of his men?"

"Positive. It's Vinny, the fella that set us up on the job in Denver."

"That son of a bitch lied to me."

"What else is new?"

Rosie poked her head out of the restroom door. "Is it safe to come out?" she asked.

Troy felt awkward. He had anticipated a joyous reunion with Rosie, one where he could hug and kiss her, but for some reason he felt no great pang of emotion as she stood before him. Maybe it was the tension caused by the two unexpected visitors that brought about his feelings of indifference, yet deep down in his soul Troy was too scared to admit to himself that he was incapable of truly loving anyone, even Rosie and their unborn baby.

"Stanley," Troy motioned for Rosie to come out of the restroom, "this here is Rosie, a friend of mine."

"I done met Rosie," Stanley was breathing heavily. "We best move to a less obvious location to talk."

"This is Stanley, a friend from Texas," said Troy.

"Yes, we've met," Rosie was feeling nauseous.

Stanley was limping noticeably, and with each breath he took came a wheeze. Troy grabbed the knapsack from Rosie as they followed behind the large Texan.

"Let's go inside this coffee shop and rest for a moment," said Troy, grabbing Stanley's arm and helping him to a table at the back of the coffee shop.

"Rosie, would you mind gittin' me a coffee?" asked Stanley, handing Rosie a twenty-dollar bill. "And a glass of water."

"Not at all." She looked at the short line of customers waiting at the cafeteria-style counter. "What about you, Troy?"

"Coffee. Thanks." He wondered what Stanley had on his mind as he watched Rosie move to the coffee counter.

"Son, I want to git straight to the point. Do you have any of the money that Mike King stole?"

Troy's hesitation was all Stanley needed. "How much do you have?"

"A bag full," Troy lied.

"That's all?" Stanley figured Troy only having a bag full of money just didn't add up, but he wasn't going to call him out. "How did ya end up with it?"

"It just fell into my lap."

"Well, we best figure a way to get it off your lap." Stanley leaned back in his chair and placed the palms of his hands on his big belly. "Where's the money?"

"In the closet at my apartment."

"Good Lord, son."

"Well, I couldn't hardly put it in a bank."

"I reckon." Stanley reached into his shirt pocket and pulled out the small tin can with his aspirin and slowly took two white tablets and placed them on the table. "Son, are you sure you want to get this young lady involved in this mess?"

"I surely don't," said Troy, frowning. "But she's already deep into this thing …"

"She's pretty," interrupted Stanley.

"It's more than that, Stanley. She's pregnant."

"Son, I know all about that, and so does your mother." Stanley placed the two aspirin in his mouth.

"Two coffees and a water," said Rosie with a hint of sarcasm in her voice, placing a tray of drinks on the table.

"Thanks, we appreciate that." Troy wanted to ask Stanley how his mother had learned of Rosie being pregnant, but he thought the discussion would be better brought up at a later time.

"No problem," said Rosie, sitting next to Troy across from Stanley.

"We were talkin' about a problem. A problem I'm feeling guilty about dragging you into." Troy looked directly into Rosie's eyes. "The other man who followed you on the airplane is the guy who robbed the bank in Denver. He's a very dangerous man who is capable of killing all of us. I'm sorry, I never in my wildest dreams would have expected them to follow you."

"I'm a big girl. I knew I wasn't on my way to a family picnic," said Rosie, emphatically.

"Shouldn't we call the police on this guy?" Rosie looked closely at Troy's face. He looked completely different than she remembered. His face was nearly calloused over and heavy with lines. The only thing that kept her from thinking she was talking to a stranger was his eyes. The glaze over his dark brown eyes was the same.

"We will get the proper authorities involved shortly." Stanley took a sip of coffee. "Troy, is there some place where y'all could go, just for the afternoon?"

"Damn, I almost forgot." Troy looked at his watch. "Charley is gonna meet me in about fifteen minutes."

"Who the hell is Charley?"

"A friend I met here in Vegas."

"Can you trust him?" asked Stanley.

"I believe I can. He lives in the same apartment complex I do."

"Write down the address of your apartment and yore cell phone number." A pen in his shirt pocket was a distinguishing feature of Stanley's. "I want you two ta catch a ride with your friend and wait for me at your apartment. Make sure ya keep that cell phone charged."

"Okay." Troy began writing.

"I'll meet you at your apartment in a few hours." Stanley's big nose had turned red during the brief stop at the coffee shop. "Keep an eye out for that thug."

"Charley's meeting us at the passenger check-in. I doubt that Vinny will be anywhere near there," said Troy.

Troy and Rosie hurried from the coffee shop as Stanley retrieved two more aspirin and placed them in his mouth. He took one final swallow of coffee and began to limp down the corridor.

Troy sat next to Rosie in the front seat of the car listening to Charley try and make an impression on them with his knowledge of the Las Vegas strip. Rather than take the freeway back to North Las Vegas, Charley drove along the congested strip. Rosie was congenial and smiled most of the way to the apartment.

Troy realized just how decrepit his habitat was when Charley pulled to the curb in front of the apartment. He was embarrassed as they walked down the hallway because of the repugnant odor radiating through the hallway, he wasn't sure, but it seemed like he could still smell the shrimp he had eaten several days ago as they walked by Charley's apartment.

"Well, here we are," he opened the door to his disgusting room.

Rosie stepped through the small door and looked out the dirty window. She didn't say a word until she sat down on the bed, "Yuck."

Troy smiled and began to laugh.

"What are you laughing at?" she reached over and slapped him on the shoulder.

"Well, I knew this place was disgusting, but I thought you might be a little more diplomatic with your reaction."

"This place is putrid." She jumped from the bed and opened the window. "It stinks in here."

"We can stay in one of the hotels." He placed his arm around her shoulder. "Until we decide what we're gonna do."

"That will cost a fortune."

Troy swallowed hard. "I have enough money to cover it."

"Most anyplace would be better than here."

"We can go tonight, but we need to wait for Stanley."

"Is there anything growing in the bathroom?" Rosie asked, opening the restroom door.

"I think it's pretty clean."

"Well, I've seen worse." She laid her knapsack on the bed and opened it. "I'm going to freshen up."

Troy placed his cell phone into the battery charger and plugged it in. He sat on the bed and began to contemplate what the immediate future held for him in regards to Rosie. Thinking about his future was something he was not very good at.

"Oh do I feel better." The fresh smell of oil and perfume followed Rosie as she exited the bathroom. She sat on the bed and brushed her hair.

Troy was preoccupied with his thoughts as he sat next to her on the bed. It was an awkward situation with Rosie handling the circumstance as though she was spending the night at her best friend's home.

"Troy." She looked away as she continued to brush her hair. "What are we going to do?"

"I think Stanley will be here at any time."

"I don't mean right now." She turned toward him. "I mean for the future, with the baby."

"Well," he couldn't believe how beautiful she was as she sat on the bed next to him.

"I reckon we have a lot to talk about before we make any decisions."

"We don't have to set anything in stone." Rosie sat her brush on the bed and turned toward Troy. "I would like to at least discuss the possibilities we have."

A light knock on the door interrupted their discussion.

"Stanley already," said Troy as he opened the door.

"Hey, man, I forgot to tell you. I caught some old guy coming out of your apartment this morning. He said he knows you and to tell you he got the package," said Charley.

"Thanks, he's another friend of mine."

"Also," stated Charley excitedly, stepping into the apartment. "I found you a gig."

"What?"

"You know, a gig. A toast gig."

"You did?"

"I have a rich friend in LA who's getting married, and I told him about your toastmaster business. He thought it was the greatest idea since apple butter." Charley's eyes were glazed over and he had a big smile on his face. "It's in three weeks."

"Well … I don't know what to say."

"I wasn't sure how much to charge, so I told him twelve hundred dollars. You have to give three different toasts, so I figured about four hundred dollars per toast." He staggered back a couple of steps before regaining his balance. "Why don't you and your girlfriend come over and have a drink?"

"I appreciate that, Charley, but we're expecting an old friend to be here shortly." Troy began to close the door. "I'll talk with you about the wedding tomorrow."

"What's Charley talking about?" Rosie straightened her legs as she moved off the bed.

"I told him I was a toastmaster," he smiled.

"A toastmaster."

"You know, I give toasts at special occasions, for money.

"I guess I am going to learn a lot about you that I never even imagined." She moved in front of him and placed her hands on his hips.

Troy was a full head taller than Rosie as he placed his hands on the side of her face and leaned down to kiss her. She pulled on his hips and they fell to the bed.

"Oh, Troy." She lay flat on her back. "What have we gotten ourselves into?"

Troy lay next to her on the bed. He placed his hand on her belly and felt the large bump. He remained silent.

"Troy, we're never going to be together." Rosie felt a terrible disconnect at a time when she should feel nothing but tenderness. "Are we?"

Troy heard a knock on the door before he could answer her question.

"Stanley," Troy's face was flushed a bright red as he opened the door.

"Am I interrupting something?" asked Stanley, with a grin on his face.

"No, come on in."

"Son, why in the hell are ya livin' in a dump like this?"

"It's just where I found myself."

"We got some work to do." Stanley sat down at the small kitchen table. He looked closely at Rosie. He had examined every part of her life over the past month and now could only hope his inclinations about her were correct.

"Did you find Vinny?" asked Troy.

"Oh yeah," said Stanley. "Our friend is staying at the Excalibur. All we need now is a few thousand dollars of that money you have, and we'll have Mr. Barrows out of your hair for good."

Troy wasn't sure what kind of reaction he was going to get from Rosie in actually seeing some of the money from the robbery for the first time. Troy went to the closet and pulled out a paper bag. He dumped a pile of newspapers on the bed.

"What the fuck is this?" Stanley asked.

"That's it," Troy stated.

"That's a big pile of shit, is what that is." Stanley looked suspiciously into Troy's dark and glazed eyes. "Do ya really think that's money?"

Troy stared back at Stanley, looking him directly in the eyes. "It used to be."

"It used to be." Stanley sat down on the bed, unsure how he felt about Troy's behavior.

"Troy, do you really think those papers are money? asked Rosie.

Troy remained silent.

"Troy," said Rosie.

"It used to be," Stanley scratched his head.

"Well," Troy lifted the side of the mattress and reached under. He pulled out four packs of hundred-dollar bills still in bank wrappings. "This is all I have."

Stanley put his gloves on and reached out to take the packets. "This is all we need."

"What do you want us to do?" asked Troy.

"I need y'all to come with me," said Stanley, looking at Rosie. "Do you have a wig?"

"No," said Rosie suspiciously.

"How about the scarf you were wearing at the airport?"

"Yeah."

"Are you up for some excitement, young lady?" asked Stanley.

"I came here to find some excitement." She placed the scarf over her hair, put on a pair of sunglasses, and seductively pulled a pair of black gloves over her tiny hands. "I am ready as ever."

Troy wasn't sure what Rosie was thinking as Stanley drove slowly toward the Excalibur.

"Stanley," Troy ruined the silence. "I suppose you know what's best in this situation. But I would like to have some inclination as to what we're plannin' to do with the money."

"Son, you're about to receive a lesson in simple economics," said Stanley, looking straight ahead as he drove slowly toward their destination.

"What might that be?" asked Troy.

"Money talks. No matter what part of the world you find yourself in, money talks."

"Are you going to pay them off?" asked Rosie.

"These aren't the type of fella's ya can buy," stated Stanley, smiling. "I'm going to plant this money in Vinny's room and call the authorities."

Rosie turned and looked over the top of her sunglasses at Stanley. She appeared quite intriguing in her makeshift disguise as she smiled at him.

"I just need a little of this money to grease a few palms in order to get access to his room." Stanley reached into his shirt pocket and removed the packet of aspirin. He fiddled with the can for a moment before motioning to Rosie to help him.

"Could ya pull me one of these aspirin out?" he asked.

"Do you have a headache?" asked Rosie with a look of concern on her face, having noticed how pale Stanley's face appeared.

"No." Stanley accepted the tablet from Rosie and placed it in his mouth. "Rosie, I need ya ta take this bag of money and place it in the room. Can ya do that?"

"I suppose so."

"I'll make damn sure that this gangster is nowhere near his room." Stanley parked the car at the far end of the parking lot on the west side of the Excalibur Hotel.

"What do I do?" asked Troy.

"Nothing. Son, I don't want yore face anywhere near one of the cameras in this place. You sit tight right here in the car, and I'll call if there is a problem." Stanley turned toward Rosie. "Are ya goin' ta be able ta do this?"

"I can do it."

"It will be a whole lot better having ya take care of placing the money in the room."

"I can do it!"

"Wait here for five minutes after I leave, and then walk to the side door, the one right over there." He pointed to the entrance. "There will be a small concession area where they sell coffee to yore right immediately after ya enter. The elevators to the rooms are just to the right of the concession. Wait there until I get yore attention. I will give ya the key to the room. Place the money under the mattress of the bed closest to the window," said Stanley, looking at Rosie's reactions to his instructions. "Okay?"

"No problem," said Rosie confidently.

"See ya in a few minutes." Stanley slowly exited the car and limped toward the hotel entrance.

"Rosie, are ya okay?" Troy asked.

"Don't worry, everything will be fine," said Rosie, adjusting her scarf.

"I can't help but be a little worried."

"Something tells me that I am in very capable and safe hands with Stanley." She placed her sunglasses over her eyes before opening the car door. She grabbed the bag of money and smiled confidently at Troy before leaving.

The noise in the lobby area of the hotel/casino was disconcerting. The cluttered sounds of the slot machines mixed with loud people moving through the area at first caused Rosie to lose her focus. She walked by a little old lady at the concession stand and into an area where blaring slot machines made her slightly disoriented. She turned and looked for the elevators; there were no elevators. She turned and backtracked to the concessionaire.

"Could you tell me where the elevators are?" she asked the little white-haired saleslady.

"Right there." The lady pointed to the elevators.

She walked over to the elevators to familiarize herself with which elevators went to which rooms. She then proceeded to the coffee bar and waited nervously. The longer she waited the more unsettling the situation was becoming, especially since she had acted so brave in front of Troy and Stanley.

"Hello," Stanley walked up and put his arms around Rosie and gave her a hug, making sure not to mention her name.

"Our room is twenty-two twelve," he placed a small cardboard key into her hand. "It's empty at this time."

"See you in a bit," uttered Rosie, remembering that she was holding ten thousand dollars in a brown paper bag.

Stanley reached up and rubbed the day-old stubble on his face before pulling out his cell phone. When he had communicated with Sam about his decision to place the money in Vinny's room, Sam had been adamant about being informed during each step of the process.

"Sam," said Stanley, watching Rosie enter the elevator. "The girl is on her way to the room with the money."

"Keep a close eye on her," said Sam, sitting at his desk in his office at the ranch. He held several reservations about being involved with the scheme in the first place, but his faith in Stanley's decisions was unwavering.

"I just talked with the maid and they finished cleaning the room only moments ago," said Stanley.

"Are you sure this is the best way to handle this situation?" asked Sam, knowing it was unusual for Stanley to go outside of the law when handling a dilemma.

"Sam, I sat face to face with the devil the other night when I met Mike King. I have never crossed paths with someone as evil as this man." Stanley kept an eye on the elevators. "The way I figure is that we can either kill him or have him think that his own men were the ones that stole the money. Otherwise, he will be after Troy for the rest of his life."

"It's a hell of a fix Troy's made for himself in such a short time," said Sam.

"It shore is. Son of a bitch." Stanley shook his head and squinted his eyes. He couldn't believe what he was seeing. Vinny, along with another man, were standing in front of the elevator.

"What's wrong?" asked Sam.

"I got to go." Stanley hobbled toward the elevator. "Vinny is at the elevator. I'll call ya back in a minute."

Vinny pushed the lit button for the elevator several times. "These are the slowest damn elevators," he said, turning toward Tony.

"Relax, man, it's only saving us money," said the muscular Italian, slapping his friend on the shoulder.

"I can't believe that asshole drew twenty-one on me. A thousand bucks! I have twenty and that prick hits twenty-one." He slaps the elevator light. The elevator door opened as though it were responding to the obnoxious behavior of Vinny.

"It's only money," said Tony.

"Yeah right, only money." The two men entered the elevator.

Stanley slipped quietly into the elevator, followed by several others. "Twenty-two," said Stanley, nodding toward Vinny.

"Already pushed," said Vinny, looking at the ash-colored complexion of the old Texan.

"Thank ya," said Stanley looking away from the men.

"Looks like you had a rough night there, old timer," said Vinny, winking at Tony.

"Yeah, it was pretty rough," said Stanley, trying to stay unruffled but wishing he could grab the cocky criminal by the throat.

"You look like the walking dead," said Vinny, turning toward Tony. "I still can't believe he hit twenty-one."

Stanley stayed calm as he followed the two men off the elevator. They turned to the right and began walking down the hall. They both stopped in their tracks.

"Damn, we did it again," said Vinny, making an about-face and walking past Stanley, bumping him to the side.

"That's the third time I've went the wrong way off the elevator," said Tony.

Stanley turned and watched the men walk toward their room. He could only hope that Rosie had taken one of the other elevators down while they had been coming up. He pulled out his billfold and took a twenty-dollar bill out before following the men. "Hey! One of y'all dropped a twenty-dollar bill."

Both men turned toward the old Texan. Stanley could see at the far end of the hall a door open and Rosie exit the room into the hallway.

"One of y'all dropped this back there." Stanley held up the twenty dollars.

Vinny walked back toward Stanley and snatched the money from his hand. "Now I've only lost nine hundred eighty dollars in the last hour," said Vinny, glaring at the smiling Texan.

Stanley watched as Rosie lowered her eyes and walked past the two men. Her composed demeanor impressed Stanley.

"Hey, gorgeous," said Tony mindlessly as she passed.

She ignored him.

Stanley waited until she passed him before following her to the elevator.

"Everything okay?" asked Stanley after the door to the elevator closed.

"Yes," Rosie was obviously irritated at having had such a close encounter with Vinny. "I thought you said that those men wouldn't be anywhere near the room."

"I'm sorry. My sources told me that they had left the room and were playing blackjack in the casino." Stanley steadied himself on the handle in the elevator. "I would have never expected them to return to their room so quickly."

"I'm still shaking." Rosie glared at Stanley as she sauntered out of the elevator and hurriedly made her way to the parked car. Stanley hobbled slowly behind her.

"Is everything okay?" asked Troy.

Rosie removed her scarf and sunglasses and looked back at Troy with her chin resting on her breastbone. "I have never been so scared in my entire life. Those two hoodlums almost caught me in their room."

Stanley opened the door and sat in the driver's seat. He pulled out his phone. "Relax now, we're gonna get away from here and you will never have to deal with Mr. Vinny Barrows again." He started the engine to the car. "Sam. Everything is taken care of. You can inform Ed and get the ball rolling. Right now is a perfect time to catch them in their room. I'm takin' a commercial flight home and will see you in about five hours." He closed his phone.

"What's Sam plannin' to do?" asked Troy.

"The FBI will be in their room before we reach the airport," answered Stanley, merging into the traffic. "Do y'all mind taking this car to the rental return and grabbing a taxi back to yore apartment?"

"No problem," stated Troy.

"I hope that's the end of our relationship with those evil men," stated Rosie.

"Son, I'm gonna tell you right now." Stanley looked through the rearview mirror at Troy. "I know ya told me ya don't have any money, but if ya do, yore gonna have a hard time finding peace as long as you keep any of it."

"I reckon your right," said Troy. "But Stanley, there's something I never told ya."

"What might that be?" Stanley continued looking at Troy through the rearview mirror.

"I know what Mike King looks like. I can identify him."

"Well, son, I'm in the process of finding out all about Mr. King," said Stanley, parking the car at the check-in area of the airport and turning around to face Troy. "One thing I want you to know, Troy. Don't ever make an agreement with Mike King because he is a liar, and he is a hell of a lot more powerful than I originally gave him credit for being. Don't trust him for even a second."

"I'm hopin' I never have to deal with him again."

"Sam's making arrangements to fly y'all back to Texas." Stanley turned to look at Troy. "You know, son, you can't go wrong having Sam Blake as a friend. He will never steer you wrong. Now that advice comes from experience."

"I'll call him when we get back to the apartment."

"Rosie, it was a pleasure seeing you again," said Stanley, opening the door and stepping out.

"Thank you, Stanley," said Rosie, unsure of how thankful she was to the large Texan.

Troy stepped out of the backseat and moved to the front door of the car. Before he could move into the driver's seat, Stanley placed his large arms around him and hugged him, something he had never done before, even when Troy was a small child.

"Look after that girl," said Stanley. "she's a winner."

"I will," Troy's words slipped idly from his mouth with no meaning whatsoever.

"Son," Stanley held the car door open and leaned down to look Troy in his eyes. "You're at a crossroad in your life right now. One road leads to heaven and the other to hell. Make yore choices carefully." He closed the door and lifted his hand in a weak wave before limping toward the airport terminal.

Troy had never heard Stanley refer to anything to do with religion.

***

Stanley enjoyed flying on commercial airlines because he was a people watcher, especially of pretty women. Sam's private jet was at his disposal, but he enjoyed the energized feeling of being a part of the crowd as they flew through the air.

Stanley made his way through the walkway to his seat halfway toward the back of the 757 jumbo jet. Two young girls stepped from their seats in order to allow the large man to take his seat next to the window. He had always preferred a window seat. And he also preferred sitting next to two pretty girls.

A young red-headed boy with a significant number of freckles looked over the seat directly in front of him. "What's yore name?" the young tyke asked.

"Rumpelstiltskin," answered Stanley, chuckling toward the girls sitting next to him.

The girl closest to him lifted her lip, shook her head, and turned in her seat toward her friend.

"Turn around and sit down right now," said the mother of the little boy.

As the plane headed skyway, Stanley opened his tin full of pills and placed an aspirin in his mouth and allowed it to dissolve on his tongue. He sat quietly looking out the window admiring the beautiful earth below on the cloudless day. He had a smile on his face as he looked at the evening sun filter across the vast earth below.

The girl sitting next to Stanley glanced out of the corner of her eye at him. He was leaning back with his arms crossed over his chest with his mouth wide open. His face was white as chalk.

She turned abruptly to her friend. "I think the old guy next to me is dead."

The young girl in the aisle seat leaned over her friend and put her hand over Stanley's open mouth. "Oh my God," she yelled.

Both girls unfastened their seat belts and stomped their feet as they fled to the aisle.

The pretty blond flight attendant, who Stanley had noticed earlier, leaned over him and placed her hand over his mouth. She slapped his hand several times yelling, "Sir. Sir." She placed her hands over his eyes and gently closed them.

She moved quickly to report the incident to the pilot. A second flight attendant began walking down the aisle, quietly asking if there was a doctor on board.

"I'm a doctor," stated an older lady. She moved to Stanley's side through the murmurs floating through the plane that someone was dead.

She reached across Stanley's body and pushed her index finger hard into his neck, causing him to leap forward.

"What, what's happening?" Stanley adjusted his eyes to the old lady hovering over him.

"Sir, you had a heart attack. Please just sit still."

"I'm just fine," Stanley tried to sit up.

"No, you're not just fine," the doctor aggressively placed her hand on his shoulder. "Half the people on this plane think you're dead. Now you sit here until we can get you some help."

"Okay," Stanley took in a deep breath and relaxed in his seat.

Medicine Bow, Texas

"I know one thing for damn certain," Sam placed his hand on his forehead and shook his head. "He is going to slow down and take care of himself from now on."

"He's a pretty stubborn man," Sara placed her hand on top of Sam's.

"I reckon the both of us are," confessed Sam, "but if I have to play wet nurse to him, I will."

"Sam, you are a very good friend to Stanley."

"About a month before Daddy passed away, Stanley and I were sitting with him right out there on the patio. Daddy was always one for giving advice, and I remember that day he gave us a bit of advice that I've always remembered." He turned to face Sara. "He told us that in order to be happy, a person should avoid any problem that could not be handled from the sick bed. At the time I couldn't understand the gist of what he was saying, but I believe I do now. We're not always going to be on the top of our game, and sometimes we need help from somewhere else, whether it comes from God or man, we all need help at some time or another. Stanley understood it better than I; he has always been there to make my life easier."

"I know he has, Sam," said Sara, picking up the cup in order to get Sam another cup of coffee.

The sun trickling through the large picture window was uplifting to Sara as she hurriedly poured the coffee so she could return to Sam's side to enjoy the beauty of the sunrise.

"Why don't you try and call Troy again?" Sam accepted the coffee.

"I'll try again shortly. It's still early in Las Vegas."

"I need to talk with him about this mess he's in." Sam looked at the floor and shook his head. "Stanley kept everything to himself, I have no idea what all he knew and didn't know about these scoundrels."

"I'll try and call Troy." Sara sat down on the couch and placed her hand on Sam's knee. "But Sam, it's time for you to become a little selfish, even if I have to force you to."

He didn't reply.

"It's time to get along with our lives," Sara sighed.

"Sara, I'm tired. I never thought a man could be so worn."

"Do you still want to marry me?" She was tired too. They had spent the night fretting about the past, but it was the future that concerned her.

"More than anything in the world." He never hesitated with his answer. "I want to help take care of you. I want to be the person you can depend on."

Sara put her arms around his thick neck and rubbed her body next to his. "When I think about that night in New York City when you proposed to me … and all that has changed since then …"

"Nothing has changed with my feelings." Sam could feel her full breasts on his chest as he rubbed her back. "I still plan on making you my wife."

Sam kissed her. They fell back into the couch continuing to kiss and hug.

"Oh Sam," tears streaked down her cheeks as she continued to embrace him as they fell into the soft cushion.

"I have never felt so tired," Sam's breathing was deep and his face was flushed red.

"Sam," Sara placed her lips to his cheek, "you need to take care of yourself too."

"That is one thing I have never been able to do very well." He turned his head and looked Sara in the eyes.

"Thank you for everything, Sam." She placed her hand on the side of his face. "I can't imagine how difficult this would have been without you."

"You would have survived."

"There would have been no other choice." Sara rubbed her thumb on Sam's cheek. "You didn't just help us survive. You've given us hope."

"You know what I hope?" Sam sat up and smiled.

"What?"

"I hope that we can get married and start living like a man and wife."

"I started preparations."

"Have ya decided when?"

"I just haven't picked a day yet." Sara placed her index finger to her upper lip.

"It's funny how fast time flies." Sam struggled to stand up. "Things can change in a blink of an eye."

Sara realized that time was not going to wait for them. "That's even more reason why we should make our wedding plans."

"I'll leave that up to you." Sam stretched his arms behind his back.

"I'm going to have Rebecca help me with the preparations."

"She has a screening set for next week."

"She's scared to death about it." Sara smiled at Sam.

"What are you smiling about?"

"You, Sam Blake." She put her arm around his neck and squeezed tightly.

"I guess I don't understand."

"I know you don't," Sara let her arms slip down his chest. Sam remembering Rebecca's doctor appointment during his own personal turmoil was as good an indicator as could be revealed for how he really felt in his heart.

North Las Vegas, Nevada

Troy pulled his jeans up to his waist and left them unbuttoned as he walked into the bathroom. He opened the bottle of lithium and hesitated for a moment before replacing the lid. He never intended to take one of the capsules. He was happy that Rosie fell asleep so quickly when they returned to his apartment last night after leaving Stanley at the airport. The image looking back at him from the mirror was different than that which he had created in his mind. He knew the anguish he had experienced since leaving Medicine Bow was festering in his mind, but his real problems were ones that had been with him since birth, the troubles that he would never lose.

Rosie was making the bed, already dressed in black slacks and a white blouse, when Troy came out of the bathroom. She was the type of woman who could feel comfortable in any situation, but had remained very quiet since they had returned from the Excalibur. Troy had been a total gentleman and allowed her to sleep in the bed while he slept in the chair. She turned and smiled at him, "Good morning."

"Good morning."

She turned and sat on the bed, staring at him apathetically.

"I know this isn't what you expected." He sat down beside her. "This is who I am."

"I really don't know you. After all I read about you, I don't have any idea who you are." She leaned forward on the bed. "Something tells me nobody really knows you."

"I never meant to hurt you."

"My life has been boring up to this point, so you haven't hurt me at all." She hesitated for a moment. "I feel really stupid for putting the baby in such a dangerous situation last night."

"That wasn't very smart."

Rosie looked at him with a confused look on her face. She expected him to tell her it was more his fault than hers.

Troy," her voice was calm. "We have to make some very important decisions here."

"With the baby."

"Yes, concerning our baby."

Troy didn't say anything, but the blank look on his face did.

"Do you want to be involved with this child?" There was a harsh tone to her voice.

"I don't know how to be a father."

"Obviously, you do," Rosie stated sarcastically. "I'm wondering if you can be a responsible one."

"I don't know," his voice was very soft.

"Oh Troy, I am so confused," she sat back onto the bed. "I came here because I couldn't stand another day of going to work and coming home to an empty apartment. I can't believe all the bad decisions I have made in my life."

"I had been down for so long that I needed someone to lift me up. You were the first person I thought of," replied Troy.

"I don't think either of us was being realistic in our approach to each other. I never once considered the depression you are experiencing."

"Depression." The color of Troy's eyes changed from dark brown to a light hazel color as he looked deeply into Rosie's eyes. "You know about my disease."

She pulled the pillow to her chest, feeling a little guilty about bringing up the subject of depression. But after the robbery, she had read all there was to know about Troy, and his disease was a subject the tabloids had picked up in a huge way. "Did your eyes just change color?"

"It's something that happens when I change moods. My mother always thought that my eyes were changing with the different colors of the surrounding area, but I know that it's my mood that changes the color of my eyes."

"That's weird." Rosie moved to her knees and placed her hands on both sides of Troy's face.

"When I don't take my medication, my eyes become very dark, almost black. My normal eye color is dark brown."

"What's it like for you when you are depressed?" asked Rosie, lying back on a pillow.

"I can't function. It's very physical, and I only want to sleep."

"I doubt that I have ever really experienced depression." She moved from the bed to again look out the window. "I know I've been sad and lonely, but I doubt I've ever been truly depressed."

"Everybody becomes depressed at some time. It's just a matter of degree. Even when I take my medication I can become depressed, but I know the difference between being depressed with my medication and being depressed without my medication." Troy moved so he could sit on the edge of the bed. "The night we met I was coming down from my manic state. Everything after that night is blurred, until I found myself here in this apartment."

"Are you taking your medication now?"

"Oh yeah. I can hardly function without it." He lied. "I take lithium. To me it's a wonder drug. If I don't take the drug, my mood will change from manic to depression."

Rosie stepped away from the window and sat next to him on the bed. She was tired and very much wanted to make her way back to Colorado.

"I know I have a problem." Troy's avowal seemed genuine, yet there was something in the tone of his voice that caused Rosie to question whether he believed it himself.

"You mean with your sickness?"

"Yes," he looked at her cockeyed, "I sometimes make people believe in things that don't exist."

Rosie sat on the bed and stared at the scoured face of the person who had kept her imagination captured over the past several weeks. What had happened to the energized and handsome man she had succumbed to on the first night they had met? She knew that love was something that never existed between the two of them.

"Did anything besides lust ever exist between us?" Rosie looked intently into his eyes.

"I don't know." He stared at the floor, knowing that it never did.

She turned and looked at a filthy wall, wondering how she could have made such a stupid mistake in making love to a complete stranger without birth control. Her only thoughts were that she should forget about the past and focus on what she had control over, the future. Her future was not with Troy, and she needed to find a way back to Colorado as quickly as possible.

His cell phone rang. He looked at Rosie fretfully before answering it. "Hello."

There was silence on the other end of the line until finally he heard his mother's voice.

"Troy"

"Ma," he grimaced, wishing he had called earlier.

"I've been trying to reach you for so long." Her voice was quivering.

"I know, Ma. Stanley told me."

There was silence at the end of the line.

"I was trying to get up enough nerve to call you." He was sorry for not making the call.

"Troy, Stanley had a heart attack last night."

"Is he okay?"

"They had to divert his flight to Phoenix. But he will be fine."

"Oh Ma, I'm sorry. He looked awful, but I never thought he was that bad."

"Troy," Sara cleared her throat, "you need to come home. At least for a little while so we can straighten up this mess you're in. The police want to talk with you."

"Ma, I need just a little more time."

"You know Rebecca has been hurt real bad … Troy," Sara began to sob, "we're so worried about her."

"What's wrong?" Troy sensed the distress in his mother's voice.

"You don't know about your sister's injury, do you?"

"No," he was surprised that neither Stanley nor Rosie would have made mention of a problem with Rebecca.

"Troy, the doctors found cancer in her leg." Sara cried loudly, "She … had her leg removed."

"Oh Ma," Troy began to breathe heavily.

"Troy, Sam wants to talk with you," there was silence on the other end of the line.

"Son, are ya okay?" Sam sounded awful.

"Yes, sir. I reckon I'm as good as could be expected." Troy felt foolish having Sam ask about his welfare.

"Now listen to me carefully. I want you to take your belongings and get to the airport in North Las Vegas immediately. I will have my jet waiting for you." Sam never hesitated long enough for Troy to speak. "Now, son, the FBI know you are in the Las Vegas area. But I want you to turn yourself in to the authorities here in Texas."

"Where should we go when we get to the airport?" Troy never even thought to question the decision Sam had made for his return home.

"Yore gonna have to call me when you get there." Sam almost asked Jackie to get him in touch with Stanley before realizing his mistake.

"There will be two of us on the plane. I'm gonna bring Rosie. She's a friend of mine."

"We know all about Rosie." Sam's voice continued to be calm. "Leave immediately."

"Okay." Troy had always felt a little weak-kneed in the presence of Sam, but suddenly he felt a sense of security in talking with the powerful Texan.

"Now y'all get movin' and we'll straighten this mess out when you get here this afternoon." He hung up the telephone.

"What happened with Stanley?" asked Rosie, knowing full well what the answer would be.

"He had a heart attack last night, but he's gonna be okay."

The cell phone rang. Troy picked it up, assuming it to be his mother calling back to remind him of something.

"Hello," answered Troy.

"Troy," the voice on the other end held a strange accent.

"Yes."

"This is Mike King, remember me?"

"Yes, sir," Troy swallowed hard.

"Who is it?" Rosie flinched when she saw the anguish on Troy's face.

Troy held up his hand and shook his head.

"I've been fascinated in reading the articles about you in all the national magazines. I was wondering if the part about you having several million dollars is really true?"

Troy could visualize the dark eyes and odd shape of Mike King's head as he prepared to speak, unsure if it might be better for him to hang up and leave for the safe confines of Medicine Bow.

"Well?" Mike King's voice was infuriated. "Do you have my money?"

"No, sir. I don't." Troy remained calm, "I believe Vinny and Tony have the money."

"Don't play games with me."

"I'm not, I never had the money."

"Where is it?"

"Vinny has it."

"Don't lie to me, you little son of a bitch," there was a loud bang.

"If you call me again I'm going to the police," said Troy, realizing he could never rationalize with Mike King.

"You know something, Troy," he waited for a reply and continued when Troy remained silent. "You come from a wonderful family and a beautiful little town. I couldn't believe that every single person in that town attends church on Sunday morning. And your mother and uncle don't even bother to lock their door when they leave. I want you to call your mother and ask her if she can explain what happened to her bottle of Eternity perfume last Sunday."

"Listen, you heartless bastard."

"No. You listen!" Mike King's voice was incensed, "Nobody has ever or will ever steal from me without paying the consequences. I guarantee you are not going to be the first one. So, I suggest we make arrangements to return the money. Now!"

Troy hung up the phone.

"Are you okay?" Rosie placed her arm around Troy's waist, worried that he was going to faint.

"Let me think," he placed his hand to his head.

The telephone rang.

"Don't answer it," yelled Troy. He walked from the apartment across the hall and knocked hard on Charley's door.

"Hey, man." Charley answered with his shirt wide open, holding a can of beer.

"I need to ask ya another favor."

"Come on in." Charley moved from the door, making room for Troy to enter.

Troy stepped inside the smelly apartment trying to think of how he should approach Charley with his needs. He decided not to give any explanation.

"Hi, Frank … uh, Troy." Jennifer greeted Troy with glassed-over eyes. She was still leaning against the kitchen counter, the same place she had been standing when he was over for the shrimp dinner.

"Hi." Troy looked around the tiny apartment trying to locate the empty boxes he had noticed when he had dinner previously. "Can I have some more of yore boxes?"

"You can have all of them if you want. Do you need another ride?" Charley staggered and braced his arm onto the sofa for support.

"No," said Troy, thinking Charley couldn't even walk to his car much less drive it. "I need to leave some of my belongings here for a little while."

"Okay," Charley looked at Jennifer. "Oh man. I almost forgot to tell you. There are some men in suits going around town asking about you. They stopped by the shop with your picture."

"Did they say what they wanted?"

"No, me and Louis acted like we had never seen you," Charley took another drink of beer.

"Thanks for doing that," Troy rubbed his chin, took in a deep breath and asked, "can Rosie come over and visit for a bit?"

"Sure," answered Jennifer. "We can talk."

Troy carried the empty boxes across the hall to his apartment. His phone was ringing.

"It hasn't stopped," said Rosie.

"I need ya to go over to Charley's apartment for about thirty minutes." Troy ignored his phone. "Please. No questions asked."

Rosie looked at the empty boxes but remained quiet as she stepped across the hall.

Slightly more than thirty minutes later the door to Charley's apartment eased open without the courtesy of a knock. Troy pushed two boxes inside the apartment and then went out to the hall and retrieved two more. All four boxes were taped shut with an exorbitant amount of duct tape.

"Charley, I need to leave these boxes with you." Troy questioned whether Charley was clearheaded enough to understand him. He didn't have the convenience of time to sober his friend. "These things are very valuable to me, very, very valuable."

"I will watch them with my life." Charley's head was moving back and forth as though he were a bobblehead doll.

"I'm going to get my things." Rosie never made eye contact with Troy as she went out the door. She was so ready to be back in Colorado.

Troy could hear his phone ringing from across the hall. He followed Rosie into his apartment and answered it.

"Yes."

"Listen, you little pissant. You better never disrespect me again. I'll kill you and every one of those country hicks you call family. Do you understand?" He sounded as though he was about to explode.

"Understood," Troy felt light-headed.

"You had better have a very good place to hide if you plan on continuing to run from me, because I'll never stop looking for you. Now, I want to meet you tonight."

"Where?"

"The Vegas Hilton."

He was in Las Vegas.

"Give me your telephone number." Troy tried to stall.

"Don't jerk me off. You have my number on your phone."

"I'm not. I just need time to find a ride."

"I'll send a car. Just tell me where."

"I don't think so."

"I guess I didn't make myself clear to you earlier." His voice was abnormally tranquil. "It really isn't the money that has me so upset. If you continue to disrespect me, and I don't have the opportunity to talk with you face to face tonight, then your entire family will be in a great deal of danger."

"I will call you in a few minutes to set up a place and time we can meet."

"I want to meet you tonight at seven o'clock at the Hilton," said Mike King.

"I don't want to meet you tonight," said Troy, listening to the heavy breathing from the other end of the telephone.

There was silence.

"All right, then. I'll just dial all sixes when I need to get in touch with you, you crazy son of a bitchin' bastard." Troy hung up and pushed the button to turn off the power to his cell phone.

"Troy, you have to give the money back." Rosie had been clenching his bicep but let go when she looked into Troy's darkened eyes. "Them boxes over there aren't worth your life."

"That money is the only thing that can keep me alive."

"Give it to the police."

"That won't get Mike King off my tail." He walked to the window and looked out to make sure there was nobody watching the apartment complex. "It would probably land me in jail. And I would place everyone in Medicine Bow in danger."

"Then let's give it to him."

"It wouldn't make any difference. He won't stop until I'm dead."

***

"I can't believe he hasn't called yet," Sam was pacing back and forth. "It's past two o'clock in Las Vegas."

"His phone is still turned off," Sara placed the phone hard onto the marble coffee table.

"Jackie," Sam waited in the door to his office.

"Yes," Jackie nudged her head out the door of her office.

"Get me in touch with Al Jones. He'll be on his cell phone."

"One second." Jackie stood at her desk as she dialed the number, "He's on line two."

"Al," Sam dispensed with the greeting, "how close are y'all to finding our boy?"

"We know he's in North Vegas."

"He was supposed to have called me from the airport a couple of hours ago."

"Sam, we need to take him directly to the authorities," said Al Jones. "My associates have paved the way for a quick release. With Agent Dodd's help, along with cooperation from Troy, he won't be charged with any major crimes."

"I want you to bring him back to Texas, even if you have to hog-tie him," said Sam.

Al knew he should turn Troy over to the local authorities in Las Vegas, but he was being paid plenty by Sam and he was in no way going to jeopardize his position within the Blake organization by disobeying him.

Jackie stepped into Sam's office. "It's Troy, on line three."

"Al, hold on for a moment. I have him on the other line." Sam looked at Sara reassuringly as she moved by his side. "Troy. Where in the hell are you?"

"Sam. I've got a big problem." Troy was standing at the window of his apartment watching the street below. "That crazy bastard Mike King is here in Las Vegas. He called me right after I talked with you."

"That doesn't change a thing," said Sam. "I need to know where you're at."

"He said he was in Medicine Bow last Sunday."

"I doubt that."

"Would you ask Ma if her perfume bottle was emptied last Sunday?"

"Who told you that?"

"Mike King told me that he was in Uncle Martin's house while everybody was in church and that he emptied Ma's bottle of Eternity perfume."

"Just one second, Troy." Sam yelled to Jackie, "Get me Tom Young on his cell phone."

"Sam, this guy is crazy," said Troy, continuing to look out his window. "He ain't gonna stop until he kills me. Now I'm afraid he's gonna hurt y'all."

"Son, there's no doubt that you are in serious jeopardy, but I can take care of everyone here," said Sam, watching Jackie who was motioning to him that she had Tom on the other line. "Now, listen to me, Troy, there is an attorney by the name of Al

Jones who is in North Las Vegas. He's a friend of mine who has been looking for you for the past week."

"I guarantee this crazy son of a bitch will follow me to Texas."

"Just tell me where you're at." Sam was losing patience. "Please, son, do this so we can end this fiasco."

"I won't turn myself in."

"For your own safety, for God's sake." Sam's lowered his voice as Sara put her hand on his arm. "Think about what your doin' to your mother."

"I need to settle this thing with Mike King before I go to the police."

"Troy, you need to think about Rosie and her safety. Y'all are in a very dangerous situation."

"Sam, he won't leave me alone. If I do go back to Medicine Bow, he'll follow me and maybe hurt Ma or Rebecca."

"Believe me, Troy," Sam turned to face away from Sara. "I will take care of your mother and sister. I'm gonna have Al call your cell phone and you need to give him your location."

"I'll talk with him," said Troy hesitantly.

"If for some reason the meeting with Al goes sour, I want you to hightail it to the small airport in North Las Vegas, it can't be far from where you are at now. Tom will be waiting for you there."

"Sam, make sure you watch after Ma, he threatened y'all, he said nobody in Medicine Bow is safe," said Troy, noticing two men across the street getting out of a blue Chevy. He moved quickly away from the window. "I think Mike King's men are in front of the apartment building."

"What?" said Sam.

Troy pulled Rosie to the wall next to the window. The men, both dressed in slacks and polo shirts, were standing in front of the apartment entrance talking and pointing in all directions. They stopped an old man who was walking down the sidewalk and showed him a picture. When the man shook his head, they allowed him to pass.

"I don't think they're police," said Troy into the phone.

"Did you meet with Mike King face to face?" asked Sam.

"Hell yes. I know exactly what he looks like," said Troy, moving away from the window and looking at Rosie. "He's not one of the men outside."

"Son, I have Al on the other line," said Sam. "I'm gonna place you on hold for a moment to see if it is him outside."

Troy turned off his phone.

"Wait, Troy," yelled Sam. He walked over to the couch and looked at the distressed face of Sara as she waited to be comforted by him. He hugged her, unsure as to whether he had made matters better or worse for her son.

Troy stepped around Rosie and moved into the bathroom. He took his half-empty tube of toothpaste and worn toothbrush and placed them in the stained sink where he placed both hands next to the mirror and stared at his reflection. Rosie quickly moved to the small wooden dresser and pulled her clothes out and pushed them into her bag. When Troy came out of the bathroom empty-handed, she nodded to him, letting him know that she was prepared to leave the decaying room.

"Let's get out of here," said Troy. "My brother Tom is waiting for us at the airport."

"I'm so ready for that," replied Rosie.

"Let's go."

Instead of going down the hallway, Troy moved across the hall and knocked hard on Charley's door. Rosie was following so close behind him that her arm brushed his back.

"Hey, man," said Charley.

Troy stepped through the door, with Rosie right on his hip, without giving Charley a chance to say another word. "I need to ask you for another favor."

"Shoot," said Charley, staggering back and bumping his thigh on the makeshift plywood table. "Ouch."

"Are ya all right, hon?" asked Jennifer, who was sprawled on top of the kitchen counter.

"I need a ride to the North Las Vegas airport," said Troy, ignoring Charley's accident. "I can drive."

Troy walked over to the telephone sitting on the counter next to Jennifer where the keys to his car were lying. He picked them off the countertop and put them in his pocket.

"Ummm," said Charley, rubbing his leg.

"We need to leave now." Troy looked out the door down the hall to the side exit of the apartment complex.

"I really don't think I should be driving." Charley's words were slurred, but he was aware enough to know that if he agreed to go he would have to drive back.

Troy pulled out five hundred dollars and placed it into Charley's hand. "Come on, we have to leave now?"

"Let me put my shoes on," said Charley.

"Hurry! We have to go. Out the back door."

They moved down the hall to the exit for the outside stairway.

As the three neared the exit, the door flung open, almost catching Troy on the chin. Two men in polo shirts charged through the door, even more surprised to see Troy on the other side than he was at seeing them.

"Troy Young," said the younger of the two men.

"That's him," said the second man, reaching inside his coat and pulling out a black pistol.

Troy didn't have time to say a word. He moved into a defensive stance, pushing Rosie back and hitting the man with the pistol hard on his flat nose. As he reached for the barrel of the pistol, he heard the loud bang before he felt a burning sensation on his right bicep. He could smell the powder as he pushed down on the gun, feeling a second bullet graze the palm of his right hand as it went through the floor. The first man through the door grabbed Troy by the shirt collar and tried to push him off his partner. Charley moved quickly and placed him into a strangle hold. Troy twisted hard on the arm of the man who had shot him, causing him to drop the gun. He overpowered the man, pushing his face hard into the dirty floor.

"Oh God! No," yelled Troy, looking back at Rosie lying on the floor with blood splattered on the side of her blouse.

"I'm all right," she quickly picked herself up from the floor.

"You're bleeding," cried Troy, continuing to push his assailant's face into the floor.

Rosie ran her left hand over the right side of her body. "Troy," she said, frantically, "it's your blood."

"Are you sure you're not hit?" screamed Troy.

"I'm sure."

Troy placed his knee into the small of the back of the man who had just shot him and hit him three times hard on the head. He looked at the gunshot wound in his bicep. He could see some broken skin and blood, and the burning sensation from the area was causing him to feel sick.

Rosie pushed some of the blood from the injury with her fingers, only to have more blood flow from the lesion. "We have to get you to a doctor," she said, placing her palm over the small gash.

"I'll have Jen call the police," said Charley, continuing to strangle his scrawny captive.

"No," yelled Troy.

Charley was surprised at how adamant Troy's denial was, so he continued to choke his skinny detainee with his strong arm.

"We need to get out of this hallway." Troy gritted his teeth as he began to drag the Frenchman down the hall. "Do you have any rope?"

"No," said Charley, "but I do have some duct tape."

"Let's take them into my apartment," said Troy.

"I'll get the tape," said Rosie, noticing that Troy was losing the color to his face. "Where's it at?"

"I'll have to find it," stated Charley, taking the strangle hold off his captive and putting him into a front headlock. "Jen would never be able to find it."

Troy twisted the arm around the back of his assailant and pulled him to his feet as Charley dragged the other thug toward his apartment. Rosie picked up the gun and pointed it at the man who had nearly killed them only a moment earlier. She could tell that Troy was weakening.

"You're a dead man," said the man, speaking with a thick French accent.

"Not yet."

"I guarantee you will be," said the Frenchman. "You are too careless. You should be miles away from Las Vegas."

"I promise you one thing," said Rosie, pointing the gun at the man. "You will be a dead man if you don't walk quietly to the room."

Jennifer blinked her eyes several times before realizing that she wasn't imagining that Charley was walking around her kitchen with a man in a headlock. She didn't say a word as she watched him search several areas of the kitchen, opening and shutting the cabinet drawers.

Charley reached into a drawer, relinquishing his hold on his captive for only a split second. The man pushed hard on the back of Charley, shoving him hard into the wood cabinet. Before the man had a chance to hit Charley, Jennifer hit him over the head with a twelve-inch frying pan.

"Who is that man?" asked Jennifer calmly.

Charley pulled himself from the floor and looked at Jennifer and then glanced at the man on the floor before rummaging through the bottom drawer. He pulled out a package with two rolls of duct tape.

"Pack our stuff up," he said. "We're going to have to leave this place."

"Okay," she said with a blank look on her face.

"I'll be right back." Charley grabbed the unconscious man by the collar on the back of his shirt and pulled him across the hall and into Troy's apartment. By the time they reached the apartment, the thug had gained enough consciousness to take orders.

Rosie cut a strip of cloth from one of the pillowcases and tied it tight around Troy's bicep, stopping the flow of blood from the wound.

Troy held his arm still as Rosie tended to the wound.

Charley duct-taped Mike King's two hooligans to separate chairs and then put them back-to-back, taping them together. Using both rolls of tape.

"We have to find a doctor," said Rosie.

"It looks like the bleeding has stopped," winced Troy.

"It's just slowed," said Rosie, holding her hand on the wound. "You have to see a doctor."

"I can't go to a doctor." Troy jerked his arm.

Rosie was surprised by his abrupt action. She sat down on the bed and placed the pistol in her purse.

"Troy, man, you need to get that arm fixed," said Charley, noticing the stunned look on Rosie's face.

"I need to ask these guys a few questions before we leave," grimaced Troy, gritting his teeth as he leaned toward the still arrogant captives. He grabbed the smaller of the two men by the hair and pulled until they were face to face. "Where is Mike King?" he asked.

"Don't worry, you'll find out soon enough," said the man, trying to pull his head away from the Troy's grasp.

Troy hesitated for a moment before releasing his hair. He had never thought about killing a person before, but he seriously considered ending the life of the man bound before him. He clenched his fist and struck the man hard on the side of his head, knocking him unconscious.

"Troy," yelled Rosie, grabbing his arm. "Please stop."

Troy again pulled his arm from the grip of Rosie before punching the smaller man. He didn't hit him as hard. "I'm gonna ask you one more time. Where's Mike King?"

"He's at Caesar's. He's leaving tomorrow morning at eight o'clock," said the man. "He knows everything about you and the young lady. Everything except where you are. He's going to kill both of you."

"Y'all are bigger liars than yore boss." Troy turned to Rosie. "Let's get out of here."

"Jen," yelled Charley across the hall toward his apartment.

"I'm coming." Jennifer scurried out of their apartment carrying a large, brown paper bag.

"Where's our stuff?" Charley inquired.

"I thought we were in a hurry." The bottles in the bag clanged together.

"So all you brought was the booze?"

"It's the only thing of value we have," quipped Jennifer.

"Charley, we need to put the boxes from your apartment into the trunk of the car," said Troy, closing the door to his apartment.

Rosie remained quiet as she waited outside with Jennifer while Charley and Troy carried the boxes and secured them in the trunk. Being killed by Mike King was something that had not been of great concern; the idea that she was in a dangerous situation was becoming very real to her. But her silence was not necessarily from the fear of being murdered by a madman; it was more from the realization that she was pregnant with the baby of someone who she really did not know. She had tried throwing reason to the wind, but the coldness she found with Troy made her realize she needed to get away from him as quickly as possible.

***

Tom's legs were getting tired as he paced the sidewalk outside a hangar at the airport in North Las Vegas. The cat and mouse game he had been playing with his brother was beginning to wear thin on his nerves. Waiting was something he was very good at. If fate had spared him of being his brother's keeper, having to wait at the Las Vegas airport, he would be back to his humdrum life of waiting for the wheat to grow in a field outside of Medicine Bow.

"I think you best call Sam agin, Tom," said Drew, sitting along the side of the metal hangar picking up several pebbles and throwing them onto a paved roadway in front of him.

"Dammit, Drew, I don't need you tellin' me to do something every ten minutes." The sun was beating down on his head. "Besides, if he knew anything he would call."

"If Twoy doesn't show up," said Drew, "let's see if Sam will let us stay hea fo anotha night. We can go to a casino and you can show me how to gamble."

Tom looked at Drew's smiling face. Drew's honest approach to life was something that made him special and unique but going to a Las Vegas casino and gambling with him would be absolute torture.

Tom assumed, from experience, that the wait for his brother would be long and most likely unsuccessful. Yet he diligently continued to watch the entrance gate and the small building that was used for the terminal at the miniscule airport.

"That's them." Drew was pointing toward a beat-up automobile next to a hangar on the far side of the terminal.

Tom was surprised at the appearance of his once strong and handsome brother as he exited the automobile. He looked as though he had aged twenty years since the last time he had seen him at the harvest festival. His two friends didn't look much better. Charley was dressed in a worn white tee shirt and a pair of old gray workout pants and his hair was greasy and disheveled. Jennifer was also dressed in baggy workout clothes and she was staring blankly through her perpetually reddened eyes. But it was Rosie who caught Tom's eye. Even though Stanley had told him that she was extremely pretty, Tom was caught off guard by how beautiful she was.

"Troy?" Tom was unsure what to say, even after the weeks of searching.

"We best find somewhere else to talk." Troy glanced at the surroundings. "We have some dangerous fellas on our tail."

Tom opened a side door to a large hangar housing several small planes and allowed everyone to move inside. He wasn't sure how to approach the situation with his brother; their relationship had always been one of respect for each other's space, but he knew he needed to get Troy on the plane as fast as he could. Before he could confront him, Troy's phone rang.

"Hello." Troy turned away from the group.

"Yes," Mike King's voice sounded calm. "Mr. Young."

"Yes." He was almost relieved that it was Mike King. "The men you sent to kill me are both …"

"They are both here with me," Mike King interrupted.

"Okay," Troy took a deep breath, "is there a way we can settle this thing?"

"You can meet me, with the money."

"You tried to kill me."

"You were lucky that I didn't."

"If I agree to meet with you, will you guarantee my safety?" His arm throbbed.

"Absolutely."

"Where do you want to meet?" Troy was feeling faint.

"Come to the sports book at the Golden Nugget. Someone will meet you there."

"I'll be there in an hour."

"Don't disappoint me." Mike King's voice was threatening. "This is your last chance before I prove to you how serious I am."

"I'll be there." Troy closed his phone and turned back to face Tom.

Tom noticed the blood on Troy's shirt. "What in the hell happened to you?"

"I was shot." Troy pulled the makeshift bandage away from his arm and looked at the dark hole in the side of his arm.

"Damn it, Troy. We have to get you to a doctor." Tom moved closer to look at the wound.

"I have to meet with Mike King before I go anywhere." Troy allowed Tom to look closely at his arm with Drew watching over Tom's shoulder.

"Troy." Tom moved back away from his brother, bumping into Drew. "You're comin' back with me right now, even if I have to hog-tie you."

"And I'll help ya, Tom." Drew was standing tall next to Tom. "It's fo yo own good."

Troy fell to one knee, before leaning onto his back. Tom knelt down beside him followed by Drew and Charley. Troy's face had gone from an off-colored gray to chalk white.

"I need to lie down for a bit." Troy lay onto his side, placing his head onto the cool concrete floor. "Just let me rest."

Tom stood up and pulled out his cell phone. He moved away from the group.

"Sam. Troy's here," he said into the phone.

"Tom. Listen carefully," said Sam. "Jerry's ready to fly y'all right now. My attorney Al Jones is almost to yore location, so …"

"Sam," Tom interrupted. "Troy's been shot in the arm and he's saying there are some dangerous men on his tail."

"Y'all can have him back here as quick as you can to a hospital there. I'll let Jerry know about the danger you're in." Sam hung up.

"We can board the airplane right now." Tom positioned himself next to Rosie, talking toward his brother.

Troy placed his left hand onto the floor and grimaced as he pushed on the concrete. Drew reached out to assist him to his feet and then helped him secure his balance once he was standing. "I need to talk to you." Troy jerked away from Drew's grasp. "We need to talk alone. I have to take care of this mess right now."

"Let's go home." Tom put his arm on his brother's shoulder. "We can take care of everything from there far better than we can from here."

"He'll follow us."

"We can handle it, even if he comes looking for you, we can handle it."

"It's not me I'm worried about, it's Ma and Rebecca."

"What about Rosie?"

"She's going back to Denver." The palpable grimace on his face was becoming more distinct. "I made a mistake with her."

"She's gonna have yore baby."

"Nothin' I can do about that now."

"Ma wants her back in Medicine Bow," stated Tom.

"Then y'all can take care of her."

"That's just what we plan on doing." Tom tried to control his rage. "Dammit, Troy, she's having yore baby. If you don't take care of her, we will."

Troy hesitated to respond to his brother's assertion. He knew that his family would never allow a member of theirs to be left uncared for. But he also realized that had he met Rosie under different circumstances, they would still not be right for one another. "Tom." The tone of his voice was much softer than before. "I will be thankful if you do."

"Let's go." Tom was becoming more irritated.

"Tom," Troy was feeling light-headed again, "I have the money from the robbery in the trunk of Charley's car."

Tom stepped back and stared into his brother's eyes. "Okay. Show me." He moved aside, allowing Troy to approach the others.

Troy fidgeted with the key to the trunk as Tom adjusted his eyes to the bright sunlight. Troy opened the trunk and moved back to allow Tom to look at the neatly taped boxes. Tom yanked away the tape on the top of the box and pulled the lid open. He took in and released a huge breath before taping the lid back shut.

"Tom and Troy?" A man with a short grey beard and medium-length grey hair approached from the front of the car. A younger well-dressed man followed him closely. "I'm Al Jones."

"Sam's attorney." Tom looked reassuringly at Troy.

"Troy." Mr. Jones ogled him as though he was worth a million dollars, and to him he was. "We have a lot to talk about."

"I reckon." Troy was exhausted and in a great deal of pain.

"We can discuss everything on the plane ride back to Texas." Mr. Jones recognized the discomfort Troy was experiencing. "Are you all right, son?"

"He has a bullet wound in his arm." Tom placed his arm around Troy's shoulder.

"Is it life-threatening?" asked Mr. Jones, moving to Troy's side.

"We stopped the bleeding," said Tom. "I imagine he'll live."

"I'll have an ambulance meet us at the airport in Dallas." Mr. Jones motioned to his young assistant. "Now mind you, Troy, I don't want to put your life on the line, but it will be much better for all of us if we handle this thing in Texas."

"I'm not leavin' without these boxes," stated Troy, grimacing. "Charley and Jennifer are in danger, so they need to come with us."

"Charley," yelled Tom, pulling the boxes from the trunk of the car. "Can you help me put these boxes on the plane?"

Charley carried each of the boxes up the steps and placed them inside the plane.

Tom looked down and saw the blood on Rosie's blouse as she prepared to board the plane. "Are you injured?" He pulled the cloth of her blouse away from her body.

"No." She was startled by the troubled sound of Tom's voice. "The blood splattered on me when Troy was shot."

Tom moved a step back and gave Troy a malicious glance. He couldn't believe his brother would allow the mother of his unborn baby to be put in such a precarious situation. To be so close to a stray bullet that blood would find its way to her clothing.

"Charley, if it's okay with you, I'm going to park your car at a parking area one of the mechanics told me about."

"Sure."

***

Jerry secured the door and stepped into the cockpit, checking his watch. Drew had taken the front seat with Charley and Jennifer sitting behind him. Rosie sat in the back of the plane next to Troy. Al Jones courteously asked her approval for

Troy to sit next to him. Rosie felt oddly relieved as she politely agreed to the switch. The decision to turn the money over to the authorities was the right one. Of course, having the money in the open would make it easier for him to tell the truth about his involvement in the robbery, along with the unlikely events that led him to his present predicament. Al Jones was watering at the mouth to hear the story.

Maliki and Tanya

"When I first read this, I couldn't believe how brave my mother was."

"So much happened so quickly there," stated Tanya.

"It was really intriguing to read about how close my mother and father were to being killed."

Tanya looked at Troy with a captivating look on her face.

Maliki noticed but didn't catch on.

"You were there too."

Maliki smiled. "I never really thought about that."

"It's interesting how both your mother and father were running from boredom, but looking for opposite outcomes."

"I think Troy relished the excitement," stated Maliki.

"But your mother wanted security to end her boredom."

"She knew very quickly after spending time with Troy that she wasn't going to find it with him."

Tanya placed her hand under her chin and looked away from Maliki. She began tapping her pen on the table.

Maliki realized there was something troubling her.

"Would you like a drink or water?" he asked, stepping away from the table and walking toward the kitchen.

"Maliki." She stopped tapping the pen and looked directly at him.

He stopped and turned toward her. The tone of the way she said his name was much different than any way they had spoken the previous three days.

"Yes?" he asked.

"Who was the old man who came to the apartment Charley referred too?"

Maliki continued toward the kitchen and poured two glasses of water. He hesitated in thought before placing a glass of water on the table in front of Tanya.

"Did the information come from Troy or Charley?"

"Charley," answered Maliki.

"And Troy never mentioned him?"

"No." Maliki sat back down. "I really don't know who it was. I know it wasn't Stanley, because I asked him. When I first read it in Charley's notes I figured it might have been another acquaintance he met in Vegas. But I really don't know."

Dallas, Texas

Ed Dodd couldn't believe he was going to be the person to bring Troy to justice. Although the glamour of the story had steadily faded over the weeks, the question as to who ended up with the money from the robbery in Colorado was still a hot item for the media. Ed knew that as soon as the press received the news about Troy Young, not only being alive, but also being in the custody of the FBI, the event would turn into a circus. In all reality, he was looking forward to finding out what happened to the loot.

It had been almost three hours since Jackie called to let him know that the airplane left Las Vegas. Ed figured he had about enough time to drink a Coke before leaving his office for Medical City Hospital. Arrangements had been made by Sam to transfer Troy from the airport to the hospital, so he didn't want to arrive until the doctors were finished taking care of the gunshot wound.

"Are you ready to leave?" Agent Travis Henry stuck his long neck through the open door and into the small office. "J.J. said the plane landed about five minutes ago."

"Tell him to stay put and keep his eyes on the plane until someone relieves him." Ed retrieved a dollar bill from his wallet. "Leave the money as is, on the plane until we get there."

"I talked with the Colorado bureau. They are on hold until they hear from us." Agent Henry stepped into the office where he towered over his boss. "They want Mr. Young back in Denver as soon as he is able to transport."

"Why don't you check the papers one more time?" Ed straightened his miniscule five-foot body and handed a stack of papers to his young assistant. "We'll go to the hospital first and then secure the money at the plane."

Both men knew that all the papers were in perfect order, and Travis knew that Agent Dodd had a Napoleon complex. So, without question, Agent Henry enthusiastically thumbed through the documents, leaving no doubt that his tiny superior was the man in charge. If he were in charge, he would secure the money first and then go to the hospital. It was not his position to question his superior.

Agent Dodd was trained to make split-second decisions, but he was happy to have the few extra minutes before he decided how to handle the scenario he was about to embark into. He, Sam, and Al Jones had been childhood buddies, and he knew that Al was as cunning an attorney as ever set foot in a courtroom. He knew there was going to be evidence that needed to be handled very careful, especially evidence that consisted of several million dollars; it would be best that he be involved in securing and identifying the stash. He also knew that there was little chance of Troy Young going back to Denver anytime soon.

Medicine Bow, Texas

"Rebecca, do you want me to make us some sandwiches?" Delphia sat close to Rebecca on the couch in the front room of Uncle Martin's home.

"I'm not real hungry." Rebecca flipped through a magazine.

"I could run to my house and get a couple pieces of angel food cake."

"I'm just not hungry."

"Are you worried about Troy coming home?"

"Not really worried." She tossed the magazine to the floor. "Just concerned."

"I hope that Troy isn't in a lot of trouble." Delphia picked up the magazine and placed it on the coffee table.

"I reckon he isn't in too much trouble that Sam and Ma can't get him out of it."

"You know what I'm concerned about?" Delphia placed her hand on Rebecca's wrist. "I'm concerned about the track meet I have next month."

"Is it almost track season?" Rebecca tightly closed her eyes. For the first time in her life, having track season approach was something she dreaded rather than looked forward to.

Delphia squeezed Rebecca's wrist. "I want you to help me train."

"I don't know how much I can help you."

"You could help me a lot." She stood up and got directly in Rebecca's face. "I'm getting really strong, and you could help me train. With your help, I don't think anybody could ever beat me."

"Now don't get too confident." Rebecca looked at her little friend's excited face. She wondered if maybe Lola or her mother put her up to asking for help with running. Something deep in her soul reminded her just how special Delphia really is, that it is Delphia's natural ability to bring out the positive aspects in any situation, no matter how difficult.

"I'm not bragging. I just know that with your help we will be the fastest team ever."

"I'll help. But it won't be easy."

"I don't care how hard it will be." Delphia placed her arms around Rebecca's neck and hugged her tightly.

"Okay, okay. We will start practice this weekend."

Chapter Seven

Dallas, Texas

The flashing red lights of the ambulance sitting several hundred feet off the tarmac was the first sight to greet Tom as he stepped from the door of the airplane. Two men dressed in suits waited at the bottom of the steps.

Tom turned to make eye contact with Mr. Jones. "Y'all have a welcoming committee out here."

"Let me go first." Mr. Jones stepped around Tom. "Please allow Troy to follow behind me."

"I don't feel so good," said Troy, holding his left hand over his injured shoulder.

"Can you walk to the ambulance?" asked Mr. Jones.

"Yeah."

"Troy." Tom placed his hand on his brother's shoulder.

"Yeah," grimaced Troy.

"Good luck." Tom wished there was something he could do to help his brother but knew that just like all the previous incidents before, Troy's destiny was completely out of his control.

Troy only nodded as he followed Mr. Jones down the steps into the custody of the federal agents.

Medicine Bow, Texas

Tom expected the ride to Medicine Bow was going to be uncomfortable to say the least. Charley and Jennifer smelled like cigarette smoke and alcohol as they positioned themselves in the back of the Chevy Suburban. Tom insisted that Rosie sit in the front seat next to Uncle Martin while he sat next to Drew on the middle seat. Uncle Martin's ability to put everyone at ease with his homespun stories even brought a smile to Rosie's face.

It was nearly ten when Uncle Martin parked the Suburban in front of his home. Rebecca and Delphia were sitting on the sofa in the living room watching television. Charley was the first to enter the house, but he quickly moved to the side of the room directly through the front door, allowing the others to enter.

"Hey, Becca." Drew hid his astonishment at the appearance of the once beautiful woman sitting on the couch before him. He tried to mask his surprise by turning to place Tom's suitcase in the center of the room. "Y'all ah gonna have some guests tonight."

"We cleaned the linen on the beds in both guest rooms," stated Delphia, looking around Drew and past Charley and Jennifer toward Rosie.

"Is Troy all right?" Rebecca brought herself up from a slouch and ran her right hand through her matted hair.

"He's at the hospital," said Drew, staring at the floor.

"I just talked with Sam," said Tom, holding Rosie's suitcase. "He and Ma are on their way to Dallas."

"Come on, y'all, move on in and make yourselves at home." Uncle Martin moved toward the kitchen. "I'll see if I can't find something to snack on."

Delphia left her seat next to Rebecca and was standing in front of Rosie, staring at the bulge in her stomach. Rosie placed her hands over her belly and stared back at the curious girl.

"I'll show ya yore room." Delphia spoke softly, holding out her hand.

"Okay." Rosie's cheeks were deep pink. "I'm Rosie."

"I know, we've been talking a lot about ya. I'm Delphia, and this is Rebecca."

"Hello," Rosie smiled warmly.

"Hello." Rebecca moved her leg off of the sofa and onto the floor without removing the blanket covering her lower body, making room for someone to sit next to her.

"Drew, yore daddy left the pickup for you to drive home," Uncle Martin yelled from the kitchen. "It's on the side of the house."

"I guess I best head home." Drew shook his head toward all the new guests as he made his way to the front door, avoiding making eye contact with Rebecca. "Y'all have a good evening."

"Nice meeting you, Drew," yelled Charley as Drew slipped out the front door.

"Go ahead and sit down." Tom motioned for Jennifer to sit next to Rebecca. "The restroom is right down the hall if anyone needs to use it."

"I'm feeling a little sick," said Rosie, surprised that Delphia continued to hold her hand. "If it's all right, I think I'll go to my room."

"Certainly." Tom stumbled over his own suitcase. "I'll put your bag in the room."

"I did change the sheets." Delphia pointed toward the twin bed, shaking her pigtails on her head.

"Thank you," Rosie whispered.

"Let me know if you need anything." Tom placed the bag at the end of the bed.

Rosie truly was thankful for the hospitality as she closed the door to the room and sat down on the navy-blue bedspread, allowing her shoes to fall to the floor. If she were home she would take a long, hot bath. Now she was content having a soft pillow to lay her head on, allowing her to doze off.

Rosie rose from a deep sleep with a jerk, unsure for a second as to where she was. Her head was aching as she brought her feet to the carpet and smoothed a hand over the still-made bed. She took two deep breaths, bringing much needed oxygen to her head before quietly moving out the bedroom door. The light from the television flickered as she unobtrusively stepped from the hallway into the dark living room. The carpet tickled her bare feet as she took two steps and waited, allowing her eyes to adjust to the darkness.

"Hello." Rebecca flipped on the lamp at the end of the sofa and noticed the surprised look on Rosie's face. "I'm sorry. I didn't mean to scare ya."

"Ohh." Rosie took a deep breath and brought a hand to her chest. "I never expected anybody to be awake."

"I've turned into a night owl." Rebecca straightened her body and patted the sofa. "Have a seat."

"I woke up with a headache and …."

"There's some aspirin in the kitchen cabinet above the sink," interrupted Rebecca.

"I think I'll just have a glass of water." Rosie took a step toward the kitchen. "Would you like one?"

"Sure."

Rosie handed Rebecca a glass of water and sat down on the sofa. She felt far more at ease than would be expected as she nestled into the warm cushions. Even though Rebecca's unkempt appearance was quite noticeable, Rosie sensed that the real Rebecca was much more refined.

"Are you excited about the baby?" asked Rebecca. She liked the idea that Rosie had taken the time to add ice.

"I'm excited. Maybe a little scared too."

"What about your family? Are they happy about the baby?"

"I don't have any brothers or sisters. And my mother is … She's in no position to help me."

"My ma is really excited," said Rebecca. "I have a feeling she is going to grill you about how you are taking care of yourself. So be warned. You might have to face some difficult questions tomorrow."

Rosie felt comfortable and somewhat joyous in seeing the fabulous smile Rebecca was showing her. It was nice of Rebecca for being so cordial when she was in obvious distress.

"Are you doing all right?"

"So so. I have good days and bad. I guess I'm a little scared of the future."

"Troy was really saddened to hear about … that you were so sick."

"I know he was."

"You are lucky to have such a wonderful family."

"I know I am." Rebecca dabbed her eyes with the blanket. "How long do you plan on staying?"

"I don't know. I hope to be able to talk with Troy in order to find out what his intentions are. Right now I don't know."

"Rosie." Rebecca hesitated for a moment, wondering if she should be so forward, before asking, "Is Troy the father? Without any question, is he the father of your baby?"

Rosie turned in her seat and looked Rebecca firmly in the eye and shook her head up and down. "Without any doubt. He is the father. But Rebecca … I just don't know how to say this."

"Just say it." Rebecca's interest was piqued. "Whatever is bothering you is best brought out in the open."

"Well," Rosie took a deep breath, "I don't love Troy, and I'm sure he doesn't love me."

"How do you know this?"

"I know, I can tell by the way he acted when we were in Vegas."

"You know about Troy's sickness."

"This goes beyond his sickness."

"You do have this baby in common." Rebecca allowed the blanket to fall from her shoulders. "You two are going to have to figure something out."

"I know we do. I certainly plan on taking care of my baby."

Rebecca stared at her approvingly. "I believe you will be a terrific mom."

"I'm so glad we can talk." Rosie yawned.

"We best go to bed. The next couple of days are going to be hectic."

"I met Stanley. I hope he's okay."

For the first time in her life, Rebecca felt a strong bond with a girlfriend, even though they had just met, she felt relaxed enough to talk about anything. "I think you will like Sam."

"What did you think about Charley and Jennifer?" Rosie brought her voice to a whisper.

"I was so surprised to see them walk in the door." Rebecca turned her body toward Rosie. "It was like, who are these people."

"I know," Rosie giggled.

"After you went to bed," Rebecca mimicked Rosie's giggling, lowering her voice. "Jennifer walked through the front room with her luggage, and it was clanging. There were bottles clanging in her luggage."

"Oh my gosh." Rosie began to laugh. "When we were leaving Troy's room in Las Vegas … there were people trying to kill us, and all she thought about was carrying the bottles of booze. They wouldn't have any clothes if Charley hadn't gone back to their apartment and packed them."

"Goodness, It's going to be an interesting few day around here." Rebecca wished they could talk all night. "Do you like southern food? Like grits?"

"I've never eaten them."

"Let's cook a big breakfast in the morning for everyone. Maybe we can get Lola to make us some angel food cake with fudge frosting for tomorrow afternoon. Lola's Delphia's ma."

"That sounds great." Rosie noticed a light in the hallway come on.

"What's going on out here?" Tom stood in the hallway dressed only in his pajama bottoms.

The girls, both in dishabille, looked at each other and giggled.

"We were just going to bed," said Rebecca.

Rosie walked by Tom without looking directly at him. "Good night."

Tom was intrigued by the way Rosie and Rebecca had hit it off after such a short time together. He assumed that his mother had asked him to bring back the pregnant girl in order to help her with the baby, but maybe there was more to his mother's intuition than he originally thought. Perhaps it was the people of Medicine Bow who were the ones to benefit from having the seemingly lost young woman in their presence.

Dallas, Texas

God knows Sara and Sam had spent their fair share of time waiting at hospitals over the past few months, so they made no qualms in making reservations at a hotel after they found that Troy's injury was not life-threatening. The doctors wanted to keep him overnight and would most likely release him into the custody of the FBI early the next morning. Sam left Sara to be alone with her son while he talked with Al.

Sam and Al sat at a table in the corner of the waiting room waiting for Ed to arrive. The attorney relayed to Sam the entire conversation he and Troy had during the plane ride home. Troy's version of how he ended up with the money seemed to stretch the truth, yet the sequence of events matched everything Sam knew about the caper. Sam was certain that Troy was being sincere with Al, but knowing Troy as well as he did, he was sure that all of it could not be true.

Al and Ed were two of Sam's oldest and most trusted friends, ones he could be completely candid with. It only made sense that when Ed arrived at the hospital in the middle of the night the three of them would have a meeting of the minds to share amongst themselves everything they had gathered concerning Troy's dilemma. Ed listened carefully as Al again conveyed his conversation with Troy on the plane ride from Las Vegas. He scratched his chin and stared directly into Sam's eyes.

"The first thing we need to do is secure the money." Ed pulled his cell phone from his coat jacket. "I'll have Agent Henry meet us at the airport and he can relieve J.J. Y'all know the money should have been placed into evidence in Nevada."

"Now, mind you. I never realized the boxes contained money until we were well over Texas." Al always protected himself first.

"Uh huh." Ed glared at his friend. "Well, let's go get it now."

"I'm gonna drop Sara off at the hotel," said Sam. "I'll meet y'all at the airport."

***

By the time Sam arrived at his airplane, Ed and Al were standing in the parking lot with the boxes of money lying on a small pallet, illuminated by the headlight from their van. Agent Henry, wearing latex gloves and holding a box cutter, was preparing to open the top box.

"I figured you wanted to be here to see this," said Ed, looking at Sam as he motioned toward Agent Henry. "Go ahead. Open it."

The agent cut the tape and pulled the lid open. All four men merged over the box and looked inside. The top layer inside the box contained only newspapers. Ed yanked the newspaper and threw it on the ground expecting to find the grand prize wrapped somewhere toward the bottom.

"What the hell." Ed's face flushed and then paled. "There's no money in here."

Sam was surprised, but not shocked, as he watched the newspapers being dumped from the remaining boxes. He knew Troy well enough to not be stunned by anything that happened concerning him.

The two FBI agents sifted through the newspapers, tossing them from side to side when one lone twenty-dollar bill floated to the ground. Ed glared at the money before motioning for Agent Henry to obtain the evidence.

Ed resisted his impulse to kick the boxes scattered on the concrete tarmac lying innocently before him. Everything would have been so much easier had there never been any boxes of money involved with the return of Troy to Texas. But now the can of worms had been opened, and he was obligated to investigate the issue to the best of his ability.

"What did he do with all the money?" Agent Dodd was directing his question toward the attorney.

"I don't know, Ed." The attorney couldn't mask his distress. "All I can do is go by what Troy told me on the airplane."

"Well …" Ed took a deep breath and turned toward Sam. "J.J. was here directly after the plane arrived. Sam, I need to talk with your pilot."

"I reckon he left for home."

"Call him and tell him to get his ass back here now."

Sam could see the concern in Ed's face as he dialed Jerry's number on his cell phone. Jerry was less than five minutes away and agreed to return expeditiously.

"Travis, I want you to search the airplane." Ed was shaking his head.

Travis hesitated after hearing his orders.

"Go on," yelled Ed.

"I thought you might call in some more help," replied Travis.

"No. Just do it yourself." Ed looked passively at the agent. "I have a feeling there ain't a damn thing to be found anyway."

"Here's Jerry," stated Sam.

Jerry drove his brand-new Ford Mustang next to the three men and rolled down his window.

"What is it, Sam?"

"Jerry," Sam leaned over to talk to his pilot face to face, "we need to check yore car."

"Why?" Jerry opened the door, forcing Sam to take a step back.

"We expected to find some money in the boxes Troy placed on the plane. But they were full of newspapers." Sam placed his large hand on Jerry's shoulder. "Now no one is accusing you of anything, it is just best that we look now so that you won't become a suspect down the road."

"Sam." Jerry waved his arm to the side, offering his car to Agent Dodd. "I have nothing to hide. I'll open the trunk."

Al Jones contemplated the entire conversation that had taken place between himself and Troy on the airplane only a few hours earlier, as he watched Agent Dodd fruitlessly search the sports car. Being suspicious by nature, he was convinced that Troy had placed the money from the robbery in the boxes at one time or another. There was no logical reason for the young man to confess to procuring the money if he didn't have it.

"Nothing here." Ed slammed the trunk shut.

"I reckon I can go home now." Jerry voiced his question to Sam.

"Did you stay with the airplane from the time it landed until we showed up from the hospital this evening?" Ed leaned on the hood of the car.

"I never left. I always clean the plane before I leave." Jerry looked at Sam. "Sometimes Mr. Blake needs to leave without much notice."

"And no one else boarded it."

"Not a soul. Your man was outside the entire time."

"I reckon if we need anything else we will contact you." Ed moved away from the car. "Thanks for cooperating."

"Jerry, hang tight for a moment," said Sam. "I need to talk with ya as soon as I finish here."

"Sure thing, Sam." There was some concern on Jerry's face. "I'll be right here."

"I think we need to talk with Tom Young." Al's abrupt declaration caught both Sam and Ed off guard.

"What's on your mind?" Sam could see the concern on Al's face.

"Tom was the one who loaded the boxes onto the airplane before we left Las Vegas."

"Tom wouldn't take the money." Sam's voice was firm.

"Mind you, Sam, I'm not accusing him; I'm simply making a statement."

"I need to talk with everyone who was on the airplane," interjected Ed. "I need to do it immediately."

"It's the middle of the night," said Al.

"We can do it the first thing this morning." Ed knew he wasn't going to get any sleep. "Travis and I can drive out to Medicine Bow in a few hours."

"I need to say something that's been eatin' at me ever since we opened the boxes." Sam took off his Stetson and ran his hand through his thin hair. "I'm not sure that Troy ever had the money from the bank robbery."

"What makes you think that?"

"I know Troy. If he had money, he would spend it." Sam wanted to make sure that Al was making note of what he was saying. "Knowing his disposition, especially without taking medication, he would have went wild spending the money in Las Vegas."

"Are you saying he blew five million dollars?" asked Al.

"Hell no. He couldn't have spent that much money without being noticed." Sam looked at Ed.

"Yep." Ed shook his head. "There was an alert that Troy might have been in Las Vegas. The agents would have been aware of him had he been in a casino, and most definitely would have recognized him if he lost millions of dollars."

"He never had the money." Sam placed his hat back on his head.

"I'll guarantee ya he convinced me he was packing around several million dollars," said Al. "Hell, Sam, he told me straight out that he had carried the money with him from Colorado."

"And he believed every word of what he told you."

Al studied Sam's posture. Sam was the one man who he would never play poker with because it was impossible to tell whether or not he was bluffing. Nonetheless, right or wrong, Sam's assumption that Troy was sick enough to imagine that he had the money from the bank robbery, along with his paranoia of being pursued by the vicious killer Mike King, would be an excellent defense for him to pursue. Certainly, any normal person would try to escape those circumstances.

"What do you think?" Al looked at Ed.

"I don't know what I think." Ed took a deep breath. "But I do need to talk with the others on that plane, especially Tom Young."

Sam made arrangements to meet both Al and Ed at Uncle Martin's house at ten o'clock, in less than six hours. He would go to the hotel and wake Sara.

With the exception of making flight plans, all other dealings Jerry had procured with Blake Enterprises had been handled by Stanley. He stepped from his car as he saw Sam approach, somewhat concerned about his boss's inquisition.

"Jerry," Sam looked tired, "I need you to set up some security for me."

"Where at, Sam?" asked Jerry, leaning on the hood of his car.

"I need ya to protect the entire town of Medicine Bow." Sam waited to digest Jerry's reaction.

"Sam," Jerry hesitated, "Stanley had me set it up yesterday. I have twenty ops already on the payroll. Nobody can come or go to Medicine Bow without us knowing. We're covered twenty-four, seven."

"Stanley did …" Sam tipped his hat back. "Well, Stanley is gonna be out of commission for quite a while. I reckon you know he had a heart attack."

"Uh, Sam." Jerry shuffled his feet. "I was just on the phone with him when you called. He's at the airport in Phoenix right now getting ready to catch the first flight this morning to Dallas."

"Are you sure?"

"Yes, sir."

"Why that cantankerous, old fool." Sam adjusted his hat and turned away. "Thank you, son. I'll be in touch."

Medicine Bow, Texas

Everyone crowded around the small kitchen table to eat the enormous breakfast prepared by Rosie and Rebecca. The two girls had scrambled every egg they could find in the house and fried three boxes of bacon. There were two pitchers of orange juice and a large plate of toast sitting at the center of the table next to a big bowl of grits. There was hardly room on the table for the plates and silverware.

"Good Lord. Did you gals cook every morsel of food we had in the house?" asked Uncle Martin.

"Not all of it." Rebecca smiled. "There's still a little milk and flour left. We couldn't figure out how to make pancakes from scratch."

"I think there is plenty to eat." Uncle Martin was happy to see Rebecca smiling. "You girls did a great job."

"Everything looks terrific." Tom smiled at both Rosie and Rebecca. He heard the girls working in the kitchen earlier in the morning but decided not to crash the fun they were having.

"Well, dig in." Rebecca pushed the bowl of eggs toward Uncle Martin.

"I'd wake up early every morning for this kind of breakfast." Charley placed a hand full of bacon on his plate and then put two pieces on Jennifer's plate.

"Not too many." Jennifer held her skinny hand over her plate. She looked as though she was still drunk or at the very least had a splitting headache.

"Well, this ain't something we have every morning." Uncle Martin took a large scoop of eggs.

"Did you sleep okay last night?" Tom was looking at Rosie.

"I slept very well." Rosie felt comfortable in the cozy home, and Tom's question made her feel even more relaxed. "Thank you."

"Is that bacon I smell?" Drew Fudderman opened the front door and knocked gently.

"Come on in, Drew." Tom stood up from his seat as everyone looked toward the living room.

"I could smell that bacon cleaw out on the fwont porch." Drew's large body completely filled the kitchen door.

"Sit down." Rebecca stood from her chair and walked to the cabinet to get Drew a plate, her perfect gait going unnoticed.

"That's okay." Drew continued to stand at the threshold to the kitchen.

"There's plenty to eat." Rebecca replaced her empty plate with a clean one.

"I was just kidding." Drew sat down. "But I am hungwy."

"What are you doing here so early?" Tom watched Drew fill his plate to overflowing with eggs and bacon.

"Sam called and told me to be hea at ten o'clock." Drew stuck a piece of bacon in his mouth.

"Sam did." Tom looked down at his plate.

"He's bringing his FBI friend by to talk with y'all," said Uncle Martin. "He called about an hour ago."

"What about Troy?" Tom placed his fork onto his half-empty plate of food.

"He's going to be all right," said Uncle Martin.

"Sam said he's gonna go home today." Drew waved a piece of toast toward Tom. "O' maybe to jail."

Sam could see everyone massed in the living room of Uncle Martin's house, so he walked in the front door without bothering to knock. Agent Dodd and Al Jones stepped in behind him with all three men removing their hats.

"How are y'all doing?" Sam looked around the room, noticing several strange faces. "This here is FBI Agent Dodd, and I guess most of you have met my lawyer Al Jones."

"Pleased to meet y'all," said Drew.

"Thank you," said Agent Dodd, stepping to the middle of the room. "I came out here this morning because I have a few questions I need to ask of y'all."

"Shoot," said Drew.

"If there is no objection, I would like to talk with each of you alone."

"No one has to talk," said Sam. "But if you have nothing to hide, it would be best to leave all suspicions behind us."

"While y'all are thinking about this, Tom, if you approve, I would like to talk with you first."

Tom was somewhat surprised that it was he rather than Rosie whom the agent wished to talk with first, but he answered, "Of course. Shall we use the kitchen?"

"If you don't mind, I would rather talk out in the van."

"That will work."

Agent Dodd loved having a power of authority over people. When interrogating a suspect, he was a control freak who felt he could always read a person's guilt or innocence if given thirty minutes alone. He had no doubt that the truth about Tom's involvement with Troy and the money would be revealed very quickly.

"Straight to the point ..." Agent Dodd pushed the seat back in the Suburban and placed a notebook on his lap, never looking directly at Tom. "Do you know anything about the money from the robbery in Denver?"

"Not a thing." Tom never flinched.

"When did you first come into contact with the boxes Troy had in his possession?" Agent Dodd looked directly at Tom.

"About a half hour before we put them on the airplane."

"You knew nothing about the boxes before this time?"

"No."

"Did you open them?"

"I opened the one box and looked inside," Tom answered. "I taped it back after we noticed Mr. Jones approaching the car."

"Did Mr. Jones see the contents inside the box?" asked Agent Dodd.

"No, he didn't. I taped it before he and his assistant were close enough to see inside it, and he never asked me to open it again."

"What happened after you closed the box?"

"Charley and I loaded them onto the airplane," stated Tom. "Then I drove Charley's car to a parking area at the airport that one of the mechanics had told me about while everyone else got on board."

Agent Dodd bit his lower lip and scribbled on the top of his notepad. "Tom, was there any money in the boxes?"

"Not in the box I opened."

"What was in it?"

"Newspapers."

Agent Dodd was surprised at the calmness Tom displayed and at how savvy he was at being interrogated. Most people talked excessively. "I don't understand something," stated Agent Dodd.

"What might that be?" asked Tom.

"Why did you bring the boxes back to the airplane if they were only full of newspapers?"

Tom shifted in his seat and squared his shoulders with the agent.

"That seems like a lot of effort for no reason," Agent Dodd declared.

"If I hadn't brought the boxes back with me, Troy would never have gotten on the plane. For whatever reason, he was convinced the boxes were full of money. He wasn't about to leave them." Tom shrugged his shoulders. "That's why I put them on the plane."

"Let me ask you straight out. Do you think Troy ever had any money from the robbery?"

"I don't know," Tom shook his head, "that is the God's truth. I don't know."

"That is all I have to ask. I may need to talk with you again." Agent Dodd opened his briefcase and handed Tom a piece of paper. "I do need you to write down the events that transpired between you and Troy from the time you met with him in Las Vegas and the landing of the plane in Dallas."

"Okay." Tom took the paper.

"I know this isn't the most comfortable place to write, but I would appreciate it if you would do so here in the truck while I talk with the others inside the house."

"That's no problem."

"Just bring it inside when you are done."

"Agent Dodd. What do you think is going to happen to Troy?" asked Tom.

"He'll be interrogated for any information he has, and a decision will be made if there is reason to charge him with his part in the robbery."

"Do you think he will be charged?"

"I think he will be charged with something. The boxes will have to be examined at the lab and the room he rented in Las Vegas will need to be processed before anything definitive can be decided." Agent Dodd opened the car door.

"I'm sure the truth will all come out," stated Tom.

Agent Dodd gave Tom a blank look. He stepped from the vehicle and closed the door. Rosie was the next person he wanted to speak with.

Rosie was very cooperative and answered the agent's questions quickly and as honestly as she could. She was extremely surprised when Agent Dodd told her that the boxes from Vegas contained only newspapers. But what really surprised her about the interview was that Agent Dodd never asked one question concerning Stanley, and he mentioned nothing about the night she planted the bag of money in Vinny's room.

Dallas, Texas

Troy's arm was stiff and the pain was much worse than he remembered it being before he entered the hospital. He sat silently as the doctor finished the final wrap on the bandage covering his wound, taking little notice of the two well-dressed FBI agents standing at the door.

"You're free to go." The doctor detected the indifferent gaze he received from Troy as he handed him his shirt. "Make sure you don't lift anything heavy."

"How bad is it?" asked Troy.

"The wound will heal. Infection is the main concern." The doctor looked toward the agents. "You should have someone look at it again in about a week, sooner if the pain increases."

Troy grimaced as he placed his wounded arm through the shirt and waited as the doctor pulled the shirt around his shoulders.

"I reckon I won't be lifting anything heavy for a while," said Troy. "It should heal just fine."

Troy stood up and walked toward his FBI escorts. Just as always, his future was completely out of his control.

***

Stanley had a quick snooze on the flight from Phoenix back to Dallas. When he got on board, he mentioned to the flight attendant that he was simply going to sleep and not to suspect him of being dead. The flight attendant had heard about the incident from the day before. She laughed and guaranteed him she wouldn't pronounce him dead. He was feeling rested as he limped through the airport parking garage.

He sat down behind the wheel of his pickup truck and pulled out his cell phone. He had missed twelve calls, six of them from Sam. He knew he was going to get a royal ass chewing, but first he needed to check with Ben Fudderman and find out if he had made progress in tracking down Mike King's alias.

"Number One," answered Ben Fudderman. It was Ben's idea to code his name.

"Ya, ummm, Number One." Stanley shook his head as he talked in the phone. "Were ya able to find anything out about the alias in Vancouver?"

"Mike King is an alias."

"Good Lord, son. I know that," yelled Stanley. "I'm talking about Jack LeClair."

"It's an alias too," answered Ben.

"What?" Stanley was surprised. "Are ya sure?"

"Jack Leclair is Jean Brochard's neighbor." Ben's voice was slow and deep. "John Brochard is Mike King."

"So he is in Vancouver," stated Stanley.

"No. Not now he isn't," replied Ben. "Number Two and Number Three have already tracked him back to Seattle."

Number Two and Number Three were Jeannie and Helen, two soldiers recommended for the surveillance job by Jerry. Stanley played Ben's game and said, "Do Number Two and Three have any idea how to find Mr. King in Seattle?"

"They know right where to find him," answered Ben. "We'll be at his place this afternoon."

"I need y'all to get me his cell phone number when ya find him," said Stanley. "Then just lie low and keep an eye on him."

"Copy that," said Ben. "Number One out."

"Good God," said Stanley, placing his cell phone on the seat of the pickup.

Stanley laughed when Jerry first recommended Ben Fudderman for the job of tracking down and dealing with Mike King. But Jerry was adamant about the local boy's qualifications. Jerry also recommended Jeannie and Helen. Jerry was accurate in his assessment; the three of them had been dedicated soldiers who, now discharged from the service, together made a very effective team.

Stanley started his truck and slowly drove out of the airport parking lot. He was going to take his time driving back to the ranch. He needed the time to figure out what to tell Sam why he discharged himself from the hospital.

Medicine Bow, Texas

"I bet you can see some beautiful sunsets from here," said Rosie, rocking in unison with Rebecca and Delphia in the chair swing on the front porch of Uncle Martin's house.

"Sometimes when the clouds are just right, they are magnificent," stated Rebecca.

"It's very peaceful." Rosie took in a deep breath. "What are planted in the fields?"

"Most of the crops are wheat," said Rebecca. "That field over there is cotton."

"We have wheat in Colorado," stated Rosie, "but I've never seen a cotton field before."

"Tomorrow I can walk ya out into that field." Delphia stepped off the porch swing. "We best keep an eye out for rattlesnakes."

"Look. There's Jennifer." Rebecca pointed to the far end of Main Street where Jennifer was briskly walking toward them.

"You shore have good eyes," stated Delphia, stepping to the railing on the porch.

"She's been walking all afternoon," said Rebecca.

"How long do you think her and Charley are plannin' on stayin'?" asked Delphia.

"I have no idea." Rebecca kept her eyes on Jennifer as she made her way toward them. "Charley has been helpful around the house."

"He replaced the toilet in the main bathroom last night," stated Rosie. "I think he's working on the sink now."

"He shore is handy," said Delphia. "I'll ask Sam if he could hire him to work for Blake Enterprises."

"You better wait and let Charley and Jennifer make their own decisions," said Rebecca.

"Hi." Jennifer stepped onto the porch and leaned on the railing in front of the girls. "Golly, am I tired."

"You walked a long way," stated Rebecca. "I've been watching you for hours."

"It felt so good to just get out and move." Jennifer's cheeks were bright red. "I walked all the way out to the old farm building west of town."

"That's the Fuddermans' farm." Delphia jumped directly in front of Jennifer.

"That's Drew's home?"

"Yep."

"The new addition they have is really nice." Jennifer stared at Delphia as though she was seeing her for the first time. "But it's so small."

"That's for the pigs." Delphia laughed. "The Fuddermans live in the old shack."

"The pigs?" Jennifer looked at Rebecca.

"It's a long story," said Rebecca.

"The Fuddermans are really nice people." Delphia crowded Jennifer and looked her directly in the eyes.

"I'm sure they are." Jennifer took a small step backwards.

Delphia crossed her arms. "What are you and Charley plannin' on doin'?"

"Delphia!" yelled Rebecca.

"Charley's a pretty handy man, and my pa and Sam could use another handyman around here." Delphia ignored Rebecca's cold stare. "But we are goin' have to find something for you to do."

"Delphia. Mind your manners." Rebecca leaned forward on the swing.

"I just want to get everything out in the open so we don't have to be wondering." Delphia uncrossed her arms and stared at Rebecca.

"That doesn't mean you have to give Jennifer the third degree."

"I guess I don't know for sure what we are planning to do," replied Jennifer. "I know Troy had talked with Charley before we left Las Vegas about some sort of business venture."

"There is plenty of time to figure that all out," Rebecca looked at Rosie, realizing that the uncertainty of the situation applied to her as much as anyone.

"Rebecca," Sara opened the screen door and stepped onto the porch, "there's a telephone call for you."

"Who is it?" asked Delphia.

"It's Jerry." Sara smiled as she handed Rebecca the telephone and went back inside the house.

"I'll bet Jerry wants to take her flying." Delphia sat down between Rebecca and Rosie.

Rebecca looked cross-eyed at Delphia as she continued to talk.

"Let her talk," said Rosie.

"He wants to take you flying, doesn't he?" Delphia grabbed Rebecca's arm when she finished talking.

"No." Rebecca handed the phone to Delphia. "Would you take it back inside?"

"Well, what did he want?" Delphia took the phone.

"Dinner and a movie."

"I knew he likes you. I've known it all along." Delphia stood up. "When are ya goin'?"

"Not this weekend, but the next." Rebecca took in a deep breath. "Jerry's really busy with work. He just wanted to make sure I am still interested in going out with him."

"We're goin' to make you look so nice," said Delphia. "Good ole Jerry's gonna think he's out with a movie star."

"I have to figure out what I'm going to wear." Rebecca turned toward Rosie and smiled. "I've never been out on a real date."

***

Sam, Lola, Sara, and Jackie were sitting at the dining room table, drinking sweet tea, when Stanley came through the front door of the ranch house. He limped by them and went straight to the bar where he poured himself a glass of Wild Turkey. The three women were all smiling, but Sam had a terrible frown on his face. Stanley sat down hard on the large wooden chair at the far end of the long table.

"How ya feelin', Stanley?" asked Lola.

"Resurrected," answered Stanley, taking a full drink of bourbon.

Sara and Jackie chuckled. Lola grinned, and Sam grimaced.

"What in the world happened?" asked Sara. "How did you end up in the hospital?"

"Well." Stanley tipped his hat back on his head. "Two pretty, young girls on the airplane ride home from Vegas pronounced me dead, and the flight attendant confirmed it." He took another drink. "Apparently, I wasn't. They dropped me off in Phoenix anyway."

"What did the doctor at the hospital in Phoenix tell you?" asked Sara.

"Just a slight heart attack."

Hearing Stanley's rendition of his illness really pissed Sam off. He knew the women were doing their best to break the ice between the two friends, but enough was enough.

"Dammit, Stanley." Sam finally yelled. "Ya had us worried to death."

Stanley sat silently and stared a hole into the table. His plan to placate Sam was to remain quiet and agree with whatever he told him.

"There is no such thing as a slight heart attack." Sam stood up from the table, never taking his eyes off Stanley. "Jackie, can ya get me the list of Stanley's appointments?"

Jackie went into her office and returned with a folder. She placed it on the table between the two men.

"Here's the deal." Sam opened the folder. "You are either going to these doctor appointments or you are no longer under the employment of Blake Enterprises. There is no more of yore telling me you might go. You are going to these appointments. Period."

The threat of being fired was comical to Stanley. He was already wealthy beyond his wildest dreams. Besides, Sam loved him like a family member.

Stanley looked at the list of appointments and tapped his right index finger on the table.

"What in the hell do I need a colonoscopy for?" He looked at Sam with an open mouth.

"Yore gonna go to every one of them appointments," said Sam. "The first one is the day after tomorrow."

"I'll be there." Stanley closed the folder.

"We're making plans for our wedding," said Sara, looking down the long table toward the two men.

"That's another reason I don't want ya fallin' over dead." Sam spoke with a much calmer timbre. "I need ya to be my best man."

Stanley felt the cold glass on his thick fingers as he twirled the remaining bourbon around and downed it in one gulp. He looked up at Sam and shook his head up and down in approval.

"Sara and Lola are trying to figure out how Lola can stand up with her and perform the ceremony at the same time." Sam looked at the ladies.

"That will be a true honor for me to stand up with you at yore wedding." Stanley stood up from his chair. "Yore daddy would be very proud of you."

Sam walked around the table and offered Stanley his hand. Stanley shook the hand and slapped Sam hard on the shoulder.

"Stanley." Sam hugged his old friend and said, "Go ahead and give yoreself a twenty-five cent an hour raise."

Stanley chuckled and let out a deep breath. Sam was the only person he could really call family. Deep down in his soul he was happy that Sam was concerned about his well-being.

***

The air was clear and there was a slight breeze blowing out of the north as Jerry crouched down, placing his knee on a clump of grass situated on the highest hill on the south side of Medicine Bow. He looked through high-powered binoculars toward a grove of trees over two miles to the east. He could clearly see three men busy adjusting their gear within the hidden confines of the low-lying area. He moved the lens of the binoculars to the right of the trees and then to the left. He knew that five of his operatives were somewhere within a hundred yards of the intruders, but for the life of him he couldn't spot them.

"Just hang tight," Jerry said into his head-mounted radio. "Let's see what they're intentions are."

Each one of the twenty men Jerry had hired at the request of Sam and Stanley was a highly trained fighting man who had seen duty in either Iraq or Afghanistan. After their tours overseas, each had been hired and retrained by private security companies. These men were the best soldiers in the world. Jerry was the pilot who flew several of the men into combat during the time of their service, so he knew firsthand of their qualifications. The others were all vouched for by members of his team. Sam was a very generous supporter of the men and women who fought for our country. He allowed the soldiers to train on several acres of land and hired them whenever the opportunity showed itself. Even with Mike King's men lurking on the outskirts of town, Medicine Bow had never been more secure or safe.

"Here." Jerry handed the binoculars to one of the two men flanking him. "I need to check in with the boss."

Jerry moved to his vehicle on the other side of the ridge they were scouting from.

Stanley just finished a bowl of Raisin Nut Bran when his phone rang. He had slept in later than usual.

"Jerry," he said into his phone.

"We have guests," Jerry was quick to the point.

"Is everything under control?" Stanley asked nervously.

"Oh yeah." Jerry's voice was steady. "There are only three."

"Where are they?"

"In the little grove of trees east of town," answered Jerry. "They're definitely professionals. They are taking their time setting up."

"I'll be in my office in ten minutes. I hope Ben has located Mike King," said Stanley. "I shore would like to confront that bastard."

"We can take these guys at any time," said Jerry. We've been listening to their conversations, and I'm confident they aren't expecting any reinforcements."

"Do you know who they are?" asked Stanley.

"They're speaking mostly English, but every now and then they say something in French." Jerry lowered his voice. "They definitely are planning on killing someone in Medicine Bow. They are equipped to do so."

"How many guys do you have with you?" asked Stanley.

"All twenty," answered Jerry. "We have all directions covered as a precaution."

"Are they communicating on a cell phone?"

"Yes, sir."

"Do you have the number where the call originates from?"

"Yes, sir. I'll text it to you right away."

As soon as Stanley entered his office, he called Sam. He sought to warn him of the impending danger and make sure neither he nor anyone else in Medicine Bow accidentally crossed paths with Mike King's men.

Sam was incensed by the audacity of the villainous Mike King in sending men with bad intentions to the safe confines of their community. He knew he had to rely on Stanley's judgment in taking care of the problem. He told his old friend that it was now time to put the threat of Mike King to rest for good.

"Okay, first things first," Stanley said to himself after hanging up the phone with Sam.

He dialed Ben's cell number.

"Number One," answered Ben. "I was about to call you."

"Have y'all found this Brouchard fella?"

"I have my eyes on him right now," answered Ben into his headphone. "He's sitting on his patio drinking coffee."

"Has he been on the telephone this morning?"

"He's on it right now."

"Do you have yore sniper rifle with you?" asked Stanley.

"I'm watching him through the telescope."

"Now listen, son," said Stanley. "Make sure ya are hid. I don't want him seeing ya and takin' off."

"The house he's in is isolated on about forty acres. I'm on a hill to the west of him so the sun won't be a problem if I have to stay until night. I'm completely covered by trees."

"Okay, what I'm goin' to tell ya now is important. If I call you back and you hear me say the word checkmate," Stanley cleared his throat, "I want you to put a bullet right between that son of a bitch's eyes."

"Checkmate. Yes, sir." Ben's voice never wavered.

"If I say Marmalade, I want y'all to disappear from there and come home," said Stanley. "Do ya understand?"

"I understand completely," answered Number One.

"If for some reason he moves from that spot, you let me know," said Stanley. "I want you to have eyes on him at all times."

"Will do," answered Ben.

Stanley looked at the text he had received from Jerry. He sat down at his desk and thought for a moment. He called Jerry.

"Take um out." Stanley spoke as soon as Jerry answered. "Don't hurt um."

"Yes, sir," answered Jerry.

"Then bring them to my office, with their gear."

"We'll be there before you know it," Jerry took in a deep breath.

Stanley went to his bar and poured a glass of Jack Daniels. He stared at it for a moment, debating if it was too early to imbibe. He took a drink, then dialed Mike King.

"Yes." Mike King sounded curious.

"Mr. King, this is Stanley getting back in touch with you concerning the Troy Young problem," Stanley said calmly.

"Ah yes. Stanley. The country hick who has my money. It's impressive you have this number. I'll change it when we finish talking," said Mike King. "Do you still think I'm a cheap hood?"

"I apologize for saying that." Stanley clenched his fist. "I want to make a deal with you to resolve this mess that has developed between us."

"Give me my money."

"I can do that," said Stanley. "I can have you five million dollars in cash delivered to a place of yore choice. We don't even have to meet."

"Wow, what a difference a few days makes." Mike King hesitated, "Here's the deal. You give me six million dollars, in cash, and Troy Young. I will then let you off the hook."

"Mr. King," Stanley held his temper. "I do want to solve this in a civil manner. Ya do know Troy is in police custody?"

"You know as well as I do that with all the money you have he will be released very quickly."

"I just want to solve our problem in a peaceful way," stated Stanley. "I can't emphasize how badly I would like to resolve this right here and now."

"Stanley, you're scared," retorted Mike King. "You should be frightened."

"No, sir. You are misinterpreting compassion and reason with fear and weakness." Stanley remained calm as he spoke slow and deliberately. "You know I almost died the other day. Almost dying makes ya change yore perspective on things. Now please, I just want to get this ordeal over with in a peaceful manner."

"Listen, you chickenshit, I told you what I want," said Mike King. "You can try and … what do you Texan's say, bullshit me all you want, but eventually you will find out I can be very persuasive."

"I will give you the six million dollars," said Stanley, taking in a deep breath, staring at the glass of whiskey. "But the boy is out of the question."

"Not everyone you pompous assholes come in contact with is for sale. I guess I'm going to have to prove that to you," yelled Mike King into his phone.

Stanley looked outside the window. Jerry and his operatives were leading three men with bags over their heads toward his office.

"Sir. Can ya give me about thirty minutes to think this over?" asked Stanley. "I would very much appreciate the time."

"You can take all the time you want," answered Mike King, shutting off his phone.

"Should I call the sheriff and have them come get these guys?" Jerry asked as he stepped into Stanley's office.

"Hell no," answered Stanley. "We're gonna pay them off. Then get all their information and use them somewhere down the line."

"You want me to just let them go?"

"We'll make damn sure we know who they are first," Stanley shook his head up and down and smiled at Jerry. "Son, that's called making a friend out of an enemy."

"Here's their cell phones and wallets." Jerry placed a small bag on Stanley's desk. "We have the rest of their equipment in the trucks."

"I take it there were no problems in apprehending them."

"No, we were on them before they had a chance to think. They were definitely surprised," said Jerry. "Their weaponry is old fashioned."

"Hang tight for a second, Jerry," said Stanley, dialing his phone. "I just finished a conversation with Mike King, and I need to call Ben to check on what that skunk is doing."

"Number One," Ben answered.

"Do you still have eyes on the target?"

"Affirmative."

"What's he doing?"

"He's still sitting on his patio looking at himself through a handheld mirror," answered Ben. "I think he's plucking his eyebrows. Wait. He put the mirror down and he's making another phone call."

"Y'all make sure he doesn't disappear on ya," said Stanley. "Let me know if he moves. I don't want to lose him."

"Number Two and Three have eyes on all exits," said Ben.

"Just keep on yore toes and …"

As Stanley spoke, one of the phones in the bag on the desk rang. Jerry pulled the phone out and handed it to Stanley.

"Hang on," said Stanley to Number One, taking the phone from Jerry.

"Yes," Stanley whispered into the intruder's phone.

"Are you in position?" Mike King's conspicuous voice echoed through the phone.

"Yes," Stanley whispered softly.

"Kill the boy's mother and sister."

Stanley almost dropped the phone. He took in a deep breath with his mouth wide open. For a brief moment, he visualized both Rebecca and Sara. He finally replied in an extremely high voice, "Are you completely insane?"

"Who is this?" Mike King yelled.

"You know damn well who it is, Mr. Brouchard." Stanley held the intruder's phone in his left hand and moved his phone into speaking position. "Or whatever yore name is, it's that country hick you are teaching a lesson to."

"How did you get this phone …?"

Stanley ignored the question and spoke into his phone. "Number One, can you put a beam on this guy's forehead?"

"One second," Ben answered, looking through the telescope of his rifle. "It's there now."

"You're not making sense …"

"Mr. Brouchard, I think you might be one of the evilest motherfuckers to ever walk the face of this earth," Stanley yelled. "Pick up the mirror in front of you and look at your forehead."

Mike King slowly picked up the mirror and looked at his face. There was a red dot moving back and forth between his neatly trimmed eyebrows.

"Mr. Brouchard," Stanley screamed. "Checkmate!"

A loud thud ended the conversation.

"Number One. Confiscate his cell phone and come on home," said Stanley, still breathing hard.

"Roger that," Ben said, removing his earpiece.

Stanley's hands were shaking as he placed both cell phones on his desk. He took a breath through his big, red nose and stared blankly at Jerry.

"Well," said Jerry, "are you making some more friends there, Stanley?"

***

Middle school track meets were very generic to say the least. The physical education teacher was responsible for the logistics of the contest as well as coaching the girls. The competition was held after school with the entire affair lasting three hours at most. Nevertheless, Delphia was a nervous wreck. She had been on the dirt track stretching ever since school ended nearly an hour prior. A big smile came to her face when she saw her mother, Sara, Rebecca, and Rosie walking toward the track from the school parking lot.

"I was worried y'all wasn't gonna be here for my first event," said Delphia, running to greet the contingent from Medicine Bow. "They're fixin' to start the first heat, and I'm in the third."

"You better go get ready to run," said Rebecca. "We'll be at the finish line."

The four women set their lounge chairs within fifteen feet of the finish line. There were approximately thirty spectators lined up along the track, so they had the pick of where they wanted to sit.

Rebecca stepped up to the finish line and held her stopwatch. The girl with the fastest time in the three heats was considered the winner; there were no preliminaries. She had the times of the winners of the first two heats and prepared to time Delphia. All Delphia had to do was beat 16.8 seconds.

Delphia broke out of the starting blocks going straight up. Her legs were locked at the knees as well were her arms at the elbows. She ran by Rebecca at the finish line a couple of meters in front of the second-place girl. Her teeth were clenched and her fists closed tight.

Rebecca looked at the stopwatch. It was 17.2 seconds.

Delphia went to the official timer at the finish line. She turned and looked at the ground as she made her way to the group from Medicine Bow.

"You ran hard, honey," said Lola.

"Well, you have that first race out of your way," said Sara.

"Good job," said Rosie.

Delphia stood in front of Rebecca completely vulnerable, with her chin down and her eyeballs looking up. Her mouth was open, but she wasn't breathing hard.

"Good gosh, girl," said Rebecca. "You can run that fast backwards."

"Rebecca," yelled Sara, "don't be so harsh."

"You ran so slow because you're too nice. You can be respectful and still give it your all." Rebecca shook her head. "Dang, girl. You have to relax when you run."

Delphia looked at Rebecca and pushed her lower lip down with her upper one. Her eyes were riveted on Rebecca.

Rebecca stared intently into Delphia's eyes. It wasn't her intention to make Delphia feel sad over something as trivial as a middle school race. She realized she had the power to help her friend, something she had not been doing prior to the meet.

"You have the 800 meters coming up in about an hour," said Rebecca, "I want you to grab a bottle of water and meet me in the infield."

"Rebecca, please be careful here," pleaded Sara.

"Trust me, Mom." Rebecca picked up her lawn chair and headed to the infield.

For the next forty-five minutes, Lola, Rosie, and Sara watched Rebecca talk with Delphia.

Finally, Rebecca walked back to the finish line with a steady gait. She had a smile on her face.

Delphia made her way to the start line.

"Come on, Delphia," Rebecca yelled.

Delphia took off running, completely relaxed with her hands open and her head steady. By the end of the first lap, she was one hundred meters ahead of her next competitor. The few fans on hand were cheering loudly as she made her way around the track and down the back stretch. Rebecca looked at her stopwatch as Delphia flashed by the finish line. The time was two minutes nineteen seconds. Rebecca knew right then and there that her little protégé was going to be a world-class runner.

Delphia stepped to the side and cheered for her friends who were still far down the track. "Come on, Emilee. Come on, Breanna." She looked at Rebecca and smiled.

After Delphia received her hug from her mother and congratulations from Sara and Rosie, they walked back to the car.

"What in the world did you tell that girl?" asked Lola.

"I told her I was sorry for being so selfish," answered Rebecca. "I had told her I would help her train but didn't follow through".

"Ya weren't selfish, Becca." Delphia put her arm around Rebecca's waist. "Remember, ya were hurtin'."

"Well, Delphia, you certainly listened well," Sara said.

"You told me not to waste my God given talent." Delphia looked up at Rebecca with a huge smile on her face. "Huh, Becca?"

"Yes, I did." Rebecca placed her arm over Delphia's shoulder. For the umpteenth time since losing her leg, Delphia never wavered in support of Rebecca.

"And that I should support my teammates when they are tryin' their hardest, because this is all about doin' yore best."

Rosie silently listened to the conversation taking place between the two young girls and their mothers, mesmerized by the unmitigated honesty of their exchange of thoughts and dreams. It was odd that Troy was intent on expelling himself from this lifestyle. For her, it was what she had been yearning for her entire life.

Maliki and Tanya

"What a great story," stated Tanya.

"I really do think Rebecca knew right then and there that Delphia was a champion-caliber runner." Maliki relaxed back in his chair. "Fifteen years later, Delphia rose above all expectations and won the Olympic gold medal in the 1500 meters."

"I never heard this story about the middle school track meet before," said Tanya, "but the Olympics were so much fun to follow the year she won."

"It was pure determination on Delphia's part in winning the gold medal. I'll never forget the tears in Aunt Rebecca's eyes as she sat in the stands after the race, looking down at Delphia pointing toward her from the track below."

"Delphia and Rebecca's friendship is exceptional. One thing I have received from hearing their stories is how much better they always made each other," stated Tanya. "I doubt Rebecca would have been more proud at the Olympics had it been her that won the medal."

"No doubt. She was more nervous than Delphia before the race."

"Great moments." Tanya stood up and made her way to the kitchen. "I can't believe our time is almost finished here."

"Time did fly." Maliki watched the beautiful woman he had spent the last three days alone with casually walk to the kitchen. He had been so engrossed in the story he failed to notice the shorts and loose-fitting shirt Tanya was wearing. "I very much enjoyed our time together."

"So did I." Tanya came from the kitchen holding two glasses of water. Her smile was bright white, framed with red lipstick. "You know, Maliki, we haven't talked much about you. Do you have a girlfriend?"

Maliki was surprised by the question.

"Well …" He hesitated. "There is a girl I have my eye on, here in Aspen. I guess I'm kind of shy."

Tanya's smile went unnoticed as she sat down at the table. She looked at him through her seductive eyes and stated, "You should never doubt yourself."

Maliki thought to himself that this beautiful, sexy, seductive woman is the most unpredictable person he could ever imagine meeting.

"One other thing I've been meaning to ask you." Tanya left a red lipstick smudge on the edge of her glass of water as she held it in front of her and asked, "Have you talked with Troy since he left Medicine Bow?"

"I have."

Tanya knew the answer before she asked the question. Maliki discerned far more information about the actions of Troy than was documented in the notebooks sitting on the table.

"I've spoken with him three different times in the past two years." Maliki leaned back in the chair. "He lives in a cabin about an hour away."

"Have you been to his cabin?"

"No. We meet in Aspen."

"Does he still live with the old man who saved him?" asked Tanya.

"No. He lives there alone. Only coming to Aspen for work."

"What does he do?"

"He's a toastmaster."

Tanya realized she should never be surprised by what happened with anything concerning Troy. But she just realized that Maliki was very much Troy's son.

Dallas, Texas

Normal is a perplexing word. With constant change being a part of existence, it is hard to think of anything as normal. Yet everyone in Medicine Bow seemed to be back to living normally. With the harvest over, Uncle Martin and Tom met at the kitchen table to go over the year's receipts.

Uncle Martin was hesitant in relaying the final figure for the profit they earned from the wheat crop. It seemed that each year's final number was lower than the previous year. Martin felt badly that after such a difficult year he was going to have to tell Tom he had made such a diminutive amount of money.

"Well, how much did we make?" asked Tom, leaning back in his chair with his Texan baseball cap cocked back on top of his head.

"Not enough to have made it worth our while," stated Martin, tossing the pen onto the pile of papers in the middle of the kitchen table.

"How much?" asked Tom, not wanting to be teased.

"Yore share is $3,240.00."

"Good Lord," yelled Tom, leaning forward in his chair and pulling his cap over his eyes.

Martin began to laugh.

"What in the hell's so damn funny?" asked Tom.

"Oh, I don't rightly know why I would find anything funny at this time," said Martin.

"It ain't hardly worth our time to farm that land if that's all we can make."

"I'm tired of planting wheat," said Uncle Martin. "What do ya think about speculating on a house?"

"What do ya have in mind?" Tom perked up.

"Several new houses popped up along Fritzler Road this last year." Uncle Martin fidgeted with the pen in front of him. "That forty acres we have there ain't hardly worth our trouble to farm."

"Do ya want to partner up on building a house?" Tom showed all his teeth as he smiled at his uncle. "I have well over three thousand dollars for my part."

"Well, we have the land," said Uncle Martin. "Can you build a house?"

"I could build a hell of a nice house. I wouldn't want to build anything but a top-of-the-line home." Tom began running numbers through his head. "We need to see how much those new houses sold for."

"I have no idea how much money is needed for building a house," said Martin.

Tom remembered back to last winter when Sam asked him about his future plans. Tom had told him he was interested in building houses, and Sam didn't disavow his idea.

"About six months ago, right here at this table, I talked with Sam about building homes," said Tom. "I'm sure he would invest with us."

"Well, son, if you can persuade Sam Blake into bankrolling this project, I have no objections."

Tom stood up and threw his cap on the table. "We best get over to the church. I told Ma we would be there by two."

"Sara left for Lola's about ten this morning. I figured she would be back before the ceremony, but I reckon not." Martin looked out the kitchen window toward the church. "We best get going. It looks like a lot of folks are already there."

"Rebecca's gonna save us a seat."

"I want a front row seat to this." Martin followed Tom out the front door. "Life around here is about to get very interesting."

***

Vases filled with yellow roses lined the walkway to the large doors of the church. Every person who resided in the town of Medicine Bow was either inside or walking to the church. Lola stood proudly at the podium at the front of the auditorium, dressed in her usual Sunday attire, preparing to speak into the microphone.

"Can everyone please find a seat." Lola held up her hand to wave to different people as they moved to the pews. "Can we leave the front row for the Young family?"

Tom and Martin slowly moved to the front pew. Rebecca and Rosie were already sitting next to the aisle with large grins on their faces. Tom stepped around them and left a spot for Martin to sit next to Rosie, but Martin leapfrogged him and sat a couple of feet farther down the bench. Tom sat next to Rosie.

How are you?" Tom looked at Rosie's large belly.

"I'm so happy for your mother." Rosie turned her knees toward Tom.

"Everyone. Thank you for being here," said Lola into the microphone. "It truly is amazing how word of mouth works in our community."

Sam walked up the aisle with Stanley following alongside him. They both were dressed in black pants and white shirts with black vests. The sounds of their boots on the wood plank of the church floor echoed off the walls.

"Sam would like to say something to y'all before the ceremony begins." Lola stepped back from the podium and gave Sam room to talk.

"This really is a surprise to see everyone here," stated Sam. "As many of y'all know, I have been engaged to Sara Young for well over eight months. When we first made our engagement, we planned on a Valentine's Day wedding, but it just didn't happen. I know that I have truly found the woman of my dreams and that she deserves a magical wedding, but those things take time. Both Sara and I are ready to be man and wife and don't want to wait a moment longer. Plans are being prepared for a gala reproduction wedding this fall, and everyone will be invited by actual invitation."

Sam stepped back from the podium and looked to the back of the church. Sara was already walking toward him, all by herself, with no music or any flare. She was dressed in a cappuccino colored, one-shoulder lace dress with the hem line well below the knee.

"Ladies and gentlemen." Sam held his hand out toward Sara.

Everyone automatically stood up and cheered.

"Please stay on yore feet," said Lola, positioning Sam and Sara before her. She proceeded to marry them.

The ceremony was quick and must have set some sort of record for having the most uninvited guests. It was Sara's idea, but to everyone on the outside it would be considered another one of Sam's unique moments.

***

"Maliki Redmond Young. That's his name," said Rosie, sitting on the sofa, watching closely over Sara's shoulder as she held the tightly wrapped baby.

"He's adorable," said Rebecca.

"He certainly is," said Sara, proudly.

"I'm going to put on a big pot of stew," said Uncle Martin. "We might as well make this into a party."

"If we're going to make this into a party, Martin, maybe you should break out a bottle of that good whiskey you have hidden," said Sam.

"We can make a toast to Mr. Maliki Redmond Young," said Tom, leaning over and touching the side of his nephew's face with his finger.

"Can I hold him?" asked Delphia.

"Girl, I think you will have plenty of time to hold that child," said Lola.

"But I want to hold him when he's still a tiny little baby."

"Come here and sit beside me," said Sara, looking toward Rosie. "Is it okay for Delphia to hold him?"

"Of course," stated Rosie. "I'll take him back for feeding and a nap after you hold him, Delphia."

Delphia gently held Maliki, cradling his head with her left arm. "He's so helpless."

"He's stronger than you think," said Rebecca.

"I've got to get this picture," said Lola, pointing the camera at Delphia and Maliki. "Smile for me."

Sara stood up and walked over to Sam. "Well, what do you think?"

"I think you looked awfully good holding the baby." He stared Sara directly in the eyes.

"Here you fellas go," said Uncle Martin, handing a glass to both Sam and Tom. "I hope you wanted Jack and water."

"That will do just fine," said Sam, placing his arm around Sara's shoulder.

"How about some wine, ladies?" asked Rebecca.

"I would go for a glass," said Sara.

"Lola?"

"I don't suppose it would hurt to have just one drink."

"I'll have one too," said Delphia.

"I don't think so, girl," said Rebecca. "You, Rosie, and I can have some mineral water."

"Someday you and I are going to have a drink of wine together," said Delphia, looking directly into Maliki's little face.

***

The top rail of the wood crib pressed firmly into the lower rib cage of Troy as he leaned over to push open the tiny fingers of Maliki's hand. The baby's open hand was not much larger than his father's thumb.

"Well, little guy, I reckon some day you will realize just how big of a fool your old man really is. I've made lots of mistakes. But you and your mommy are not one of them. You're safe here and y'all will be well taken care of. Now I have to go. I wish I was normal and that I could be here and watch you grow. I just can't."

He pulled his hand from the crib. He placed a spiral notebook at the base of Maliki's feet.

"This should help answer a lot of the questions you will have in the future. I'm sorry son." A tiny tear formed at the corner of his eye.

"Troy." Rosie stepped into the room.

Troy held his hand palm up toward Rosie but didn't say anything. Rosie placed her hand in his and squeezed.

Troy leaned down and whispered in her ear, "I'm sorry."

She looked up, showing the whites of her eyes, and said, "You have nothing to be sorry about. Coming here is the best thing that ever happened to me."

"Ya are where ya should be." Troy put his arms around her neck and hugged her to his chest. "But ya know I have to go."

"I know." She moved back. "I know."

Troy stepped out of the bedroom and walked past everyone in the living room and outside to the porch. Tom followed him.

"Troy," Tom said, "can I talk with ya?"

"I was just fixin' to find you. We need to talk before I leave."

"This isn't the best time for you to be leavin'."

"I hope you will understand, Tom. I have to go."

"How could you even dream of leaving your son?"

Troy's shoulders slumped as he looked away from his brother. "This place is almost perfect. As soon as I'm gone, it will be even closer."

"Don't talk crazy. You have a responsibility here you can't ignore and run away from."

"Every fiber of my being knows that."

Tom squared his shoulders with his younger brother's broad shoulders and looked him directly in the eyes. He could see beyond the mist to the glaze covering his pupils. He remembered the first time he had seen the shiny finish and how incorrigible his brother was at that time, as he asked, "What about Rosie?"

"We had one night together. It could have been any girl."

"It wasn't any girl." Tom's face turned bright red. "You have a baby with her."

"Don't get mad at me," Troy stood toe to toe with Tom, "I want to be able to tell you the truth."

"The truth?"

"I know. I wouldn't believe me either. But you have to believe me now. This is most likely the last time we will ever talk."

"Come on, Troy. Quit the dramatics. You can stay here if you want. There's nothing, outside of what's in your mind, that's making you leave."

"I'm leavin'."

Tom sighed.

"If I stay here, this is as clean as you will see me for the rest of my life." Troy placed his hand on his brother's shoulder. "I have to leave for the good of everybody."

"Dammit, Troy! You made a hell of a mess here."

"I know I did. And just like always, I need y'all ta clean it up for me."

"Well, I'm not going to do it this time. You have Maliki and Rosie to think about now."

"Tom, you know as well as I that Rosie would rather be with you."

"What are you talking about?"

"I could see it in her eyes the first time she saw you in Vegas."

"Yore sicker than I thought."

"I'm not asking you to drop everything and marry her." A slight smile formed on Troy's lips as he witnessed his brother's halfhearted denial. "But I've thought about this, and I can't think of two people who would be better for each other."

"What would you say if I told you I'm not the least bit interested in her?"

"I'd most likely call you a liar."

"Oh Lord, help me here. I made three thousand dollars last year. How am I supposed to take care of them?" Tom stared at his brother. "Now you're gonna leave just like nothing never happened. Sometime in your life, Troy, ya have to look farther than the tip of your nose."

Troy hesitated and stared down at his worn-out boots.

Tom looked at his brother's weathered face and could make out moisture forming in the corners of his dark brown eyes.

"I know it seems like I'm runnin'." Troy sniffled. "But this is something I have thought about greatly. For the first time in my life, I am looking forward for the good of someone besides myself. The way I feel chose me, I didn't choose it."

"Troy, there's other ways …"

"I can't change who I am. It's who God made me." Troy shuffled his feet, causing a small cloud of dust. "I know who you are, Tom, and there is more good in you than anyone I know."

"Man, Troy." Tom blew out a breath of air and looked up toward the blue sky. "Ya have to try to make yourself better."

"So do you." Troy smiled and put out his hand.

"Okay," Tom shook his hand, "I'll turn and walk back inside that house and not say a word, if you tell me one thing."

"What might that be?"

"The truth."

Troy let go of Tom's hand.

"Do ya have the money from the robbery?" Tom asked. "And did you know when we were in Vegas there were only newspapers in the boxes and not money?"

Troy turned and walked to his pickup. He opened the door and pushed his suitcase up against the passenger side. He slid into the driver's seat, started the engine, and rolled down the window.

"Well?" Tom asked again.

"Yes and yes." Troy spun the tires as he drove toward highway ten.

Chapter Eight

Maliki and Tanya

"Did Tom believe him?" Tanya asked.

"He didn't," answered Malaki. "I asked him point-blank if he ever believed Troy at any time after they came back from Las Vegas. He said he didn't."

"Do you think Troy actually thought the newspapers he packed was money?"

"Troy was a lot smarter than everyone gave him credit for, but I can't believe he could think that far ahead." Maliki couldn't help but notice Tanya's exposed legs as she sat across from him in his recliner.

"Maybe he was going to use the newspapers to trick Mike King." Tanya placed her hand to her chin.

"I flat don't know," stated Maliki.

"He might have only had the money that Stanley and Rosie planted in Vinny's room." Tanya leaned forward in the chair. "Did you ever ask Rosie what she thought about whether he had it or not?"

"I did." Maliki hesitated for a moment. "She truly didn't know for certain, but her best guess was that he did have the money somewhere, or Mike King would not have been so adamant in pursuing him."

"Makes sense." Tanya stood up. "How about a glass of wine for our last night together before everyone shows up?"

"Sure," answered Maliki. "Sit back down and relax, I'll get it."

Tanya watched him walk toward the bar.

"Another thing I find intriguing is how Tom went from nearly destitute the morning of Sam and Sara's wedding to becoming a very wealthy man that afternoon," stated Tanya.

"From all the notes I read, it was a total surprise to Tom and Rebecca how quickly their relationship changed regarding Sam. He immediately claimed them as his son and daughter." Maliki was taking his time pouring the wine.

"And Sam Jr."

"I'm more like a big brother to him than a nephew." Maliki placed a glass of wine on the table in front of Tanya.

"One thing I'm happy about is that the Fuddermans were so inept at taking care of the pigs that Sam finally stopped having the greased pig contest."

"I never was a part of the contest," said Maliki. "I still love going to the harvest festival."

"Medicine Bow is a place that is so far behind the times that it is most likely a place people will try to emulate in the future."

Maliki stared at her with a puzzled look.

"It's what your mother saw that made her want to stay, and why your grandmother stayed when she moved there after the death of your grandfather."

"I understand."

Tanya sat deep in thought. She never realized how talking about other people's lives would cause her to become so introspective about her own existence. "The people of Medicine Bow found a way to find positive results from every hurdle they faced."

"They sure did," Maliki responded, despite not grasping the full meaning of what Tanya was getting at.

"Case in point, you, Maliki." Tanya sensed he didn't understand what she was getting at. "Your life would have been much different had the people of Medicine Bow not been so persistent in finding Troy."

"True." Malaki stood up from the table. "I can't overemphasize how enjoyable this weekend has been, spending it with you."

"I've enjoyed it too," stated Tanya, smiling. "We'll have a house full tomorrow."

"It's why I bought this house, so there would be enough room for everyone to visit comfortably."

"So we have Sam and Sara, Tom and Rosie, Rebecca and Jerry, and Stanley spending the next two nights here. Delphia and her husband Jon are going to meet us tomorrow night in Aspen for supper. Lucky this is a six-bedroom, six-bath home." Tanya watched as Malaki opened the door to the dishwasher. "Why don't you have the cleaning company come in?"

"Grandma and Ma both like to resituate everything when they come, and they are going to vacuum and clean anyway." Malaki began filling the dishwasher.

"What question do you most want to ask tomorrow?" Tanya stood next to Maliki but never attempted to help him clean.

"Lots I would like to know, but there has been something that keeps coming back to my mind ever since I began all this research." Maliki dried his hands with a dishtowel and tossed it on the counter. "It's concerning Stanley."

"What?"

"Well, Stanley is such an easygoing man. A good man. I wonder how it affected him after he made the choice to have Mike King killed."

"Good question. We need to decide the best way to handle this information."

"This will be written as fiction."

Tanya gently placed her hand on Troy's arm.

***

Malaki held the front door open as Sam and Sara slowly made their way up the long walk toward his house, followed closely behind by Stanley. As far back as Malaki could remember, Stanley had limped around as though he was on his final leg. Who would have ever thought he would not only live into his nineties but still walk on his own.

"Take your time, take your time ..." Malaki helped the three as they inched their way inside. He leaned over and kissed Sara on the cheek. "Hello, Grandma."

"Hi, sweetie." She gently patted him on the side of his face with her gloved hand.

"The air gets thinner every time we visit," said Sam, wiping his feet on the mat.

Tom, Rosie, Rebecca, and Jerry waited patiently for everyone to get inside.

Everyone milled around the kitchen area as Stanley slowly made his way to the bar before gradually walking outside onto the deck. He sat low in the comfortable chair right outside the large picture window staring heavenward at the bright stars, every now and then taking a sip of Jack Daniels over ice.

Maliki allowed Stanley time to settle into the chair before excusing himself from his conversation with his grandmother to exit to the deck.

"How you doing, Stanley?" It was cold enough outside to see his breath.

"My knees are killing me." He took a sip of whiskey and held up the glass. "But this stuff seems to have a little more kick at altitude."

"I can warm it up for you, if you like."

"It's fine." Stanley hesitated for a moment in thought. "I suppose I have drunk whiskey baked by the Texas sun on more than one occasion."

Maliki moved to sit in the chair next to Stanley. They sat in silence for a short time.

"Son, it shore is beautiful up here," Stanley smacked his lips.

"Yes, it is. I'm damn lucky."

"That you are."

"You know, I've been up here for the past few days researching the book Grandma wants us to write."

"I do know that." A smile came to Stanley's face. "That must have been very interesting spending time alone with Miss Springfield."

Maliki smiled and stole a look inside the large picture window at Tanya sitting with legs crossed and her red skirt at midthigh. Something that hadn't gone unnoticed by Stanley.

"If it's all right with you, I have some questions I would like to ask you to clarify in my own mind some things that happened."

"I'll do my best to answer." Stanley's demeanor became more serious. "I tried to be as honest as possible in the notes I gave you."

"You were more than honest." Maliki sat his glass on the table. "The day you ended the Mike King situation."

"Yep." Stanley nodded his head up and down.

"Tanya and I have decided to represent our book as fictional so as not to incriminate you or anyone else."

"Never entered my mind that it would be necessary to do so." Stanley swirled the last of his whiskey in the glass before downing the final drink. "But I reckon it makes sense."

"What I really want to know is …" Maliki struggled to get his words right. "How did it affect you having Mike King killed?"

Stanley's eyes were bloodshot and his nose a brighter shade of red than before as he sat up straight in his chair. He contemplated the question, wishing he had another drink.

"You don't have to answer." Maliki shuffled his feet.

"No, no, it's something you should know about."

"It's just that you are one of the most sympathetic people that I know."

"Well, son, Mike King was the most evil person I ever crossed paths with or even imagined to have. He would have killed your Grandma, Rebecca, and Troy, and that's a cold hard fact." Stanley took a deep breath. "I knew when I met him in Washington state that he would either kill me or I would have to kill him. I just happened to have the means to get the better of him."

"Does it ever bother you that you didn't resolve it differently?"

"Not even for one second. He gave me no choice. You have to go with what's thrown at you." Stanley struggled to stand up from the cushioned chair. "What ya say we go in and get another drink?"

"Thank you, Stanley." Maliki placed his hand on Stanley's shoulder to steady him.

"My pleasure." Stanley stood looking at the rest of the group through the picture window. "Now I have a question to ask you."

"Yes, sir," said Maliki, "anything."

"How was it spending all this time up here alone with Tanya?" Stanley had a big grin on his face. "Be honest with me. My heart can still handle the minute details of all that transpired."

"I hate to disappoint you, but nothing happened." Maliki laughed out loud. "I swear, Stanley, I was a gentleman."

Stanley started slowly walking but stopped and turned toward Maliki and said, "For all four nights?"

"A gentleman, from start to finish, a complete gentleman."

Stanley shook his head back and forth. "Son, something tells me ya just don't want me to have a heart attack."

***

A single teardrop rolled down Tanya's cheek as she stared out the window at a small lake surrounded by snow-covered pine trees, cradling her glass of Pinot Noir, deep in thought. She had been in the same spot for nearly fifteen minutes.

Maliki rented the room at his favorite steakhouse in downtown Aspen to better accommodate the vociferous group from Medicine Bow. He observed her from afar and decided it was time to bring her out of the catatonic state.

"You look very content," he said, standing next to her and looking out the window.

"It's so beautiful." She turned toward him. He noticed the tract of the tear.

"Are you all right?" He felt a great sense of sadness.

"I'm fine." She turned and looked at the group behind her mingling around a large dinner table. "The time here went quickly."

"I wish we would have had a little more time. I really enjoyed these last four days." He was unsure how he should handle her obvious distress. "Is there something bothering you?"

She smiled at him, but it wasn't the confident smile he was accustomed to. It was more of a frown.

"Tell me." He clutched her hand tightly in his. He wished he could give her a hug but decided not to embarrass her in front of everyone from Medicine Bow.

"This is something totally uncharacteristic for me. I'm just being silly."

"No, you're not. Please tell me what's wrong." Maliki was beginning to think something he had done was the reason for her angst.

"It just dawned on me that I'm every bit as stuck in life as Troy."

Maliki was surprised and unsure how to respond.

"I'm the same now as I was twenty-five years ago. Everyone else around me changed, but I stayed the same."

"You mean beautiful, famous, and successful?"

"Oh, I love that country charm." Tanya gave him an authentic smile.

"We are about ready to sit down to dinner." Maliki held a sense of relief.

"Give me a moment and I'll join you." She pulled out her compact mirror and looked into it. She wiped away any evidence left behind by the teardrop.

"I can't express how happy I am to have all of us together tonight," said Maliki, sitting at midtable.

Maliki turned toward Delphia, who was sitting between her husband Jon and Rebecca. He pulled out the gold medal from his coat pocket and handed it to her. "When you won this medal, being at the Olympics was one of the most amazing moments I will ever experience. And to have you allow me to keep it for so long is the epitome of who we are as people from Medicine Bow."

"I wouldn't have won it if it wasn't for y'all." Delphia took the medal and placed it in her purse. Delphia had grown into a beautiful woman; she no longer was an awkward child, but her fabulous, toothy smile was still the same.

Rebecca reached over and squeezed Delphia's hand. The bond the two shared had grown even stronger over the years. Sam realized how valuable Rebecca's competitive spirit was in the business world. He worked side by side with her running Blake Enterprises for over twenty years. When Delphia returned to Medicine Bow after winning the Olympic medal, Rebecca coaxed her into working for Blake Enterprises. For the past five years, the two women were in complete charge of all operations and decision making for the very lucrative company.

"I wish Lola were here tonight." Sara leaned toward Delphia.

"It's been almost three years since she passed," said Delphia, lowering her eyes to a glass of wine. "You know, Maliki, when you were just a newborn baby, I told you someday we would have a glass of wine together." She held up her glass.

"Tanya and I just read that in your diary." Maliki held up his glass of wine. He then turned and looked toward a double-wide door at the back of the dining area where he could hear a speaker addressing the people in the other room.

"Pardon the noise," said the waiter as he filled water glasses. "It's a fiftieth wedding anniversary celebration."

"Sam and Grandma," Maliki turned toward Sam and Sara. "I know next month will be your twenty-fifth anniversary."

He turned toward Tom and Rosie. "Mom and Dad, it will be your twenty-fourth anniversary."

The speaker in the room celebrating the anniversary was very loud. Tom and Sara both stared intently at the room. Walking slowly toward them, between the room and their table, was a tall man in uniform.

"Sam," Sara yelled as she pushed her chair back.

"Hi, Ma." Sam Jr. placed his arms around Sara and kissed her on forehead as she hugged him tightly.

Sam stood up and placed his arm around his son. "I thought you were on your way to Hawaii."

"They let me divert here for the night on my way to San Diego." He smiled at everyone at the table.

"Sit here." Sara moved over to allow a waiter to place a chair between her and Sam.

"Maliki, did you know he was coming?"

"Of course I did, Grandma." Maliki smiled. He and Sam Jr. were close friends.

Tanya quietly took a seat next to Maliki at the table.

"Are there any questions you have for anyone?" Sara asked Tanya.

"How is Drew Fudderman doing?" asked Tanya.

"That boy still pesters me every chance he gets," stated Sam.

"The Fudderman family still has the same buildings now as they did a hundred years ago," said Stanley. "Only difference is Drew's now in charge of the big mess."

"They just never wanted to change," said Tom.

"How about Charley and Jennifer? Whatever happened to them?"

"They left about a month after Troy left," stated Tom. "Nobody's heard from them since."

The applause from the back room became extremely loud as the speaker finished talking. Tom was the first to notice the old man dressed in a tuxedo walk through the doors from the celebration and move slowly toward their table. Although he felt the voice he had been hearing was familiar, it took him a moment to realize it was Troy.

Troy walked up to the table and placed his hand on his mother's shoulder. There was a tightening around his eyes as he looked at Rebecca, then at Rosie. "How are y'all?"

It took a moment for everyone to realize it was Troy.

"Here, sit down." Rebecca made room for her brother.

"No, no, I can't stay." Troy put his hand up. "Thank you."

"Why not?" asked Sara.

"I just need to go, Ma." He squeezed her shoulder. "I want to let ya know that I'm doing well."

"Sit down and tell us," said Tom.

"Just want to let ya know that I keep track of y'all." He ignored Tom's plea and pulled his hand from his mother's shoulder. "And I do love ya."

"Troy. Please sit …" He was gone before Rebecca could finish.

Not a soul moved to follow him.

Rosie placed her hand on top of Tom's hand and looked him in the eyes. "God only knows, as long as I live I will never understand that man," she whispered.

Tanya blamed her earlier melancholy on being tired. Deep down she was happy to be a part of the Medicine Bow family. As she watched Troy disappear from the room, she had a premonition; the old man who Charley spoke about coming to Troy's room in Las Vegas was Steve from the mountain cabin. It was clear as day; Troy was much more in control of his life than anyone ever suspected. Somehow it made her feel better.

Phoenix, Arizona

The little, old man could see his reflection in the mirror behind the various bottles of booze as he waited to order his customary Dewar's on the rocks. The bartender tossed a napkin onto the bar.

"By gosh. It took me a while to realize that old son of a bitch looking my way from behind that bottle of Jack Daniels is actually me."

"Nothing we can do about getting old," said the barkeep, leaning an elbow on the bar. "The usual?"

"Yes, sir. Too old to change now."

The bartender poured the drink and set it on the napkin in front of the old man. "You retired?"

"Yes, sir. Retired, shelved, and put out to pasture for several years now. Just moved to Arizona from Texas three months ago."

"This must have been your first stop; it seems like you've been coming in here for a lot longer than three months. We've been here for a little over twenty-three years."

"That's a long time to be in one place." The old man offered his hand. "By the way, my name's Ed Dodd."

"Nice to meet you, Ed. I'm Charley, and the little lady over there is Jennifer." He pointed toward a skinny older lady with a cigarette hanging out of her mouth, being supported by the bar at the far end.

Ed took a drink and smacked his lips. "You know, son; I believe we have met before."

"Yes, we have," said Charley, shaking his head up and down. "I recognized you the first day you came in here."

"Yep, yep." Ed took a big drink. "Hard to believe it's been twenty-five years."

"Time flies."

"I'll take another one of these." Ed held up his glass. "Have ya seen Troy Young since then?"

Charley lifted his eyebrow as he looked at Ed. He poured the drink and set it in front of him. "Yes sir, we've crossed paths quite a few times."

"That was a heck of a mess. I never had an incident in my whole life where I was as surprised as I was when I opened those boxes of newspapers."

"Hi, hon." Jenifer approached, having noticed Charley talking with the old man. "Who's this?"

"This is Ed Dodd." Charley tried shouldering Jennifer away. "He was the FBI agent we met in Medicine Bow."

"Oh. Hi, I'm Jennifer." She held out her hand.

"My pleasure," said Ed, shaking her hand. "What brought y'all to Phoenix?"

"We had a mutual friend with Troy Young," Jennifer slurred.

Charley tried to elbow her away from the bar.

"Quit, Charley." She slapped him on the shoulder and pointed toward a picture of an extremely old man hanging on the wall. "Steve Dalbey. He made a fortune when he sold his mountain land in Colorado and came here and bought this bar. He passed six years ago."

Charley just lowered his chin to his chest and stared at Jennifer with his head going back and forth.

"We invested with him and Troy. Steve left us his part after he died," alleged Jennifer.

Charley looked at Ed and took in a deep breath.

Ed started laughing as he watched Charley relinquish the breath. "Don't worry, son, I wouldn't touch that case again with a ten-foot pole, even if I was still working." He lifted his drink and slugged the rest of it down before slamming the glass on the table. "I'll see y'all tomorrow."

Epilogue

Troy sat on a wooden bench on the porch of his cabin. Even though it was cold enough for him to see his breath, he remained outside dressed in jeans and a charcoal-colored T-shirt, embracing a cup of hot coffee. He'd been watching a mountain lion in the tree line wandering back and forth about a hundred yards away. The sun was slowly setting in the west over a billow of smoke from a chimney no more than a mile away.

"I knew your grandmother," he yelled.

The mountain lion pranced back and forth, making a screeching noise.

"You crazy, old, cantankerous cat," Troy yelled.

The cat stared back.

"You best go find something to eat. It'll be dark soon." Troy looked at his Rolex watch.

The lion made a faint growling noise.

"You're just playing with me, aren't you? You know I live here and you live there," he yelled. "Did I ever tell you that you inspire me, Ethel number three?"

Troy walked into the cabin and retrieved a pen and notebook. He sat back down on the porch and began writing. Courage, strength, different.

"Different. That's the word," he shouted toward the forest.

"A toast, Ethel." He held up his coffee cup. "To different. Today is different from yesterday and tomorrow will be different from today. We know it will be different, but who knows what tomorrow will bring."

The End

Everybody has a story. Humanity is full of intriguing and compelling people. Cutting wheat on a harvest crew in west Texas during the 1960s inspired many of the characters in Toastmaster.

About the Author

Dan Peavler lives in Littleton, Colorado with his wife Helen. He grew up on the eastern plains of Colorado in the small town of Bennett. Dan has a BA in Psychology from the University of Colorado, Boulder (75)

He has worked as a counselor, a coach, a real estate broker, and a bricklayer. By far the most important part of his life has been that of a family

You can see his other books and reach him through his website - danpeavler.com.

2051 War on American Soil

What would your family do
if foreign powers used gangs
to paralyze American cities
and the heartland?

What would your family do
If EMPs knocked out power
and society was on the
brink of chaos?

2051 is a novel about the Lisco family, who work together with friends, as the unthinkable happens, War on American Soil. It is a tale of the strength and resolve of the family as they struggle to endure the escalating threats. It becomes apparent that everyone will need to fight as the danger grows in ferocity and magnitude from enemy forces attacking from Mexico across the southern border.

The passion and fighting spirit of Colonel Deb is illustrated as she battles to save the country from the approaching enemies. Colonel Deb, along with her brother, Colonel Ted Lisco, fight the insurgents. Their brothers Jon and Hank, along with the rest of the family and friends work to protect the farm and people who live there. The encounters the family have with strangers show the best and worst of the human spirit.

2051 Books 1-3 contains all three books of the trilogy. Or Book 1, Book 2 and Book 3 can be purchased separately.